THE FIERY SYPHON

LEO LYSUCOR

authorHOUSE

AuthorHouse™
1663 Liberty Drive
Bloomington, IN 47403
www.authorhouse.com
Phone: 833-262-8899

Published by AuthorHouse 09/29/2022

ISBN: 978-1-6655-7094-7 (sc)
ISBN: 978-1-6655-7093-0 (hc)
ISBN: 978-1-6655-7092-3 (e)

Library of Congress Control Number: 2022917142

CONTENTS

PROLOGUE

Continues from first book: *And The Sun Taketh* . . .

Virginia drives down to the gate explaining to Glenn, "My mother (Velvet) started me driving the car when I was twelve years old. She said that since I didn't have any friends, after we moved to the farmhouse and took me out of school, I would have fun learning new things on my own. I was very excited when my mother brought home all the computers, and very upset when my mother told me that I couldn't touch them. But after a few weeks, she gave in. Then when she got sick, the only thing she enjoyed was watching me work on the computers, understanding what they did and how they worked."

Glenn says to her, "That is very impressive, a young girl like you learning all that on your own, you're really very intelligent!" He's thinking, "She's very well developed for her tender age, it's probably more baby-fat than woman." Her voluptuous chest swells, his approval makes her eyes glow. She is not used to receiving compliments. She stops the car at the compound gate and opens the door. Then Glenn adds as an afterthought, "By the way, what did you say your name is?"

As she is stepping out of the car, she turns her back to Glenn and painfully bends over, as if she had just been kicked in the stomach. "He doesn't *even KNOW my name!*"

Glenn is anxious to get back into the Propeller-Basket', (not a hot-air balloon - but a hydrogen/helium balloon with self-contained compressor & storage-tanks, heat-pump with solar batteries and a hybrid gas/electric motor that propels a fan-jet engine). He is frantic to float its balloon twenty miles up and get the hell out of there. He picks up his rifle and helmet and goes and opens the gate, telling her to pick up her stuff and follow him. He puts down his things in the basket and turns looking for her. Then he walks back and sees that she is still bent over, standing at the car door, holding on to it as though she is paralyzed with a memory. He picks up her few possessions and forces them into her hand saying, "Come on we have got to go, quickly!" He steers her into the Propeller-Basket and sets it to ascend, thinking, "She's not even surprised; she should be excited to go on a balloon ride. I will set the autopilot to take us southwest out over the Pacific twelve-mile limit, hopefully I'll avoid more trouble from the Mexicans."

As they are climbing to ten thousand feet, Glenn sees that the girl had just been leaning with her back against the railing, bent over looking at the floor of the basket with her possessions still enclosed in her arms. He takes them from her and stuffs them behind the elastic netting along the inside wall; this secures her personal things from falling out. Then she slides down to the floor and sits saying, "My name is Virginia, the same as my mother's, I thought you would have *known our names*, Velvet is the nickname that Jake gave her, he is the only one that ever calls her that."

Glenn says, "Okay, put this space-suit on, we have to climb high to avoid the border patrol." He thinks, "Jesus, this girl is not even excited to put on this space suit." Then he thinks about what she had been saying about her mother, and feeling guilty he lies, saying, "Yeah, that's right, Virginia, that's your name, I remember now. She told me that she had to get you out of that ghetto school, to get you away from those filthy boys who wouldn't keep their hands off you. She said she was going to send you to a Catholic all girl school or home school you."

Glenn helps her into the space-suit and explains its functions. Now she is becoming interested. They put their helmets on and speak to each other via their headset radios. He ties a safety-rope around her waist and then another around his. He invites her to look over the railing at the world below. She says, "I really can't see anything." and then goes into her things and picks up her iPad. She holds it up over the edge and looks at the screen and then zooms-in so she can make out details on the ground.

Glenn is quite impressed by this and enjoys looking with her at the ground below. He tells her, "We should be crossing over the Mexican border right about now." He is thinking, "The spy satellites can see details from 170 miles up, in high-depth resolution, for all I know they may be in a geosynchronous orbit at 24,000 miles up and still see that detail. Mount one of those iPads on the Skyhook, or even in this Propeller-Basket; I would be able to see insects on the ground, in many different light rays: infrared, ultraviolent. Maybe I can also install in an ultra-enhanced directional microphone and be able to pick-up conversations on the ground too." He calls Professor Natzi and asks him to look into this.

The Professor counters, "We would have to use the Pequadorian military connections to accomplish this, and we are not in their good graces to be asking favors of them."

Glenn commands him, "Well then call Arturo, my lawyer, and tell him I insist that he makes these inquiries!" The Professor grudgingly acquiesces.

Meanwhile Jake and Bernie are sitting in the plane on the runway, with the two Mexican thugs who are discussing how they can fire their weaponry out of the plane at their targets when they only have access to the one door, the right-side passenger seat. They are discussing the possibility of removing both of the doors when the FBI Regional Director's voice comes over the radio and gives Jake the GPS coordinates of their target and tells him to take off immediately. He confirms that it is the same balloon that killed their friend in Mexico. Jake starts the engines and begins taxiing onto the runway which ends all the speculative conversation. The Cessna takes off heading southwest toward the Mexican border. Jake cannot see Bernie who is sitting directly behind him, but they share a palpable fear.

Glenn remembers he has not called Margherita, he tells his headset to call the hotel in Acapulco, Mexico and then he asks to be connected to her room. There's no answer and he leaves a message trying to explain in his limited Spanish that he was unable to call before this time, and that he will call later, and he hopes she is out enjoying herself with her family. Virginia, Velvet's daughter, is trying to get his attention and finally pulls on his sleeve. He tells his headset to switch from external cellphone to space-suit radio communications. "Yes, I can hear you . . ."

"I could see a funny looking plane on my iPad viewer before, it was coming in our direction, but it was far below us. Let me see if I can find it again." Glenn is not alarmed as they already crossed the border and are now reaching 70,000 feet, miles above any normal aircraft. He decides that they are far enough away from any foreseeable trouble zones and sets the controls to slowly descend to 40,000 feet. "Oh, I got it; I can see it more clearly now. It looks like one of those Military Drones you see on the news; like the ones the CIA uses in Afghanistan." Glenn thinks it's cute that this mere teenager watches the international news.

Then he thinks it's probably an unhealthy sign of her being socially ostracized; she should be listening to MTV and all that rapper nonsense. He had concluded that the only way anybody could understand what these rappers are saying, is to research the songs on the Internet. Then he thinks, "Maybe not, back in the days of Led Zeppelin and the Rolling Stones, they said you had to be under thirty to understand the words to their songs." He looks over her shoulder and sees that it is in fact a drone. He is surprised that the Mexicans have them. It is inclined up pointing directly at them, but he can't tell how far away it is. Probably miles away, he figures, as it assuredly cannot approach this altitude. "You're right, it is a drone. You have made a very astute observation."

Virginia continues with pride in her voice, "They are controlled by someone on the ground, he has video. I'm sure he can zoom in, so he can see us." She shifts the iPad to her left-hand and waves vigorously with her right-hand, trying not to shake the iPad so that she can still focus on it.

Glenn attaches a bungee cord connection around her left wrist onto the iPad so that she doesn't drop it overboard. Then Glenn joins her happy salutations, waving both hands in the air thinking, "Maybe the remote pilot will respond with a friendly rocking back-and-forth of his wings by way of a reply."

Then Glenn shouts,

"Mother Fucker!!"

He draws his pistol and fires repeatedly in its direction as he sees a projectile being launched from the drone pointed directly at them. He quickly empties his automatic pistol, reaches for his rifle and throws the controls into rapid ascent. He again starts firing in the general direction of the drone using only his right-hand, and with his left-hand, pulls Virginia by the shoulder down to the floor of the basket. Just as he empties the clip, he sees the missile appear, up from under them and then sees an explosion.

×

She screams *in shock!* He instinctively falls down on top of Virginia, covering her protectively.

The impact on the balloon pushes it forcefully away and the basket swings violently from side to side. He clings to her as they are thrown up and out of the basket with each swinging arc, then jerked back down into it by the safety-ropes around their waists. When the arc of their violent swinging subsides to less than 180 degrees and they are able to stay inside the basket, Glenn tells his head-set to switch to ship-to-shore, channel 16: the emergency hailing channel; and shouts, "Are you out of *your fucking mind!* You're **shooting at us?!?"**

The regional director of the FBI is looking over the shoulder of the drone pilot at his monitor, then presses the microphone switch to speak, saying in English, "You must land immediately, return to the US border and land immediately or you will be shot from the sky."

Glenn replies, "Are you crazy, we're in Mexico now, you have *no jurisdiction* here!"

The stern voice repeats the message more menacingly, "You must land immediately, return to the US border and land immediately or you will be *shot from the sky!*"

Glenn switches back to space-suit communications and asks Virginia, "Are you okay?" She says she thinks she is. Glenn tells her, "You have got to find that drone again, use your iPad to pinpoint it." She struggles to stand up and grabs on to the railing and tries to steady her iPad and look for it. Glenn sees that she is now looking to the south; he yells, "It is on the other side!"

She creeps along the railing, as the basket is still swinging. Shaking nervously, she begins to look again. Glenn is reloading his automatic rifle with its largest clip and attaching a telescopic scope to it. Virginia says, "I had it for a second, then I lost it." Then as the basket swings back, "There it is! Wait, I lost it again." Glenn tells her to keep her finger pointing in the last direction where she saw it. As the basket swings back she says, "There!!" and extends her hand, pointing at a downward angle. Glenn leans the rifle over the railing holding tight with his left forearm and sights the telescopic scope in exactly the same direction she is pointing. Then he gently moves it around in a millimeter – circular arc, and spots it. He squeezes the trigger allowing the full clip to unload.

He switches communications back to channel 16 and hears the same command again with the addition of, "This Is *Your Final Warning!*" Apparently, they don't know that Glenn is shooting back at them. He switches back to space suit communications and tells her to find it again, to keep pointing at it, while he replaces the empty clip with another large clip. He returns to the railing and sites in the direction she's pointing and repeats his millimeter circular search. When he finds the drone this time, he waits and tries to keep it insight until the swinging reaches the top of its pendulum-like arc and then fires another few bursts. When it swings back to the other side of its arc, he fires again. As it is swinging back again Virginia says, **"I think you got it!!** I see *black smoke!* It wasn't there before, – there was white smoke when it fired the missile at us, but now I see *only black smoke!"* As the pendulum reaches the top of its arc Glenn catches it in his sights again and fires emptying his clip. He can see she is right. It is smoking and angling down away from them. Then she says, "Wait, it fired another missile, it's falling down, but it fired another missile." They can see the white vapor trail going first westerly and then almost straight down, and then a fiery explosion on the ground. Apparently, the missiles guidance system was damaged. They are now watching the drone's trail of black smoke going down until they see another impact cloud of black smoke on the ground.

Glenn switches back to channel 16 again, and shouts, "I want the whole world to know that a United States military drone has just fired two missiles at a peaceful passenger balloon carrying only myself and my daughter on a sightseeing trip, twenty miles inside Mexico's border. That is twenty miles south of the US border and seventy-three miles east of the western coastline of the Bay of California. Thank God the drone malfunctioned, or we would be dead now." Then Glenn gives his estimation of the drone's crash site's GPS location and urges everybody listening to contact newspapers and local authorities to have it investigated and find out who was behind this cowardly attack on an unarmed, peaceful sightseeing balloon.

Glenn slides his back down the wall of the basket and sits on the floor, emotionally drained. Virginia sits down beside him and snuggles her space-suit up close to his space-suit asking softly, "Are you some kind of a drug smuggler?"

When he doesn't answer, she tugs on his space-suit sleeve and when she hears him breathing heavily repeats the question, saying, "Are you some kind of a drug smuggler?"

Glenn had been breathing deeply, meditatively, looking up at the red balloon above him. It is covered with nanotube wire-netting interspersed with the shining, silvery solar batteries. Glenn suddenly jumps up, inadvertently flinging Virginia to the side. He sees black smudges to the one side of the balloon! "Were they damaged? Did the missile hit them? Where they now falling to the ground?" He frantically walks around the basket looking up at every possible angle, looking for damage. Then he checks the controls and sees that once again they are approaching 70,000 feet. "Obviously, there is no catastrophic leak." He stops the ascent, and he checks the pressure: it is holding. "These balloons are stronger than I thought; with that exterior layer of rubberized Kevlar, they can take a beating." Virginia is looking at him nervously. He says, "It's okay, I was afraid that the missile had caused the balloon to rupture. It did get burnt somewhat, you can see the black smudging on the solar batteries and on the red balloon surface. Maybe we should not go too high, we don't want to stress the balloon, those burn marks may suggest that it is weaker there. When we land, we should clean the burn residue off the solar batteries, if possible. Then I can look to see if the rubberized Kevlar material shows any signs of burn damage. The only way to test it is to stress it by ascending into the high altitudes – maybe 100,000 feet – which has really low atmospheric pressure and see if it explodes. Not a good idea!" he says, smiling at Virginia. Then he adds, "No! I'm not a drug smuggler, I could never do that. I have too much respect for my own brain to have anything to do with helping other people destroy their brains - and their lives." Then he sets the controls to descend to ten thousand feet and explains to her their current dilemma, as he squats down beside her. "We are now about fifteen miles straight up above sea level, too high for any local aircraft to come after us. But they know where we are, and since we can only move slowly at this altitude, it will make it easy for them to find us again. So, I am floating us down to where we can maintain good speed and get out of this area more quickly. But we may be at greater risk if they do catch up with us at the lower altitude."

She asks softly, "If you're not a drug smuggler, why are you hiding from the government? It's okay if you are a drug smuggler. You don't have to lie to me. My mother said that somebody is going to sell the drugs and she wishes it could have been her." Then he gives her the entire history of his Big Cannon and how the FBI tried to interfere with him; and then, when he accidentally created the Big Syphon's Whirlwind, how they accused him of terrorism. She replies with warm affectionate relief in her voice, "So that's why you had to abandon my mother and I."

Glenn's eyes roll up toward his wrinkled forehead. Then he continues explaining the damage that his Whirlwind was doing and how he was able to stop it in Pequador. Then he adds, "When I heard in the news that the Whirlwind came back, I knew that somebody must have fired up my Big Cannon again."

Virginia sits up in shock, saying, "You mean I started another Whirlwind?" She continues in a fright. "That I'm the person who is causing all the air and water to be sucked off the Earth!"

Glenn replies, "No, you did not start another Whirlwind." Glenn hears a sigh of relief exude from her; then he quickly adds, "You started *two new Whirlwinds,* which will now suck the Earth dry *twice as fast.*" She screeches out in emotional anguish ~ but Glenn mercifully adds, "Don't worry, I stopped the whirlwind before and I will be able to stop them again, everything is in place. We just have to wait until September 21 when it gets to Pequador." Then he softly adds, "And it's going to cost me several million dollars." As they come down to ten thousand feet, Glenn takes off his helmet and then her helmet. All the while she is saying how sorry she is, and she will make it up to him; she'll work day and night every way possible and give all her money to him. He just laughs saying, "Don't worry; it's my fault; I should have destroyed all that equipment before." Then as an afterthought he adds, "I should also destroy that tower: my Big Cannon."

Virginia is offended by his laughter and says as she starts to cry big tears, "I made over a half million dollars since I got your Big Cannon working again. It's for you, I thought you would be so proud of me when you finally came back to get me, that I was able to make this money for you."

Glenn is genuinely surprised and bewildered, but he tries to comfort her saying, "I am proud of you, very proud of you, what you accomplished is a remarkable achievement, especially for a fourteen-year-old. But I don't need your money." She protests through her tears trying to tell them that it's not her money, but it's his money. Glenn thinks, "Thank God a pimp did not get a hold of this voluptuous young girl. Velvet was right to isolate her." He continues saying, "No, you keep the money. We will have to transfer it to a different account, probably a Swiss bank account. You will need it for your education, you're a smart girl and you need to go to college."

With this she breaks down into total despair, blurting out between tearful sobs, "I just found you, and now you want to send me away to school?!?"

Glenn wonders, "Does she think that I'm her father?" He hugs and comforts her telling her not to worry, that she doesn't have to go to college until she's eighteen years old, they will have four years together and even then, he will see her on all breaks and vacations. When she hears this, she bursts into loud, heartfelt crying, squeezing Glenn, and blurting out between sobs that she has been waiting for him all her life and she never wants to leave him. Glenn finally gets her to calm down, then gets toilet paper and wipes her face and tells her to blow her nose. He gets sandwiches and drinks from the little refrigerator. He encourages her to eat. As they are eating, he thinks, "Maybe she is mentally unstable. She doesn't mind if I'm a drug dealer; maybe she's a sociopath, a genius sociopath: the worst kind!" When they finish eating, he helps her up to her feet and they look over the railing and see the Sierra Madre Mountain range approaching in the distance and beyond that they can see the blue waters of the Mexican Bay of California.

Remembering the incident of being shot at while crossing over the mountains the preceding day, he decides not to take any chances. They put their helmets on and he sets the controls to slowly ascend to twenty thousand feet. Virginia becomes alarmed and runs to Glenn when she hears the O2 alarm blasting in her helmet. He calms her down and shows her how to change the O2 canister. Shortly after his alarm also sounds and he has her change his, just so she can get the practice. They are enjoying the view when Virginia spots another plane trailing them. She gets her iPad and zooms-in on it. Glenn gets the rifle and installs another large clip.

Then Virginia says, "Wait… that looks like Jake's plane."

Glenn asks, "Where would Jake get a plane?"

She replies, "He has a pilot's license, and he bought his own plane. He took my mother and I flying in it once, before she got too sick."

Glenn is thinking as he spies on the plane through his automatic rifle's telescopic lens, "This guy Jake must really be on the ball if he can afford to buy an airplane."

Then she zooms in even closer and says, "It *is his plane*, I'm sure of it." Then adds, "***Don't shoot him***, maybe he came to rescue me, maybe he thinks *you are kidnapping me . . .*"

Glenn is nervous and does not know what to do. "I survived two separate attempts to shoot me down; early this morning I shot a Mexican who was shooting at my balloon, maybe I killed him." He feels that he will be pressing his luck to allow this plane to get too close. He sets the controls to go back up to 70,000 feet, "The altitude before I discovered the missile's burn marks on the balloon - it didn't burst at that elevation before - hopefully it will not burst now."

Then he tells Virginia, I am going to call Jake, but I have to disconnect from you before I can do that." He hails on channel 16, "Jake flying in the Cessna, is that you? I am here on the balloon with Virginia, Velvet's daughter. She thinks you're following us because you are worried about her. Is it true? What are you doing here?"

Jake is dumbfounded when he hears Glenn's voice. He looks askance at the Mexican gunmen next to him. Then he is totally shocked when he hears that Virginia is on the balloon. He responds whispering, "Yes Glenn, it's me. Listen closely! Do you remember what you paid Velvet for traveling expenses; change to that channel now." Jake changes to channel #70 and hails Glenn. Then Jake's tone changes its intensity to casual conversation as the Mexican felons are wondering who he's talking to, "I've got a pair of very malevolent representatives here with me who insist you return to port of origin. They have sophisticated armament and lucrative motivation."

Glenn is pondering Jake's speech, 'sophisticated armament and lucrative motivation.' "I never heard him talk like that?"

Then Jake speaks more quickly as the thug next to him picks up the passenger's headset and listens. "You cannot take any chances with Virginia on board. Turn around immediately!" The Mexicans are now alarmed; they can't understand what Jake is talking about, nor who he is talking to; they tell him to shut up.

Then they spot Glenn's passenger balloon, and the Mexicans order Jake to get closer and keep it on the right side where he can shoot at it. Jake tries to explain that they are circling under it, but that this plane will not go any higher. The shooter opens his door and leans out as far as his seat belt will allow, then sticking his AK-47 straight up, begins firing even though he cannot see the balloon.

Virginia is looking on her iPad and sees the muzzle of **the** gun sticking up and spitting fire as the plane is turning and coming under them. "My God! Jake is *shooting at us!!*"

The gunmen in the rear squats down low behind Jake and looks out Bernie's window shouting that he can see it on the pilot's side. He pushes his AK-47 in the back of Jake's head and tells him to turn left. Bernie is sitting next to this gunman and feels he should do something. All he can think of, "Is there some way to release the front shooter's seat belt; he's leaning far out of the plane's door and he might fall out." Bernie is paralyzed with fear, "They will see me if I make a move toward the thug's seat belt latch . . ."

Glenn grabs Virginia and throws them both down onto the floor, squeezing into the corner by the toilet and stammering with contempt, *"Fuck – you - Jakie!"* He can see pieces of the wicker basket being shot away out of his peripheral vision. He rolls Virginia on top of him, placing himself between her and the bullets coming up through the floor, then squeezes himself with her on top of him further into the corner.

Jake continues turning the plane left as he was ordered; it continues to circle around until the shooter is now facing away from the balloon. The shooter says in Spanish that he hit it; the felon in the back is lying down low with his head on Bernie's lap looking up out of the left-rear window; replying that he doesn't see any damage, and that it is still floating up there. Then he prods Jake in the back of the head with his AK-47 and commands him to open his doors so he can take a shot. Jake does as he's commanded. The felon leans over the back of his seat, pushing Jake forward and to the right causing Jake to lose control; the plane swerves to the right and begins to dive as the AK-47 sounds loudly in his left ear. The shots go wide, not even coming close. Bernie seizes on this opportunity and releases the front passenger seat belt latch. But his would-be victim is already pulling himself back inside the plane. He yells at Jake for losing control of the plane and for going the wrong way, to turn the plane around so that he can shoot at it from the right-side of the plane, again. Then he commands Bernie to give him a grenade from the grenade case. Bernie does as he is told and as Jake is now flying the plane toward a counter-clockwise loop around and under the basket, the shooter is loading the grenade to his AK-47 which has now become a grenade-launcher. Jake and Bernie are shaking with fear as the shooter yells to lean the plane on its left side so he can see where he is shooting. The gunman in the rear prods Jake's head again with his AK-47. Jake responds and the front passenger opens his door sticking the weapon out and then leans out, seeing that he has a clear shot; he is ready to pull the trigger when he feels his seat belt slipping across his waist. He screams and pulls himself back into the plane as he inadvertently pulls the trigger; the grenade goes wide missing its target. His face glows red as he looks at his unfastened seat belt and shouts in Spanish, "I'll be the son *of a whore* if I don't plant *these two pussies* under the sand today!"

Glenn is lying down on the floor inside the basket. He sees the vapor trail soaring up past him then an explosion. He remembers that Jake said, 'sophisticated armaments.' "Some kind of missile launcher? Maybe a laser?" He pushes Virginia off him and squeezes her into the corner saying, "Stay there! They are still shooting at us. I've got to do something!"

As Jake nervously tries to level the plane, he overcompensates, and it leans far to the right. The passenger door springs open - the felon screams again as he starts falling out the door. He seizes on to the loose seat belt to support him. Simultaneously the felon in the back sees that he has a direct shot at the balloon through Bernie's rear window. He places the muzzle of his AK-47 up against the glass and fires repeatedly. The glass shatters as Bernie leans to his right to get away from the hot muzzle flashes. The front-seat shooter's eyes are burning with rage as he yells at Bernie to give him another grenade from the case, as he latches his seat belt.

The plane levels. Now that there is no glass in the rear window, the felon climbs on top of Bernie then pushes him to the right side, sticks they AK-47 out the window, slouches down so that he can look up and again begins to fire as he sees a small section of the bottom edge of the basket.

Glenn is about to get up when he sees more chips of the wicker basket being *ripped away again*, he rolls against Virginia to protect her. He sees the wicker around the toilet near Virginia's head ripping away, then the toilet shatters. Glenn jumps up screeching, **"You Mother FUCKER!!!"** He picks up his automatic rifle and leans over the railing looking for the plane. He's walking all around the railing. He can't see it. "Virginia … are you all right?" She replies that she thinks she is okay. "Bring your iPad over and see if you can find Jake's plane." She gets up and soon sees it and zooms in on it with her iPad while pointing directly at it. The balloon's basket is not swinging. He is calmly resting the rifle on the basket's railing. Everything is steady. Glenn's sights along her directing line and he sees the cockpit through his telescopic lens.

He is about to squeeze the trigger when Virginia anguishes, *"Don't Shoot Jake!"* He moves his aim to the right engine just as he sees someone leaning out the passenger door and pointing a weapon up at him. He pulls the trigger and holds it down until he sees smoke coming out of the engine.

The missile fires wide again as the suddenly pale-ish grey thug scrambles back into the plane; he is terrified realizing that Glenn is firing back at him and his bullets are impacting the engine near him. The plane leans to the right and begins to dive when Glenn sees another weapon appearing through the left rear window and begins firing. Chips off the basket are splattering all around them. Glenn shifts to the left engine and pulls the trigger again, holding it down until he is out of ammo. He scrambles for another clip when he hears Virginia saying, "You got it, both engines are smoking, *it's falling down!*" Glenn replaces the clip and hurriedly moves to the railing next to her. "It is going down. They are above the bay." Glenn watches the two smoke trails coming from the two engines. Virginia is continuing to watch it on the iPad, zooming in closer every few seconds. In a minute she says, "It's hitting the water . . ."

The felon in the rear of the plane is the last to realize their dire circumstances. When he loses sight of the balloon, he grabs a grenade and attaching it to his AK-47 turns and looks at the others saying that he is sure he hit it. But now they are all paralyzed with fear as smoke is coming from both engines and they are falling fast. Jake is instinctively pulling back hard on the rudder, trying to level out from the dive. Finally, the plane's nose comes up and they come down parallel to the surface with waves slamming into the tail section and then the bottom of the plane, causing it to bounce repeatedly. Then the nose plows into a big wave which covers the plane as they are all flung forward. The cockpit is submerged and then floats up onto the surface. The ocean water comes pouring through the shot-out window and is now up to their knees. They take off their seat belts and hurriedly scramble to get out. The Mexicans are demanding life preservers. Bernie is trying to explain to them that they were removed a long time ago to make room for the drug shipments. There were none on board. The felon in the rear angrily hits him with the butt of his AK-47 and scrambles over him to get out of the plane before him. They take Jake's lead who scrambles out of the plane and up onto a wing and then sits down on top of the fuselage. Jake did not think to send out a 'Mayday' message. He knew that they were somewhere in the middle of the bay with land on either side, but it could be more than twenty miles in either direction. He knew that the plane would not stay afloat for long. Bernie is the last one out of the plane following the Mexican with his AK-47 strapped around his shoulders, with the grenade loaded into its muzzle. He is trying to climb up to the roof of the plane without getting his weapon wet and he kicks at Bernie, preventing him from getting out of the water.

Virginia is still looking and can see the plane floating on top of the water. She cries out to Glenn saying, "We've got to save Jake, we can't leave him there!" Glenn agrees to go down lower and take a look. When they get below ten thousand feet, Glenn and Virginia take off their helmets and scan the area to see if there are any boats around that might be in a position to rescue Jake. There are none.

Glenn says that they can call for a rescue boat to come and get them. They are close enough now that she can see Jake clearly sitting on the top of the plane. She sounds like a love-sick child when she says pleadingly, **"No** ... *we've got to go get him!?!"* Glenn gets closer and closer to them and doesn't see anything menacing. He comes to them from the right- hand side, the Mexicans are the first to see them coming and they conceal their weapons. Jake sees what they are doing and yells to Bernie in the water, that they still have their guns. Virginia is screaming, **"Jake! Jake!** *We're coming for you!* **Hold on!"** Bernie starts swimming toward the balloon. Glenn is looking at them suspiciously, steering the propeller-basket with one hand while holding on to his automatic rifle with the other.

Bernie is now close to the basket, and Glenn stops the propeller-basket, allowing it to hover four feet above the water. Waves are slapping up under it and seeping up through the wicker floor. Virginia opens the gate, throws out a rope to Bernie, kneels down at the opening and helps him to climb aboard. Jake seeing this quickly stands up, and dives into the water, swimming toward the balloon. Bernie, catching his breath and seeing that Jake is now clear of the plane, is begging Glenn, *"Shoot them ... shoot them, quick ...* **Hurry,** *they've got guns!"* Glenn ignores Bernie, keeping his eyes on the Mexicans. Virginia is calling to Jake, encouraging him to keep swimming.

As Virginia helps Jake on board, he joins Bernie's pleading, "Shoot them, *kill both of them . . . they* **were trying to kill you!"**

Bernie shouts in desperation, "Give me the gun, **I'll kill them!"** Then Bernie gets up and hastens toward the guns lying in the corner of the basket.

Glenn points his rifle at him menacingly saying, *"Get back there and sit down!"* Virginia is hugging Jake who is trying to free himself from her grasp while imploring Glenn to listen to them, to kill the Mexicans. Glenn sets the balloon controls to elevate and begins to fly away when the Mexicans start cursing and pull out their weapons. Bernie shouts that they have a grenade-launcher. They hear gunfire. Glenn raises the rifle and pulls the trigger aiming first at the grenade-launcher and then at the pistol. Everybody else squats down inside the basket as bullets rip through the wicker. The grenade-launcher fires straight up into the air as the two Mexicans fall into the water on top of the submerged wing with blood oozing out of their bullet wounds. They can hear them crying in pain and pleading for help as the balloon slowly ascends.

Virginia says, "We can get them now, they are hurt, they cannot shoot at us anymore. We can get them to a hospital." Glenn simply shakes his head no. She gets the iPad and looks down on them again. Jake and Bernie move on either side of her and share her view.

They hear them shrieking,

"*El tiburon?* – **Auida!!** - *TIBURON!!*"

~

While lust consumed
These wanton thieves
The Zenith of their history,
Has gone past forever.
How calmly does this endless breeze,
Attack these waves, eternally.
Without a cry, without a prayer,
With no betrayal of despair.
Oh courage - could you not as well,
Select a second place to dwell,
Not only in these rugged seas,
But also in the heart of me.

~

The Mexican's blood is readily evident in the water. Suddenly there are shark fins circling the plane. Viewing the scene below with the iPad, Jake, Virginia, and Bernie cry out in turn as they become aware that the jerking motion of the Mexican's legs is due to sharks biting off their flesh, as they cling to the wing and scream in horror. Glenn does not want to look, as he once again suffers the horror of the big shark's teeth clamping around his own head, sending shivers through his body . . .

I

❖

RETURN TO THE HACIENDA DESERT VALLEY

Glenn is watching the sunset in the far West horizon over the Pacific Ocean as they are flying 'Alcarracho' (bastardized Spanish for El Alcatraz Borracho: the Drunken Albatross bird) his Propeller-Basket, to South America. He is beyond thinking. The fantastic orange-orb with its golden spray of rays reflecting off the darkening blue Pacific is lost on him. That fiery orb will be burning-up the first load of nuclear-waste that he successfully launched a few days before. It would take about two months to travel to the surface of the Sun's south polar region; but they should burn-up before that in the Sun's Corona. Glenn sighs forlornly. He's responsible for the shark attack on the two Mexican hoods. He shot them and left them bleeding in the Ocean. How could he live with this haunting memory? Their ghastly screams will echo eternally in his mind, "*El Tiboron! **Tiboron!!!**"* He had summoned the sharks to feast on them.

Virginia has settled in comfortably sitting in a corner on the floor talking happily to Jake and his young drug smuggling friend. Finally, he is safely flying his balloon to his Pecuadorian sanctuary, to his volcanic crater Hacienda high above the city of Pequito. He should be able to relax.

The Pecuadorian President's military dumped thousands of tons of nuclear-waste barrels all around his leased Hacienda Valley. He needs to start launching them to the Sun with his magnetic-levitation (mag-lev) Railgun from his 'Skyhook': his near-earth space platform. It is a massive structure of reinforced – dirigible like – square shaped hydrogen- balloons floating over 20 miles up above the equator. He got the idea when he learned that the Hindenburg hydrogen dirigible (zeppelin, blimp) that exploded in New Jersey a hundred years ago (killing many passengers – 'Oh, The Humanity!'), could carry a 60,000 pound payload – That's 30 tons!

But there is so much worrying him. "I now have these three new unwanted American guests to deal with. The drug smuggler Jake: I mistakenly thought was a good guy and an industrious person. His young accomplice, Bernie: a cub reporter who was somehow involved in me being ostracized from my 'Big Cannon' project in Southern New Mexico. And then there is Virginia: my former prostitute's daughter, whom I had never seen before. Her now deceased mother, professionally named Velvet, had been my only friendly female contact with civilization. Jake had been his only male contact, and he transported Velvet to me. Virginia, who has a Japanese complexion and their beautiful almond shaped sloping eyes; seems to think, for some unknown reason, that I may be her father? - Or just a father figure - as her father was obviously Japanese. She is emotionally distraught; and as such, susceptible to exploitation, being young and voluptuous and naïve. Although, she was able to reassemble my computerized 'Big Cannon' control system and reactivate it. She's only 14 years old! Maybe she's a genius? I wouldn't help those Mexican thugs and she was alarmed that I refused to radio for an emergency rescue. Well, I couldn't risk the possibility of the authorities tracking us.

Virginia needs protection and apparently has nobody but me - or Jake the drug dealer - to rely on. Very distressing. Not to mention that I have CIA Jane hopefully imprisoned with Elena, my cook/second mistress. Since she is no longer under my control, God knows what she may be doing by way of trying to communicate back to her CIA bosses about my project?"

Glenn sets course into the darkening sky: south/southeast off the coast of the Baja Peninsula at 10,000 feet; heading straight for Pecuador. He sits down in a corner and falls asleep, finally. Virginia is relieved to have the only other adult male in her life to talk to and is sitting beside him on the floor. Bernie is already fast asleep, exhausted from the days frightening encounters with the drug cartel and their criminal associate: The Southwest Regional FBI Director.

Virginia is happy to be playing hostess on the balloon flight, acquainting Jake and Bernie with the use of the toilet, providing them with refreshments and food and enjoying their conversation. The next evening, they arrive at the Hacienda in the ancient volcano crater. They throw together a quick meal and then retire for the night. Glenn insists that they each take a separate cabin, with Virginia in the cabin next to his, where he can keep an eye on her. She wants to be with Jake in his cabin. Jake also says she should stay by herself, but he will take the next cabin - to also keep a watchful eye on her.

The next morning Glenn wakes up late and, peering out his window, sees there are no signs of anybody intruding into his Desert Valley. Convinced now that the Pecuadorian Military has made all deliveries that they could possibly fit into his Valley. So, they have suspended further deliveries of the toxic waste and are probably piling them up on the docks. If word got out that it was being imported for storage near Pequito, it could lead to serious problems. Like the Yucca Mountain storage site; people will be protesting the train carrying the material and perhaps blocking it: killing his project.

He must get things going again immediately. He had launched two Loon-Evator (bal**Loon**-el**Evato**r, ie balloon-elevator) nuclear-waste loads from his Skyhook (his near-space floating platform: a 50 square miles network of thousands of hydrogen filled, 10 foot cube shaped balloons. (They have internal metal structure which maintains the cube shape allowing them to be lashed together into the space platform. Each balloon has an open access hole in the bottom allowing the heavier atmospheric air to flow in & out the bottom. Each balloon has internal computerized elevation controls, electric heaters, compressors & hydrogen storage tanks, solar batteries & thermo-electric generators, all wired together and connected to Glenn's central computer). All this is supporting his solar launching Railgun tracks - floating above his volcanic-mountain- crater, at about 22.7 miles straight up - 120,000 feet in altitude. He had to get back up there as quickly as possible with another load and resume the launchings. He had to get his crew back the next day, so that production could resume. And, what about *CIA Jane?*

But for today, he would get Jake and Bernie working on the ground with the forklift loading up the Loon-Evator. He must get into his space-suit and ride up with the first load. Then, using the forklift on Skyhook, unload the Loon-Evator, then send it down for them to reload it again. Meanwhile he'll be reloading the automatic feeders while monitoring the launching of the nuclear-waste to the Sun.

"Well, was it a premonition, or simply a coincident? Was it a dream or was there actually an Alien talking to me - that made me look again at the satellite pictures of southern Arizona - where I saw that the firing of my 'Big Cannon' had resumed?"

The electric company czar (chief executive officer) had warned me about a new solar flare. He reminded me: 'The solar flare in 1989 damaged the electric grid in Canada's Quebec Province.' Dammit! Another problem to have to deal with. I don't know if the heat from the solar flare will overwhelm my Skyhook or if it will dissipate before it collides into the upper-stratosphere." So, Glenn goes into his office cabin and checks the solar flare activity on his computer. He sees that it had already passed and had caused electrical failures in China, Vietnam, Thailand and Malaysia. He checks his control computer and sees that each of his Hydrogen-squares are holding their hydrogen, none were leaking. So apparently, the solar flare had passed with no effect in this area. Otherwise, he would have had thousands of collapsed balloons and very probably Skyhook would have been falling from the sky, or at least hanging down. Glenn calls the Electric Czar and relays his findings about the solar flare only impacting Asia. The Czar confirms this and then asks Glenn if there has been anybody snooping around his electric power stations. Glenn says, "Nothing unusual; only the military has been dumping trainloads of the nuclear-waste all over my Valley."

The czar explains that he has had several inquiries, lately threatening inquiries, about his recent failure to purchase Venezuelan oil for the generation of electricity. "I would expect they will be trying to sabotage your supply source. These supposed communists are kleptocrats who feel entitled to steal the Venezuelan oil income that they were getting from my country."

Glenn replies hesitantly, "I wouldn't be too concerned about them; but, if the big oil cartels get involved . . ."

The Czar gravely finishes his sentence, "We could be dead ..."

An ominous silence – then Glenn mutters as they disconnect. "Another *fucking problem . . .*" Then he puts a call into his lawyer, Arturo, and requests that he contact his crew and ask them all to return to work the next morning. He inquires as to any military activity around his Valley and what is happening around the ports. Arturo makes a few calls and then confirms that there was nothing unusual to report. There are still several ships waiting to unload their nuclear waste. The dock warehouses are full. Glenn rousts Bernie and Jake and Virginia from their cabins and explains what he'd like them to do during the day, while they are making and eating breakfast. He says that he will put them on a payroll commensurate with their ability to do what he asks. They agree as they have no other options available to them; and have no idea what the future may hold.

Glenn teaches the men to work the forklift, loading the skids full of barrels from each railroad car to the center of the railroad tracks, through the fencing gate, up the ramp and onto the Loon-Evator's cargo deck. As he is doing this, he is cautioning them on the dangerous cargo, toxic nuclear-waste, and to take care not to drop or puncture any of the barrels. He also reminds them that the FBI and the Mexican cartel, and God knows who else, are looking for them with probably a reward for their heads. "I mean literally – your heads!" He expresses his anger that Bernie and Jake are drug dealers. He makes it clear that no further drug activity will be tolerated. Bernie protests saying as far as he knew they were only smuggling marijuana.

Virginia is tagging along insisting that she too could drive the forklift and participate in the work effort. Glenn says to her, "What's the point; you're going to have to go back to school daily." She is alarmed at that and looks to Jake, as if to rescue her from that fate. Glenn is assured that they can each handle the task of loading the Loon-Evator. He prepares a lunch for himself and carries it to his space-suit which is hanging on a clothesline and takes off his pants, underpants, shoes and shirt and climbs into the legs of the space-suit. He attaches a plastic fecal bag between his legs and secures it around his waist; then inserts an O2 canister into each hip pocket and connects the intake regulator valve.

Then he picks up the trunk of the space-suit over his head and seals it around his waist. He moves his arm up through the neck opening, takes his food and drink inserting it into the chest pouch on the inside the space-suit. Then he inserts his arms into the sleeves forcing his fingers into the gloves. He picks up his helmet, walks back with his exaggerated gait, bearing the weight of his space-suit. He sees they have finished loading the Loon-Evator and explains to them that it will be back down in about two hours. They finish tying down the dangerous cargo as Glenn re-acquaints himself with the controls on the Loon-Evator and the emergency cabin to make sure that everything is operational, and that the Pecuadorian Military – 'The drunkards!' - didn't damage it while he was gone. His three new guests watch him with suspicious curiosity as he is proudly explaining his Loon-Evator contraption, then adding facetiously, "and now I am setting it for a two-minute delay, now I am pushing this control lever to up, giving you all just enough time to get off."

He sees that 'mad scientist' fearful glare lights up their eyes. As they are scurrying down the ramp he says, "You can watch channel 13 on any TV to see what I'll be doing up there." Then he puts the space-suit helmet on, giving it a quarter-turn twist and hears it lock into place; the O2 canisters 'fwist' as one of them releases O2 into the space-suit.

Suddenly electric motors hum, noisy valves open, tubing vibrates, the loading ramp lifts and folds into place, and the Loon-Evator rises-up and rapidly disappears into the sky as the new employees gawk with amazement.

The Loon-Evator arrives at Skyhook and Glenn unloads all the skids of nuclear-waste and then sends the Loon-Evator back down to be reloaded. Meanwhile Glenn takes each skid to the Railgun's automatic loaders and gently slides the barrels into it. Then he fires up the Railgun which accelerates each barrel to 25,000 miles-per-hour: the Earth's gravitational escape velocity. The Railgun launches one barrel every 15 seconds, on 3 distinct trajectories, so they will not form the magnetic/gravitational channel that started the 'Big Syphon's' catastrophic Whirlwind. Each barrel has a strobe light and radio, transmitting temperature and location, as it soars silently into deep-space on its long journey to the Sun's South Polar region. Within 12 hours, after having emptied two railroad cars, Glenn returns with the now empty skids stacked on the Loon-Evator. Virginia had managed to cook dinner for them, and they enjoy a late-night meal. He looks at Velvet's daughter with admiration, thinking, "Thank God I can NOT be responsible for her mother's E.coli demise as I refused her *sexual-delight bonus*. Maybe it was Jake; maybe he let go a little *methane toot* that she inhaled, or it adhered to his skin, and she *licked it up*. Even though he was paying her, he must **feel some guilt . . .** " Then they all retire to their cabins.

The next morning Glenn awakens to the sound of his truck horn beeping. He is surprised that it is not the train whistle; but then realizes that the train track had been clogged with the excess nuclear-waste deliveries. His crew had to leave the train near the tunnel entrance and drive the truck back to the Hacienda. Glenn quickly dresses and runs out to greet them. He sees Sancho and Professor Natzi assisting the obviously half sedated CIA Jane back to her cabin as she is mumbling something about a promise to take her to the Pequito Airport. Everyone is anxious to know what he has been doing and what involvement, if any, he had with the Mexican military since he's been back. Elena is going to the kitchen and asks if she should deliver his breakfast to his cabin with a raised eyebrow. He replies, "No, I have to go up there, pronto." with his right-hand pointing up to the sky. He yells for Sancho to immediately load up the Loon-Evator. Glenn ushers everybody to the kitchen area including Jake, Bernie and Virginia who are stumbling out of their separate cabins; wearily confused by all this activity. He introduces them to all his employees and asks the Professor to keep them fully employed, as they are now on the payroll.

Then Elena lasciviously eyes Virginia's ripe, young body, and questions, "Why isn't she married with children?" Glenn stresses in English and Spanish that she is an American, only 14 years old, and still a child. Elena sneers, "Virginia won't be a virgin for long around these horny old Latinos." She cast a suspicious glance at Glenn then at Jake and Bernie. Without pausing she adds, "I have a young cousin, Miguel, who is perfect for her! He is *too smart* and *too 'elegante'* for these *used up* mountain girls. Senior Glenn, can I bring him here to work for you?"

Glenn shakes his head with an alarming expression somewhere between 'I don't understand you' and 'you are insane!'

Elena returns to searching the cabinets and refrigerator, then yells, "There's not much food left . . . what's a matter with Margherita? That stupid bitch forgot to order the food!"

"Oh Christ!?!" Glenn had forgotten about Margherita and her family; he had abandoned them in Acapulco days ago and was supposed to return to vacation with them – "Boy; **is she gonna be pissed!!!**" Glenn gets on his phone as he is climbing into his space-suit and tells Arturo to apologize to Margherita and her family saying that it was impossible for him to call as he had to get back to the Hacienda immediately. "They should stay and enjoy the vacation as long as they want and then they can return at their leisure. Explain to her that the military has gone from their valley, and everything seems to be okay here: just like normal." Elena brings him his lunch, which he stores inside his space-suit's pouch; then an egg sandwich to eat immediately with a cup of coffee. He wolfs it down then mounts the now loaded Loon-Evator and floats-up into the sky.

At lunch the men are talking about the strange shape of Jake's penis. They are working in the sandy desert and piss in the presence of each other. They are laughing and have nick-named him 'Pene-Flor' ('Floral-Penis). He speaks Spanish so he joins their laughter, bragging about how the woman like to taste his flower. Elena hears this and thinks it's fascinating. She cannot imagine such a thing. By the time she was married, she had probably seen every penis in her village; there wasn't much else to do by way of entertainment. But every one of them looked like a menacing spike; not a flower. After dinner she quietly asks Jake to help her fix the water-bed's temperature, saying that it's too cold. Then she takes him by the hand and leads him to Glenn's cabin while sensually bumping into him. He responds by putting his arm around her hips and pulling her close to him. As they are going up the 3 steps into the cabin, she pulls his hand tighter around her waist and grinds her ass into his crouch. As they enter the cabin, he closes the door behind them and pulls her close, grinding his erection into her and squeezing her titties. She pushes him down on the bed as he pulls off her sweater. She pulls down his pants and marvels at the flowery head of his penis. She fondles it while examining it closely; she has never seen one like it before. It doesn't seem to have any foreskin, but has a ridge behind the head. She exclaims, "It is like a flower! But, it's too big . . ." She tastes it with her tongue, and then sucks it a little bit while complaining, "it's too long!" She drops her pant and mounts him; inserting him just beyond the head. He thrusts his hips forward and she repels away saying, "No, it's too big . . ." while thinking, "Nothing special except for the funny flower". She gets off of him and quickly finishes him off with a hand-job. He tries to be romantic as he is expecting more from her; but she quickly shuts him down demanding, "You have to leave now, I don't want to see your Pene-Flor anymore!"

"What the fuck?!?" he grumbles, then exits the cabin muttering, "Que loco muher!?!" Elena cleans-up, leaving no trace of their 4-minute encounter. She returns to the kitchen and gets Virginia to assist in the after-dinner clean-up. She doesn't give Jake a second look.

II

❖

SPLIT THE NIGHT

That evening, Glenn returns to find that Jake is excitedly trying-out his spare space-suit. The Professor had determined each working 12-hour shifts in Skyhook, splitting the workload, was necessary to clean up this mess of rail-road cars; with each of them taking half of the night to minimize their sun exposure to solar radiation. Although Glenn is of the opinion that they are sheltered with dozens of overhead balloons which support the miles of elevated Railgun tracks. But Glenn is glad to have help as they must launch 24 hours a day, 7 days a week to get rid of all the nuclear-waste cargo.

Elena spends the night with him and now she is able to take his whole penis into her pussy. It takes Glenn longer to climax which they both enjoy; even though she is still chanting her sensual phrase, *"It's too big!"*

The next morning Jake rides up with Glenn and is thrilled with the fantastic view over the mountain tops into the Amazon jungle and out into the Pacific. And then the stars piercing through the daylight. Glenn cautions him to never look at the Sun and to keep his sun visor down. He explains the availability of the emergency pressurized cabins so he can remove his space-suit if needed. Jake is overwhelmed and amazed with all these innovations that Glenn has achieved. Anybody who can operate a forklift can do this job, Glenn believes, so he takes the noon to midnight shift and Jake takes the midnight to noon shift, operating seven days a week, 24 hours a day. Bernie works with Juan, the train conductor. They spend their time maneuvering the clutter of railroad cars around so as to return the empty ones and position the full ones for unloading, without blocking the main track in and out of the valley. Elena, enjoying her superior position, has Virginia helping her with the cooking and cleaning.

Jake whispers to Glenn a worrisome comment that he had heard from Elena. "Apparently, she was oblivious to my presence or thought that I could not understand enough Spanish. She said to all the men in front of both Bernie and Virginia, deliberately pointing at Virginia's breasts, saying, 'What big tits Gringa women have?!?' We all understood her including Virginia, and she was quite embarrassed." Jake wants Glenn to fire Elena over this. But he simply replies that he would speak to Elena.

That night before sex he tries to admonish Elena saying, "First of all Virginia is not a lady, she is just an embarrassed young girl . . ." - at which point Elena talks over him before he could finish explaining that she should not be talking about Virginia's breasts to the men.

Elena exclaims, "She's not a girl - she's a woman. All the girls I know are having sex by the time they are 12 years old, with older men; as soon as they start to *grow their tits!* That's when they **become a woman!!**"

Glenn is outraged by this, saying, "That's not how it's done in civilized countries; men go to jail for that. At least they wait until the girls are out of high school . . . high school boys no doubt try; but most are discouraged by their healthy moral upbringing."

Elena says, "We girls never got to go to school. I know a lot of **fathers** whose **daughters** would ***send them to jail!***" Then she raises the question, "Maybe that's why I cannot have babies, because I started having sex too early? When my father started fucking me? I cried so hard because it *hurt so bad*; my mother told me to **get used to it!**" Glenn is too shocked to answer. As they are having sex later that night, Elena pants, "Is it true in other countries that young girls are protected and don't have to have sex? – *It's too big!* – We have to get Sancho's wife to send more food supplies on the train. **It's too BIG!** I am going to stay with you every night until Margherita comes back. *It's too big!* We are going to make sure that you are satisfied and don't need any *big titted Gringa* coming here to satisfy you! ***IT'S TOO BIG!!***"

Glenn is too **engrossed** to follow her broken English conversation - ***engrossed in her tight little pussy.***

The next morning Glenn goes to the kitchen area where Elena is busy cooking lunch and Virginia is setting the table. In the presence of Elena, Glenn apologetically says to Virginia, "Elena is sorry for commenting on your breasts to the men. The social attitudes are quite different in this country. You should not be offended nor embarrassed by it."

Virginia replies, "I wasn't really offended, but I was a little embarrassed in front of Jake, because I'm in love with him . . . I know he loves me too, - and we will get married . . ." her eyes light up with this confession that she has uttered aloud for the first time to anyone.

Glenn replies, "He's much too old to marry you; you need to find someone your own age - when you get old enough; which will not be for years - until you finish college."

"People in this country have babies when they're my age, they get married!" Virginia says in retaliation, "That's what I heard from Elena! I always thought of my breasts as baby-fat until I started going to this new high school. The boys there wouldn't leave me alone, groups of them would back me into a corner and touch my breasts. It was in an awfully bad neighborhood and when I finally told my mother about it, she took me out of school, for home schooling."

Glenn says doubtfully, "The school agreed to that, that your mother was going to teach you? I don't think she even graduated from high school."

Virginia replies, "At first my school Principal objected, but when my mother showed him my bruises from the girls punching me and told him what the boys were doing to me *at **his school***; the principle signed the papers and no longer objected . . . He was staring at my breasts when he signed the papers."

Glenn says, "Anyhow, Elena apologizes, and it won't happen again." - timidly hoping that Elena doesn't understand what he is saying to Virginia in English.

Elena understood that Glenn was whispering to Virginia about her and also that Glenn said she is too young for Jake, that she will find a boy her own age when she is older. "But she's already old enough to get her juices flowing." She decides that it's her turn to whisper to Virginia and pulls her out of view. Elena slowly fondles Virginia's tits while squeezing her ass as she purrs with blazing eyes, "You are a pretty young thing and todos hombres are all gonna want these big titties and your sexy ass. But mio cousin Miguel is intellighente, es clean hombre who is perfecto por tu. Es muy guapo! He gusto tu mucho; gusto marry tu. You two make beautiful babies. I fix for you. Shush; donna say not-ting a Glenn o noboty." Virginia is surprised by all of this, but is more surprised at the stirring in her loins.

Workers are now coming into the kitchen area responding to the smell of sausage and potatoes being fried. Jake arrives, still in his space-suit after finishing his first 12-hour shift on the Skyhook. CIA Jane is walking on her own, apparently not under sedation, and sits opposite of Glenn. Elena is busy cooking while Virginia is busy setting up the tables. Virginia doesn't like the idea of them treating her as if she were a child. The Gringos join Glenn, all sitting together at his table, when she loudly proclaims to everyone how sexually aware she is. "When I was in grade school the kids used to look at my breasts as though they were baby-fat, and tease me for being top-heavy, but in high school I realized how sexy I was. Even the high school seniors were after me. It was quite a change. My mother told me that I was just growing up too fast, and she didn't want anybody to take advantage of me. But she was always trying to protect me." Virginia pauses with sparkling eyes, enjoying being the center of attention. "She didn't want me to have too much fun . . ."

"Yes, your mother told me that those filthy boys would not keep their hands off of you." Jake says protectively, "That was a violent, ghetto school you were in. They sold drugs out of that school to all the ghetto children; even turned some of the girls into prostitutes."

Bernie says, "No! That's disgusting! First year in high school!?! A seventh grader! I can't believe it!!" CIA Jane looks at him with surprise.

"You better believe it!" Virginia proclaims, "I was there for about a month and it's all true, it's even worse than that! It was an accident if anybody learned anything in that school. Everybody who wasn't members of the controlling gangs were constantly afraid of being beat up. They would shame you every chance they could get. They said that 'I think I am too good for their ghetto boys!' I was the butt of their nasty pranks. One of the boys snuck up behind me in the cafeteria, when I was carrying my food tray to a table, and he pulled his dirty, smelly jock strap over my head onto my face. Another time they sent a girl to talk friendly to me, just as a distraction to turn me away from my food. I realized it when I bit into my sandwich: a used rubber came sliding out of my sandwich and was hanging from my mouth. Everyone was laughing at me as I ran crying from the cafeteria."

Now Virginia has captured everyone's attention, "The gang would force students to buy their drugs, they would take your lunch money away from you. They would force you to join them in smoking pot and then sniffing cocaine, and finally they would have you smoke crack and even inject heroin: to get you hooked on it. This way you could become a friend of the gang without having to become a member. Of course, the members of their gang wouldn't do the heavy drugs. But they would make everybody else do it. The girls mostly all had to join the gang and be initiated by having sex with all the gang members one after another. When they saw I wasn't going to join their gang, they had the girls punch me saying that I think I'm too good to have sex with their friends; that I was prejudiced against them. They had a new girl and boy in the cafeteria surrounded by the guys - but having me pinned in so that I had to watch their initiation: They had this new boy on the floor on his back with his tongue in a new girl's crotch, while she was kneeling over his head, while she had their leader's dick in her mouth . . . They were all looking at me, saying stupid things like, 'your next baby', 'look how she likes to suck on it', 'you know you want some' – 'you're gonna suck it and love it' and 'your titties are gonna be special to all of us.' That's what they did after I refused all of their more friendlier advances. That's when I told my mother she had to get me out of that school. All the other students knew what was going on. I believe the teachers and cafeteria staff deliberately avoided that section of the cafeteria where the gang had me cornered, knowing full well that something bad was happening to somebody." She studies each of their shocked faces thinking, "I guess they'll consider me a woman now - no longer as a child."

Jake is the first to break the silence after Virginia returns to setting the tables. "I know that neighborhood, it's controlled by a drug-lord . . . That high school is the heart of his operation. It's his cash-cow. To think that she had been exposed to that! If I had known at the time, I would have probably got myself killed over it."

Bernie is seething with emotion, "Couldn't you have gotten our FBI Director friend to do something about it, to raid the high school?" Jake replies with a negative scowl. "Well, we should do something; this is happening in an *American High School – **<u>TODAY!!</u>***"

CIA Jane chimes in saying, "He's right, you should do something . . . *it's **intolerable!*** We should all do something ***to stop it!!***"

Glenn shakes his head in dumbfounded disgust thinking, "What horrific lessons these poor children must endure . . . What **cruel purpose** *does it serve –*"

{other than the *enlightened evolution* of the *Cosmic Consciousness* . . .}

III

MARGHERITA RETURNS

Margherita is back the next week and is livid with rage towards Glenn for abandoning her on the roadside near Acapulco, with a strange limousine driver to take her to the hotel. She was all alone until her family arrived the next day.

He asks if she had a good time. She retorts, "What 'good time' could I have *had without you!*"

He replies, "Well at least your family had an enjoyable vacation; I hope.

She says more calmly, "SI they did, and they said to thank you very mucho."

Glenn replies, "You're welcome." happily.

Margherita screams, "Yo non dice **gracias a tu!!** (I was not **thanking you!!)*"* and runs into the kitchen. CIA Jane follows after her.

Elena hears this and tries to calm Margherita down, saying, "I wish Boss-Man would send me to vacation in Acapulco. You know he has to work; we will always come second to his project."

Jane gives a snickering laugh saying in Spanish, *"Second?!?* You count for nothing with Glenn; you are **slaves!** *You count* for **ZERO!!** He can replace you in a *minute!* And Elena, as for you pleasing Glenn sexually – you count for *less than zero!"* Margherita gives her a cold stare in return for her callous comment; Elena looks like she's been *slapped in the face.* Then Jane continues, "Did you tell Margherita: *'No mas sanque'?"*

"E vero; no mas sanque . . ." Elena replies, her lips trembling with emotion. Then asks, "Did you miss your period too?"

Margherita shakes her head, "No; I got mine when I arrived in Acapulco."

"But we always have it at the same time?"

Jane scolds her saying, "Wake *up stupid;* your periods are synchronized because you're fucking the same man. 'Synchronized periods': It's nature's excuse for men to find *some new - strange* pussy. I would sooner die than let that **terrorist's dick near me!**" Turning to Margherita, "She thinks mine is going to synchronize with hers because we spend so much time together. When he finds out she's pregnant; he's gonna throw ***her ass out!!*** Then you'll see what a ***'Good Man'*** he is! Just because he showers before sex don't make him a *'good man'."*

CIA Jane is recuperating and is up and moving about on her own. She no longer requires constant sedation, although she is still on the addictive steroids because of the massive amounts of bruising all over her body. These steroids are meant to help her body absorb the bruising from her prolonged period of depressurization while going into the stratosphere without a space-suit, and while they were falling back to Earth from the Loon-Evator at 30,000 feet, with Glenn clutching her in his arms - till the parachute finally opened. She will have to go through a prolonged period to become un-addicted.

At breakfast, Glenn tries to socialize with her, but she is too livid with anger towards him. Glenn attributes it to the steroids. "How stupid do you think I am that I would believe your story of that ridiculous cavern - to hold all the world's nuclear-waste that you are receiving?!" Had she somehow learned it was not just the United States shipping it here; his eyebrows raise questioningly. "It's written in foreign language on every barrel: *Hazardous Toxic Waste'!* And it is hap-hazardously piled up all over this place! Any fool could tell that the cavern was never going to be a tenable solution with the ocean water penetrating into it!"

Glenn is surprised as he says, "What? Ocean water? I have never seen that. You must be mistaken." Anyway, now it's obvious to him that she knows that we're carrying it up on the Loon-Evator and she must conclude that we're doing something to get rid of it: which is obviously launching it to the Sun where it will burn-up harmlessly.

Then she says, "I don't know exactly what you're doing with it, but I fear that it is once again being bombarded into cities around the world as was attempted in Southern Arizona by that stupid, crazy, mad scientists."

Glenn gives a sigh and a wry smile answering her saying, "Maybe that stupid, crazy, mad scientists was planning on shooting those toxic barrels into the Sun. And maybe that's what *caused the Whirlwind*. And maybe that same crazy, *insanely stupid* mad scientist was the one who managed to **stop the Whirlwind!"**

She replies, "Do you know this crazy mad scientist?" Accusingly, "Is he a friend of yours?" Her eyes narrow into menacing daggers, "You can be assured that you both are going to suffer severe consequences *for your terrorism!"*

But Glenn replies, "What if however, they were able to accomplish their final goal: successfully launching this nuclear-waste from near-space," pointing his finger up, "into the Sun; thus, eliminating this horror from the world," adding sanctimoniously, "and for *all future mankind as well!?!"*

She says, "If that were ever possible, it is no more than an interesting development, and they would still have to pay for the terror that they had caused the world."

Glenn pleads earnestly, "But, what of the greater good that they've accomplished?"

She retorts, "What about the loss of life and the injuries and property damage around the world."

Glenn denies this by shaking his head negatively, "To my knowledge there was minimal loss of life. Henry Ford's invention kills thousands - hundreds of thousands - which was developed to benefit mankind: why is this so much worse? People die doing construction, and airplanes crashing, and ships sinking – accidents: but mankind has benefited in the long run."

"Bullshit!!" she screams, "- And are you telling me that you are that mad scientist - that you built that tower?!?" The dawning realization is coming to her gaze of contempt. Glenn says nothing and walks away from her.

The next day Sancho has bad news: "Every railroad car that they empty returns the next day filled with more skids of nuclear waste. Also, Juan says that Bernie is *another* **loco Gringo** because he wants to lay more railroad tracks in the Valley. We just laugh at Bernie asking where? - There is no more room."

Glenn is thinking, "I guess I am the *first* **loco Gringo** that they were referring to."

Glenn is relieved to see Margherita when he gets off the Loon-Evator at midnight. She helps him out of his space-suit as usual and has hot coffee and food for him. She joins him in the shower, bathing him and does everything to please him; but she remains mostly silent and distant. He orgasms quickly and although she moves appropriately; she gives no indication of enjoyment.

Glenn asks Bernie at the next morning's breakfast, "What was your idea about laying new train tracks?"

Bernie says, "We're wasting so much time because of the north tunnel entrance. Everything must come and go through there on a single track, so we must juggle everything around in order to return the empty railroad cars. If we keep one return track clear and put transfer-tracks with switching across the center of the valley, we could have everything moving in a continuous circle instead of going backwards and forwards." Bernie sketches out what he means, and Glenn agrees to have it accomplished using the Pecuadorian Military who laid the tracks throughout the country.

Everybody protests about having the extorting military back in the Valley - for any reason whatsoever. Glenn asks Sancho, "Are you still paying that military railroad engineer 25% of the profit from your mule train operation?" Sancho looks at him with raised eyebrows as his eyes are about to pop out of his skull. Glenn continues harshly, "You remember, you promised him and that other piece of shit, 25% - and the other 25% you were SUPPOSED TO PAY ME - out of ALL your profits; if he would re-route the train tracks to run through YOUR property - THROUGH YOUR TOWN; so that you could get tourists there: instead of having them run my train the shortest way possible - like I wanted. But I *paid extra because of your interference!*"

Sancho replies guiltily, "Si, I know the railroad engineer . . ."

"Good," Glenn's tone is now more gentle, "tell him that you could give him some private work if it can be kept a secret from the military and the government officials."

He says, "Okay," relieved that Glenn is speaking more softly to him, "I'm sure he want to do that because he knows everybody in the government stealing everything they can: so if you get the military to do work through General Garcia everything costs more, because the Generals and the President and everybody who see the papers have to make money on it."

"Okay Sancho" Glenn says, "That's good. This way you do not have to pay me back that 25% you promised me for taking the long way with my train tracks." Within a few days there are military men working on Bernie's plan for the cross-desert track switching. It is quickly completed without interfering with the main project of launching nuclear waste. Then Glenn thinks that it would be useful to have another tunnel at the southern end of his Crater Valley. This way it will help relieve the congestion at that northern tunnel and allow access to the southern portion of Pecuador; without having to go through Pequito. Then he might be able to have some deliveries without the knowledge of the government, who has no doubt been screwing him on everything he ordered. He has this same Military Engineer put a plan together for a new southern tunnel and for his railroad tracks to connect to the existing southern public tracks outside his valley. The Military Engineer will keep this money-making project for himself and those few military personnel that he trusts. It will take about a week to complete, working around the clock with two crews dynamiting both sides of the tunnel. Then they will begin working on laying the tracks.

Glenn asks the Electric Czar to secretly provide the electric wiring and to put another meter on that southern connection of his tracks to the Ecuadorian public railroad tracks, as he envisions his electricity will be flowing into those tracks as well and he wants to get paid for it. The Electric Czar agrees happily; but then says, "I was interrogated by an agent of the Venezuelan Oil Company. I told him that we get overflow electricity from several different locations that are connected thru our electric train tracks. He was escorted by a Pecuadorian Military Major who told him that we get the cheap electricity from your valley."

Glenn sighs saying, "Always got to be some stupid fucking problem . . ."

That night after his shift on Skyhook, Glenn is elated to see Margherita serve him his midnight dinner . . .

With everybody busy working, Virginia is happy to be going to school and glad to be away from slaving in the kitchen all day. She rides the train back to the Professor's house and stays in the girl's dormitory that he has set up. She is happy to be around children & have the female companionship and the educational environment provided by the Professor's wife. She returns to the Valley Hacienda on weekends. The workmen at the Hacienda had all been eyeing her suspiciously but staying away from her as they did not want to antagonize the Boss-Man. They no doubt thought that she was Glenn's fourth mistress. Elena tells Margherita, "I am helping my cousin Miguel by having him marry Virginia, and this will keep her away from Glenn's pecker. He is staying at my house."

She replies, "Miguel is too shy for any woman . . . Your X husband won't like him staying at your house . . ." but, she quietly fears he will be attacked by her town's rugged mountain men - for being too girly - a sissy.

Elena says, "I already told him to go to their new school to help teach – and don't ask for any money. This way he can get friendly with Virginia – she must be getting horny and will want a pecker from a nice, clean, smart boy like Miguel. She is sleeping in that dormitory with all the other girls; she can't even play with herself . . ." Margherita just rolls her eyes in reply.

As usual, they take turns staying with Glenn as he must be satisfied sexually every day. They fear that the other females would jump into his bed if they weren't already there. They had to protect their lucrative jobs. He is usually too tired for more than once a day. Every morning they bring him breakfast after everyone else has eaten. They wake him with sex - either one or sometimes both of them. He gets back from his 12-hour shift from the Loon-Evator every night at midnight and is exhausted. But he looks forward to the affectionate warmth of their bodies as he snuggles close; and then promptly falls asleep.

IV

CONCEPTUALIZE
SPACE/TIME

Glenn spends the rest of each morning checking on the devastation of the new Big Syphon2's Whirlwind, anticipating its destruction again by his H-cube (10'X10'x10' cube shaped, heavy-duty, hydrogen filled) balloons choking it. He's thinking, "My balloons now cover my entire Valley, so we do NOT have to intercept it like we did with the first Big Syphon. It must pass somewhere over my valley at noon on the equinox and suck up my frigid hydrogen filled balloons which will absorb the Whirlwind's heat, causing its cooling air to compress and fall back to Earth: thus, choking off the Whirlwind's attachment to the Sun – at least that's how I think it works. Whatever - as long as it chokes it like it did last time." His 50 by 40 square miles of balloons are all attached to each other, and are now 1 mile higher than they were when the first 'Big Syphon' invaded. That is the height to maximize Skyhook's electricity harvesting. Wherever this second Whirlwind hits, it will suck most of the other balloons into it. - He wonders, "Did the Electric Czar tell me that there were Solar Flares or CME's; or was it both?" He wasn't sure technically if there was a difference between them and he resolves to try and ask Professor Nazi (not so lovingly nick-named by the Mickey Mouse News Network after he derisively exposed their androgynous weather forecaster). He is always busy, and grouchy, and reluctant to engage in conversation. Glenn decides to bravely address the Professor and hesitantly enters his office cabin. As expected, he finds him hunched over his computer laboring diligently on their project. But then, he is surprised to see something different on his computer screen: He seems to be writing on a subject completely unrelated to their work . . . Glenn quietly spies over his shoulder:

Conceptualize Space/Time

I found it difficult to grasp the concept of Einstein's **Space/Time Fabric** and, the speed of light being the absolute maximum anything can attain. Also, (1) the **SPEED** travelling through this *fabric*, decreasing the object's actual passage of **TIME (i.e., time dilation)**, while (2) increasing the actual **MASS** of the object; that is the **DENSITY** of this travelling object actually gaining **WEIGHT** with the speed.

We accept that its true, but that doesn't help us grasp the concept. We need a mental image:

    ~   something we can sink our teeth into . . .

Also (3) black holes crunching down and disappearing all matter; and (4) the acceleration of galaxies away from each other with the creation of new Space/Time Fabric between intergalactic space.

Why isn't there a concept allowing we average dimwitted peons to wrap our feeble imaginations around? - Isn't that what Astrophysicists are getting paid for?

The existence of Einstein's Space/Time *Fabric* was proven with the Hyades group of stars – being observed from beyond the eclipse - appearing simultaneously on both sides of the Sun. This Space/Time *Fabric* was *warped* (bent, squeezed, stretched) by the Sun's gravity; so that this one star's pinpoint of starlight was visible at two different locations simultaneously. The starlight was bent around both sides of the Sun.

Therefore, this **fabric** must have dimensions if it can be warped by gravity. Within our universe these four dimensions are: 1-Height, 2-Width, 3-Depth and 4-Time (as in one cube of this microscopic Space/Time Fabric in a single instant of **Time** - but at different times of day: at this very moment {i.e. **NOW**}, or a moment before, or a moment in the future ~ but at the same physical location: yesterday, today, or tomorrow.)

So, let's call this single point-in-time, the smallest divisible portion of this **fabric**: Einstein's '**STUBIT**' (**S**pace/**T**ime C**ub**e), and envision it as a microscopic cube.

The *Stubit* must have mass as it can be warped by gravity. (To be affected by varying degrees of gravity, these *Stubits* must therefore have mass.)

Relative speed of an object is the factor: the objects mass is increasing while its elapsing time (actual passage of time) is decreasing, simply because the objects speed has increased while passing through each **Stubit**?!?

~   This did not compute in my shallow mind . . .

I guess my subconscious was percolating on the subject while I was consciously observing my emptiness from the perspective of my navel. (EEEUUGH! There is a disturbing image for your subconscious to percolate on: My brown eyed bellybutton seeking longingly.) After many months of meditative pondering, I got this small return on my contemplative investment: I was suddenly struck with this simple concept;

~ not to suggest that this concept will ever
be construed as scientific fact ~:

We concede that Space/Time – these microscopic *FABRIC STUBITS* – actually occupy every scintilla of everything we can see, and touch; in this dimension that we exist in. This includes every tangible thing that we know of including **EMPTY SPACE** – even in a vacuum; but does not include Black-Holes, Dark- Energy, Dark-Matter; Dark-Gravity, nor Dark-Magnetism. The Astronauts took an atomic clock around the Moon, confirming that time is relative to speed. People who live on mountain tops age slightly less than people living in valleys. We are all traveling:

> rotating around the surface of the Earth,
> *while orbiting around the Sun . . .*

> ### *while our solar system is orbiting around our galaxy!*

> ## *AND OUR GALAXY IS ? ? ?*

An identical twin Astronaut, Scott Kelly, on the Space Station for a year, aged less than his earthbound identical twin brother.

He was traveling faster and consequently aged less.

But why?!?

With your total *concentration*, please try to build an *image* of all this:

Travelling, we are passing through these *STUBITS* of Space/Time *Fabric* and that is what causes the passage of time and makes us age. What if (in our dimension) you can only pass through a limited amount of these fabric stubits at a given speed; beyond which you do **NOT** pass through it – **BUT** you **PUSH** some of these stubits aside.

~ Consequently, you would gain the **mass** of these *Fabric Stubits* that your **INCREASING speed** is pushing aside. And, as your speed increases, you are pushing aside more and more *STUBITS* of Space/Time's Fabric, increasing your mass - and therefore - pushing these stubits aside, you are travelling through less of the Space/Time Fabric. Consequently, your time would be less, you would actually age less.

Therefore, you could never reach the speed of light (in our dimension) as you would have to push aside an infinite amount of this **Stubit *Fabric*** –which would mean you must gain infinite mass, -which must require an infinite amount of energy to be able to accelerate to that speed.

Thus: a concept of Einstein's Space/Time Dilation you can sink your teeth into ~ although it is undoubtedly far removed from the scientific reality . . .

This also suggests that if there was absolutely *NO* movement at all through these Stubits of Space/Time Fabric, *time* would stand still, 'NOW' would not exist, ~ there would be no such thing as *TIME* . . .

Now if we can throw in Wormholes, Multidimensions, Dark-matter, Dark-energy, Dark-magnetism and Quantum Entanglement, we can retire the Astrophysicists for this century.

Imagine a Blackhole crushing everything into oblivion, including Einstein's Stubits (the micro fabric of Space/Time). We know that deadly gamma rays are a byproduct beaming out of the Blackhole's magnetic poles. (New discovery: Blackholes have magnetic polar regions!) Now, imagine this crushed matter being *smashed into Stubits* and then (like gas bubbles in champaign) *bubbling out* from the crushing density at the center of the Blackhole, this great pressure forcing these crushed Stubits through another dimension, and reappearing in the least dense place in our dimension - *our universe's intergalactic space.* Thus, adding *new Stubits*: separating the galaxies, accelerating them further and further apart from each other.

(Except for our Milky Way's crashing through Andromeda. Their gravitational attraction must be increasing the density of the Stubits between them. Thus, preventing the new Stubits escaping from blackholes to bubble up into this denser intergalactic space.)

The Professor pauses in reflection and then becomes startled that Glenn is spying over his shoulder.

"I didn't see you there" he says apologetically, but then more retaliatory, "I am free to pursue my other interest while I work for you . . . After all, I am *an Astrophysicist!*"

Glenn says apologetically, "Oh, I didn't, eehhh, 'Stubit'? aahhh, I became engrossed in your space/time concept for this book you are writing and . . ."

"It's not a book, it's just an article. I used to submit them to science magazines before I became a cog in your *waste removal **assembly line!***"

Glenn stammers. "It's truly hard to get a grasp of Einstein's concept . . ."

The Professor interrupts with derisive contempt, "HUMPFFSS . . . What did you want, anyhow?"

"AAHHH . . . ***FORGET ABOUT IT!***"

"Our contract doesn't say I have to remain a cog in your **waste removal *assembly line!***" the Professor shouts as Glenn stomps away, "I'm free to spend time pursuing my career."

V

❖

MALCONTENT CIA AGENT

Jane is becoming more uncontrollable daily as she is getting better, and her steroids are being cut back. She has virtually no pain anymore and is making all sorts of crude, sexually teasing overtures to all the men. Of course, she is also bored. She is closest to Elena who has helped her through most of her convalescence and talks to her whenever she can. And through her, she also has become friendly with Margherita. They laugh a lot together, making sexual innuendos about each and every one of the men that work there and how humiliating it would be to have sex with them. Elena says she saw Jake's Pene-Flor one day when she was looking through Glenn's binoculars; he was pissing in the desert while working. She quips merrily, "It is so strange looking, it makes me laugh every time I think of it. It really does look like a sad, pale, dying flower. It has no skin to go over the head, not even to cover it a little bit."

Margherita says, "The only gringo dick I ever saw is Glenn's and it's not like that; it's pale and big, but otherwise it's normal."

Cia Jane explains the whole history of circumcision for them. "It's better because it is desensitizing for the man so he can last longer for the woman; and it's cleaner because germs grow under that foreskin."

Elena is surprised to hear how common it is in rich countries and that the Jewish religion requires it. But she chides, "Those poor men – desensitizing – that means they can't enjoy having sex as much as they are supposed to. Just because you Gringa Bitches are so afraid of a little dirt, a little smell . . . I like that smell; it makes my pussy wet."

Jane retorts, "It prevents CANCER in woman; cervical canc . . ."

Margherita affirms, "All your Gringo men must have **cancer of the hand!**" ~ Jane guffaws, dumbfounded. ~ Margherita continues, "You Gringas throw away so much money on smelly cosmetics! No wonder you people divorce and gotta go to the pussychiatrist doctor and can't enjoy sex . . ."

Jane's eyes bulge, "**Pus-sy-chi-a-trist** Doctor! **HA!!**" Then recovering slightly while walking away, "I guess if you woman *enjoy being* **dirty cocksuckers**; there is nothing more to say . . ."

CIA Jane always speaks badly of Glenn and the fact that he is holding her there as a prisoner and that he will never let her go because she has sworn to put him in jail for the rest of his life. She relays the history of the Southern Arizona tower, his 'Big Cannon', that he built and threatened to destroy American cities. The women are surprised and disbelieving; but choose not to challenge her. They agree that Glenn is wrong for keeping her there as a prisoner when all that she did was try to report on the work that he was doing. They think that if there's nothing wrong with this work, why is he keeping her there to prevent her from reporting on it . . .

Elena whispers to Margherita that Jane wants me to help her escape from the valley. She says she'll take me to Washington, D C with her if we help her. You can come too."

Margherita replies dismissively, "You can't walk out of here, the cliffs are too high and sheer; the military patrols the tunnel. Anyhow, we never had it so good; why would we want to leave Glenn . . ."

CIA Jane also befriends Bernie saying that she heard he used to be a reporter in Arizona, and therefore he must know about that FBI tower seizure? They talk about it, but his understanding of it is as vague as hers. He tells of their heroic escape from the Mexican Thugs, and their history together. The local FBI director originally hired him to spy on the tower; but then, more importantly, to recruit the pilot Jake for the FBI's drug smuggling from Mexico. Bernie brags that he made the hook-up between Jake and the FBI. He knew Jake the pilot from before, while doing a video report on skydiving. Bernie was trying, but had failed once again, to make the TV network shows. Jane says when she is physically better and free of this captivity, she would introduce him to a Network acquaintance. Her eyes are suggesting she would be interested in him romantically. He has no other prospects, but he fears Glenn: he had murdered someone in Mexico, he had seen him shoot another two Mexican hoodlums, (which he would've done himself if he had the opportunity) - so don't fuck around with Glenn. He doesn't know where he could go and is still fearful of the Mexican drug cartel and the American FBI. So, he is indebted to Glenn and worries at Jane's attempt to slander him. But she's his only possibility of female affection.

Glenn flies Alcarracho (his motorized floating balloon/basket), his Propeller-Basket, to the southern end of his crater valley to check on the tunnel plans. He takes Bernie and Sancho with him so they can survey from the air all that has been done with the tracks and how they can now take railroad cars from the northern end and circle them around, unload them, and then send them back through the northern tunnel. Sancho was afraid to ride Alcarracho, but he did it anyhow as Glenn promised to not go too high; he was getting some nerve back after seeing Jake repeatedly going 'up there' on the Loon-Evator and returning every day. Deliveries keep coming from different countries, which is alarming to Glenn because he cannot imagine that there is still more coming with what is already piled up at the docks.

After checking the marked-off tunnel site he decides to investigate the cavern thinking that crazy woman, CIA Jane, said that there is saltwater in it. They tie down Alcarracho to a big boulder then he goes into it with Bernie and Sancho following. After he has gone down a crevice into the cavern a short distance, he sees that indeed the pathway is wet, and he is only about fifty feet down into it. Now he pauses and looks up and down the sandy pathway. He bends down and forces his fingers into the sand, then licks his fingers, actually tasting it for salt content. *He can't believe it! It's definitely true: it's salty!* He pushes past Bernie and squeezes past Sandro then runs back to the entrance. Sandro follows in a panic, so Bernie follows after him. Glenn suddenly stops and bends over again. Sancho falls over him and Bernie must grab on to the walls to keep from falling on them. He is struggling to try and help the ample Sancho to his feet while asking if Glenn is alright. But Glenn scrapes a handful of sand and puts it into his mouth without any thought of getting up. Bernie and Sancho are alarmed. Glenn shouts while spitting it out, "It *is salty!* It's Fucking *SALTY!!*"

Bernie looks to Sancho incredulously. Sancho nods knowingly with intense despair in his eyes. Glenn is continuing to spit out the sand, while springing to his feet. Sancho jumps back away onto Bernie's feet who curses with pain. Glenn growls, "That fucking stupid *cunt is right!*" angry at himself for being embarrassed by her intelligence. He runs up the crevice near Alcarracho and takes another handful of sand and puts it in his mouth. "IT'S SALTY!! HOW COULD I HAVE **NOT** NOTICED THIS BEFORE!!! I'VE BEEN HERE *FOR MONTHS* AND SHE SAW IT *HER FIRST FUCKING DAY!*" he shouts as he is spitting out the sand.

He gets water from Alcarracho and rinses his mouth out. Then he aggressively walks down the crevice pushing past Sancho and Bernie saying to himself, "But we are inland, miles *away from the ocean!* AND two miles *ABOVE the ocean!!* I cannot *understand it!?!*" Glenn stomps a couple hundred feet down into the cavern; they follow, each lighting their flashlights. The path ends at a steep decline and Glenn tells them to wait there for him. He gingerly climbs down eighty feet of the steep loose rocks to get to the cavern floor, as he walks around, he notices the sand is soft and wet under his feet. He tastes it again then spits in anger. "How *fucking stupid* could I be!" He senses some kind of activity deeper in.

As he is walking around the cavern, Bernie and Sancho are on the path above him cautioning him not to go too far, not to go out of sight, to keep the light on so that they can see him. He waves them off, annoyed by their concern. He had been this far into the cavern before and now he was going to go a little further to see what he is sensing. It is like a musty current of air that sounds like a distant wind.

Sancho yells, "Boss-Man, I no see you, shine your light at me."

Bernie shouts "Wait, I'll come down with you." Their voices reverberate to a hollow echo.

That distant wind sounds closer, and Glenn walks toward it, he can feel it on his face. He comes to a wall that goes far to his right, but he can see a large opening ahead to his left. He goes there and shining the light thru he sees a pathway going up into another immense cavern. He wants to go in there but feels a sudden whooshing wind coming from his right. As he turns to walk there, he steps on a hard shell. He finds it has attached itself to the rock wall and he tugs it loose. He thinks, "Another curiosity to investigate . . ." Resuming his walk to the whooshing wind; he sees in the beam of his flashlight, droplets streaming up to the surprisingly high ceiling. Then he notices rocky debris everywhere on the ground ahead of him. Now the sound is quickly increasing; it beginning to sound like Niagara Falls. Frightened he turns and runs back towards the entrance. He can't see their flashlights. He turns and flashes his light behind him in time to see a gusher of water squirting with ferocious force and impacting the high ceiling, then cascading down everywhere. He runs faster, but in an instant the water is covering the ground.

The next thing he knows the water is around his feet as he starts to run faster. The water is up to his ankles, then his knees, then his hips and – it's FREEZING cold – but fortunately, it's carrying him in the direction he wants to go.

The next thing Glenn knows he can no longer walk, he's floating. "AAGGHHH!" he cries out in frightened surprise and drops the shell, as he must swim to stay afloat. Sancho and Bernie suddenly see water is climbing higher and higher up the cavern walls and then they see Glenn's flashlight beam coming towards them within a flooding tidal wave. They scream for him to be careful and swim towards them. Glenn tries, but the water is taking him past that rocky slope where they are standing above him. Glenn leaves them behind as the tidal surge carries him further away.

Sancho tells Bernie to go get the long ropes off of Alcarracho's basket. He quickly runs up and gets them and runs back down. Sancho ties one around Bernie's waist, "You swim?" Bernie answers with a wide-eyed nod. "Bueno! *You go get him!!*" as he anchors the end of another rope around a large boulder then ties the other end to Bernie's rope. Bernie does as he is told and dives into the water as Sancho feeds the rope out to him, while trying to keep his light on him. Bernie screams in shock from the freezing water. Sancho is yelling, "Bernie, he went where I am shining my light; go there! You see it? *Swim THERE!!*" Bernie swims in the direction Sancho's light illuminates on a far wall. He quickly swims several hundred feet as the flood is still coming in, carrying him in that direction. He arrives at that far wall. Feeling the current on his feet, he knows that the water is continuing under him thru an opening.

Bernie's mind races, "Certainly must drown to be stuck under there! Can't swim against this current; but I have *the rope!* Glenn must be dying on the other side, just beyond me. Must be drowning as the water is rising so high; he'll be trapped against the roof." He can hear air bubbling out from there as the water is filling up that cavern. Diving down below with his flashlight, he is able to see underneath and realizes the current is carrying him through the opening. He sees a faint glimmer of the other flashlight through the mist of sandy surf below him. "I can't *dive down* that far?!?" He sees the glassy surface above him and thinks "I don't want to *get trapped up there!*" Then he hears coughing and gagging from up above him. He swims up and breaking the surface sees Glenn *frantically treading water* trying to keep his head up. The water is almost against the ceiling. He doesn't see Bernie's light shining on his face as he is too busy *choking on his vomit* after swallowing this freezing salt water. Bernie throws two loops from his rope over Glenn's head, down to around his waist and calms him down saying, "We're gonna dive down and follow the rope back to Sancho: we'll be *all right!* Take 3 deep breaths *then we dive!!*" They both have their heads cranked up against the ceiling to avoid the water that is now up to their chins. They dive down *but don't seem* to be making any headway against the strong current.

Sancho senses something on his end of the rope; did it *lose some tension?* He starts pulling it in and feels *tremendous resistance* against him. He passes the rope over his shoulders and leans forward with all his weight, he *strains up the crevice*, then hand over hand he pulls on the rope as he walks back, and again turns and struggles his way back up the crevice. After 6 exhausting times he *finally sees them*, and *he pulls them back* to the top of the rocky slope. The water is now up to Sancho's feet and *he falls* as he starts to run away; Bernie and Glenn are half crawling, *half swimming up* the crevice. They scramble to their feet undoing the rope and *run out* into the valley. The water is following them and spreading out calmly across the valley's desert floor. Sancho unties Alcarracho and they quickly jump into the basket. Glenn sets it to rise. They are *freezing* as that water is so cold . . . "Jesus!" Bernie says through chattering teeth, "It is saltwater; where the hell is *that coming from?!?*"

Glenn says shivering, "Yeah, I even saw some kind of a small fish; strange looking - like I've never seen before. White, almost transparent, with some sort of a glow to it."

Bernie says, "Sounds like a fish I had seen in a nature TV program about deep-water, ocean floor fish. They live down thousands of feet; down around volcanic vents."

"You guys earned your pay today; you *saved my life!*" Glenn says gratefully. - A quiet instance of reverie for all, then - "I picked up a large spiral shell and was bringing it back when the water caught me." They quickly fly Alcarracho back to the Hacienda; Glenn and Bernie are still shivering from the freezing cold water. The Professor instructs them to take a hot shower and rest to recuperate. Sancho tells everyone how he and Bernie saved Glenn's life, detailing how he struggled to pull them both from the water. They exchange sneers saying Boss-Man too stupid, not know he can't go deep into unknown cave all alone, with no safety gear.

Elena tries to have sex with Glenn in the shower, but he roughly pushes her away and goes to bed to rest. He misses his noon shift on Skyhook. At dinner, Glenn describes to Bernie the fish and the shell he saw. Bernie draws the images from his description and says, "I'll look them up on the internet. It's possible that I could identify those fish and their habitat on-line - using the Professor's computer; that is if the 'great man' wouldn't object to me using his computer."

Glenn says smiling, "No, I wouldn't risk it; but you can use mine. But only for this . . ." Then Glenn repeats, "*Only for this* - not for anything else. Do not try to contact anybody as it will be a risk to everything. We are only hiding; but we are not out of the reach of the Mexican cartel."

Bernie explains, "The FBI Director said that cartel was going after somebody floating in a red balloon who shot one of their people in Mexico."

Glenn says, "Yes that's true; but they were shooting at me and I shot back, I guess I hit someone." Bernie solemnly relays that the FBI Director said he died. "Sorry to hear that but I had to shoot back because he was going to cripple my balloon, and then God only knows what they might have *done to me!* There were others also shooting at me; but they scattered when I returned fire."

Bernie meets with CIA Jane and confirms what she had been claiming all along: that it is ocean water going into the cavern. Bernie intensely relays his heroics and the mysterious fish Glenn saw. Replying, she says with a 'come hither' radiant smile, "I told you that; even this sandy desert floor here comes from saltwater - because volcanic craters don't have sandy floors; they have rocky gravel floors from the lava rock. This is not volcanic rock - any fool could see that this sand does not naturally occur here."

The next morning at breakfast, Bernie has print-outs of the shell and the fish and confirms they live on the deep ocean floor, maybe near volcanic vents.

The workers are all talking about the deadly Covid19 virus infection going around the world and how they need to keep a distance and maybe quarantine from each other; maybe even their children. Elena is saying how terrible to think a parent would stay away from a sick child. She and Margherita would give their lives to have children and to be with them when they were sick; "Can you imagine your child is dying and knows that you won't go near them out of fear of getting the disease? We played at being mothers as children and want nothing more out of life than to be good mothers. - Then to abandon them to die alone?!?" They share a moment with tears welling up in their eyes.

Then Margherita says, "Maybe you are going to be a mother." More wet eyes. "I asked Glenn what if I get pregnant, he said he would pay for my abortion . . ."

Elena's eyes pop, her mouth drops as her brain screams, *"ABORTION!!!"* She senses a strange new twitching in her abdomen. She asks fervently, "Did you tell him I might be pregnant?" Before Margherita can answer, she sees Glenn walking out, bending over and eating sand. She's thinking, "He has to take care of my baby . . .

But

Glenn WANTS TO MURDER <u>MY BABY</u>!!"

Bernie had just told Glenn, according to Jane, this whole valley's crater floor is ocean sand. He goes outside, bends over, and picks up a handful of sand and puts it in his mouth – Elena comes *running* out from the kitchen and *tackles him* thinking he must be suicidal because of her pregnancy. - then Glenn spits it out; barely noticing Elena on the ground next to him. He stands-up saying, "That CIA-bitch is right . . ."

All the men bust out into frantic laughter, *"Como stupido; he's eating sand,* que Gringo! Little Elena threw him on the ground, she tackled him and *rolled him around* and he just gets up talking to himself and spitting out sand *like nothing happened!!"*

CIA-Jane and Margherita run to Elena; Jane is ready *for action!* Margherita scolds, "What's a matter with you, are *you loco?"* as they help her to her feet.

"He was eating sand; he has to take care of my baby. He can kill himself after he *signs the 'Birth Certificate'.* Did you tell him that I am going to have his baby?"

Margherita says, "No, you don't even know if *you're pregnant!* You got time; no sense saying anything until you are sure. Anyway, he was talking about paying for *my abortion,* not yours!"

Jane says, "He'll never sign anything for you. Who *gives a fuck* if he swallows this *whole desert!* I hope *his brains* turn to sand ~ and his cock too!!"

Elena cries putting her hand on her abdomen. "I am sure *I'm pregnant;* I just felt something here when we were in the kitchen, and I am never this late . . . He can't make me *have an abortion!"*

Margherita replies negatively, "When I said 'abortion', you just got scared for your baby. That's what you felt."

"We should all *kick the shit out of him!"* Jane says, "One day, sooner or later, he is going to throw you both out; and he is *gonna murder me!* We got to *do something!!"*

"Maybe you got to do something, *not us!"* Margherita replies with disdain, "We are much better off because of Glenn and his project. *All men are pigs;* why should we think he is gonna be different."

"You have a right to a healthy relationship with a man; if you keep thinking like that your men will never treat you right." Jane lectures, "I'm telling you we should get together and *kick the shit* out of him. That will make your Pecuadorian men think twice about the way they treat their women."

Margherita's eyes narrow into daggers, "Don't bitch to us about how our *men treat us!"*

Jane retorts, "If the Boss-Man finds out that Elena's cousin Miguel is trying *to fuck Virginia* while she's at that school; he's going to throw you both out and take her *for himself!"*

Elena says, "I don't need a man, I just need money to raise my baby proper. I don't even *want a man!*" Jane shakes her head seeing the tears well up in their eyes again; then turns and walks away.

Glenn stops her and asks irritated, "How the fuck did you know that this is *ocean sediment?* You're not a *geologist!* I've been here for months, and I *never noticed it?!?*" Everyone is watching to see if Glenn is going to continue the scuffle with this other woman.

Jane is aware that she is the center of attention. So, to impress everybody and shame Glenn, she translates his question into perfect Spanish and then answers it in Spanish only, thus excluding him. Glenn recognizes a few words: 'Suo Petrone genio, yo non sono geologicolo; como tu sabe, aqua de mare'; but he knows she is not complementing him. She finishes her speech, saying in Spanish, "I got tired, so I sat down on the ground, and I *got my ass wet!*" while sticking her ass out and brushing it off. Everyone but Glenn bust out laughing; he *is humiliated!* The Professor, through laughter, finally explains what she had said; Glenn laughs too.

Glenn sees her later and says, "So you got your ass wet; but, how did you know it was *salt water?*"

Without saying a word, she leans as if to sit on the ground extending her painted manicured nails into the sand, then brushes her hand off on her thigh, then looks at her nails, and then puts them into her mouth, and then squinting, protrudes her tongue with a cute little, tiny spit, then says . . . *"salt."* She dismissively walks away.

CIA Jane is impressed that Bernie is trusted to use the computer. She catches him alone and asks, "Can you use it again whenever you want, for whatever you want?"

Bernie replies, "The Boss-Man told me that I can only use it for his project."

"Well, you're able to get on the Internet, so you can get outside." He nods yes. "Can I give you an email address for you to look up."

He says, "I guess so," but adds an after-thought, "I ah - I don't know - if Glenn will ok it."

"You can't even look something up *for me?* Please try? I don't want to get you into trouble with your Boss-Man. I just want to let my mother know that I'm all right, that I'm not afraid, that *I'm alive,* and that I'm going to be okay, that nobody's hurting me. I just need to *let my family know!*" she says tearfully.

Bernie says, "Give me the email address; I will try to get it past that *fucking dictator.*"

She thanks him with hugs and kisses. Then she says, "He'll trust you more after you tell him that your friend Jake is spreading nasty rumors about our US Government's having a phony election process . . ." his eyebrows raise up, "because they are considering NYC businessman Ponald Prump for President - Jake's labeling him a white supremacist . . ."

Bernie looks at her questioningly, "But, he thinks the black boys accused of raping the white woman in Central Park should have been executed. Even after somebody else confessed to it, he was in favor of them remaining in prison; one of them is still in prison. Also, he was found guilty of stealing from a Children's Cancer Charity. And, 25 million dollars was paid in restitution for Prump University for fleecing the students. He also is notorious for underhanded dealings in real estate and refusing to pay people and getting them tangled-up in lawsuits." Jane withdraws from their embrace. "Isn't that all true?" Bernie queries.

"Even if it is true, Americans shouldn't be promoting this negative image of our democracy. Especially not to foreigners in a foreign country. *That's SEDITION!*"

"But isn't he already saying, before the election, if he loses it will be because the Democrats will have stolen the election from him? He is already *undermining our democracy* as a candidate. They say that his campaign is colluding with Russians in obstructing the elections in the United States."

"Well, if Glenn is such *a humanitarian*, I am sure he will want to know about how unpatriotic Jake is."

Bernie is thinking, "What does *being a humanitarian* have to do with supporting a *kleptocratic fascist* for the presidency?" but elects to return to the warmth of her embrace and follows up with *a tender kiss.*

Later, Bernie introduces this information while in conversation with Glenn and Jake, asking how it came to pass that he was speaking in Spanish to Juan and others at the dinner table about U S politics. Jake replies, "They were curious about our presidential candidate becoming famous around the world for saying that - as a television celebrity - he was free to *grab any woman's pussy* and they let him do it!"

Glenn simply replies with a chuckle, "Yes, you can understand how that piece of news would spread to these remote mountain villages. But nothing about the millions he had to repay to the Vets charity that he had fleeced from them. But I have other problems to worry about." as he walks away abandoning them to their gossip.

"So," Glenn is thinking, "the Cavern-Gusher is eating away at the rocks there in the cavern and carving out a higher ceiling. Eventually that pressure is going to break through, and a saltwater cascade will flood down into the jungle below; washing out the railroad tracks and maybe some native Indian villages. Somehow or other I have got to make sense of this."

He asks the Professor, who predictably replies, *"Listen!* For the second time: I am an Astrophysicist, why don't you hire *a geologist!"* Glenn doesn't want anybody snooping around his project, making waves and possibly trouble for him. He knows it's got to be the deep Pacific Ocean water traveling up two miles above sea level and two miles inland. That seawater was flowing into this valley crater over the millennia, then it stopped and turned it into a sandy desert.

Glenn had only gone down into the cavern a few times. He guesses that whenever he had gone the seawater all must have evaporated, or it seeped down between the boulders, filling the old volcanoes' main lava-tube. He needs to go back into the cavern with flood lights and set up camera so that he can monitor what is actually happening there. But he has got to work on the mag-lev launchings from Skyhook – 12 hours a day, 7 days a week. "I'll get Bernie to do it, he was a reporter. He should be able to handle setting up cameras, and I'll get Juan to run electricity from the train tracks into the cavern: they can help each other."

After breakfast the next day, Bernie and Juan take the truck and equipment and go there to accomplish the task. To Glenn's surprise, Bernie invites Jane along for the ride. Sancho and the Professor both agree for once that it is a relief not to have her around causing trouble. (She playfully grabbed Sancho's fat ass in front of all the men. He was shocked and had to endure much derisive laughter.) They drive there and Bernie cautions them not to go down into the cavern beyond the rock slope. But Jane had been there before, and she chides them for being afraid; so, they follow her. As the men are setting up the lights and the cameras, she brazenly approaches the opening that gushed the seawater and studies it, taking video of it while commenting on what she can deduce about it. Glenn is impressed when he views it, "Just like a real reporter; less like a CIA Agent?" He studies the steep edges down into the gusher tube and musingly thinks, "She might have fallen in, and it looks like we could have never gotten her out . . . She would have simply disappeared . . . Hhmmm? - Wouldn't that have been *a tragedy?!?*"

Over the next week, using Glenn's computer Bernie monitors the cavern video feed along with Jane who seems to have developed an interest in the flooding phenomena: or an interest in Bernie. He reports the prior day's viewing to Glenn at breakfast and finally comes to the conclusion that it is tidal, as the gushing matches the Pacific coast tidal schedule, 3 hours before high-tide till 3 hours after. It, more or less, reaches the same level up into the valley every 12 hours. And the seawater that remains in the cavern basically all flows back down the same lava-tube by the time of ebb tide. Glenn insists on gaining the Professor's attention and points all this out to him, "It gushes 2 miles or more above the ocean level and it's about 2 miles inland: whoever heard of the ocean water traveling inland - up hill like that?"

In spite of himself, the Professor is also amazed by this. "I did . . ." The Professor surprises Glenn with this quick retort. "The bore tide in the Bay of Fundy between the Nova Scotia peninsula and the Canadian mainland."

"*What?!?*" Glenn is amazed. "That tide travels *uphill* - far in land?!?"

"Yeah. As much as thirteen miles as I recall, against the river's current. The tidal weight of the whole Atlantic Ocean is leaning on the coast during high-tides, funneling the pressure that propels the bore tide up the river." he says. "It does it regularly twice a day with its arrival timed down to the very second; it's an amazing thing to see. You should go there sometime."

Glenn's bewildered mind is further confused while trying not to aggravate the Professor, "Yes, but if this is ocean water, it more or less had to come up an elevation of two miles above *sea level!* It had to come from the deepest part of the ocean; which must be - probably - *3 miles, at least,* off the continental shelf of South America. I must research that. It would have to travel underground, and up this mountain, at the time high-tide is just starting to come in. So, for another three hours beyond the time that we were in the cavern; it wasn't even high-tide - that can't be disputed. What's the answer: could there be a hidden ocean that's above sea level within the mountain; if that's true, why would it suddenly gush up like that; and why would it not just fill up this valley and stay here until it all evaporated?" Glenn's meandering confusion continues, "It's gushing up with such great force, it shoots all the way up to the ceiling, blasting rocks from the ceiling. I was walking towards it. If I had been caught on top of that it would have slammed me up there and crushed me against those rocks."

The Professor replies too casually, "Well then, stay away from it . . ." And returns to his work; Glenn's face betrays his mental exhaustion.

That night while loading the Railgun's automatic feeders, Glenn's mind wanders to other consideration about the Cavern-Gusher. Somewhere he had heard there's a lot of precious metals dissolved in the ocean: gold and silver. He drives the forklift back to the Skyhook's loading-bay and waits for the next load's imminent arrival on the Loon-Evator. "Computer: Search Bay of Fundy, Canada." His heads-up space-suit display shows tourist info only: 'The highest tides at super-moon raise up fifty feet on the coast, carving island that look like huge flowerpots'. The map shows the Bay is in the shape of a funnel pointing inland to a river which goes further inland. Glenn looks up 'Fundy Bore Tide' and sees it flows at least thirteen miles above the city of Moncton. Then he searches 'metals in ocean sediment' and finds that there's more than just gold & silver. There are rare metals used for the electronics industry that are in great demand; his entrepreneurial mind is surging.

At their next breakfast he mentions it to the Professor, who isn't happy to have his meal interrupted, "I am here to assist you in your humanitarian project - your *original project!* It's still not solved; there is *another 'Big Syphon' sucking the fluids off the Earth*. It's killing people; shouldn't we be concentrating on choking it . . ."

Glenn replies offended, "We're all set for it, it has got to cross over this crater valley, and we have more H-cube balloons in the stratosphere than we had the last time we choked it. *We can't miss!*"

"Well then, hire a geologist, an aquatic engineer, an oceanographer, and all the other Professors you'll need to get your distractions resolved.

There are plenty of other experts with Doctor's Diplomas dying to get experimental research work. Remember, that's how you got me here."

Glenn's lip curls as he sneers with contempt, thinking, "Yeah, now I want more like you telling me how stupid I am . . . to rub my nose in their Doctoral Diplomas."

The irritated Professor reacts, "Now you want ME to go prospecting for gold?!? Don't you have enough money? Why do you need more money? You said you wanted to work on saving the environment . . . *It's still dying!*" The Professor's voice has gotten louder attracting everyone's attention; Jane's eyes alight with pleasure. "You are the only one getting filthy rich off this whole operation: selling your electricity and launching your nuclear waste; we all are still *working like dogs* and most of your employees are living like dogs! Well, at least you're *getting rich!* I'm still no closer to getting my project started . . ."

Glenn retaliates by pointing out their success, "By providing cheap, clean electricity from Skyhook's balloons, these Central & South American countries are no longer burning the polluting coal & oil! The world was running out of space to store all the nuclear waste; it was a disaster waiting to happen! We are all instrumental in accomplishing this! Also, we are gonna stop Armageddon: 'The Big Syphon', for *the second time!!*"

"Yeah; *Armageddon! –* Your 'Big Syphon'!! – WHICH WAS *YOUR IRRESPONSIBLE CREATION!!!*" The Professor's blood pressure is cooking his face red. "I studied to be an *ASTRONAUGHT!* NOW I am working in a fucking assembly line; exactly why I went to school for *twelve fucking years*: to become a cog in *your fucking assembly line!!!*" the Professor snaps. Glenn promises him again that he will fund his project, that he can start his Antarctic Ocean Plankton Production project after they clean up this mess and get it down to a regular schedule. But the Professor replies, "Yeah, but after the next equinox your economics gets *FUCKED!* You're going to have one million exploded H-cube balloons laying all over this Valley – again - and we will have to start all over – again - with no income from electricity coming in and no means of launching the toxic waste!! So that means we repeat everything – *again* – with absolutely no money coming in – *and* all money spent on rebuilding – _AGAIN_ - and nothing left over for my project for another couple *of years!!* Once we finally get started - again; who knows what else will delay my project: *I PUBLISHED* my book

3 years ago where I said I would have accomplished my Carbon-Dioxide (CO2) reduction project within a year – Now I look like a *FOOL!!!*" He brusquely gets up from his breakfast and stomps away.

The next morning before breakfast the Professor stops Glenn saying somewhat apologetically, "I was curious about those strange emails I found in the historical backup of our computers."

Glenn queries, "What strange emails are you talking about?"

The Professor elaborates, "I was looking for an old purchase order that I wanted to duplicate and went into the historical file and saw that there has been recent activity: emails that I didn't recognize." Glenn's expression questions the nature of these emails. "Oh, it's just a comment saying that 'I am alright' and 'do not worry', and 'I can't say any more yet', and 'do not tell anyone, especially the police or the government'; strange stuff like that."

Glenn thanks him and returns to his office and looks in the historical file and sees several emails that are obviously from Jane going to her mother. He stomps his way to the kitchen, brusquely passing the men who are being drawn to that pleasant smell of bacon cooking. Breakfast is on the verge of being served. Elena and Margherita are busy cooking, Jane and Bernie are sitting at a table talking. Glenn goes directly to them shouting, "What emails have you been sending out?!?"

Jane says defiantly, "I simply told my mother that I was all right and not to worry about me." Everybody stops what they're doing to pay attention.

Glenn glares at Bernie. "I told you not to have any outside correspondence . . . You are supposed to use my computer *for research only!*"

Bernie defends sheepishly, "She only wanted her mother to stop worrying; my God, she thought Jane was dead."

"You *fucking compromised everything!*" Glenn challenges. "I trusted a drug smuggler . . . *I should feed you to the Mexican cartel!!*"

With that CIA Jane jumps up, takes two steps and throws her right leg forward into a snap kick directly into Glenn's balls. He *gasps* with the shocking pain. It bends him over, clutching his groin with both hands; Jane takes one step back and then, with the same leg, throws a front snap kick to his throat. He *yelps* with this surprising new pain and falls backwards and rolls over.

Everybody's eyes bulge out of their heads; *"Get him!"* she screams. But nobody moves. Glenn painfully turns over and scrambles to his feet. Still bent over, he goes towards Jane, straightens his spine, keeping his left-hand on his balls, his right-hand is balled into a fist behind his back. She jumps in the air in a circular spin and throws a round-house kick towards his head - which he easily dodges. As she is going back down to the ground, with all his weight he slams a solid hard right behind her right ear. It sends her sprawling down to the ground, crashing into the leg of the picnic table. She gets up dazed and approaches Glenn with trepidation in her voice shouting, "Come-on *everybody* ~ let's get him!" She tries to attack him with an overhand right, which he quickly blocks with his left forearm while delivering a solid right-hand deep into her stomach: Jane collapses to her knees, vomiting. "Come-on ~ get him . . ." she cries, speaking Spanish while gagging and holding her stomach. Everybody is standing in wide-eyed amazement. Bernie then jumps up and goes to Jane, kneels on the ground comforting her while blocking Glenn's access to her. His two women come running from behind Glenn. He spins around anticipating violence. They stop – frozen in fear. Bernie is helping Jane up, who now pleads in Spanish through her tears, "Come on - let's *get him!?!*" Glenn whips around glaring hatred at her.

His two women slowly make a wide berth around Glenn, walking towards Jane. They grab her by the arms and start talking to her in Spanish saying, "Come with us, we'll go to your cabin. What's a matter with you?!? You must *be loco* from that steroid medicine . . ."

Jane breaks down, crying in defeat, "You people help him - *against me?!?* You don't care if he kills me! You're supposed to *help me*! I'll never get out of here; are you just going to watch *while he's murdering me?!?*" Jane is sobbing uncontrollably as the girls are leading her away, "It's not fair; you're my friends, why won't you help me?"

"It's needlessly cruel . . ." Bernie says as he continues blocking Glenn from attacking her while watching her slowly hobble towards her cabin. "Now she's even got me wondering if you mean to kill her."

Glenn snarls through gritted teeth, "If I wanted her dead, she would have been dead long before *you got here!* I saved her life - risking my own life!! She was shooting at me and shot my 50,000-pound helium storage tank - she *blew it up!* Stupid cunt almost ruined *my entire project!* If I let her out of here, she's going to do it, and we'll have to stop launching the nuclear waste." Bernie backs away from Glenn and sits down at the table as Glenn continues accusingly, "You must have told her that I shot those Mexicans? How can I ever let her leave here now?!? I was going to let her go when she gets over her steroid addiction, after we finish launching all the nuclear waste; when we start launching the other toxic waste." Glenn's lungs are heaving with anger and from the pain in his balls and under his chin where she kicked him. "She's not a reporter; *she's CIA!* She tried to kick me in my throat; that would have *KILLED ME!!*" After a moment of silence Bernie sighs and resumes his breakfast.

Suddenly all the workmen begin an animated chatter, laughing and frolicking saying what a great place this is to work:

"There is always some exciting drama going on . . ."

"The loco Gringos are always finding something to fight about . . ."

"It's better than a cock fight . . ."

"Next time I bet on Jane kicking the *Boss-Man 's ass!*" "It looks like all Gringos hate each other . . ."

"Maybe because they have too much money and don't have to work hard like we do . . ."

"Too much time on their hands - nothing important to do . . ."

"Nobody has ever seen Jane doing any work . . ."

"Who knows what they do when the gringo men go up on the Loon-Evator?"

Another man answers singingly, "They go up there to *make love to the stars . . .*"

- Then exhaling a prolonged spiritual sigh while looking longingly, he points his left-hand at the sky.
    - Then he sticks his tongue out the corner of his mouth while grimacing orgasmically.
        - Then does the jerking-off motion with his right-hand . . .
            - The workmen all bust out *laughing heartily!*

Glenn rages with anger while suffering in pain and thinking, "Stupid CIA should have trained her against combat with anyone – man or woman - who is much heavier than herself. She should have grabbed a knife or a fork, or smashed a dish on my head; then *cut my throat* with a fragment. Next time *she will* use a weapon against me . . ." He aggressively hobbles to the kitchen and goes into the medical supplies retrieving a syringe and a vial of fluid. He remembers Jane's prescription dosage and he fills the syringe to that level. He manages a quick walk, disappearing behind the row of cabins, then he painfully jogs to Jane's cabin and goes inside and hides behind the door. As Jane hobbles through the doorway, supported by Elena and Margherita on either side, he viciously stabs her in the ass with the needle. She shrieks with this sudden new pain and the other two girls respond by backing away from her. Jane arches her back and turns towards Glenn. He continues to inject the syringe of medicine into her ass. They all stop and look on as Jane's eyes glaze over and she crumples to the floor.

Glenn resolves he must get her away from everybody. He tells them to throw her on the bed and pack up all her clothes. Then asks Elena to go finish serving the employee's breakfast. She asks if they should all eat in Jane's cabin. He says yes and tells Margherita to pack up a lot of canned food and frozen food, anything that can be refrigerated, and milk and a can of coffee and a big jug of water. Glenn gets an empty skid and lays a tarp on it, then puts an electric heater on it and sets it to 50 degrees and places it in the middle; then places Styrofoam coolers surrounding it. The two women carry the food to the skid and put it in the coolers.

Elena asks, "Why you taking all dis food? You gonna go live up there?"

Glenn replies angrily, "Just do what I tell you to do. And don't say anything to anybody – nothing about Jane or the food – NOTHING!!" Glenn ties down the tarp completely enclosing its contents. The three of them eat a cold breakfast while keeping an eye on the sedated Jane. Then Margherita feels a bump on Jane's head were Glenn punched her; she gets an ice pack for it. Glenn says, "Get me one for my chin . . ." then adds "and one ***for my balls!***"

Just before noon Jake returns with the Loon-Evator and gets out of his space-suit. Glenn has recovered from the kick in his balls and the kick to his chin, so he goes and takes Jake's space-suit off the clothesline, gets the forklift and drives it back to Jane's cabin. He puts on his space-suit while he has the girls put Jake's space-suit on the comatose Jane. He makes sure it is properly sealed at the waist and sets her communicator so that he can talk to her if need be; then they slide her head into the helmet, he locks it into position and sees that the space-suit inflates properly. Then they all carry Jane to the skid and lay her on top of it. Glenn picks up the skid with the forklift and drives it on to the now fully loaded Loon-Evator. Everybody is looking but does not quite understand what is going on, it is strange to see Jake in his space-suit laying on top of the skid – or – it could be just his inflated space-suit. They don't know – but, it could be Jane in the space-suit. However, they're not really that interested. They talk about the entertaining fight:

> "It must have been a lover's quarrel between the crazy Gringos."
> "Horny Boss-Man has to fuck all his mujers the same day."
> "He too stupid to know there's gonna be big trouble."
> "We're gonna get to watch them all *kill each other!*"

Glenn unloads the skid, drives off the Loon-Evator, walks up the loading ramp, plugs in that heater to prevent the food from freezing solid and ruining it on its way up into the minus 50-degree stratosphere. Glenn pushes the switch to up. As the Loon-Evator begins to rise, he verifies that Jane is still breathing okay and lowers her sunshield. He is further reassured as he observes both their space-suits fully inflating simultaneously. He feels a little better and reaches to the groin of his space-suit to gently massage his aching balls; all he feels is his gloved hand rubbing on fabric.

When he arrives up at Skyhook, he can see that she is still sedated, and oblivious to anything that is going on.

He expects her to remain totally unconscious for the next several hours. He drives her off with Skyhook's fork-lift and notices that her feet are now hanging down over the edge of the tarp. As he slows down by the cabin, the skid bounces a little on the fork-lift-prongs and he hears her interrupted breathing as she slides off and hits the floor with a painful groan. Glenn jams on the brake and frantically runs to the front, she's still unconscious and is now breathing normally again. He places his hands under her armpits and drags her through the air-lock-doors and inside the cabin. He places her on the couch and proceeds to remove her space-suit. Seeing that she is sedated and resting comfortably, he feels a surge of vengeful anger - complicated by a sudden erection. "I should give her a *punishingly violent fuck!!*" he thinks - then his sub-conscious mind inquires,

{"Is this my pride or my penis re-acting?"} Glenn's conscious mind thinks, "Maybe it's just my adrenalin subsiding; making my mind and body react strangely?" He surrenders to an irresistible impulse and slides his thickly gloved hand under her bra and squeezes her titty; he sees her eyes moving under her eyelids. He experiences fleeting guilt remembering how the N Y Congressman/former comedian Alan Franken had to resign as he jokingly felt up the life jacket of a sleeping female on a military flight; as if he could feel anything other than the thick fabric. Glenn could only feel the fabric of his glove. He whips his hand away leaving the top buttons of her blouse open. He leaves her, taking Jake's space-suit back to the Loon-Evator. He is fearful of leaving Jane up there alone in Skyhook's cabin; but then dismisses it as the cabin is under video surveillance.

He unpacks the skid of food placing it into the entrance air-lock, then pressurizes it, and then goes into Skyhook's cabin carrying the food in and stowing the perishables in the refrigerator and freezer and everything else into the cabinets while thinking bitterly, "She could use the microwave to warm up the canned foods and there's a toaster for her to toast frozen waffles and bread. There's butter, peanut butter, jelly, and some eggs, she *won't starve!*" He places a fresh jug of water next to the water cooler, so it will be immediately available for her to replace when the other one is empty. He checks that the toilet is functioning and gives himself a reminder to have Jake replace the sewage tank daily. "He's going to love that," he thinks sardonically, "Well he did it on my Winnebago in Arizona when he was making a lot less money – of course - not counting his drug smuggling business with the FBI." He looks toward Jane on the couch thinking, "Could she have had any connection with that South Western FBI Director who was harassing him? No! That would mean they would know where I am, and they would certainly have me arrested - or have a hit man kill me." Continuing to look at the sleeping CIA Jane he thinks, "She is still on a decreasing dosage of the steroid to wind down her addiction. I forgot to bring any up here for her." He dictates a reminder to bring it up the next day, then he says aloud to no one, with some small feeling of justice, "For today, she'll just have to suffer the withdrawal symptoms." Again, he is fearful of leaving Jane up there alone in the Skyhook cabin; but resolves the video surveillance will have to suffice. He locks the cabin from the outside disabling the air-lock mechanism so that it could not de-pressurize in case she tried. Now she cannot escape without a space-suit as there is no air outside the cabins and the temperature is -50° at that 120,000-foot altitude, up in the stratosphere. He makes sure that the cabin has adequate oxygen tanks and C-O2 scrubbers to support her breathing for several weeks and records reminders to check it daily and to order additional refill tanks. Glenn resumes his work of launching the nuclear waste.

By 7PM Jane awakens, sits up, very groggy, looks around the familiar cabin layout - except that out the window - she can see a spaceman walking around in an unusual gate; "It must be Jake or Glenn, but where are they?" She doesn't recognize anything out the window. She goes into the bathroom and sees that two top buttons of her blouse are open, and her bra is askew, "Was Bernie trying to get her tit out again? No," she now starts to remember, with that dry taste of bile in her mouth, she feels the pain in her stomach where Glenn had punched her, "It must have been *that pervert*, Glenn! I am going to kill *that motherfucker!!*" She uses the bathroom and washes out her mouth and throws water on her face to wake-up. "Something is very different about this cabin . . ." She surprisingly finds her suitcase in the middle of the floor. She takes out her toothbrush, goes back into the bathroom and brushes her teeth.

By the time she finishes, her mind has cleared, and she is back to full realization. She responds to a surging vindictive anger at Glenn as she pounds ferociously on the window. He sees her and responds by turning an imaginary crank with his left-hand while slowly raising the large middle finger of his inflated glove on his right-hand! She angrily struggles to open the door, then frantically kicks it.

Then she recalls her first days here, spying on Glenn from inside the Loon-Evator's cabin and then it floating upwards. She remembers how she had propped both the inner and outer doors open on the Loon-Evator and how it led to her almost suffocating - also the freezing cold; but not much after that until she woke up several days later. "They said I was recuperating from the 'bends' as a result of low air pressure when I was at 30,000 feet. They said I shot at him and exploded his Loon-Evator's 50,000-pound helium storage tank. They also said he risked his life to save me by parachuting while holding onto me, from 30,000 feet up." She feels her attitude towards him start to soften.

Now she remembers today's fight,

"He punched me in the stomach and *made me vomit!*" She says aloud to no one,

"That was then . . . this is *now!*
– It's on *NOW*!!
- **WAR *Motherfucker!!!*"**

She maliciously pounds on the window again and finally attracts Glenn in his space-suit, "He's strutting *around moon-walking*, like he's some kind of a *ridiculous Astronaut!!*" She takes three steps back, stepping in and jumping gives a full force round house kick onto the window. Glenn's eyes bulge. Then he gratefully remembers that these pressurized cabins are built with reinforced, unbreakable construction, including bullet-proof windows. She would need power tools or explosives to break *out of there!* Glenn still fears Jane's withdrawal rage. He can see she is screaming as she grabs a plastic ashtray off the coffee table and throws it with all her might. They watch it bounce harmlessly off the window. In angry desperation she goes to the refrigerator to find something heavier and grabs a gallon of milk. She heaves it against the window, it breaks the plastic carton splashing milk everywhere; but that's all. She sees Glenn doing an exaggerated Santa Claus laugh at her, then he gives her the finger again with a slap of his left-hand into his right elbow. He goes back to work, leaving her to endure her raging anger in that solitary confinement. He smiles with contentment knowing that she is *also suffering steroid withdrawal.*

In an hour he takes his lunch break while sitting in the fork-lift facing Jane's window. He frees his fingers from the space-suit's gloves and pulls his arms inside, then he ducks his head down into the trunk of the space-suit and takes his sandwich out of the chest pouch and eats with an occasional sip from the beverage straw. Ordinarily he would be eating inside the cabin while sitting in the oversized club chair with his feet up on the ottoman; but, not with Jane in there. He was used to sitting on the floor of his old Jet-Basket, so this was still better than that. He knew she couldn't distinguish his face with the glare of the lights reflecting off his visor and her window, unless they were within a foot of each other. He enjoys the idea of her thinking that he is staring at her. He finishes eating and the next thing he knows, his alarm wakes him up. He returns to loading the automatic feeders and monitoring the launchings of the nuclear-waste barrels.

Glenn bangs on her window just before midnight distracting her from a TV show. He waves goodbye to her with a gloating, rhythmic rocking of his head and hands. He thinks that he could never trust her to be reasonable; to not sabotage his project. That night he tells Jake of Jane's violent anger, "Don't go into Skyhook's cabin for any reason short of a life-threatening emergency. Jane must remain inside there - alone. She's not simply a reporter; she's a trained CIA agent working for the U S Government. She's here to sabotage *our project*. She thinks that I am a terrorist and believes the nonsense that the Mickey Mouse News channel and the FBI were spreading about my 'Big Cannon' project." Jake finds this hard to believe and is surprised that Glenn includes him on the *'our project'* concept; but has no thought of interfering with Glenn's plans. He's very tired working 12 hours a day, seven days a week, but he is content as he's got no alternatives. He's making good money and he has financial obligations to his family back in the states. Glenn had arranged to send support money from his pay. Also, he witnessed Glenn very casually shoot those two Mexican thugs. Jake feels threatened from what Glenn might do if he felt betrayed. Jane is going crazy trapped inside the Skyhook's cabin with nothing to do but watch television and look out through the glass at the launchings and try to communicate through the glass with whomever is in the space-suit working there. The video security displays can be viewed on all the TVs but there's no sound, so she cannot speak to anybody. However, she does find pencil and paper and writes messages and holds them up to the camera in the hope that Margherita or Elena would write back to her. They have very little written skills and can barely read, so no communication goes between them. They are laughingly fascinated by her last word which they pronounce, "Hane" (Ha Ne) and cannot figure out what it means; did she mean Juan? Glenn does not tell them that it's her signature – 'JANE'. He is not alarmed by Jane anymore and assumes the whole issue is behind them; except for Margherita asking Glenn why Jane can't go home. Why is he afraid to let her go? Glenn finally explains the whole history of everything that happened to him including showing her historical newsreels of his 'Big Syphon'. He explains what they were saying about him, and that the FBI is still after him: he is still on the most wanted list. They're calling him a terrorist and he elaborates on what would happen if they captured him. "And" he explains, "That is why I cannot take you to America. I only feel safe here in the valley and this corrupt government in Pecuador is making enough money off me, so they are not interested in my history - other than the fact that they call me the 'Ugly American'. As far as they know, I am not from the U S A, I am from Canada; but to them it's the same difference. I have not even contacted any members of my own family for fear that the FBI may trace my where abouts through the computer connections; and for all I knows they may have accomplished that already with the emails that Jane and Bernie sent out."

But Margherita's mind is stuck on the phrase: 'that is why I cannot take you to America.' She feared being arrested by the military ever since they murdered Corporal Tomas. She has often pondered: 'Glenn says he loves me, but- not even to save my life - will he take me to America.' How could he love her and not protect her by taking her away to his American home? Tears come to her eyes as she finally realizes that it was not possible for him, that he had no other alternatives.

Bernie wants to know what happened to Jane. Glenn explains to him as he explained to Margherita, everything that has transpired. "That is why we cannot let her go until the world can see that all my efforts were humanitarian. Therefore, I should not be punished for anything, and that incarcerating me would be a disservice to humanity. I do not know if they will ever understand; but that is our only hope. Until then, we keep her here as a prisoner, because she is definitely a 'loose cannon' on our environmental ship's voyage to save our planet."

Bernie is not impressed; however, he knows he has few alternatives. He was thinking of contacting his own family but now respects Glenn's restrictions for this humanitarian project. He apologizes to Glenn saying Jane shouldn't expect to be violating security when Glenn does not allow himself to do it. He remembers his discussion with Jake about when Glenn releases her, "The Mexican cartel is not after her, so they wouldn't be apt to hunt her like they would for Glenn, Jake and me. But what if she reports their location to the CIA and the drug smuggling Southwestern FBI

Director finds out? Political corruption is running rampant in the States. The international news talk shows are saying the Presidential Candidate will not accept that he could lose an election. And, he is letting everybody know that his 'Department of Justice' will penalize anybody who opposes him. He will award 'Federal Judgeships', 'District Attorney's', political offices & jobs, Cabinet positions, political support *and even criminal pardons* to his faithful. But they must visibly *KOWTOW to him* – like his press secretary repeatedly insisting that a million followers came out in the rain to support him, while the video showed a few hundred only. His VP obsequiously repeating Prump's name (instead of using the pronoun) in every uttered phase, while praising him."

VI

❖

THE GUSHER WITHIN

When Glenn's mind calms down, his thoughts go back to the cavern and the gusher within. He theorizes that the seawater must be coming-up from the deep depths of the ocean. He concludes that one of these deep ocean trenches must be running all the way to their shoreline, or maybe even further under the Continental Shelf, maybe even under this mountain peak. Volcanic hotspots over millions of years have created the Andes Mountains and the volcanoes within, and as these hotspots move, they may leave empty lava-tubes behind. Glenn has now surmised that a lava-tube from his volcanic crater must go down deep into the crust where it has somehow connected to a deep ocean trench. What did he remember from that old Rock Hudson & Ernest Borgnine movie 'Ice Station Zebra'? "They were concerned that the submarine would get crushed at 1200 feet saying that the ocean water pressure was 40,000 tons per square inch? NO! It must have been *40,000 pounds* per square foot. But wait - that doesn't make sense either . . . {I'm afraid to ask the Professor to calculate it.} Imagine what it must be like in the deepest ocean; maybe seven miles deep in the Mariana's Trench." He looks it up: "17,506.7 pounds-per-square-inch. At 1200 feet it is only 550 psi: is that enough to crush a submarine?" Then Glenn spends hours researching and finds there is a 5-mile-deep ocean trench, the 'Nazca Ridge & Trench' off the Pecuadorian Coast, resulting from the Pacific Tectonic Plate subducting under the South American Tectonic Plate. "The already deep ocean water pressure, plus that tidal pressure must cause it to gush up a lava tube into my valley, 2 miles above sea-level and inland 2 miles, with frightening force . . . *Twice a day!* That is a tremendous volume of seawater - I see it on Bernie's video of the cavern. There must be tons of naturally occurring metals dissolved within that ocean water, including gold, silver and other precious metals. That would include a concentration of dangerous metals too, like mercury, lead and whatever else. Oh well, I could launch that *into the Sun*, too."

VII

❖

EMPLOYEE PROBLEMS

Jane had spread the word amongst the workers that Glenn and the Professor were arguing about them all working like dogs and living like dogs while he is getting filthy rich. This hurt Glenn deeply. He was paying them more than they ever could have earned anywhere else. They were all fortunate to have jobs. Also, he had always intended to give them a fair share of his profits by way of bonuses. So, he devises the plan to have a 51%/49% corporation set up where the employees would ultimately own 49% of the company and share in its profit ratio based upon their salary, which is proportionate to their value to the corporation. But they would not become fully vested until they had worked for 10 years. That 49% would then become invested at 10% per year, after having worked for one full year. Meanwhile he would pay health insurance for them and provide life insurance. After 10 years he would continue paying it, but it would come out of their profit-sharing. Meanwhile he would continue to collect 51% of all the profits, as opposed to 100% of all profits now. Glenn explains this to the Professor. His face glows with appreciation.

Glenn seizes upon this moment saying, "By the way, I didn't know that you had studied to become an Astronaut?"

The Professor demurs, "I studied with that intention, but I knew I couldn't physically qualify. I got fat by the time I got out of Graduate School. I settled for environmental work as an astrophysicist – it's secondary to my lofty ambitions."

The Professor explains Glenn's profit-sharing plan at an employee meeting. The employees are suspicious, they cannot believe their ears. Sancho, Margherita, Juan and Elena had already been with him over a year, and he presents them each with the first year of their profit-sharing earnings in cash. And he does it in front of everybody so that they all can see how much money they are getting - everybody is totally floored by this.

Margherita says, "I am going to buy a red convertible and I'm going to take everybody in my town for a ride, I'll be the first female they ever knew that *can drive a car!"*

Elena clutches the money to her abdomen as she whispers to Margherita, "Soon I will have enough money for my baby!"

Margherita says, "Why? Are you sure you're pregnant now?"

She says, "Yes, you got your second period already. I should have mine by now; **but I don't!** I'm having *his baby!!* And if Glenn tries to make me have an abortion, I will use this money to pay somebody *to kill him!*

Margherita says, "*Stop talking stupid!* I will speak to him; I am sure it is not a problem for you to have his baby." That night in bed Margherita asks Glenn, "What if I get pregnant?"

Glenn says, "You know you can't get pregnant, why are you asking?"

"I just like to know what you would think if I got pregnant."

"I already told you, I would pay for your abortion."

"But, what if you get Elena pregnant?"

"I would pay for her abortion too." Glenn cannot help but think of those self-righteous white politicians who proclaim their religious convictions against abortions; but who routinely pay for their many mistresses' abortions using pilfered campaign funds.

"But what if Elena would want to keep the baby and not have an abortion?"

Glenn says, "Why these questions, *that CANNOT happen!"*

Margherita watches his expression closely as she answers, "Why? Because she says she is pregnant . . . ?"

Glenn says suddenly in shock, "She has to agree to **an abortion!** ~ I cannot have *a bastard child* running around . . . She's already married - why would she want to *have my baby?"*

"She's not really married; her husband is married to another woman."

Glenn says questioningly, "So she's divorced?"

"No, we poor mountain people don't bother with that sort of thing. It's no big deal here, the Priests would rather people be married and commit bigamy, than to not be married and having babies, and the men not feeling a family obligation. At least it lasts for a while till the men start looking for younger women again. Like my husband did. So, what you gonna do if it's true - Elena's pregnant?"

"What would I do if she doesn't want an abortion? Well, - we would have to get married - then; ~ just like everybody else does around here."

Margherita's eyes pop ~ tears well up, ***"You will marry her?!?"***

Glenn says, "But, how can your people get remarried without getting divorced?" too shocked to notice her distress, he explains, "Of course, if she's going to have my baby - and she agrees to have at least two more; because - I don't want my child to grow up alone. I spent a long time alone: I want my children to have brothers and sisters; siblings - that they can rely upon for help, - which look out for each other, that want to be together - and have holidays together. That's what life is all about. ~ It's not just working - and making money – and . . ."

Margherita runs out of the cabin naked and crying. Glenn yells out to her, "What's your problem? You're gonna *catch a cold!* **What's a matter with you;** *have you gone crazy?!?"*

She turns around and screams at him "Elena *is **pregnant!!**"* She comes back to bed later and finds Glenn sleeping.

The next morning Elena sees that she has been crying and asks, "What is the matter, did the Boss-Man say I must have an abortion? - Did he *beat you up?* I will **kill him** if that's what he did? Jane ***was right!*** We should have kicked the shit out of him."

"No *abortion!"* Margherita starts crying again, "No . . . He didn't beat me up." Sobbing she adds, "It's worse **than that!"**

"No abortion; but worse than getting beat up? Well then, tell me *what's the matter!"*

Margherita sobbing replies, "I told him you were pregnant, and you won't have an abortion; that you want to keep his baby."

She begins to shout, *"He'll make me have an abortion or else **he'll fire both of us?!?"***

"No; he says you have to **get married!"**

"Married . . . to who? Does he know someone he wants me to marry?"

"Yes, he wants you to ***marry HIM***

~ *AND*

he wants you to have ***three babies!***"

Margherita gasps, catching her breath,

"*or **even MORE!!!***"

Elena's eyebrows arch, "That's *what he said?!?*" as her eyes pop. Her mouth drops as Margherita nods in confirmation. Elena shouts, "**aaii*ieeeee!***" She jumps-up, then goes prancing and dancing around the Hacienda singing loudly, "I am going to **get married**, he's going to *marry me*, we gonna have ***three BABIES!! Yo sona PETRONA!***" Margherita bursts into tears and runs in to Glenn's cabin, crying profusely.

Glenn sees that and runs after Margherita saying "What is the matter with you? What's a matter with Elena?" Not understanding what she's saying to everybody.

"I told her what you said last night and now she's telling everybody that you're going to marry her, and you are going to have three babies . . ."

Glenn retorts, "I said I would pay for the abortion - and *I will* pay for it!"

"We would never have an abortion ~ all that we ever wanted was to be mothers and you think we would kill our babies: our only chance to be what we always **wanted to be?!?**"

"Uh, ahh, okay ~ so I will *marry her!* Why are **you crying?!?**"

Sobbing between painfully deep breaths, "You have to ask that! ***YOU STILL DON'T KNOW!!*** I have been with you from the **beginning!** You say you *love **ME**!* But you're going ***to marry Elena!!***"

Glenn starts to laugh uncontrollably ~ Margherita loses control and starts pounding her fists towards his face hitting him in the chest. While laughing he grabs her arms and falling backwards pulls her down on to the bed on top of him and then rolls on top of her. He holds her securely and starts kissing her tears as she turns her head angrily from side to side. He grabs her hair and restrains her, continuing to kiss her tears away and licking her tear-soaked face while whispering softly to her. "I do love you; I would marry you if you were pregnant; if that's what you wanted."

Margherita cries, "You know I can't get pregnant. I tried all the time and I never use protection like Gringas do. I just *can't get pregnant!*"

"Well, if you wanted it that badly you should have told me. There must be a reason why you can't get pregnant, and we could find out what it is. Maybe the Doctor can fix the problem . . . And if you're sure that is what you want, I will be happy to make you *pregnant!* But you have to agree to have at **least three babies!"**

Margherita calms down and is listening wide-eyed, comprehending – "Glenn will pay for the Doctor? The Doctor can fix my problem; *so that I can have a baby?!?"* - then she screams again and cries like a little lost child.

Glenn is surprised, but still soothingly says, "What now? What did I say to make you cry like this?"

"Now you tell me that you could marry me, and we can have babies - maybe - but it's too late; you gonna *marry Elena!"*

Glenn says, "Oh my God? *Now what!"* then continues soothingly kissing her *{kiss}* with each phrase, "Okay, *{kiss}* then I'll marry *{kiss}* both of you. If the Priests don't care *{kiss}* about men leaving *{kiss}* their first wife *{kiss}* to marry a second wife *{kiss}* without getting divorced, *{kiss}* then *{kiss}* why should they care *{kiss}* if I marry both of you!?! *{kiss}* What about *{kiss}* the laws *{kiss}* of this country; *{kiss}*is it legal *{kiss}*to have many wives, *{kiss}* to be a bigamist. *{kiss}* I'll have to check it out. *{kiss}* But you know *{kiss}* there are Muslim countries *{kiss}* where men can have many wives. *{kiss}* If need be, *{kiss}* we could change religions *{kiss}* and even *{kiss}* go to those countries *{kiss}* to get married. *{kiss}* In America, *{kiss}* these people are only allowed to have one wife in the country at a time. *{kiss}* Anyhow, *{kiss}* I am the law here. *{kiss}*On my land, *{kiss}* in my Valley, *{kiss}* my Skyhook, *{kiss}*and *{kiss}* we could do whatever we want."

Margherita is thinking, "In a Moslem country, with all your money, you could buy a beautiful young teenager; why would you want to *marry me?!?"* She dismisses this unpleasant reality and clings to hope. "I can refuse to go there ~ I *can* **refuse** to change my religion." Now she is feeling much better and says, "You would do that for me? You would send me to the Doctors to see if I can **get *pregnant?!?** And if I can get pregnant, you *will* **marry me?!?"**

Glenn says, "Of course; you know I would rather marry you than Elena; but I cannot allow any of my children to grow up without a father." Now Margherita starts to cry again and is really letting it all hang out. Glenn says, "Now what's **wrong!**"

She says, "I'm so happy, I want to tell Elena and my mother and everybody." Suddenly she is restless and tries to get out from under him. Then she stops, "But this is only stupid talk - if I cannot get pregnant."

Glenn says, "Ah, - aarrhh – Ah - Si, yes . . . I agree."

She relaxes, melting back into the mattress, pulling Glenn tightly against the whole length of her body. "But what are we going to do for you to have sex if Elena and I are both pregnant; you will not want to have sex with either of us?"

"I can live without sex - for a while . . ."

Margherita cuts him off abruptly. "That's what all you men say, then your pecker smells a sexy ripe teenager . . . "Then her face squelches into anguish as she resumes crying like an injured child, "You won't want *either of us!* We are both gonna *be fat and ugly!!* Then you won't want **our babies either!!!**"

Glenn grabs her by the shoulders and shakes her violently til she stops crying; then says, "You can't believe that *I would ever abandon* **my babies!!** ~ ~ I will always want to have sex with you; but you won't always want to have sex with me. You will have to satisfy me every day, even when you are pregnant and don't want to be bothered - because I cannot be distracted from my work by being horny all the time."

"Okay . . ." she says kissing him, her tears subsiding. "Elena and I will always make sure you are satisfied every day, even if we have to show you pictures from those made-up American Putas in those dirty magazines."

Glenn says knowingly, "There are better visual aids than magazines . . ."

"What do you mean, 'better visual aids'?" Margherita is puzzled. Glenn takes out his cell phone and revisits an internet site from his lonely days in the South-Eastern desert of Arizona. Margherita's eyes glow as she sees a naked bosomy young blond woman licking a muscular young man all over his genitals and the crevice below, then with intense concentration the Puta swallows every inch of his giant penis deep down her throat. Margherita's concentration becomes more intense: she duplicates the video's actions while fervently grinding into Glenn's leg.

Then they have great sex. Glenn's orgasm is particularly acute, beyond consciousness, beyond sub-consciousness: beyond anything the human mind can conceive – *simply **BEYOND!***

~

{An overwhelming gushing of euphoria sending convulsive spasms throughout his whole body, ~ tears and saliva ensuing simultaneously with an enthralling rapturous consumption – penetrating beyond his awareness, ~ toes curling, lungs heaving, a descending whimpering crescendo exhaling, ~ the light of his consciousness convulsively being squeezed out of his brains; ~ then . . .'la petite mort' - the little death' ~ and then upon returning from beyond this timeless non-being – only then one knows he's been gone; ~ yet – irony of ironies - struggling to cling to that profoundly penetrating emptiness, ~ the timelessness of that little death. ~ ~ An intense longing for being totally consumed in that *alternate universe!*

~

The *experience* that broadens humanities *'**experience horizon**'!!}*

~

Invasive reality too quickly steals from that blissful emptiness; we then encounter the undeniable longing to return to that deep, plush emptiness. Is this simply God's reward for evolutionary procreation?

Or in that dark emptiness, are we closer to the Light? Or - Are we enduring an overdose of endorphins?

Is it our creator beckoning from afar; or, is it just endorphins. A deeper meaning to our existence; or, just endorphins.

The call of our *never-ending quest* for the **ultimate truth** of our personal *'**Sound & Fury**'* – or just endorphins . . . As our heroine stated in the finale of that beautiful movie:

'Kama Sutra: A Love Story'

~

"Any way –

__Life is Correct__ . . ."

~

{**Dios Mios,**

please don't let it be *just the endorphins* . . .}

Margherita prayerfully remembers why Glenn is screaming: The angels were assisting God in creating humans when Gabriel cautioned God about installing an excessive number of nerve endings in the sex organs. But God continued adding more & more. The other angels asked why so many. God replied, "I want them to remember ___my name___."

They take a brief nap and then Margherita pouts saying, "I hope you don't get tired of both me and Elena and want a young teenager like all these Latino men do; and all those Moslem men that continue to marry younger girls."

Glenn replies, "There is a religion in America that is even worse, but it's not legal there."

"How soon can I go to the pregnancy Doctor? We must keep it a secret from Elena . . ."

Glenn takes her to his office and gets on the computer and calls a 'fertility clinic in Pequito', and insists on an appointment for the next day, emphasizing that she'll pay cash. He introduces her as Senora Margherita Glenn and explains, "We know she has a problem becoming pregnant and want to know what, if anything, can be done about it."

Margherita cleans up and cheerfully goes to enjoy Elena's celebration. Everyone stares at her red swollen eyes.

Margherita explains that she was only crying because she is so happy for them to be getting married. Elena whispers as they walk away from the workmen, "When you went away crying and did not come back, I was sure you are angry with me. What took you so long?"

"I needed time to adjust my brains; then I was with Glenn - your *fiancée*" - She says smiling - "*I had to fuck him again!* - Are you going to **forbid me** to fuck him anymore?"

Elena says, "Please, fuck him **all you want!** Sometimes I *will help you!* You can help me get pregnant two more times, maybe even more. Remember when you jumped on top of him, *pushing him deep* all the way into my pussy for the first time ever. Remember, you told me I had to take it all the way inside, and you forced him into me all the way *by jumping on his ass?* You were screaming, *'Fuck her Gringo!'*

I am going to give my baby *your name!*
~ because ~
I believe *YOU ARE* the *FATHER* of my baby!?!"

They both laugh hysterically and hug each other.

Margherita confesses, "Of course I am sorry that I didn't get pregnant and end up marrying Glenn; but I am still happy for you, Elena:

- As you would be happy for me if the *situation were reversed"*

– Elena concurs, "Of course *I would be!"*

Elena plans on going home to tell her mother the good news; but Margherita tells Elena to stay with Glenn the next two nights because she must go into Pequito tonight - to pick up medicine for Jane - and she will not be back for 2 days. When Glenn comes out of his cabin the men are all watching closely as Elena runs to him, jumps up on him, then kisses him fervently on the lips. He responds positively, holding her, smiling and laughing, confirming for everybody that it's true; she is going to *get married to El Patrone: El Boss-Man, Signor Glenn!*

Sancho says, "You see, that's how to marry a Gringo; you tackle him in the desert rolling him around ~ then he's afraid not to marry you!" They are all laughing hysterically.

Juan adds, "But first the Gringo has to be crazy enough to eat sand! And then you get a *Gringa bitch* to kick him in the balls; this way he learns *not to* **marry a Gringa!"** They continue laughing uncontrollably.

Then the Professor shakes his head looking at Glenn saying, "What are you doing, you cannot play with these people *like that!* You're going to turn her **into Madam Butterfly?!?"**

Glenn retorts offended, "I am not playing; we're *going to get married!"*

"But I know Elena is already married, her husband lives near me with another woman, with their children."

Glenn scoffs, "I know that . . ."

"Well, she's not divorced; how could she get married to you?"

Glenn says, "They do it in this country all the time; so, we'll just do it too."

The Professor shakes his head ominously, "I don't think her husband – I mean X husband – is going to like this; he's a prominent man in town; everybody kowtows to him."

Glenn says nonchalantly, "What right does he have to object to her re-marrying?"

Since he seems to be in a talkative mood Glenn brings up the ocean water sediment again and the precious metals. The Professor gets angry, saying, "Okay - we like your profit-sharing plan. But you still have a long way to go with this project before you start fucking around with something else. Why don't you donate this money to something worthwhile . . . like NASA's space program? The only way you can get this shit out of their is boiling off all the seawater and then centrifuging the sediment and going through some chemical procedures to separate whatever; and it's going to cost more than it's worth in terms of money, time - and the pollution, - the electricity . . ."

Glenn interrupts saying, "I know 'Astronauts and space exploration' is one of your pet projects, but I don't think NASA is looking for donations."

"NASA has big financial problems. The Boeing Starling is far behind on development and over budget, it is supposed to replace the Space Shuttle to resupply the ISS. Otherwise, NASA has to depend upon the Russians, or Jeff Bezos or other billionaires who are only in it for the money. The stupid government – playing political funding - took away the Shuttle's contract from McDonald Douglas which was developing successfully, and gave it to Boeing which was unsuccessful. They are now far behind schedule with continuing software problems. Can you imagine; the U S SPACE STATION is dependent on the *Russians* to *resupply it* from **Kazakhstan!** Russia loves Presidential Candidate Prump; he is indifferent to their invading Ukraine's Crimea Peninsula. But they hate Obama, because he enacted U S Sanctions against them. Russia is threatening to stop supplying the ISS. Now there is trouble with the hardware on SpaceX, and NASA has no funding."

Glenn is perplexed thinking, "They have a satellite still in orbit from the 1950s. It was only supposed to last a few years and it's still in orbit. They have other launched vehicles that have long outlived their projected lifespan. They have robots on Mars that were supposed to stop working years ago and are still functioning. How is it possible that they cannot get a new space Shuttle operational? How is it possible that they're running out of money? If the United States Government can't give them enough money, what good could I do?!?" Then he returns to his idea to recover the wealth from the ocean, "Anyway, we got free, non-polluting electricity here to centrifuge the precious metals from the seawater sediment."

"Yes, but you haven't delivered our electricity to all of South America yet, and the plan is selling it to Central America and even in the United States and – remember - what we're doing here is to save the environment - not to make you rich - or now, all of us rich. You don't need that! Don't surrender to your 'gold-fever' - Just leave it alone! If the seawater squirts through the top of the cavern and cascades down the mountain; we'll deal with it then. I'm sure we'll have some warning and if need be, we'll evacuate the area and shut down the trains until we divert the seawater, or build bridges, or do whatever we have to do; but there is no sense in letting that little bit of gold dust cloud your thinking. You got to keep your mind on what we're doing."

Glenn whines, "Yes, but I'm getting burnt out working up there and so is Jake; this seven days a week 12 hours a day shit - it's really getting exhausting."

The Professor reasons, "What about having Bernie take five days a week, relieving Jake for two nights and you for three days?"

"Bernie is driving the fork-lift on the night shift, loading the Loon-Evator. Besides, I don't know if I trust Bernie anymore to do anything. Jane has convinced him I am a terrorist and that we are sending these barrels of nuclear-waste into cities somewhere around the world. *How **ridiculous!***"

"You can always hire a local to drive the fork-lift on the night shift . . . Well, take Bernie up there and let him see what you're doing and then he'll know that it's not true; just like you did with Jake - that should solve the problem."

"I'm holding CIA Jane up there; I can't risk them being alone together. God knows what plot they may hatch."

"Well, they'll only have one space-suit and I'm sure she *now realizes* that people cannot go outside up there without it, - and Bernie and her might be a romance. They seem to have been developing that way - and maybe, if things work out between them, they can have a life together . . . that will be interesting for them."

Glenn says, "Professor *Natzi!* You old **matchmaker!** – I'll consider it . . ." Then, after 15 seconds he says, "Okay, send Bernie up to take 2 of Jakes night shifts and 3 of my day shifts."

But Glenn's *gold-fever* haunts him. He fills a Styrofoam cooler with seawater from the Gusher-Cavern. Then he adds it to the skid carrying the supply of food going up to Skyhook for CIA Jane. When it arrives at Skyhook, 5 miles up, he removes it from under the heated tarp that was keeping it at 50 degrees. He quickly uncovers it and watches as it immediately evaporates into a disappearing mist with the last few residue droplets of ice silently popping all along the inside of the container. Then he sees a residue lining the container. He has it analyzed: it contains trace amounts of gold and silver with other elements. Now his *gold-fever taunts him.*

His subconscious draws his thinking back to his old 40,000-foot tower in S E Arizona. It was going to blast containers of nuclear-waste into the Sun using only air pressure. His failure - destroying his childish dream of being awarded the Nobel Prize for helping to save our environment. He is aware, however, that he left this Big Cannon's air intakes open and wonders if it is constantly sucking and drawing surface air up into the stratosphere. There were high concentrations of ozone (tri-oxygen, $O3$) polluting the breathable air for COPD (Chronic Obstructive Pulmonary Disease) victims all across the southern USA. Ozone pollution from California across the Mohave Desert through Arizona, New Mexico and into Texas, has long been a life-threatening problem. Is it somewhat better now? He researches the 'ozone layer depletion' in the stratosphere and sees it began healing when he shot-up his Big Cannon. He knew that Fluro-carbons were found to be destroying the ozone layer. Obviously, the 1978 banning of these chemicals from aerosol sprays was a factor; but it would just now begin to have an effect as it takes about 40 years for these Fluro-carbons to float up and finally arrive at the ozone layer's height in the stratosphere . . ." He concludes, "It must be due to my destruction of my 'Big Cannon's' computers, leaving it inert: that turned my 'Big Cannon' back into my 'Big Straw', sucking up the ozone at ground level and spitting it out up at 40,000 feet into the stratosphere, where it ultimately floats and levels out to patch the holes in the ozone layer.

"YES!!"

"So, after I shot-up its control computers, my Arizona 'Big Cannon' became my 'Big Straw 'again. So, my invention – though I didn't intend it - is taking ozone laden air from ground level and syphoning it into the upper atmosphere where it is rebuilding the ozone layer. Preventing, or limiting, - or at least reducing - skin cancers." He gets Bernie to verify the improvement of the ozone layer weekly, which is normally only 5 mm thick on average. He knows over the South Atlantic there definitely is an ozone hole where excessive solar radiation is getting through and causing problems. "We should be able to see if there is a noticeable recovery of it."

Bernie confirms there's a slight improvement, but then reads from his research:

'Australia's ozone hole has depleted by 50% since the 1970s and accounts for 95% of all their skin cancers, as a result of the subsequent increase of Solar Ultraviolet Radiation.'

Glenn laments, **"SHIT!** Now I guess I am supposed to construct another 'Big-Straw Tower' *In Australia?!?"* Bernie continues droning on about the San Juaquin Valley's sandstorm causing low visibility with air and ozone pollution.

Shunning these new obligations, Glenn's mind wonders, "Could a 120,000-foot tower – a taller, 'Bigger Straw', all the way up into the vacuum of space - could it possibly siphon-up the lava-tube seawater from his Gusher-Cavern?"

As the Professor had lectured, using electricity was too expensive to boil away the Gusher's seawater. Glenn is thinking, "I am already operating Skyhook at almost 23miles up, at 120,000 feet elevation. I wonder if I can build a tower all the way up there." He knew of a proposed plan to build an elevator tower all the way up to a geosynchronous Space Station orbiting

24000 miles above the Earth, where the Space Station would maintain its fixed position, connected to the top of this elevator-tower. "Could I, using the cavern's gusher as its base, build the tower - exactly as I had done before – but all the way up to the Skyhook, where this 'Gusher-Tower' would spray the evaporating seawater? Up there, the vacuum of space would boil away the seawater and I can collect its sediment from the roof top of Skyhook. Then I could centrifuge the gold out of the sediment. It would be quicker to install another Loon-Evator over the Gusher Cavern from which I can mechanically install each segment of this new Gusher-Tower. I can install them myself, from a platform off of this 2nd Loon-Evator, through a 5-foot diameter hole in that platform, which will fit around the Gusher-Tower. Every fifth sewer pipe segment would contain a high-speed pump to boost the seawater up the Tower if needed, it would automatically turn on when it detected that the upward seawater pressure was beginning to fall. (Then, as the tied ebbs, the seawater falling back down the Tower would turn the pump backwards, which would generate some electricity.) I can use a laser to verify that each tower segment is mounted perpendicular, so that its slight weight is not leaning." He goes on-line and researches an industrial size centrifuge . . .

Then he buys one . . .

Despite the Professor's strenuous objections, he proceeds with the project. The southern tunnel was finished, and tracks are being laid. So, Glenn has the Military Engineer investigate the Gusher-Cavern with him. He explains that he wants a cement level platform over the Gusher-hole, which will have a 5-foot diameter for the Gusher to spray up into. The engineer says, "Why don't we just pour cement down there and seal it off." Glenn explains he may find use for the water at some point in the future; so, he wants to be able to open & close it at will. "I will have to dynamite a bigger entrance into this cavern and build a ramp down and then lay railroad tracks to supply it. You have electricity here and railroad access close by." the engineer continues, "It's pretty basic cement construction with a heavy-duty electric motor that can seal the opening whenever needed with a heavy, movable concrete slab. The major problem is diverting the water during construction."

The Engineer comes up with a 5-foot diameter PVC sewer pipe that he secures around the gusher opening and builds it up thru the ceiling. The Gusher-Spray is directed west where its seawater rains down the mountain's western side and harmlessly flows to the Pacific Ocean. The Engineer is quite surprised by the volume and force of the water and suggest that it could be used to turn a dynamo to generate electricity. Glenn lies saying, "You deduced my plan, I will put the dynamo on top of the cement platform."

VIII

❖

SANCHO GETS AMBITIOUS

J ane had told everybody that 20% of Pecuadorians are rich and collect 50% of the income, while the poorest 20% collect only 5%. Then Sancho is humiliated when Jane tells him that the Gringos make more money than him. He doesn't want to risk upsetting Glenn, but finally confronts him. Glenn explains, "Jane is not getting paid at all, only free food and no rent, no matter what she told him. And she does not do any work for me. I could not trust her to do any work. Bernie has been a newspaper reporter, has gone to college and has knowledge of computers and good English. He has been very useful while helping me deal with supplies and doing research on the Internet. Also, he is publicizing the fact that their 'Hacienda Electric Company' is providing clean, cheap electricity to each country."

Sancho says, "All I see him do is drive the forklift at night to load the Loon-Evator. He doesn't even take the nuclear-waste skids off the train; we do that for him in the day so he don't have to do that at night."

"Yes, but he does a lot more for me."

"What about Jake? He did not go to college; why should he make more money? It is because he is a Gringo; you pay them more because you are -"

Glenn retorts, "That's not true, I would pay you just as much if you would be willing to do the work that he does. And I need someone to *help up there!* Remember when we started here, you laughed telling me that you would go as high-up as I wanted, as long as you could keep *one foot on the ground!?!*"

Sancho says, "All he does is drive the forklift up there. I drive the forklift down here; what's the difference?"

Glenn says, "It is a **big difference;** just understanding how to work with the space-suit and know the dangers involved. To be brave enough to go up there and do the work. You're right it is not difficult; but it is very different, and you have to know a lot more."

Sancho insists, "I know as much as Jake, how hard is it to push a few buttons on a computer? Any fool can put *on a space-suit!*" Glenn challenges him to try it. Sancho doesn't say anything.

The next morning after breakfast Glenn sees Sancho trying on his space-suit; it is a little difficult for him to seal it around the waist from within as his stomach bulge gets in the way, but he is able to suck it in. Glenn goes to him and explains everything that is happening with the space-suit and all the complications involved with the O2 canisters, the heads-up display and what it's messages and alarms mean, and what is to be done about them, if anything. Sancho is ready to try going up in the Loon-Evator. Glenn puts on his spare space-suit, sets the communications for four of them including Jake and the Professor, and they ascend the loading ramp. Sancho holds onto the railing for dear life, Glenn has to pry him away to move him to the control post to operate the controls. Sancho does as instructed, but then, won't let go of the control post. Glenn activates it immediately; he can see the fear in Sancho's eyes as they start to rise. Glenn is patting him on the shoulder and telling him it is okay. Sancho's heart rate and blood pressure alarm flashes red; he seizes with fear. Glenn calmly explains what it means, "It is okay; take long slow breaths." The Professor translates into Spanish with a rough, accusing tone. They can all hear Jake laughing and Glenn yells at them to keep quiet. In spite of this ludicrous effort, Sancho manages to lower his blood-pressure. Glenn continues softly, "Breathe naturally, but deeply, take long slower breaths, see the alarm has gone off, now just breathe naturally." Finally, Sancho calms down.

They go up above 10,000 feet and Sancho space-suit starts bulging out and he becomes terribly concerned at this change, screaming at Glenn, **"I want to go down!** *I want to go down… **Now!!**"*

Glenn says as Sancho's heart-rate alarm flashes red again, "Don't look at the controls, breathe deeply, look at the beautiful view, breathe . . ."

Sancho complains, "But my space-suit, it's squeezing me, something is wrong; *it's blowing up!?!*"

"No, that's normal. Breathe slowly. It has to do that because there's less air up here."

Sancho demands, "What you mean *less air.*"

Glenn says patiently, "The higher you go the less air there is; the less air pressure . . ."

"What air *pressure?!?* Air has no pressure; it's not like water squirting *from a hose!*"

"I know, but; it still has pressure . . . of another kind, the weight of the air from up above is pushing down and causes this air pressure . . ."

Sancho exclaims, "What weight - air has *no weight!* It *don't **weigh nothing!!**"* Glenn tries not to laugh but can't help himself as Jake and the Professor are both laughing uncontrollably.

Glenn says, "I will show you, do not be afraid because the suit is going to blow up more. The higher we go, the less air pressure there is, and the suit has to give you more air, so it is the same pressure that you are used to on the ground."

Sancho insists indignantly, "There's no pressure on the *ground!* **Only here!!**"

"You see my space-suit is expanding too. If it doesn't, we get sick like Jane got sick - with all those bruises that she had."

Sancho insists, "That is because *you threw her* off the Loon-Evator! Now you want my *space-suit to* **explode!!** ***With me in it!!!***" The alarm flashes red with a beeping that matches the flashing.

The Professor barks through his laughter, **"No!** He didn't throw her off, he saved her life by getting her back down to Earth as soon as possible by jumping off and parachuting with her in his arms."

"So how she gets all those bruises?"

Now Jake chimes in, "Because she was up on the Loon-Evator at 30,000 feet without a space-suit and her inside blood pressure was busting her blood vessels causing all those bruises. Because there was *no outside air pressure* to hold her blood in!"

Sancho says, "I thought it was because she was cold."

Glenn responds, "Yes, that is true; it is very, very cold up here because there is no . . ."

"**No air?!?** What you mean: *'there is no air'?!?"* Sancho blurts-out.

"The higher up you go, the less air there is and the colder it is."

Sancho insists, "That's *not true!* I come up the mountain from my village to the top of the mountain every day and it's hot too; just like it is in my village."

"Sancho, we're going up tens of thousands of feet; you only go up about a thousand feet from your village, maybe 2000 feet. We're going more than 10,000 feet, more than 20,000, were going 30,000 – 40,000, 50,000, 60,000, 70,000, 80,000, 90,000, 100,000 feet *strait up*! That's **twenty miles** straight up!!"

Sancho's alarm silences as he is listening intently to Glenn's explanation. "You mean in heaven; how does God breathe if there's no air in heaven?"

"Heaven!?!" Jake guffaws, "I give up!" They can hear the Professor trying to stifle his shocked response.

"Sancho, it's not heaven; we're just going up into the sky, but higher than airplanes fly."

The Professor says, "This is just his fear talking, it's defensively objecting to anything we might tell him."

Sancho says, "Take me down . . . I want to go back down." As his space-suit balloons out more.

Glenn notices Sancho's voice is much calmer and there are no alarms. "Alright Sancho, I will take you back, but we are almost there already. Look up, you can see it. Remember all those balloons that you launched?" As Sancho looks up through the Loon-Evator's donut hole he sees the wires going into the familiar helium/hydrogen balloon-cubes comprising the vast network which is Skyhook. Glenn sighs with inevitable surrender, "Look, I do this every day – Jake does this every day, this is why he gets more money; if you want more money - I need your help. Or I have to find somebody else and pay them more money *than you make!* You could be making more money working up here instead of on the ground; I think you'll find it more interesting. You will like this work much better."

Sancho whines, "I don't know, I don't think I like this . . . You stay right by me Boss-Man?" he looks into Glenn's helmet pleadingly. "Okay Boss-Man, you stand right here next to me."

"Okay, Sancho okay." Sancho's gloved hand slides around Glenn's arm drawing him close. Glenn tries to make him enjoy the view, tries to tell him something of the beautiful blue Pacific Ocean; to look south at the Andes Mountain peaks punching through the clouds. But he would have none of it, keeping his eyes focused directly on the post in front of him.

The Loon-Evator slowly stops their ascent with a slight bouncing; again, Sancho is terribly alarmed. Glenn leads him, arm in arm, up the ramp on to Skyhook's loading-bay. They walk through the loading-bay, past the forklift that Jake is operating; he is very shaky as he walks and is looking around wide-eyed with terror. Glenn knocks on the cabin glass and tells him to look inside through the glass. Jane is sitting in there watching television; he knocks again. She glances at them barely noticing, not wanting to give Glenn the satisfaction. She should have been surprised to see two more space-suits. Sancho says with surprise, "I see Jane, she's okay? She is not dead?"

"No, she's not dead. She's fine." Glenn tells Jake to take the rest of the day off and he gets on the forklift with Sancho sitting beside him. He drives the forklift onto the Loon-Evator, Sancho holds on to Glenn's arm again as they go down the ramp, the fear in his eyes subsides after a while. Glenn thinks, "Thank goodness I had Jake put up that railing around the Loon-Evator portal where the loading ramp is; otherwise, he would have really been afraid. But it is good to be afraid, you do not want a false sense of security just because there is a railing around the ramp. One could certainly drive the forklift through the fence and *over the edge!* And fall perhaps onto the top of the Loon-Evator which can be as far as 120,000 feet down." So, Glenn thinks about how he could reinforce the fence to prevent that eventuality from happening. "That would be a catastrophe on the ground as well." Sancho takes over driving the forklift and finishes unloading the skids of nuclear-waste. Then Glenn shows him how to send it back down using Skyhook's remote computer as Jake gets aboard to go down. Sancho watches it, looking down from the railing, and becomes frightened as it disappears from view - below him. He can only see *empty sky - **below him***. He is very disoriented and fearfully shakes his head.

Glenn takes the driver's seat of the forklift again with Sancho beside him and transports a skid full of barrels of nuclear waste, that they had previously unloaded, from Skyhook's cargo bay to the Railgun's automatic feeders. It continues to launch as there are still barrels in the automatic feeder. He shows him how to raise the skid up to the feeder, then cut and remove the metal straps securing the barrels on the skid, then gently tipping it so that the barrels slide into the top of the automatic feeder. He shows Sancho all this as several barrels are being launched by the Railgun, disappearing almost too quickly to be observed. They are piling up the empty skids back in Skyhook's loading-bay. When that is done Glenn shows him on the computer with a few keys, how to stop the launchings, and then to re-start them. Then to single step each instruction so that he can see how the conveyor belt receives a barrel, runs it down to a point where the tracking mechanism is clamped on to the barrel. Then it continues down onto the Railgun's Launch-pad, and then the Railgun becomes activated. The barrel floats up, suspending it freely two feet above the rails; and then as the magnetism increases, the barrel accelerates up the rails. He shows Sancho how fast it works automatically. Sancho is amazed to see all this action going continuously without anybody touching it. All he has to do is load it and let it run; it will stop automatically when it is empty - or should anything jam, which it never does. He also shows him how to load the tracking mechanisms into its feeder that automatically clamps them onto the bottom of each barrel.

The ground crew has sent up another load on the Loon-Evator. Glenn motions for Sancho to handle the cargo on his own. Glenn talks him through it. With the next load Sancho is competent enough to do the job on his own and Glenn is glad to let him. He has had other things on his mind; probably dangerously so. It is no place to be working with your mind being distracted by other things. He could do a lot of damage carrying a ton of nuclear-waste with that forklift. The least of which would be puncturing one of the toxic barrels. The worst of course would be crashing through the cabin exposing Jane to the stratospheric elements; or crashing the forklift over the edge of the Skyhook. Glenn is relieved to see that he has another person able to work up there and he tells him, "Now Sancho, if you can come up by yourself like Jake and I do every day and keep it launching all day, you'll be making as much money as Jake plus a little extra, because you've been working with me longer." Glenn repeats, "You will be making *more than Jake!*" Sancho's eyes are beaming with pride. "But I have to trust you to be able to do this every day; we have to launch all that nuclear-waste and we can't afford to miss a day."

Glenn is concerned because they have so much more just sitting on the docks. The military is letting the earlier shipments wait and just sending up the newer shipments, because that means less handling. He is worried that the tracking of the billing of those earlier shipments from United States will reveal prolonged open invoices, showing that it is not being handled promptly and may provoke another investigator, like CIA Jane, to come snooping around in his valley. Also, stupid thieves may think they could get away with stealing barrels if they see them staying in one spot for a long time. He sighs, "As if I didn't have enough to worry about."

Glenn thinks about the Big Syphon2 coming over his valley on the next equinox. His H-cube balloons will explode as it sucks up their freezing cold hydrogen. This sudden chilling will condense the Syphon's ground air, causing it to fall back down towards the Earth, breaking the Whirlwind - separating it and fizzling it out. At least that's how he surmises the Syphon's destruction; as does the Professor .

Glenn enjoys watching Sancho perform the task. His mind returns to the Big Syphon2 wreaking havoc daily as it circles the Earth. It is still traveling around the Earth once every 24 hours, now angling south approximately 18 miles each day. It flips over cars and destroys house trailers, wrenches off roofs, sucks up small vegetation, animals . . . and babies. Fortunately, most of the world is informed and knows to move 25 miles to the north or south away from its predicted center. That center is well plotted by the weather channel and announced in every country that it's going through. Still, when it reaches the jungles of South America and Central Africa and some remote islands, they may not be getting the information. Glenn shudders to think what might happen to those people. His screaming tornado will hit them at high noon. Also, there is concern for those who are too stubborn or do not have the means to move away. It wobbles more or less 35 miles north-south off-center, so the 50-mile distance is more than adequate.

The time comes too soon for Sancho to return to the ground to catch the train home. Glenn wants to send him down on the Loon-Evator alone; but Sancho it too afraid. Glenn lets the automatic launchings continue. He takes Sancho down who immediately grabs onto the same post he clung to on the way up. Glenn finally gets him to take in the view when he tells him the Hacienda is visible below. Sancho slowly looks, his curiosity and relief at arriving, conquers his fear and he peers over. "I can't see it." he says.

Glenn lies saying, "I can . . ." as he points to where he knows it is. I can see the train tracks there, where it goes into the tunnel. Look there, you can see Pequito, and on the other side you can see the Ocean, and south of us you are looking at the Andes Mountains in Peru. Sancho is now taking it all in, forgetting his fear. The pressure begins to lessen in his suit, and he becomes alarmed. Glenn tells him why it's happening and not to worry. As they are enjoying the setting Sun with their visors down, the Hacienda comes into view. Sancho is very happy now. Glenn tells him to go back up the next morning and work with Jake who will already be there. When they land, Sancho swaggers off the Loon-Evator while removing his helmet and shouting to all the men at how exciting it was way-up there, a couple of thousand feet in the sky. Glenn returns with the next load and works until midnight.

IX

❖❖❖

GOLD FEVER!

Now Glenn presses ahead with his Gusher-Tower project. He takes Bernie away from the launchings putting Sancho and Jake back on the 12 hour/7 days a week schedule; but now it's sunrise to sunset so Sancho can catch the train home each night. Glenn & Bernie construct a 2nd Loon-Evator next to the Gusher-cavern. Bernie is excited but fearful of the work. "Are you sure the parachute will open if I fall?" They drop electric supply cables down through its donut hole from the Skyhook. Then they build a separate balloon-floating construction-platform right next to Loon-Evator2, which has a hole so that it floats over-top of the tower construction. It has a conveyor belt on it which will carry the tower segments to its center hole from Loon-Evator2's cargo deck. They simply have to lower the sewer-pipe segment thru the hole and turn it on its connecting threads. The construction-platform floats up to the top of the tower as each new segment is added.

Glenn has the 5-foot diameter PVC sewer-pipe segments delivered from the southern port city of Caraquez, via train up into the Valley through the southern tunnel entrance. He hires locals to operate the forklift to unload the tower segments from the train onto Loon-Evator2's cargo deck. From Loon-Evator2, these sewer segments slide off onto the platform's conveyor belt which carries them right to the edge of the hole in the platform. Then each one is gently dropped through the hole on top of the previous segment, and with a slight turn, it locks into position. The computerized laser verifies that the alignment is proper. Loon-Evator2 and the platform are programmed to operate automatically, floating to the top of the new segment after each installation is confirmed by the computer's laser. Glenn works for six hours on the platform at low-tide and Bernie works the other six hours. During high-tides, Loon-Evator2 and the construction platform are floated back to the ground. The seawater Gusher-Spray is directed southwest by a 45-degree angled PVC segment which they install after each shift. When the Loon-Evator2 is empty, it goes back to ground and is reloaded. Working seven days a week like this 12 hours a day they soon complete the Gusher-Tower, twenty-two miles straight up into the stratosphere. Then they transport the centrifuge up to Skyhook and installs it at a lower level creating a pit for it to operate within.

Glenn is surprised to see how instantly the Gusher-Spray's ocean water evaporates; but the misty seawater vapor spray continues going far away. He has it pointed to the southwest thinking that it will condense and rain down on the west side of a nearby mountain and cascade down its steep cliffs into the ocean harmlessly. The evaporating seawater mist yields its sediment that glistens in the sunlight as these tiny grains surrender to gravity; a fine dusting that settles down on top of a 4900 square foot of a 7 by 7 section of H-cubes. Glenn has the computer lower the pressure in these balloons, producing a gentle slope which causes the sediment to slide down into the centrifuge pit, feeding the centrifuge, which automatically separates each element by its density.

At the end of the first day, he's recovered just over a pound of gold and silver. Still in his space-suit, he swaggers back to the Hacienda and plops it down on to the Professor's desk, arrogantly asking, "Do you know what the going rate of gold and silver is?"

The Professor looks at the bags of the metal dust and says, "No, however, I heard some interesting news from a South American weather station."

Glenn responds, "What? Our Big Syphon can't be in South America already?!?"

"No, it's not about **YOUR 2nd BIG SYPHON!** It reported that there was serious flooding from a freak storm near the southern border of Peru . . . on the southern coast. . . It lasted for six hours, and was more intense halfway through . . . Kind of like your 'Tidal Gusher'! It was a very freakishly cold storm – even snow and ice, even at lower elevations - there was no prediction of it. Any idea where it may have **come from?!?"**

"Oh shit!" Glenn says and runs to view this news feed on his computer:

'South of the town of Los Palos, Peru a freak ice/hail/snowstorm raged for about 6 hours with its peak arriving after 3 hours. It covered a small area of only about 4 square miles. Of course, everything melted on contact with the hot ground and then proceeded to flood and cause some mudslides on the steeper mountain slopes. So far there are no fatalities reported; but some property damage. It had a very cooling effect, some report as much as 20 degrees cooler, but the residents say it was too high a price to pay for that cooling relief. Stay tuned for updates.'

The Professor picks up the bags of gold and silver and goes to Glenn's office cabin, gloating, "So, you squeezed out some gold & silver. What are you going to do with it; throw it on your money pile? Stack it up till it fills your cabin? Then you can hide it in the walls . . . bury it under the sand. Just like the *Drug Lords do!* You'll have to hire hoodlums, also just like the **Drug Lords do!** You cannot have these people living in abject poverty while seeing you living with unlimited wealth."

Glenn is upset and irritated by the Professor's pointless haranguing, "Don't you have anything productive to say?"

"Remember, this is *your fiasco!* I told you that we don't want to have anything to do with your *prospecting!* Well, now what are you going to do - shut it down? Just abandon the whole million-dollar Gusher-Tower?" He plops the 2 bags of Gold and Silver on Glenn's desk.

Glenn replies with guilty contempt, "Whatever I do with *my pile* of money and my project is ***my business!"***

The Professor retorts with ironic contempt, "Too bad you didn't dump your industrial wastewater 50 miles further east where it only rains once a year. But that's what you get when you don't think, you don't plan . . . you *don't **test!"***

Glenn hurries back to the top of the Gusher-Tower as Bernie is just ending his shift. He explains to Bernie that together they must divert the Gusher-Spray as it is inundating the southern Peru coastal region. Bernie says, "That's to the South; about *1500 Miles Away!* That's not possible!"

"Impossible or not, that is what is happening . . . ***And***, we must stop it. The Professor said that there is a drought east of there by about 50 miles inland. Maybe we can spray it there. The fucking Professor - arrogant bastard - he could have been useful with the mathematics, calculating how much to adjust the spray to the East, and up and down so as not to have too much fall at any one spot, as it had done there."

Bernie says, "How difficult can it be, like squirting a hose; we just move it a little bit side to side."

Glenn replies, "It's Not That Simple; if it's traveling 1500 miles, moving it here 1° could result in hundreds of miles of movement there - 1500 miles away. We need to computerize and calculate this whole thing." Glenn directs Bernie, "You get online and see if you can find anything by way of mathematical calculations or formula on 'Degrees of the Earth's Angle moving south away from the equator.' We must program this sprayer-nozzle's control-motor to spray where we want. Calculate it for 50 miles East. We want to spray the length of that desert plain, maybe you could look that up, it would be east of the town of Tasco in Southern Peru, right near the Chilean border on the coast. Meanwhile I will manually operate the gusher-spray-nozzle so that it's not going back to the same spot it flooded before."

"Okay, but you had better get started because here *comes the gusher!*" It sprays directly in the direction it had before and with the same energy propelling its seawater vapor far off into the distance. Glenn moves it a degree east and then gently moves it up and down every five seconds while he speaks to his helmet computer to tune in the news channel that he had seen before.

The same announcer comes on after a while saying that this freak storm is returning once again, but then he adds, "Wait a minute, it is moving east, we can see it passing over the Andes. We have a helicopter crew standing by. Weather Helicopter Pilot, can you please follow it and report on the storm?"

Through the background plop-plop-plop-plop whirring of the helicopter-blades Glenn hears, "We shall follow after it at a distance because we don't want to be caught in it. I will report on it as much as is possible." The Pilot reports that he has to fly through mountain passes in the lower part of the Andes which will take some manipulating, but he can see snow falling ahead of him where the freak storm is depositing it and that it is moving further east. Then as he flies out of the mountain pass, he says, "Yes, I can see it is on the desert plains and I can see that it is moving south now; it's a wide and long storm of falling ice and snow, I don't want to get too close to it, I do not want to be caught in it. We never have this kind of weather on the eastern side of these mountains." And then, "I can see that it is moving north again. I will travel north and then wait – this is crazy – now it's moving south again. I'm on the southern end of it and it's moving south again – this is *really freakish!* I'm going to get out of here because it doesn't make any sense to me . . ." He turns his helicopter and flies back towards the mountain pass and his home base saying, "I'm signing off because I'm afraid that this doesn't make any sense and it is too dangerous for me to report from here. Wait; now it's on me, the temperature, it - it dropped ~ **it's freezing?!?** Even for this altitude- it's ridiculously cold . . . Wait - now I got an ice storm - my screen is icing-up - the engine is suddenly laboring – I can't hold my altitude – I, I'm caught in a downdraft – **I, I'm crashing!** . . . **I'm - *CRASHING!!*"**

We hear the anxious breathing from the pilot and then the metallic impact into the ground and metal parts breaking against rock and whizzing through the air. He's calling SOS and MAYDAY on his radio and giving his location.

The pilot scrambles out and runs away as his helicopter bursts into flames. The broadcast station is stunned and then suddenly says, "OK, we've got that; we will send relief *to you immediately!* Are you alright? Are you hurt? **Please come back!** Let us know - *are you OK?!?* Shall we send an ambulance? We're sending an ambulance anyhow . . . We can't hear you; you're not talking to us anymore. ***Speak up!*** ~ Maybe his radio equipment broke up inside the - the helicopter? Maybe that's why he's not answering us? OK we're getting the rescue service on the phone immediately and they will take care of him. Maybe all other aircraft should avoid that area? Maybe we should advise them to totally avoid the area of this *freaky storm?!?*"

Then in the background there can be heard a female radio station director saying, "Have the ambulance swing by here and pick-up our reporter so he can do a live broadcast from our helicopter crash site." When she is challenged for delaying the rescue, she retorts, "Do we want to have the TV reporters scooping us on ***our own incident!?!***"

The reporter comes back on, "Ah… Okay; and we'll have somebody from Lima drive over there immediately and see what is going on."

A Lima reporter says, "We will get on that right away and report back to you within an hour; when we'll be able to see this freak storm over the drought area." It's apparent that they'll wait to hear a report from whomever drives over there.

Another voice comes on, "This is the Lima Weather Center speaking now; since we have been listening to your broadcast, we have obtained a radar report showing the freakish downpour is still coming down on the eastern edge of the Andes." A brief pause, then he continues, "It looks like it might cause as big a problem here with mud slides as it did on the western side; however, it does not seem to be coming down as heavily as it did before. It seems to be covering a much wider area; perhaps 30 or 40 miles as opposed to the 4 square miles that it had covered before, and even a much wider area: from the eastern edge of the mountains into the torrid desert. It's covering the western portion of this desert plain." Glenn hears that and moves the spray another half degree eastward; then in a while he hears the reporter saying, "Our radar does not show this storm coming from any direction. Neither *East, West, North nor South!* It just suddenly happened, and it is continuing; materializing spontaneously. It's not emanating from any weather front or temperature differentiations: Mother Nature is certainly capable of some freaky storms . . . Though I've never seen anything like this before! On the radar, the storm has moved further east, away from the mountains and is now entirely over the region covering the eastern to the middle section of the desert plain, about one half of it." Glenn then, in addition to moving the spray up and down every five seconds, every two seconds he moves right and then left. In a short time, it's reporting, "Now the storm is covering the whole desert area – apparently it is irrigating the *whole desert area?!? **Believe it or NOT!!** That's what the **radar indicates!**"

Glenn must keep this up for six hours while Bernie is frantically working to find whatever calculations they can come up with to arrive at this Gusher-Spray projection. Glenn is shouting at him, "It is going to be a factor of gravitational attraction, and the angle of the spray above the global contour of the Earth, ah - including its ultimate high altitude, ah plus - including the gravitational attraction formula, ah, and ah then include - at the speed that it's being sprayed . . ."

Bernie interjects befuddled, "How in the hell do I know what speed it is gushing at?!"

Glenn replies desperately, "Can't we arrive at some sort of measurement that will tell us? It can't be traveling any faster up here than it was traveling up the gusher-tower. When we look at the cavern video, can't we tell how long it took the first drops of spray to go from out of the lava-tube up against the ceiling; we can approximate that height and then multiply . . ."

Bernie interrupts saying, "Took less than a second."

"Well, the video is 32 seconds per frame; can you single step that video and determine how many frames it took to get here?"

Bernie says, "I'll try and see but I think that it's going to be even less than 1/32 of a second - we seen those first drops get up there immediately."

"Well, the time the first drop you see plus the time you see the first impact against the ceiling."

Bernie searches thru the video that he had taken in the cavern and slow motions to the point that he can isolate those two frames, "So that's one frames at a 32nd of a second and twice that is a 16th of the second and multiply that times 3600 seconds per hour equals 57,600 feet per hour; divided by 5280 equals 10.9 mph."

"It has got to be much, *much faster* than that. We need that ***fucking Professor!***" Glenn growls angrily.

Bernie grumbles, "It was already splashing off the ceiling in the second frame."

"The news reporter first noticed the storm in about a half an hour after the gusher started here. So, let's just say 3000; no, make that 2700 mph." Then, "**WAIT!** Record the motions of the spray-nozzle that I've been doing, and we will start adjusting *from there!*" He programs it using that history into the control formula for the directional-motor attached to the spray-nozzle of the tower. At long last, Glenn does not have to move it manually; it switches directions automatically, right or left for West or East, and for North or South it tilts up or down.

THE TIPPING-POINT

Glenn and Bernie are both emotionally exhausted as result of this Herculean effort. Listening to the live Peruvian radar report, they fine tune the program so that by the next tide it is fully operational.

The radio announcer reports:

> 'There is a once- a-year rainfall which creates a vast growth of wonderful flowers. I can't wait to see it. But this rain/ ice storm is so heavy that it will probably drown them out, if it happens again. And it's happened now twice within one 24-hour period. And I fear it has wiped out the *Nazca Lines! You know those pre-historic massive drawings in the sand* which only make sense when viewed from an aircraft high above.'

"Oh shit!" Glenn is thinking, "I didn't want to wash away those 'Ancient Alien Lines' carved into the desert plane, (~ My Alien visitor might *be pissed! -* Wait, - *wasn't that a dream?*) But, other than that, it is just a vast wasteland. The indigenous people struggle to survive in those areas and if they could have some form of agriculture, it would be a tremendous value to them. My fresh pure water is a good thing; but too much of anything is bad." Glenn pulls up a climate map on the Internet and expanding it he sees that that desert plain extends south into Chile's Atacama Desert. He enters new coordinates.

About half an hour after the next high-tide, Peru's radar reporter states:

> "Mother Nature's Freaky Storm has started again in the same area. Wait; now it is moving further south, and it is irrigating the Chilean Atacama Desert Plains; which is an even larger area."

Glenn gets radar from the weather station in Lima, Chile and looking at the maps and listening to the reporting he estimates and enters how far and how wide to send the spray. "Thank God I am able to complete this using the computer; I don't have to be up there on top of the Gusher-Tower manually controlling it." He worries that he'll flood it out; but the area he's now spraying is thousands of square miles.

Then he wonders about the vast Mexican deserts and if his gusher water could do some good there. Perhaps people can grow enough food so that they can at least support themselves and not have to migrate to the United States illegally. Also, they can leave the crowded cities to farm in this area and be spread out far enough that they won't constantly be fearful of the drug gangs. He calculates the direction for spraying the Mexican desert, points the Gusher-Tower's nozzle almost 180° to the north and then he anxiously awaits the next day's reports. Bernie laughs, "Too bad we can't warn the weather forecaster: they're gonna go crazy trying to figure *this one out!*" So, Glenn has Bernie create an anonymous blog which they name 'Mother Nature ' and then boldly submit 'Breaking News' to talk shows, news media and weather channels:

Prediction 1 - Mother Nature's Freaky Storm is going to move from South America up north to Mexico's desert area between 2:18 AM thru 8:18 AM for six hours the next day.

Prediction 2 – Airports should consider flight patterns to avoid the freezing rainfall. Desert dwellers should be wary of flash floods.

Prediction 3 - Weather Station reporters will not be able to explain it.

The Weather Channel's pretty-boy announcer derisively picks up the challenge and does his own prediction saying, "There is no way it can **possibly be true!** There is no temperature differential weather front and not an ounce of moisture to be squeezed from that desert atmosphere. I'm sorry to say Mother Nature's Blog *is pure fantasy!*" The next day's reports verify it, using weather station's radar marking exact location and movement of the freak storm. It is slightly off center, so Glenn adjusts the program to compensate for surface winds.

The Weather Channel's announcer is ***flabbergasted!***

Bernie's anonymous blog has now gained sudden notoriety. There's news that the satellite is showing fires in the Amazon Jungle. Opportunists are clearing the trees by burning. So, the next Gusher-Tide they spray into that area - putting out the fires. They laugh heartily at these gold miners and drug dealers trying to clear the land with no consideration given for the environment. (The gold-mining is open pit and causes a lot of toxic pollution to the land, ground-water, and total environment.) Then they turn the Gusher-Spray on each of the South America deserts wherever they find them on the map and continue irrigating them weekly. And then back to Mexico; and then the rest of Central America where there are deserts. A Pox News naysayer points out that the tourist trade for the Peruvian NASCA lines is being destroyed as well as the tourist trade for the Chilean Geoglyphs. Glenn says, "What the fuck are Geoglyphs?"

The Professor pounces saying, "You didn't even investigate where you were dumping your industrial waste-water?!? They are large ancient artworks carved into the desert. It brings a lot of tourists. You went off half-cocked again without considering the consequences of **your greed!**"

Glenn retorts, "My so-called industrial waste-water is as *pure as rainwater!* There is also a noticeable cooling of temperature in those hot arid deserts. I am sure those local residents prefer self-sustaining farming to a hit-or-miss tourist trade. Pecuador had been suffering from the increase of torrid temperatures which had been attributed to Global -Warming. That had come down noticeably after we built our first Skyhook. Then the temperature went back up again after that Skyhook was destroyed by the 'Big Syphon.' But then, when it was rebuilt, the temperature cooled drastically and *has remained so!* Understandably because our new Skyhook covers this whole mountain valley blocking the hot Sun in the afternoon. In the evening it cast Skyhook's shadow in the eastern section; from sunrise though mid-afternoon the shadow is in the western section. Nobody **is complaining** about that!"

Bernie interjects, "Maybe that's why Sancho's mules do not have enough green grass to graze on. Maybe it's because we're blocking the sunlight and the grass isn't growing as robustly as it usually does?"

Glenn glares at Bernie, then continues, "All that solar energy is being either reflected back into space off the top of Skyhook or being gathered by the solar panels and turned into electricity, and the radiant heating of the solar batteries is also being converted to electricity with our *thermal-electric transducers!* It's reducing **Global-Warming!!** There is a name for negative people like you; I wish I **knew what it is!!!**"

The Professor huffs sarcastically, **"Humph!** You discovered your electricity supply source **accidentally**; Ben Franklin got electricity from the atmosphere *200 years before* **we** did it! You are basking in feelings of superiority ~ from your Gusher Irrigation invention ~ which was an **ACCIDENTAL BYPRODUCT of your GOLD FEVER!!** I am surprised you have not found a way to make money from your *water supply!"* Then he repeats mimicking Glenn, "Your fresh - *pure* **water supply!?!** Maybe you can *collect a pint of blood* from each of these poor farmers you're irrigating . . . You don't want to know it; but I must keep reminding you about your other *fiasco!* Your *second 'Big Syphon' - September 21st - The Equinox is coming soon!!"* The Professor stomps away.

Glenn shouts after him, exasperated, "How many times must I say it; we are prepared for it already, we have *1000 times more* H-cube balloons to choke it than we did for *the first Big Syphon!* What more **can we do?!?"**

Bernie hurries out the door and catches up with the Professor, "You know that the Mexicans are protesting because Americans are sucking the Colorado River dry before it reaches them . . . You know it is really a good thing - this irrigation we are doing; we are providing fresh water, cooling the deserts, and this new vegetation will remove C-O2 from the atmosphere . . ."

The Professor glances at Bernie questioningly, "By the time it has an effect, the Artic Tundra's permafrost will be melting and releasing *tons of methane gas*, pushing **Global-Warming** over the *tipping-point.*"

Bernie has no retort, so he continues, "We could have really used your help. We couldn't calculate the speed of the seawater mist spraying out of the Gusher-Tower, trying to pinpoint its target destination. We were using the video frames per second to calcula . . ."

The Professor interrupts without even thinking, "Subtract the beginning time of the high-tide appearing in the Gusher-Cavern, from the time it first gushes out the top of the Gusher-Tower, divided by the height of the tower. *Simple* . . ."

Bernie is dumb-struck with humiliation.

XI

❖

TOP OF THE WORLD, MOM!"

The next day's news reports:

> 'Due to the inevitable effects of Global-Warming, we are rapidly approaching the tipping-point; that is the point that Global-Warming will be accelerating beyond our ability to stop it. Earth will become a smoldering cauldron – like the planet Venus – its surface temperature is over 900 degrees Fahrenheit. One California City reported a new record high of 130 degrees F. There are massive forest fires on the west coast once again. They are threatening vast areas including the two-thousand-year-old Red-Wood Trees and all of Yosemite Park.'

Glenn follows the news, pinpointing the locations of the fires on the map and then directs the Gusher-Spray there. Then he moves it as needed to the location of other fires, thinking, "What a miraculously great tool I *have invented!* I am amazed at the range that I can spray my *seawater vapor!* Despite the Professor's demeaning tirade, it is pure water – resulting from evaporation, just like rainwater, only much colder." Within six hours the Gusher-Spray has extinguished all the fires. His chest swells with pride.

The next day he hears *Australia is now* **on fire**: virtually the **whole continent**. It got so hot that the trees are spontaneously igniting. Firefighters are begging for volunteers as it is threatening the city of Sydney. The other cities are suffering from the thick, caustic smoke. "Oh my God, that's really far away, across the Pacific; it's got to be *10,000 miles southwest of here!* There are vast deserts there as well. That's bigger and further than any place I have attempted to irrigate so far." Glenn is fearful his effort will not succeed. "Anyhow," Glenn figures, "worst case scenario is, I will miss it. Cold rainwater won't be a problem for the ocean." So, he calculates Australia's distance then tilts the spray nozzle upward and points it towards the west-southwest. Glenn is listening on the shortwave radio to Australia's weather; he hears the horrific price the fire fighters are paying. "Bernie let's take a chance and declare on the blog that Mother Nature will put out all of Australia's fires . . ." Bernie becomes increasingly pale as he nervously writes this prediction on the blog. They wait in hope for hours. Glenn demands an answer from no-one, "Did it fall into the ocean!?!" He can't concentrate on anything else; he just waits for 'Mother Nature's Freaky Storm' to impact.

Bernie relays a conversation he had with Jake who has been listening to radio news talk shows while working on Skyhook. "They are saying that Candidate Prump's campaign is coordinating the election with the Russians. There have been arrests, but Prump promises to pardon them when he wins the election. He is insisting that he can only lose by Democrats stealing the election. He is undermining the U S Democracy and setting himself up to become the dictator of his U S Kleptocracy." Glenn only nods in polite acknowledgement.

Bernie is passing the time by researching Pecuador's volcanic continental shelf. "I read that there is a section of tectonic plate subducting under Pecuador that left a deep trench, named the 'Carnegie Trench & Ridge', that runs east/west - not north/south like the rest of the plates do; our Gusher- lava-tube must go down to that deep trench. The pressure in the deepest ocean, the seven-mile-deep Marianas Trench, is about 8 tons. *Mother of Jesus!* Imagine that: ***16,000-pounds-per-square-inch!!***"

Glenn speculates, "We don't know how deep-down in the ocean our Gusher-Lava-Tube goes. But our Gusher-Tower reaches the vacuum at the highest point of the Earth's globular shaped atmosphere: my Skyhook is floating at the very top of that globular shaped atmosphere: every place to the south and north is below us so we should be able to spray our Gusher's seawater everywhere."

They are anxiously awaiting the Australian weather report . . .

   ~ The mounting tension is becoming palpable . . .

     ~ Their anxiety is building into an explosive outbreak . . .

      ~Bernie's catharsis breaks thru as he *screams like a maniac!*

"TOP OF THE WORLD, MOM!"

Glenn simply looks at him askance . . .

~ (Bernie is flashing back to James Cagney's maniacal death cry, while shooting at police from the top of a huge gas storage tank.)

Bernie reflects back to Glenn's discourse, "It's just a matter of spraying the seawater high enough so it goes far enough; then gravity takes control. *That fucking Professor!* He could calculate the formula for targeting our spray in a minute. It's the speed of the Gusher-Spray times the angle – gives us the height to arrive above the target area, then the formula for gravity-free-fall, gives the arrival time. Somehow he would factor in the decreasing forward momentum due to the atmospheric resistance. And we're sitting *here like idiots* waiting for hours . . . If it falls into the ocean, we'll *never hear ANYTHING!!"*

Then Bernie relays the Professor's comment about the Artic Tundra's methane emissions and the tipping-point. "Why can't we simply lay your empty balloons on the tundra capturing that methane within, then we could use the internal tanks to compress it? We could collect these tanks periodically. Then we can donate or sell them with small portable gas burners that poor people can use instead of burning wood for cooking and heating. That's what Rockefeller did with his kerosene lamps." He gets no response from Glenn, "We can use silver-colored shiny balloons that will reflect the sunlight back into space and further reduce Global-Warming . . .? Or, they can be covered in solar batteries, just like your H-cube balloons are, and we can wire them into Canada's electricity supply *just like we do here!"*

Glenn is annoyed and finally replies, "You're getting rich with your share of the Gusher profits; you can do whatever you want . . ."

"Can I take Jane with me to work on it?" he asks sheepishly.

"Of course *NOT!* **How stupid it that** – she'll have the CIA all over me the second **she is _free!!_**"

"Maybe I'll get my college friends to work with me on it . . ." Bernie responds demurely.

Glenn softens his tone, suddenly alarmed by the prospect of losing his enthusiastic assistant, "That's a good idea. You can use our Mother Nature's Blog to fund it while still keeping our location a secret. But manage them anonymously thru the blog - don't let them know it's you hiring them; nobody can know where you are, or that you're *associated with the blog!* Your idea could make a dent in Global-Warming. You know that permafrost covers about 25% of the Earth above the artic circle, millions of square miles. In addition to greenhouse-gases, it also releases anthrax and other deadly diseases when it melts. People *have died* from it."

Bernie interjects, "I presume that burning the sequestered tundra gases will kill the anthrax and other bacteria."

Glenn nods continuing, "The communist would *kiss your feet* it you could deliver that cheap electricity to them *from Siberia's Tundra!*"

Finally, the Australian weather news comes through:

'Their firefighters are at the point of exhaustion . . . Now, suddenly **they are elated!** They can back away from the flames and get out of their heavy, hot suits while Mother Nature comes to *their rescue!!* There *is celebration* in all of Sydney! Thanks to Mother Nature's freaky **life-saving rainstorm!!!**'

Glenn feels elated; his spirit is soaring at this wonderful success; probably saving the lives of the firefighters, he can't sit still and just prances around with joy . . .

Then he recalls feeling this way before, when he thought he had successfully tested his 'Big Cannon' – immediately before it started the apocalyptic 'Big Syphon.' He begins to wonder how the Professor will complain: on behalf of the deadly poisonous snakes he will drown; and how many of their kangaroos might object to all the fresh, cold water that he is dumping on them. Glenn's jubilant euphoria has been curtailed by the criticism he expects from the Professor; however, he is still quite satisfied with himself. This is a *magnificent accomplishment!* He wonders, "Could we do the same for the Sahara Desert?"

The fires are completely extinguished within two days; but Glenn decides to rotate the Gusher-Spray around Australia's whole desert region, attempting to irrigate it. "Imagine that, in just a few days how many tons of carbon dioxide and toxic smoke we prohibited by putting all *those fires out!*" He says, congratulating Bernie on their accomplishment, "No, you don't have to imagine that Bernie ~ **because it's true!!** Maybe we can irrigate the whole Saudi Arabian Peninsula. They would become independent and farm. All those Palestinians living in Jordanian refugee camps for decades. All the ones that are *fleeing from Africa* to try to get into Europe! My God, the camps they have in Syria - if Dictator Assad's and the Russian's bombing *left any survivors* there – also, there are millions of Syrian refugees in Turkey. . . the Kurds *could finally have* their Kurdistan – The **Bangladeshi refugees!** – The Gobi Desert: The ***Chinese Uighurs!!*** Maybe even the Sahara Desert ***can be irrigated!*** That would give all the refugees in the world plenty of land to escape to. *AND* all the new vegetation our irrigation will enable – it will suck all the excess C-O2 from our atmosphere ~ and

~ put

~ an

end to

GLOBAL-WARMING!!!"

Bernie sees Glenn's eyes flashing wildly and his eyebrows bouncing erratically up his forehead . . . He is fearful that Glenn is having a brain seizure:

~ "will he fall and *convulse violently* while frothing at the mouth?!?!" ~

"You are right Bernie, *scream it to your mother* - and to **Mother Nature's Blog.** We are on ***top of the world!*** Our Gusher- Tower is the ***top of the world!*** " Then he whispers breathlessly, "If we find that our atmosphere is becoming too rich with oxygen, we can simply stop irrigating the least desirable desert areas. We won't irrigate any part of Israel until they return the housing that *they have stolen* from the Palestinians. Also, we should have your Blog insist that the United States build a *Palestinian Embassy* across the street from their U S Israeli Embassy in Jerusalem. We can irrigate *the Dead Sea* for the Palestinians; or create another 'LIVE SEA' in their eastern region. Bernie, you won't irrigate any country that does NOT encourage **birth-control!** Over population is going to be the Earth's final apocalypse . . . I wish we had more Gusher-Towers!!" Glenn voice raises, oozing with enthusiasm, "You could build them on every mountainous coast along the equator and be able to irrigate constantly using the various high-tides. I wonder if this tidal-phenomenon of 'lava-tube-gushers' exists elsewhere - that you could tap into. Why can't you just drill down at an angle, creating your own Gusher- Tubes; there must be other lava-tubes that go deep below this mountain range near the ocean? This crater valley got its long oblong shape due to the fact that its volcanic hotspot was moving over the millennia. *Bernie!* You can find these lava-tubes using ground-penetrating radar, then you can begin drilling from the bottom of them at an angle down into **the deep ocean!! "** Glenn quickly reviews Bernie's' research, "That Carnegie Tectonic-Trench is between two tectonic mini-plates near our northern Pecuadorian border; Bernie – you've got to start drilling into the deepest part of that trench, *immediately!?!?"*

Bernie's eyes are bulging with the burden of these Olympian tasks. Glenn now sees how he is overwhelming his young assistant and then calms himself down, saying, "You can get a few of your college friends to start working on it . . . AND, maybe instead of this one gigantic 5-foot-wide Gusher-Nozzle, we can somehow insert several dozen nozzles squirting independently of one another, in various directions, accomplishing the same thing. That might increase the pressure as we're reducing the diameter, but then each one of them could be individually programmed to point at different targets. We could concentrate the sprays to the more populated areas at night when people won't be bothered by it; and then in the daytime, we can aim it at desolate areas that are unpopulated, like the Mojave Desert, and the Sahara Desert, and all those other deserts around the world. And we can alternate our Gusher-Spray to each area maybe once or twice a week. After an initial good soaking, vegetation will be able to grow." Bernie now gazes wistfully as Glenn muses on, "I remember seeing somewhere that grass creates more oxygen and absorbs more C-O2 than trees do. I imagine that all these desert regions are going to naturally spring up with grass, as grass-seed will be blowing all over the place." Glenn's fantasies end as he laments, **"My God!** Elephants are starving because their grasslands are turning into deserts. In Kenya and Uganda, the villagers are *killing each other*, stealing cattle and water from each other. Jake told me that *35% of their livestock* has died from the draught. The giraffes are even *dying from it!"*

Bernie is thankful for a task he can handle, as he works on the installation of the maximal number of 6-inch nozzles into the 5-foot diameter Gusher-Nozzle. Bernie calculates, "The diameter Gusher-Tower's sewer pipe covers about twenty sq/ft so we might get 40 six-inch nozzles into there, each of which can be programmed separately to point in any direction. Yes!" Bernie exclaims to Glenn showing his diagram of the proposed forty new Gusher Nozzles, "We are reaching Australia; I analyzed the angle and determined that our Gusher-Spray can reach anywhere in the world and when there is any excess, we can point it to the North and South Pole to rebuild the polar ice caps." Glenn's eyebrows raise questioningly. "These ice-caps are melting into the oceans due to Global-Warming. There's one the size of Connecticut that is sliding into the ocean off of Antarctica. It's already raising the ocean levels – that plus the heat-expansion caused by the warming of the oceans. Bangladesh and some Pacific Islands are being inundated. Don't you know about the Saltwater Conveyor Current? Greenland's massive glaciers are sliding into the Atlantic. Didn't you see the movie, 'The Day After Tomorrow'?" Then Bernie's eyes light up as he loudly demands, "*Wait!* ***STOP EVERYTHING!!"***

Glenn's joy turns to fright as he jumps up out of his chair, "***What is it?!?*** *- Calm down! -* You're going to give me a heart attack . . ."

"You said the elephants are starving; it reminded me of today's news: Jake heard that there's a pending famine as a massive swarm of locust are destroying all vegetation in Asia Minor. ~ We can flood them with 6-hours of ***freezing water!*** Program the Gusher Nozzle to start at 100 miles east of Istanbul and then continue east for another 50 miles while I research that *news report!"* Glenn is shocked with indignation; but he does as his young assistant commands . . . Bernie soon has the GPS-coordinates, and they joyfully enter them into the computer. Bernie shouts gleefully,

"They can scoop- up the frozen locusts and use them *for animal-feed!*"
Glenn tells Bernie to post that new 'protein supply' with the 'Locust
Demise Prediction' on Mother Nature's Blog. He breaks out two bottles
of Champagne and invites his two mujers to join them. They wait for the
news reports on the locust swarm – the girls seeing the champagne are
anxious to start partying and can't understand why they must wait.

As the Gusher-Spray hits, the Dictator Perdogan is basking in praise as
Allah has justified his dictatorship by answering his prayers: thus, ending
the locust plague.

Laughing with *triumphant joy* they begin dancing around: Jake with
Margherita . . . Bernie with pregnant Elena. The girls are happy to be
partying, but *are perplexed* by their understanding of this celebration:

    "Many grasshoppers got <u>wet</u>?!?"

                  Because **it *rained* on a *<u>turkey</u>*!?!"**

When the celebration ends, Bernie feels impotently ostracized and
suffers post elation let down – as he watches Glenn lustfully clutching
both women, practically dragging them to his cabin. Bernie Is green with
envy thinking, "Glenn will have a wonderful night with both ***women in
his bed!***" As he is finishing the last of his champagne, he shuts the lights
and peers into Glenn's dimly lit cabin. He can see the silhouettes of the
voluptuous Margherita lowering her breasts into Glenn's face while Elena's
head is slowly bobbing up and down in Glenn's crouch. Bernie brushes his
hand over his own crouch while longing for the imprisoned CIA Jane . . .

The next day Bernie reiterates their success with the locust-swarm
in Asia Minor, then adds that there is another infestation on the Horn
of Africa and awkwardly ask Glenn if he can direct the Gusher-Spray
there. Glenn replies, "*Of course!* Why do you even bother to ask? Don't
forget to post these predictions on your blog." Bernie proceeds to direct
the spray without answering. Glenn continues, "You should also set an
internet alarm for African flying-ants and driver-ants that regularly plague
the continent." Then he is thinking, "But those countries probably don't

practice birth-control. I don't want to help them over-populate the world. We'll have to investigate Moslems and birth-control."

Bernie responds with an indifferent tone, "Okay, and I am proceeding with the Blog hiring my college friends to construct new Gusher-Towers and laying the Green-House-Gas sequestering balloons on the tundra. Jake heard that the desert in Mexico has become much cooler and inhabitable as a result of the Gusher-Spray's regular cold watering. There is an element of temperature control associated with this. Equatorial Africa would be an ideal place for the new Gusher-Tower; but they have so much trouble with the war-lords."

Glenn replies glibly, "Well, have your college friend check it out." He wonders, "Can it be used to minimize the temperature differences between warm-fronts and the colder jet-stream which causes so many tornadoes with life threatening damage. Might a cooling Gusher-Spray in front of the warm-front minimize the temperature clash of the hot and cold air and destroy the murderous tornadic effect." Then he speculates, "What about hurricanes?" He knows they are fed by the hot or warm ocean; though there's no hope of cooling off the ocean, might there be an opportunity to intercept the low-pressure center as it comes off the African Coast? He had seen that many Atlantic hurricanes develop from low pressure centers blowing off the Sahara Desert. Not all of these low-pressure sand swirlers take on this ugly cyclonic effect; and even less take on more energy and expand becoming tropical storms, and then even fewer materialize into hurricanes. – "But those that do can be **KILLERS!** Wouldn't *that be wonderful!* We can make sure that that portion of Western Africa is well irrigated in the hope that it will *stop this cyclonic evolution.*" He assigns Bernie the task of looking into all that, too. "And, if you please," he says with some joyful arrogance, "elaborate for the Professor all the environmental recovery work that *you and I are accomplishing!*"

Bernie laughs confidently, "Gladly, I can barely wait **to rub his nose in it!**"

The Professor's reply to all this is a dry, "Congratulations . . . but you still have *Glenn's second 'Big Syphon'* circling the Earth every 24 hours and **wreaking havoc!**"

Glenn wonders, "Could I possibly use my Gusher-Spray to *choke or drown* my **2ⁿᵈ 'Big Syphon'** . . . I wouldn't think so."

He timidly raises the question to the Professor who retorts, **"What?**
Are you trying to accelerate YOUR *APOCALYPES?!?*

It is already sucking up tons of the Earth's water every day - *you want to give it more!"*

A tense silence follows. Then the Professor plays a 'News Commentary' he recorded of the helicopter crash in Peru's Andes Mountain:

> 'The pilot survived with some injuries but is crying in anguish as his personally owned helicopter has been destroyed and his livelihood with it. "I have a mortgage to pay on it and children to feed. I do not know how I am going to tell my wife that our prosperous future has ended." The Reporter asks about his accident insurance. He replies, "The insurance has loopholes; it is only for the bank's protection not mine, as they only insure flights with a pre-approved flight plan, which is unrealistic to get on short notice. I am only approved for good weather flights for my 'traffic reporting' job in the city. Otherwise, I have to solicit pre-flight approval from the airport's Weather Department which is expensive and time consuming and must be obtained 24 hours in advance.'

The Professor is looking coldly at Glenn. He responds by getting his lawyer on the phone saying, "Arturo, buy a top-of-the-line new helicopter for the Peruvian Weather Reporter as a reward for his heroism. Yes, he is a hero. He bravely faced his fears and reported the news as best he could. Besides, the world needs more heroes. Make it appear as a donation from Mother Nature's Blog." Then he calls Bernie, "Make sure your blog notifies all airports, weather stations, and police & fireman in advance of our irrigations in their areas so they can schedule any safety measures that might be necessary."

XII

❖

CIA JANE'S PAROLE

IA Jane gets a message to Bernie through Jake, telling him to watch for each other on Channel 13. Each security camera gives a 5-second view (no voice) throughout the Hacienda. He waves to her when he sees himself on the TV and she has written a note which she shows when she is on the TV. She states how bored she is imprisoned there and wants to know everything that he is doing. He is happy to list all the progress they are making; and what impact they are having on the environment. Jane is disappointed to know that; she wants him to join with her as Glenn's enemy. She is actually angry with him for becoming so cooperative. He explains that he's being well paid, and the work is very gratifying. Bernie is concerned for her and approaches Glenn, "What's going to happen with Jane. You cannot conceivably expect her to stay up there, all by herself, with nothing to do but watch TV?"

Glenn says dismissively, "Doesn't she have a hobby . . . besides *trying to kill me!*"

Bernie protests, "Even in jail prisoners can communicate with the outside world. Must you be so cruel?"

Glenn speculates, "Well, if she wants something to do to preoccupy her mind, at night she can access the telescope room from her cabin without going outside. There is a stairwell that goes up to the top level of the Skyhook with a cabin there just like the one she's in; except that there is a telescope in it, from which she can view the heavens. I have notes there that I don't want her to fool with: I had been tracking asteroids and watching the launches that we are doing. I used to do it while working up there; one day I hope to renew my interest when I'm not so busy. I will unlock the stairway automatically from down here with the timer during the night only, so she doesn't blind herself: trying to use the telescope in the daylight."

Bernie scoffs, "I'm sure she's not that stupid."

Glenn retorts, "She was stupid enough to hide in the Loon-Evator without a space-suit ; stupid enough to prop open the *safety doors!*"

Jane is grateful to Bernie. She climbs the spiral staircase from her cabin up to the top of Skyhook and finds herself in another cabin with the computer-controlled telescope. She studies Glenn's forbidden notes. Then she keys in specific locations and is enjoying the view all night long. She goes back regularly every evening at sunset and utilizing Glenn's notes she is watching the launchings and follows their various tracks; all of them on their way to the Sun's south polar region. She discovers that there are Morse-Code radio transmissions and blinking lights uniquely identifying each barrel of nuclear waste. She can determine their spatial location relative to solar system mapping. She subsequently calculates how far a given barrel has traveled and is surprised to see their speed is over 40,000 miles-per-hour when they reach half-way to the Sun. Beyond that they accelerate forming a straight line towards the Sun's south polar region.

There is a solar blocking mechanism on the telescope which she could use to watch the barrels start burning-up as they get closer to the Sun; however, she is fearful that she may do something wrong and cause herself to go blind.

She would like to have some instruction on using it with somebody who has done it before. That can only be Glenn, as the Professor never goes up there. She would rather die than asked *Glenn for anything!* Going through Glenn's notes, she also sees that he has an obsession with asteroids. There is a fascinating one called Cruithne that tracts the Earth's in a 'horseshoe pattern' orbit:

> When it is on the Sun side of our orbit; as it gets closer,
> it gravitationally speeds up and then shifts to the far side
> of the Earth. That is now a wider diameter orbit (hence
> slower), so the Earth pulls away from it.

When the Earth catches up with it again in another seven-hundred years or so, Earth's gravity attracts it once again and pulls it past the Earth's orbit again, shifting it back into its narrower diameter orbit. Then the asteroid goes faster than the Earth and catches up again in probably another 700 years and then, once again, crosses beyond the Earth's orbit – completing its horseshoe shaped orbit.

Glenn's note states a frightening concept: what happens if the Moon is closer when this 3-mile-wide iron asteroid is crossing, or if the Moon is in between, their gravitational forces combining - that's a catastrophe just waiting to happen. Additionally, there are over 10,000 Apollo Near Earth asteroids. At least 1,648 of them are Earth-crossing asteroids that could possibly collide with the Earth. It is apparent from Glenn's notes that he fantasizes about eliminating these apocalyptic asteroids.

CIA Jane learns how to change the telescope's lenses and studies all those Lunar Craters: it was indeed something to worry about - meteors colliding with both the Earth and the Moon. The Moon's 'Sea of Tranquility': God what an impact it must have been to have created that monstrosity. The supposition is that our Moon is the small remnant of Earth's impact with another Mars sized planet called 'Theia', causing its total devastation; and there are some humongous craters on the Moon - suggesting that's where the impact occurred. The remaining debris from that planet got blown into space – probably forming the asteroid belt between Mars and Jupiter. Astronomers say that logically, in planetary evolution, there should have been another rocky planet orbiting there.

Another of Glenn's notes shows his morbid fascination with the last toxic-waste barrel that was launched from his Big Cannon in Arizona. That was not so long ago. He seems to think that it must have been magnetized somehow or other; although, it was not launched with the massive magnetism of the Railgun - but blasted with air pressure from the Big Cannon. She had heard from Virginia how he had shut down the Big Cannon without waiting for the launching to finish. He shut it down by shooting the computer controlling it - totally destroying it. She surmises that launching never did accelerate enough for this rogue barrel to totally escape the Earth's gravitational pull; but fast enough so that it was caught in an elliptical orbit around the Earth. The telescope could track its orbit; he had plotted it with the help of the Professor. Glenn's notes concentrated on the fact that you could see the barrel's flashing signal pointing directly to the Magnetic North Pole when it is just above the equator, - when it is below the equator, it tilts away towards the Sun. Glenn can understand that it would tilt towards the north magnetic pole as a result of some slight magnetism acquired by the metal barrel from the Earth's magnetic-field, but he cannot understand why it would turn and point towards the Sun's southern magnetic pole. Can the Sun's magnetism be a factor - reaching all the way - 93,000,000 miles from there to here? Of course, he knows our solar system's magnetic-field extends out further than Pluto, and he knows that our Sun's solar wind protects us from inter-galactic cosmic rays - deflecting them away from our solar system; the same way that the Earth's magnetic shield protects us from the Sun's deadly radiation.

Having little else to interest her, she becomes engrossed with plotting the paths of these meteorites. She is also fascinated by Asteroid 3753 Cruithne. Other asteroids (2003-YN107 & 2002AA29) follow in the Earth's orbit in a horseshoe pattern: this sounds especially dangerous to her. She also spies on that rogue barrel. Initially, she was convinced that one day it will fall down to Earth into a city, finally fulfilling Glenn's terrorism mission. But, now seeing thousands of launched barrels are in fact going to the Sun, she is beginning to soften her attitude. Also, her steroid addiction is calming down as she was being weaned-off them and she is no longer excessively abusing her clitoris. She was never thinking promiscuity, but admits to having been very horny as a result of the steroid's side effects. She's hot for Bernie now, especially since she had not seen him in person for a long time.

Finally, she breaks down and asks Glenn if he will allow Bernie to show her how to use the sun-blocker on the telescope and if she could update his notes on the plotting of the asteroids. He says that Bernie doesn't know how; but he will show her. He cautions her about any nonsensical attempt to attack him or to try to escape. He is thinking, she could kill him then take his space-suit and escape - or just incapacitate him; or maybe seduce him and fuck his brains out until he falls asleep then take his space-suit. He agrees to instruct her if she will go up to the telescope and stay there - alone. He will lock her in up there by way of a remote-control lock on the stairwell (which he had installed to prevent the possibility of depressurization of the cabins, should there be any sort of incident in the stairwell). Then he will go there, but he will keep his space-suit on. He will enter through the cabin's exterior pressurizing entrance.

Then she explains that Bernie is writing to her by way of the closed-circuit television which is very tedious as she only has a short number of seconds to read it and asks if they could facilitate their communicating. Glenn says that they can exchange video or writing materials with her food deliveries. She is grateful but wonders if there isn't any way they can have a constant communication like email or Facebook? Glenn gives a flat "No."

With her next food delivery, Jane sends telescope-videos to Bernie that she took of the launchings, and of Glenn's wayward nuclear-waste barrel. Also, pictures of the asteroids that Glenn had been tracking, both the Earth crossing and the other few that were orbiting around the Earth. Bernie shows them to Glenn, and he is quite impressed; obviously, she's a very intelligent young lady. Bernie wonders if he can go there and use the telescope. Glenn is reluctant, but he's beginning to feel sorry for Jane's situation and the fact that they do have a romance going. He agrees to a halfway measure as Jake and Sancho are both becoming burned out working essentially 12 hour shifts seven days a week. Bernie can now work on Railgun launchings four days a week giving them each off two days and still continue his work on research and Mother Nature's Blog.

Bernie mentions that the blog is getting a lot of comments and requests for delivery of water, suggesting that since it's always so accurate with predictions about where the next freaky irrigation will occur that it must have some control. If it can spray at Vale Ski Slopes, they would pay for it. Glenn says, "Okay, I'll have Arturo open a Swiss Bank Account in the name of Mother Nature and we will charge them $5,000 per hour to start and see how it goes."

XIII

TELESCOPE-CABIN

Sargent Aguilar of the Pecuadorian Military delivers a new Jet-Basket, replacing the one that Glenn had destroyed when he was flung into deep space by the Big Syphon1. That evening Glenn takes Bernie up on Loon-Evator1 to Skyhook and teaches him everything about the Railgun launchings again. He can see however, that Bernie is terribly distracted by the mere presence of CIA Jane imprisoned in her cabin. He chastises Bernie telling him to pay attention, reminding him that this is nuclear toxic waste that they are handling 20 miles up above the ground and cannot afford any mistakes or accidents. After he is assured that Bernie can handle it on his own, he gives CIA Jane a note telling her to go up the spiral stairway to the telescope-cabin where he will train her on the sun-blocking-filter. He warns her that she had better **not** try any *funny stuff!*

Glenn returns to the ground and then immediately takes his new Jet-Basket and flies back up to the top of Skyhook where he will enter the telescope-cabin through its external pressurized doors. He is thinking of the irony that he had to float the Loon-Evator down 20 miles to the Hacienda Valley, to then float Alcarracho back up that same 20 miles plus 15 feet to arrive at the front entrance of the telescope-cabin. Somehow, he just feels this is safer for him dealing with Jane; he is embarrassed by his physical fear of this woman. To be opening the door of Jane's prison cabin, with Bernie behind him and Jane in front of him, seems a little frightening. He can control the locks on the spiral stairway between her prison cabin and the telescope-cabin. So now she is locked in the telescope-cabin, while

Bernie is working. The security cameras verify their location - he enters the telescope-cabin through the pressurized air-lock and sees Jane face to face for the first time since their fist-fight.

She gives him a cheerful smile and asks, "How are you?" in a grateful tone; and then quickly adds, "I am so impressed with the work you've been accomplishing; Bernie has been telling me all about it in the videos that we exchange."

Glenn replies, "The thing I remember most from our last meeting is your foot digging into my throat ~ Fortunately ~ just missing my Adam's apple - or I *would be dead!*"

Jane apologizes profusely, "It was the steroids that were driving me crazy. I couldn't understand what was happening. I didn't know - how could I believe that you are actually doing humanitarian work. I understand now that you have to keep everything a secret."

Glenn wonders how much of that Bernie had coached her to say. Then says, "All right, but don't get too chummy; I don't trust you - nor your motives."

She says with earnest intensity "All that I really want is to be a part of your project's humanitarian effort; I feel I must be able to contribute in some way. Also, I need to have some communication with my mother, let her know that I'm alive and well. We can shoot a video of me in front of the TV news showing the date and time. We can instruct her not to notify anybody about it. She will listen to me. Bernie's email message to her was weeks ago; there has been no effort to locate me. You see, she didn't reveal anything; we told her not to – *and she didn't!*" After a moment of silence, "Also, I would like to be able to have a civilized dinner with some people; at least I could sit down with Bernie, look into another human face - have a decent conversation. It's really not fair: I didn't *break any laws!* But *YOU kidnapped me! ~* **I'm *not the criminal!*"**

He challenges, "You did not attempt any further contacts with your mother? You didn't have Bernie send out some videos or emails to her?"

"No, I didn't ask him to, and I don't believe he did. I'm sure he would've told me if he did."

Glenn says, "Well let me think on it for a while." They review all the information on the solar blocking mechanism while concentrating on all the safety procedures, and then activate it through the telescope's computer control system. For the balance of the night, she points the telescope at all the available sightings referenced in Glenn's notes, glowing with pride. "I told you to keep your hands off of *my notes!*" But then Glenn is very interested to see her study of those objects, where they are in their orbit - in particular, a couple of the large metallic Earth crossing meteors. Also, his rogue toxic waste barrel stuck in its hundred-thousand-mile equator crossing, slightly elliptical orbit. He speculates with Jane about the Big Syphon2 passing by it, "It might latch onto it and suck it in, returning it to its previous trajectory, to burn-up in the Sun's Corona. Wouldn't that be nice! How naïve . . ." he says with a submissive smirk on his face. "As if things ever go right. ~ Never seen that in Murphy's Laws."

Then he conveys his concern, "A magnetic-field has been created on my rogue barrel orbiting the Earth. North of the equator it points to Earth's northern/positive magnetic pole. But South of the equator it points to the Sun's positive/southern magnetic pole? I want to know what happens to that rogue barrel when it passes near (or possibly thru) the Big Syphon2. You understand that its siphoning was created by the Sun's gravitational/suctioning power? Now that you have the sun-blocker you can video the Big Syphon2 between 11AM and 1PM on the days when my rogue barrel is orbiting on our side of the Earth, to see if they come close to each other and if they interact. Maybe crashing through its siphoned fluid will cause it to explode? Maybe it's traveling too fast to be affected? Maybe its magnetic-field will deflect it?"

"No." CIA Jane interjects enthusiastically, "Why should your rogue barrel have a magnetic-field, it wasn't launched from the mag-lev Railgun, it was blasted into space with air-pressure?"

Glenn replies, "They say anything can become magnetized under the right circumstances. I don't understand it either, maybe it's the rogue-barrel's orbital speed passing through the radio-active Solar-wind? Could that cause it to become magnetized? I would like to see how it is effected as it travels through the 'Big Syphon's' magnetic/gravitational channel."

Jane's eyebrows arch with intensity as she questions, "Space/time – orbital speeds effect time? That barrel is orbiting at around 100,000 miles higher, which means its orbital speed is much faster than the satellites?"

Glenn looks at her askance thinking there must be something more worthy of his time . . . She continues with her convoluted questioning, "I am confused . . . Because of the speed of the communications satellites - their clock-time is slower and has to be adjusted to earth-time? You said to video it between 11AM and 1PM - Does a satellite's radio signal, or a voice transmission, or my telescopic image of the rogue-barrel, come faster as their orbital speed makes their time slower?"

Glenn's eyebrows scrunch in confusion . . . then he commands glibly, *"Figure it out . . ."*

He turns and walks away from her entering the bathroom. He is too ashamed to shit into his fecal bag with CIA Jane around. It's still 3 hours before the Sun comes up when he can show her the sun-blocking on the telescope. While struggling to drop the pants of his space-suit, he ponders her bizarre question to him: "Does NASA Ground Control notice time differential from Space Station and satellite clocks. – When they transmit live video from the Space Station, - there's not even a second lost in viewing time? The rogue-barrel's orbiting, speeding thru the Earth's magnetic field or through the solar-wind, must be creating its own magnetic-field ~ therefore, *creating slower space/time?* But time slows down with greater speed? ~ Is it only the speed? ~ Maybe not only speed, but rather . . . ***can a magnetic-field slow time?"*** His eyes brighten as he is feeling a sense of accomplishment, "Maybe my tortured reasoning has arrived at something concrete?"

{But then, his doubting mind chimes in, "Einstein
would have considered that . . ."}
Then a diverging afterthought, "They say everything
can become magnetized to some degree."

Resuming his slow thought process, "Maybe it's not because of going fast, as much as pushing the fabric of space/time aside, and therefore not passing thru that space/time fabric. Therefore, passing thru less time, less aging?" Recalling the Professor's article, "Pushing aside these stubits of space/time fabric would account for increasing mass with speed. But that would mean a rocket launched into space would get heavier as it accelerated and should require more fuel to accelerate to overcome its greater gravitational attraction

but Galileo proved that gravity attracts everything equally, at the same rate?

maybe inertia?"

Glenn is lost in a vacuum of meditative speculation . . .

Recovering: "But, somehow speed is still creating a magnetic-field around my rogue barrel. (Maybe creating a time-warp, or maybe a wormhole.) What about my magnetic-pyramid construction – turned into a dream of an Alien?

The Alien was pissed because I built it and told me not to re-construct it for at least an hour. How did he know about it?

He suddenly appeared several times, dismantling my pyramid. He materialized aboard my Skyhook from no-where, repeatedly within minutes - without a vehicle - 20 miles above the Earth. He must have been able to look thru something from a distance and see me. How could he see me?" Glenn is totally perplexed; he calls the Professor on his helmet communicator. "Professor, I just had a revelation on space/time being a factor of the solar magnetic-field . . . and also our Magnetic . . ."

The Professor abruptly cuts him off, shouting, "What good is *your idle* **speculation**; it can ***never** be tested* as we are trapped within *this – our own -* **Solar magnetic-field**?!?

It's the *middle **of the fucking NIGHT!!!***"

Glenn remembers how he glibly dismissed Jane's questioning with a flippant, 'Figure it out.'

Mouth agape, Glenn stares through his space-suit-helmet at the bare bathroom door - as he visualizes himself forlornly shrinking - his space-suit pants below his knees, sitting on the toilet, confined in a small room, 20 miles above the Earth, enveloped by a crushing empty blackness . . .

When the Sun is beginning to come-up Jane demonstrates how well she's learned to use the sunshield. Now they can look close to the Sun and watch the stream of blinking lights from the toxic barrels as they begin to glow red-hot, their lights extinguishing, lost in the hot glow. They hear the squelching of their Morse Code radio signals, their scalding screams turning into a squawking cry of death; and then a fiery – silent – explosion: a radiant plasma-like spray as it burns away to nothing but ionized debris. One after another, every 10 seconds or so. It is a sight to behold. "Wow!" she says, "I had no idea. I thought we would see them splashing onto the surface of the Sun."

Glenn replies, "The Professor says that the Sun's core is 27 million Degrees; but surprisingly, the surface of the Sun is only about 10,000°F - while the corona is *about 1,000,000°!* Of course, our barrels never reach the surface. They burn-up in the corona. Whatever might survive that million degrees, if anything, I imagine would be atomized and would continue to be gravitationally pulled into the Sun. But I've got no idea about that. Even the Professor says it's just idle speculation. Maybe it will become part of the solar wind."

She says, "Well whatever is happening to the nuclear waste, it is better there than here - this is a wonderful thing that you and the Professor are accomplishing."

"You mean," Glenn replies suspiciously, "that you no longer think that I'm trying to bombard cities around the world with *nuclear waste?!?* You no longer think that I'm **a *terrorist*?**"

She replies defensively, *"Of course not!* I remember the network news reports that were being broadcasted alongside of the FBI's conflicting report; but they both agreed that it was a terrorist attack that they each individually claimed to have thwarted. When I realized it was you, that you are still wanted by our government, and that you had taken me prisoner, naturally I felt the need to escape. I feared **for my life!"**

Glenn replies seriously, "Maintain that *justifiable fear!* Don't forget; you are in the stratosphere, the outside temperature just beyond that wall is

50° below zero, the air pressure is just about zero. When you were at 30,000 feet and shot a hole in my helium storage tank, you had the possibility of surviving a few minutes. At this altitude you *wouldn't last a second!* Fear is justified and, believe me, I've taken every precaution against the possibility of you escaping. Every space-suit is programed to function only when worn by its assigned operator; it will only operate when its assigned person's voice matches, and there is also a DNA matching requirement." Glenn thinks that last lie might have stretched her credulity.

"I understand." she says. "I just want to help now - with the understanding that one day, when the nuclear-waste is basically off the planet, and you are then, for the most part, just launching other toxic waste - that you will find the means to let me go. But I couldn't think of any more interesting work than what you're doing here, and I would be glad to help - if I could at least have on-line visitations with my family. I am their only child . . ." She has tears in her eyes now; Glenn is feeling guilty.

Then, he realizes her release plans are repeating what he had told Bernie; and obviously, he had relayed them to her. *"That bastard!"* Then he says to her, "You're still not ready to admit that you are CIA? How else could you have gotten that plastic gun with its plastic bullets? And I'm supposed to trust you!" She returns a practiced stare of bizarre confusion. Looking at TV channel 13, he can see that Bernie is on the Loon-Evator floating back down to the ground and he feels it is safe to allow CIA Jane to return to her cabin. He exits through the exterior air-lock and as he starts floating Alcarracho back to the ground, he hails the computer through his headset and instructs it to unlock the spiral staircase doors. He gets to the ground again and gets out of his space-suit. He checks channel 13 and sees Jane has in fact returned to her cabin and he instructs the stairwell doors to lock again. Then he programs them to unlock during Bernie's shifts automatically, in the hope that she will show more interest in going to the telescope than gazing at Bernie through her window while he is working in Skyhook.

Through the next two days of Bernie's shifts Glenn is gratified to see that she is in fact working on the telescope. That is when Bernie has taking over Sancho's daytime shifts. But Bernie is turned on by the mere presence of Jane, and she, being a prisoner is delighted for his attention. At first through the glass window, then, during his first night shift, he slowly opens the pressurized door and uneasily enters the air-lock. Then he anxiously enters her prison cabin as he removes his space-suit helmet. She comments, "Oh, the smell: how can you bear it?"

"I'll take it off and leave it air-out in the air-lock." She looks at him askance. He responds excitedly, "I can cover with a towel. I'll come back after I finish stacking the next load, to keep the automatic launchings going." He soon returns and she hands him a towel at the pressurized vestibule. He gets out of the smelly space-suit and enters asking, "Is this better?" with a romantic air of anticipation.

She shakes her head while holding her nose and leads him to the bathroom, *"Take a shower!"* He quickly showers and comes out to find her stepping into his space-suit. He rushes over to her and viciously grabs her arm. **"Ouch!** What are you doing?" She yells as she whips her arm free of his tightly pinching grip. "That's gonna *leave a bruise!* I just wanted to see why you all walk around like you're on the Moon. It's heavier than I imagined."

"Three minutes ago you couldn't stand the smell and now you're trying it on?" He angrily throws the towel in her face and gets back into his space-suit, leaving her alone.

However, on his next night shift Jane has lured Bernie back into her cabin.

Glenn glances at the TV and sees that Bernie is inside Jane's cabin with his space-suit off. He is wrapped in a bath towel. Glenn speculates where they may have found privacy from the security cameras - only in the stairwell or the bathroom. He locks the stairwell access and turns off the automatic unlocking. He is angry; but somehow fascinated, watching the two of them. This strange fascination prompts him to reach down inside his pants to his testicles and rub them sensuously; his face contorts into a lusty scowl.

Professor Natzi happens to walk in and sees that Glenn is painfully transfixed on the love-birds. "What - you need to watch them to *get your rocks off!* I would say you got bigger fish to fry; look at **your personal fiasco** instead of spying on them. *How do you feel about this!*" He turns the TV to the news channel:

'The High Noon Whirlwind is causing devastation within its quarter of a mile swirl around the world. At one point there were two of them; but they had combined into one.'

The Professor derides Glenn, "Of course, you are too busy *jerking off* to notice that it's wreaking havoc all around the world - **every day!** ~ You've heard of the 'Jews for Jesus' movement . . My young brother is a *crazy,* **Born-Again** *Rabbi* and he's leading a couple thousand Pilgrims *right into it!*"

Glenn is surprised about his brother and thinks, "Maybe worrying about his brother is what makes him so nasty all the time." but replies with a practiced calm, "Well one Whirlwind is better than two . . . I am surprised that it did not double in size when it combined with the first one; it is still only a quarter of a mile wide . . ."

Glenn uses his remote to change the channel back to the video surveillance. Then his computer sounds a remote alarm: his centrifuge at the top of the Gusher-Tower has stopped. Glenn looks at the TV and is relieved to see Bernie – and not CIA Jane – getting into his space-suit. He phones him; Bernie responds with a guilty jerk. Jane looks on in fright as he puts his helmet on saying, "Yes sir?"

"Bernie, when you finish fooling around up there, can you change the bags on the centrifuge. I got an alarm saying that it stopped working."

Bernie says, "Sure, this is my last load for today. I forgot; I haven't been there since I started working on the Railgun launchings. I'll drive down there in the truck and take care of it. I should have it working again within two hours."

"Thanks Bernie." Glenn says warmly.

As the Professor leaves, he gives a warning, "You're going to be a billionaire - but you're going to get *that kid killed*; sending him up the Gusher-Tower to *work all by himself!*"

Glenn challenges, "I'm already a **billionaire!! AND!** It didn't bother you when I went up into the stratosphere ~ *alone!*"

"He's just finishing a *12-hour shift*, and I didn't send you . . . It's *your project*! I told you to hire *professionally trained Astronauts!*" the Professor's retort fades in the distance.

Glenn yells after him, "He was laying around naked with Jane . . . Bernie was smuggling drugs before - now he's doing honest work . . . he's *not a **kid!!***"

Glenn is frustratedly reconsidering; even though he doesn't like the idea of employing another 'high-falutin' scientist! He looks up Astronauts online and gets 'NASA Space Training & Funding' ~ and happens to see that they are selling the old Space Shuttles for $50,000,000. Recalling the Professor's childhood ambition to be Israel's first Astronaut he mutters vindictively, "Maybe this will soften-up that **arrogant bastard!**" He calls his Lawyer, Arturo, and tells him to buy a Space Shuttle from NASA and have it shipped there immediately.

XIV

❖

SPHINCTERED INTO
THE NIGHT

Glenn sulks through his attentive fiancée's dinner, not knowing which of the day's events are weighing most heavily on him. He tries to enjoy a movie with Elena, but cannot get his head into it.

Bernie comes off Loon-Evator1 and waves a hello to Jake who is starting his night shift. Bernie goes immediately to the truck and drives to the Gusher-Tower and floats up on Loon-Evator2, twenty-miles to the top of the Gusher-Tower. It is still high-tide, and the Gusher-Tower is still spraying. As he walks off Loon-Evator2 an awe-inspiring chill runs up his spine. He sees the golden glow of the rising Moon. It is sparkling off the flecks of golden sand that is surrounding him. The ocean floor sediment, containing the precious metals, is raining down everywhere. He is admiring their accomplishment. The multiple Gusher-Spray nozzles are irrigating several distant locations in virtually every direction. Now he realizes the consequences of not servicing the centrifuge since he started working on the nuclear-waste launchings. He decides to wait in Skyhook's cabin2 a few hours for ebb-tide when the Gusher-Tower will stop spraying. He makes a cup of instant coffee and enjoys some cookies. He looks out the window and, in the moonlight, sees what looks like a flat desert. Then he sees the top roof of the centrifuge protruding above this wasteland. Then just beyond that the top of the Gusher-Tower is glowing in the moonlight. He is thinking, "Since the centrifuge has not been working, the ocean sediment has piled up high. It was supposed to gently slide down into the pit that feeds the centrifuge. It will take days for the centrifuge to catch up and process all this sediment . . ."

Bernie abruptly wakes up with a start, sensing when the Gusher-Tower stops. His O2 alarm sounds as soon as he places his space-suit helmet on. He changes the O2 canister. Carrying a spare O2 canister and a shovel, he walks out onto the wasteland to the centrifuge stairwell. It is totally buried in the sand-like sediment. It overflowed the spillway pit and went into the stairwell - filling it. It will need to be shoveled out which means that he must carry each shovelful up the stairs, freeing enough space so that he can maneuver and remove the filled precious metal bags along the stairwell, replacing them with empty bags. He needs to shovel out 2 feet of space down the staircase to be able to walk down the stairs to replace the collection bags and then restart the centrifuge. He must start shoveling from the top stair obviously, but as he clears a few stairs, the sand falls through the 4-inch gap of the railings and covers the stairs again. He starts shoveling from the outside of the stairwell. He is reaching down with the shovel into the pit and trying to shovel it away from the centrifuge staircase. As he is bending over and shoveling deeper the sand keeps falling back into the hole that he is digging. He realizes he must carry each shovel full and dump it some 20 feet away.

Bernie is already exhausted, not used to doing this type of work. His space-suit alarm starts flashing red because his heart rate is elevated. He thinks about phoning Glenn for help; but is fearful of bothering him. He is standing on the outside of the stairwell and is bending low in his heavy space-suit, shoveling down into this hole. His feet slip ~ and he is falling headfirst into it, screaming, **"OhhhHH S H I T !"** His space-suit monitor instantly senses his panic and his emergency alarm blares in his ears as his helmeted head jams down into the sand hole. He is upside down; his helmeted head is being covered with the sand that is sliding into the hole. He tries to lift his head by pushing his hands down, but they simply go deeper into the sand. Fear seizes him as he questions, *"Now what?"* Each of his movements take him deeper and deeper into it. The sand's weight is pressing heavily on his space-suit as he goes deeper: it's increasing the air pressure within his space-suit. The air he is breathing is compressing and he is rapidly using the O2 all up. Another alarm sounds as his space-suit cannot alleviate this pressure. He reasons, "My space-suit was not made to endure excessive external pressure, it only protects against less than 15 pounds per square inch of internal pressure. There is no way for me to struggle against this greater outside pressure?!?" Bernie suppresses a fleeting image: {'A medieval executioner is laying heavy stones on a victims chest.'} He tries to activate his helmet headset and call for help. But now he has become completely buried in the sand, so there is no radio transmission. "With each motion that I make, the sand beneath me is parting allowing me to sink deeper and deeper into it." He moves more aggressively in panic thinking, "I will soon reach the floor level and hopefully can drag myself to the edge, and then out of this pit. I know that these 10-foot H-cube balloons are tied together side by side; they comprise the floor and walls of this pit. Maybe I could force them apart, and crawl in between them, to escape the weight of this sand . . . that is pressing down on me". Now he feels bitter bile welling up his esophagus, searing into his mouth. **"Oh God!** Don't throw-up inside my helmet - while I am upside down . . ." Then Bernie seems to have an out-of-body experience; as if he is observing himself from afar. "It is like this sand is alive - it's rhythmically sucking me down . . . Like a churning digestive activity, a repeating wave gravitationally squeezing me down. It's as if I'm inside the Skyhook's muscular intestines and I am being peristaltically ingested."

His breathing has become laboriously exhausting. He feels his sweat running up his back, up his neck onto his face, into his mouth and up his nose, and burning into his eyes. He clenches his eyes tightly shut against an attack of nauseous dizziness. Now he is only hyperventilating: desperate shallow breathing against the heavy weight pressing on his chest . . .

He whimpers . . .

~   *"MOMMA! . . . "*   ~

The couple try watching a movie together. Glenn realizes that he is lamenting his decision to spend 50 million dollars on a Space Shuttle to pacify Professor Natzi. They go to bed and he takes his wrath out on his fiancée as he viciously stabs his pecker into her vagina. She gasps a small shriek with the sudden ferocity of his violent penetration. He growls, ***"Shut the fuck up!"*** Her eyes disappointingly pop open as his penis withdraws from her. He pulls her hair as he rolls off her and guides her to his crotch.

She winces in pain and grabs his wrist restricting his hair pulling, but then grinds her hips into his leg while licking under his testicles. She is only slightly alarmed at his sudden violent behavior; she has seen it many times before from other men who translate their unhappiness into sexual aggression. But his intensity has somehow stirred her loins, narrowing her eyes into passionate slits.

Glenn is distracted by a blinking, faint red glow. He glances around and notices that it is on his bedroom window, which is facing his office cabin. *"What the fuck!"* He pushes her away and runs naked to the cabin next door. It's his computer screen, flashing a warning signal that there's no communication from Bernie's space-suit. It shows the prior 3 reports: 3-high blood pressure, 2-high heart rate, 1-his air pressure was too high... "How could that be? I never saw that alarm before, except when I was deep in the ocean. Also, his blood pressure and heart rate were too high." Glenn screams into the microphone, *"Bernie! Bernie, talk to me!* **What's happening!***"* When there is no answer, he runs from the cabin towards his new Alcarracho, his new Jet-Basket. Elena runs after him carrying his clothes and shouting that is dangerous to be out at night with no shoes. They stop at the clothesline where the space-suits are hanging to dry out after their daily rinsing. He climbs into his space-suit, explaining, "Bernie's space-suit is failing, and I cannot locate him on *his GPS locator!* He went to restart the centrifuge operation. That **was hours ago!** Wait here for me." Elena won't hear of it: now that she is going to be the Petrona, she must be involved in every emergency, even though she doesn't understand anything that is going on. She gets into the spare space-suit. Glenn climbs into the Jet-Basket and has to help little Elena as the spare space-suit is ridiculously large on her. They quickly fly into the night sky to the top of the Gusher-Tower.

Glenn maneuvers the Jet-Basket into the gap between Loon-Evator2's loading ramp and Skyhook's cargo-bay2. He climbs over the railing and must help Elena as she is dragging the feet of her space-suit behind her. She grabs onto his arm and won't let go. He wants to run ahead to find Bernie, but sees that her eyes are agape with amazement as she has never been in the stratosphere before. Then Glenn's eyes bulge with the golden lunar reflection: he is dumbstruck, **"So Much Sand!"** He sees that there is a light on inside of Skyhook's cabin2 and they go there immediately.

He searches everywhere for Bernie, calling his name out. Elena is anxious to take her helmet off as Glenn had done, but he yells at her to leave it on, as he is already replacing his. They go back outside and stare at the desolate silent emptiness. He feels pangs of anxious guilt, "The Professor warned me not to send him up here alone . . ." Glenn doesn't recognize this sandy wasteland. He's never seen it like this before: inundated with ocean sediment. He screeches into his helmet, *BERNIE!*"

Then Elena notices faint imprints in the sand some distance away; remnants of Bernie's footprints, leading towards the centrifuge-pit. They follow these imprints and discover they end at the buried stairwell to the centrifuge-pit. Glenn wonders, "Maybe my friendly Alien abducted Bernie." There is no place left to search for him, other than on Loon-Evator2. He hurries there pulling little Elena behind him, with the feet of her space-suit dragging. They go on to Loon-Evator2 and explore both levels and its interior cabin. No sign of Bernie . . . Then he thinks, "Bernie must have parachuted to the ground. He *must be hurt!*" Glenn insists Elena stay on Loon-Evator2 in spite of her insistence on remaining with him. He says, "I have to hurry and fly back down to the ground in the Jet-Basket: you *float Loon-Evator2 down!*" He sets the automatic start dissent for a one-minute delay and he quickly scrambles back onto the Jet-Basket and flies below Skyhook. He flies a little to the side to watch Elena as it lowers; to re-assure her that everything is alright and that he is nearby.

The interior lights of Loon-Evator2's cabin shine as it lowers below Skyhook and Elena is scanning around when suddenly she screams. As Glenn is asking what's wrong, she points to an area up under the Skyhook beneath the centrifuge-pit. Glenn shines the Jet-Basket's spotlight where she is pointing. Elena then shines Loon-Evator2's spotlight on it. They see the helmet and shoulders of a space-suit appearing from under Skyhook, upside-down and rocking with a rhythmic undulation. Then unexpectedly more of the space-suit is squeezed out. Suddenly Glenn hears Bernie's low oxygen alarm sounding. But not his high blood pressure nor his high heart rate alarm. With the next spasm Glenn shouts, *"That's Bernie space-suit!"* Then with another spasm, the abdomen of the space-suit slides out and its two arms fall out, hanging limply.

While still pointing with an incredulous gawking stare, Elena shrieks,

"That's Bernie?!?! ~

it's <u>shitting</u> him <u>out!!</u> ~

Go get him!"

With the next spasm Bernie's right leg squishes out and hangs lifelessly to the side. Glenn is wide-eyed as he tries to fly the Jet-Basket next to him. Another spasm . . . Now Bernie is hanging only by his left ankle, swaying with a slight turning, side to side. As Glenn gets close, he can see that Bernie's eyes are closed, "Is he sleeping *or is he dead?* I can almost reach out and grab him . . ." Then there is another ejecting spasm from the anus of Skyhook and Bernie's foot *plops out* - he falls, freely tumbling - rapidly out of sight, into the dark oblivion. They shine their spotlights down on him as Glenn races to catch up with him, but it's impossible. He leaves Elena far behind. She spies Bernie and immediately loses him from the light - and then searching, regains his tumbling image; then, nothing but empty darkness.

Glenn finally gets his spotlight on Bernie as his space-suit's parachute automatically opens. Glenn is afraid he will get totally entangled in the parachute cords - prohibiting it from opening properly. But then he sees Bernie swinging wildly from side to side under its canopy. Then he sees him hit the ground and being dragged with a violent tumbling. Now Glenn notices below him where Bernie has landed, in the dim light, the ground seems to be *unnatural* in an *undulating* - AND - *haunting way* . . . Then he sees as he is floating-down closer, that Bernie seems to be *disappearing* underneath that *unnatural haunting,*

his legs are disappearing,
as if being swallowed by that *undulating* . . .

rhythmic . . .

undulation . . .

~   ~   ~

"~ NO ~ !!!

~ AAAHHH ~

~ SNAKES ~ !!!"

Glenn lands the Jet-Basket and grabs a canister of O2 and also the igniter from the propane stove. As he is about to step off, he realizes that there are thousands and thousands of snakes there and they are entwined and totally involved with each other. *"It's an orgy! It must be mating season".* He is about 20 feet from Bernie and can see the snakes crawling and biting into his space-suit; all over his legs and arms. He steps down onto the snakes and they immediately respond by springing up and biting onto the legs of his space-suit. He quickly steps back onto the Jet-Basket and *shudders with revulsion*! He sprays oxygen from the O2 canister on these snakes while holding the igniter close to them. He pulls the trigger igniting it, instantly catching fire to the snakes attacking his space-suit legs. They writhe and curl in agony, falling away from him, trying to escape the flame as they die. He tentatively walks across towards Bernie igniting a pathway of snakes before him. He tip-toes across their flaming, writhing bodies. He gets to Bernie and begins burning the snakes off of his arms and away from his neck and helmeted face. He can see that Bernie still has his eyes closed. **"Is he dead?"** By the time he clears the snakes away from his torso, his legs, and then his feet; the snakes have returned to his helmet, neck and shoulders.

Then he hears Elena on his radio, "I down on the ground. I see truck. I drive to you."

Glenn yells, "You don't know how to drive. Wait there for me. There are snakes all *over the ground!"*

"No serpentas here?!?" she yells, "I see Alcarracho's light."

Glenn hears the ignition start and then the engine racing loudly. The next thing he knows the lights from the truck are bouncing rapidly towards him. He yells, "Slow down - *stop*. You can't even reach the brakes - you can't *see over the steering wheel!* **STOP!!** - The pedal next to the gas - put *your foot on it!"* Now she is practically on top of him as she pushes hard on the break. The truck slams into the Jet-Basket breaking the spotlight sending it flying another 20 feet away from him. She also breaks a headlight on the truck. The snakes are covering Bernie again. He pauses to switch O2 canisters. The first one is empty. Glenn tells Elena, "Keep burning the snakes."

She doesn't want to harm them. *"It is just snakes - being snakes!"* she exclaims thinking she can gently pull them off with her thick gloves. But that is tediously slow; it's futile. She resorts to burning them as Glenn instructed. He goes to the Jet-Basket and flies it back beside them. He realizes these little eyelash-viper poisonous snakes cannot bite through the thick space-suits. He replaces one of Bernie's space-suit's O2 canisters and then ties a rope around both of Bernie's feet as he tells her to get into the Jet-Basket. He floats it straight up lifting Bernie up by his feet high off the ground, with snakes still adhering to him. Then he notices that Elena is burning snakes inside of the wicker Jet-Basket. She screams as the wicker catches on fire.

Glenn grabs the water jug and extinguishes the flames while yelling, "Sit still and **do not do anything!**" They grab the remaining snakes and throw them over the side, shaking their biting teeth off their space-suit's hands and arms.

Glenn flies back to the Hacienda and gently lands, easing Bernie to the ground. They get out, and quickly burn-off the rest of the snakes using the O2 torch. Then he gets Bernie's helmet off and still can't tell if he is alive or dead. His face is pale in the dim lighting around the Hacienda.

Glenn's mind shrieks a silent plea to the heavens: *{"GOD PLEASE! NO!!"}*

Glenn abruptly gives him mouth-to-mouth resuscitation while pressing rhythmic heart-beats on his chest.

Bernie suddenly wakes-up with a violent jerking motion that startles them. He sits-up and vomits down the front of his space-suit. Now Bernie is astonished to see that he is not only free of the sand pit but also back at the Hacienda. Then he screams and kicks his feet as a snake slithers out from under the ass of his space-suit. It slithers away, instantaneously disappearing into the darkness. They help him out of his space-suit and go into Bernie's cabin. Glenn raises the cabin's air pressure control and tells Bernie he can gradually lower it over the next few days. This will minimize the possibility of Bernie suffering from the 'bends', allowing time for his body to equalize. Elena fixes them both a snack and hot coffee. Glenn instructs Bernie and Elena, "Do **NOT** tell anybody about this incident - most especially *the Professor.*" Then, Bernie drifts off to sleep and they call it a night.

Elena is anxious to tell Margherita, about her astonishing experience:

"I was seeing Bernie *being shitted-out* into the night sky!"

Glenn cannot rest; Elena's available body does not stir his loins. He sneaks out the door as she drifts off to sleep. The thought of that last snake impudently slithering away into the night is unnerving. He flies his Jet-Basket to the electric generator and mule-hauls the spare 50-gallon gasoline barrel onto it. Then he flies back above the snake orgy and dumps all the gasoline onto them, spreading it all around. Then he flies to the perimeter of the orgy, lights a flair, and tosses it into the serpent orgy. He watches with a vindictive glare as the flames sweep across the orgy. His subconscious gleefully imagines the sounds of their orgasms turning to gruesome gasps of gory terror.

XV

COVID19

The next day Glenn sees that Skyhook is still shitting-out the sand from its anus, below the centrifuge-pit. He lowers the pressure in selected balloons to facilitate that amassed ocean sediment's falling out the bottom of Skyhook; sacrificing it to blow across the Andes Mountains. He's lamenting philosophically, "It's a good fertilizer . . . So - I lose a hundred pounds or so of gold . . . It's the safest way to deal with the problem." Then a question pops into Glenn's mind, was it the Electric Czar or was it the Alien who had raised it. He turns to the Professor asking, "Did you hear anything about a CME?"

"No, I didn't. Not surprising with all the other news in the world: there's a virus called Covid-19 that is forcing people to stay isolated indoors because it is highly transferable and it's killing a solid 3 percent of the infected population. It's getting 20% hospitalized; and the other 80% that don't get noticeably sick are also contagious - while being asymptomatic. Do *you understand?!?* It is highly communicable, even the pre-symptomatic *are contagious!* So eventually, we're all going to get it. It will be a year or two before they get everyone vaccinated. Meanwhile, they don't want everybody to be sick at the same time, so they are asking that everyone isolate all around the world."

"Jesus, I never heard of anything like this before. What about Africa? ‑ I guess they are hopeless . . ." Glenn answers his own question in response to the Professor's squinting smirk.

The Professor continues, "The closest thing to it is probably the 1918 Spanish Flu which killed 50,000,000 people worldwide. This seems to be worse because it's not as selective as the flu. Apparently, everybody gets this. What this does to people's lungs is terrible, unlike pneumonia, which is just a spot or two, this infests most of a person's lungs. In 3 months, it killed over 100,000 in the States."

Glenn says, "Oh my God . . . You better explain that to the employees."

"Isolation should be at least two weeks; maybe more, and they should try to keep a '6-foot social distance' from each other, and wear masks too."

"So," Glenn asks, "are you recommending that we all shelter in place – here …?" The Professor replies with a blank stare. Glenn suddenly prances around in outrage as he shouts, **"Jesus H. Christ!** I got to provide living accommodations for all my employees for 2 weeks - up here - *in my Hacienda!!"*

"Yes, we should. Your project will come to a grinding halt if these people get sick; and if they go back home after work, they are sure to pick it up from somebody. Then just riding on the train together – we'll all be sick with it. The best thing would be for them all to stay here. We have a few empty cabins, and we can get tents for the rest. The workers can shower at the water tower and sleeping bags will keep them warm enough at night. We can get a lot of food shipped in right away, let's say enough for two months, mostly canned foods, boxed pasta, rice and beans and whatever else that doesn't have to be refrigerated; - powdered milk. Each tent will need a small propane stove for cooking. We'll still have our daily train deliveries, and we'll have to get 2 extra water deliveries. But everything should be disinfected when the train arrives inside the tunnel, spraying everything with disinfectant. Everybody and everything getting off the train would have to be disinfected. We cannot trust that it will be handled properly before the train gets here, so we must do it ourselves."

"OK," Glenn says, "Take care of that."

"Great! Another fucking job for *me to do!"* the Professor bitches.

Glenn joins his anger, "Jesus H. *Christ!* Another fucking catastrophe for me **to deal with!!"**

"Oh YEAH! This worldwide pandemic is all **about you!** Sorry for the *inconvenience*!! I guess you'll have a use for all that gold you're centrifuging . . ." he guffaws as he leaves, laughing heartily.

The Professor gathers the workers and explains Covid19 pandemic in Spanish. The men laugh at this, saying, **"More Gringo nonsense!"** But Elena is very curious and asks more questions. She is concerned about her pregnancy. Also worried about her relatives. The men mount the train, and the Professor dozes off listening to the men discuss it on the ride home. Elena's fears had undermined their confidence.

After resting a day Bernie returns to work and Glenn restores the centrifuge and its spillway pit to proper functioning. Bernie puts it on his work schedule to maintain it regularly, 3 times a week. He brings the precious metal bags into Glenn's office asking, "Where shall I put these?"

Glenn nods his head towards the corner, already piled 4 foot high with these bags, saying, "Throw them on the pile."

Glenn is surprised to find the next morning's train has no workers. Only the Professor and of course Juan, the train conductor, and Margherita, who is coming back from her secret Doctor's appointment. She grabs Glenn and leads him away brushing by a disappointed and now suspicious Elena. "The Doctor say is possible with 'in-vi-tro fer-til-i- za-ci-on'" Margherita's whispers as her eyes dance with delight. "Tu comprende what dis means?"

"Si, it means I have to jerk-off into a bottle . . ."

"Ohiieee! Ha Ha! Por questo de nurse give me dis bottle!?! She say keep it in refrigerator, Ha HA, but I look inside *HA HA HA – it's empty!! HA HA HA!!* ~ Don't worry - I make sure you get it in de bottle!!! *HA HA HA!!!* De nurse, she know I don't understand about de bottle and she make the motion with her hand. I look at her like she is crazy ~ because I think she want me to do something with *her!!! HA HA HA!!!* " He joins her laughter. They start walking towards Glenn's cabin, filled with anticipation. Elena's eyes narrow into piercing daggers, she is not happy with these two laughing conspirators.

The Professor catches Glenn and explains, "Our workers were talking on the train last night. Elena's questions convinced them that they should not leave their families to suffer this Covid19 infection alone - that if it was so dangerous, they all needed to stay together with their families. Meanwhile - the nuclear-waste deliveries are still *coming in!*" The Professor proposes, "We should have them all come and live here at the Hacienda, including their families, until the whole thing passes . . ."

Glenn says, **"Holy shit!** We've got 14 workers and now I have to accommodate all their families *for two weeks!"* Margherita continues into Glenn's cabin, alone.

The Professor replies, "For at least two weeks; they could be here for several months. We're going to have to order big tents and they need to have heat because we can't expect families to suffer the cold nights up here in sleeping bags. They should all probably be cooking their own food, which means we will need additional refrigeration and stoves and toilets. All kinds of problems... That's going to keep me busy for weeks."

Glenn says, "Forghettaboutit! I'll just order another 15 pressurized cabins, and each family can take one. We should be able to cut a deal on quantity as they are old US Navy surplus. Arturo had been dumping them on me before claiming that we would need them for employees; I guess now he's proven to be right."

"This is good; it's a relief that all we have to do is pipe in the water and do the electrical connections from the railroad tracks; and quadruple the food and water deliveries. I will get a hold of everybody and tell them to come to work with the first delivery."

Glenn gets Arturo on the phone and, sure enough, the cabins were dumped on the Pecuadorian government as part of a foreign aid deal. And their President, not knowing how else to make any money from them, was still trying to sell them so he could pocket the money. Arturo negotiates a deal for 15 of them and has them on the next morning's train. The Professor instructs everybody to come back with their families where they will be safe from the virus. "Great, that's one problem solved. Now, if I can just fix those fucking Chinese pricks?!?"

Glenn questions, "Why, do we know for sure that Covid19 originated in China?"

"It's not that; they launched a weaponized satellite to destroy other satellites. It's like they don't care about creating dangerous orbiting space debris."

Glenn is glad to have the Professor in a conversational mood for once, "What do you mean, 'Fix those Chinese pricks? What did you have in mind?"

"If I was with NASA, I would insist that the military shoot it down. But that's never gonna happen . . ."

Glenn reflects, "It can't be flying very high if it's going to be a threat to our satellites, can you plot its orbit? "

"I can plot any orbit – I'm a fucking *ASTROPHYSICIST!*" His eyes narrow, "What are you thinking?"

"Maybe their 'weapons satellite' **is getting** *thirsty* . . ." Glenn says with raised eyebrows and a knowing squint.

"HUH?"

"We can squirt the Gusher-Spray 12000miles around the world, their satellite shouldn't be too hard to reach . . ."

The Professor's eyes bulge as he inhales a deep sigh, "I'll get right on it, we'll have Jane track it with the telescope.

Maybe we can flood it with water-vapor with the next high-tide, which should make it slow down and come out of orbit within a half orbit; say 50 minutes. I have got to make sure we don't impact any other satellites."

Glenn says, "Hurry up, the Gusher-Spray is coming in just over an hour." He returns and sends the satellite's orbital coordinates to Jane who immediately tracks it on the telescope. They will be able to see it on the monitor in Glenn's office. It's flying over the Indian Ocean on an equatorial orbit approaching Africa. They exchange a profoundly serious glare at each other . . . then inhale deeply as they enter the Gusher-Spray coordinates into its control computer.

High-tide arrives and one of the Gusher-Tower nozzles squirts a narrow column of its seawater east, 300 miles up into space, above South America, then across the Atlantic Ocean. Skyhook's telescope monitors as the Chinese Weapon's Satellite encounters the invisible gaseous water-vapor as it is falling back to Earth.

The Chinese Satellite immediately begins to lose altitude over western Africa. Jane has difficulty keeping track of it.

They turn on the TV and see the Weather Channel has breaking news reporting:

'As it is approaching the coast of South America, the Chinese Satellite has lost almost a hundred miles in altitude and must inevitably crash if it doesn't accelerate. As it begins flying over South America, it will be descending much more . . .'

Glenn shouts, "It's gonna crash into our *SKYHOOK!*"

The Professor raises his hands to calm him down, shaking his head. "No, I plotted this so that it will burn-up over coastal China at twilight so that they can't hide it from their Chinese citizenry. It should be passing 80 miles over us right about now." Jane confirms that.

Bernie comes into the office expressing concern that the Gusher-Spray is out of whack, then he reprograms it to its regular schedule. He notices the tense atmosphere in the office and concludes that Glenn and the Professor must have been arguing – again.

Glenn says matter-of-factly, "The Chinese tore down the statue commemorating the Tiananmen Square Massacre."

The Professor adds, "They have been flying fighter jets over Taiwan. They are also a threat to Japan and South Korea."

Glenn responds blithely, "They shut down the last free newspaper in Hong Kong and reneged on that treaty with the U K."

Bernie is bewildered as the Professor replies in the same tone, "They are illegally building an Island in a channel of the South China Sea . . . They blame the USA for having to move their Space Station's orbit to avoid collision with the Starlight Satellite."

Then the Weather Channel announces: 'The Chinese Weapon's Satellite is crossing the Galapagos Islands and is descending rapidly. Our scientists think it may reach China and burn-up harmlessly in its atmosphere just after their sunset. Some small debris may hit the ground.' Then the international news picks up the story and is broadcasting it around the world. Glenn and the Professor exchange guilty – excited looks of proud responsibility . . . As plotted, it burns-up in full view of the Chinese People while being broadcasted live on international news coverage.

A news commentator laughingly suggests:

> 'Chinese space program administrators are going to end up in education/prison camp for the rest of their lives. Probably joining their military geniuses who thought a weapons satellite was a good idea.'

The Chinese Government refuses all comment. The Chinese space program comes to a grinding halt.

The unusual narrow strip of rainfall stretching from Africa's west coast, across the Atlantic, over South America, does not gain any attention.

They all walk in silent contentment side by side into the kitchen area.

Then Glenn notices Elena's concerned expression as she approaches him, "Hey, what about us getting married?"

"Yes, we're going to get married; as soon as you say." He says as he embraces her close to him. "Wherever you say, in your village, or here, or Pequito; and you can spend as much as you need to." Elena has never heard that concept before – 'spend as much as you need to'. You always had to sacrifice one thing to get another.

"I not know how do this; I want you be happy. Like Gringo wedding should be; you gotta help me?"

Glenn tells her, "No, I am too busy. I want the wedding to make you - my little Mama – happy. You and Margherita can figure it out. You can order whatever you need on the computer. Margherita has to go back to Pequito to exchange the medicine tonight; but she will be back in a day or two and you can do it then."

"Margherita not know how do Gringo wedding - get Jane to help me? Bernie say she on top of the Loon-Evator. She comprende Gringo weddings and computers."

Glenn does not want to disappoint her, "Ah, let me think about that . . . I can have Bernie help you?" Her expression tells him that she is disgusted by the idea. "All right, let me think about it."

The Professor was standing nearby, as Elena leaves, he says, "I was going to offer to translate for you, talking to Elena; but then I thought better of getting in the middle of anything with you two . . . So, you're really going through with this marriage thing; you really did not learn anything from 'Madame Butterfly'." Glenn looks at him with consternation. "Did you think how this might affect her life in her village; about her past history with all her relatives and friends?" Glenn's sharp gaze intensifies. "Do you know that her husband is telling everybody he will kick her in her stomach - and any baby she pretends to be having?" Glenn is now shocked. "He said he will not allow her to humiliate him with that fucking balloon-man-Gringo! Yes, 'balloon-man-Gringo': that's what they all call you. Her husband is like the leader of the town gang, nobody wants to cross him. I live there with my children; I am not going to do anything to piss him off. My wife does not like the way he has been looking at my oldest daughter, so I've been thinking of moving out of the village."

Glenn is taken aback as the Professor continues, "Elena's X barged into Virginia's school room - maybe in an attempt to intimidate my wife, or maybe lusting after my daughter, but then he locked his gaze on Virginia. The men of the town had been talking about her luscious ripe body; how it needs to be harvested. Maybe he just wanted to check her out? Little Ricardo ran to my wife, pulling her away from her classroom to intervene in Virginia's classroom. He was intimidating and very macho; I fear for Virginia. Nobody would blame any male for lusting after Virginia as she is considered a mature woman in this country. But my daughter is so scrawny compared to her? Also, I fear that Virginia may be attracted to him, like most other young women are." Glenn shakes his head and walks away, trying to fathom this new dilemma.

Glenn finds Margherita in his cabin and asks her if she knows anything about all this. She says, "Si, the only reason her husband married Elena was because she has one of the bigger houses. It has a nice view. It is on top of the cliff with a nice big porch looking out over the valley. He will be embarrassed because a Gringo got her pregnant when *he couldn't*. He thinks he will take her house; that she will leave the town when she sees she will never marry anybody there. He and his gang run the town. He is the biggest, strongest, sexiest man in the village. He told everybody Elena is too small to get pregnant and that's why he left her for a younger girl, who he never married; but now has two children with. But he still fucks other girls. It's like - he has to fuck every virgin when they start growing tits. Pedro is very friendly with him. You remember Pedro, who had the lightning bolts bouncing off the truck, who gave me trouble when he quit working for you."

Glenn is pissed. He calls Arturo. Then he hands the phone to Margherita telling her to explain exactly where Elena's husband lives, how to get there, and when she thinks he will be home. She is pleasantly surprised by this executive assignment and is speaking animatedly in Spanish to Lawyer Arturo. Glenn pulls off her blouse, tangling the phone in her sleeve and confusing her. He unfastens her bra, kneels and starts sucking on her titties. She is alarmed as she never had this sexploitation performed on her while talking on the phone – and now, for the first time in her life, she's talking like an *executive* - to a *LAWYER!* She is quite flustered, but surprisingly turned on. When she finishes explaining that he is home every day for siesta time; she throws the phone away and clutches Glenn to her bosom. Glenn looks up, disturbed and then struggles to free his head from her arms and boobs and walks on his knees over to the discarded phone. "Arturo are you still there. Sorry, she dropped the phone. Here is what I want you to do." Now Margherita is not going to be put off. She tackles Glenn to the floor and unbuckles his pants and slides them down with his underwear. She grasps his erection and licks it, stroking up and down with one hand and pushing his legs apart. Glenn's voice is thickening as he continues talking angrily to Arturo. Laying her head on his thigh she licks his testicles, then up and down his cock, pausing to suck on it firmly, and then returning to his testicles, then below. She grabs a pillow from the couch and puts it under his ass and pushes his knees high, spreading his legs wide open. She licks and then sucks on his testicles; then she continues her progress lower.

All the while Glenn is having an animated angry conversation with Arturo, interspersed with curious groans. His anger is giving his erection a ferocious quality, her eyes alight with anticipation. She stops and rummages through her bag and pulls out the little thermos bottle the gynecologist gave her. She brings it back and then lays her head down on his inner thigh as Glenn continues his conversation; his erection is not losing its intensity. She resumes her licking and sucking. She kisses his penis and pushes her tongue hard against the tip and slurping loudly sucks up all her saliva. Arturo has difficulty understanding Glenn. She does a rotating massage on his pecker while tickling his balls with her tongue, and then going down under, licking everywhere. Glenn is groaning as he tells Arturo to call back as soon as the paper is signed. As he hangs up the phone, Margherita has the bottle in her right-hand, his penis in her left-hand, and his testicles in her mouth - and she is humming with an anticipatory loud moan: *"HHHOOOOOMMMMMM!"* She feels his testicles contracting on her tongue and she points the tip of his penis into the bottle opening. Her unblinking eyes are looking with a frightening intensity at the eye of his erupting penis; she wiggles her lips and tongue back and forth on his testicles. Glenn's mind explodes as he feels her vibrant humming resonating through his brain. Every muscle in his body contorts with each spasm. Intense white light drowns out his perception, his consciousness fades into oblivion while his saliva filled throat strains out a gasping growl. Margherita continues her sensuous moaning while milking every drop of his orgasm into the bottle . . .

Glenn's convulsed body slowly relaxes, and Margherita puts the lid on the bottle then hurriedly puts it into the refrigerator. Glenn rolls onto his stomach and crawls up into the bed. She strips off the rest of her clothes and joins him, wrapping her legs around his thighs. She would like to have an orgasm; but somehow feels totally satisfied. They drift off to sleep.

XVI

❖

ELENA'S FIANCÉE

Elena brings lunch thinking that they will all eat together. She finds them naked in bed sleeping and placing the food on the night-stand, mutters, "I should have known." And then she says loudly, "Margherita, are you doing any work today or did you just come here to fuck my fiancée?"

Smiling sleepily, she explains, "I am too tired from the past two days in Pequito and I have to go back again on the evening train; I'm too sleepy to do any work."

Elena leaves saying, "Enjoy *your lunch!*" The phone rings and Glenn jumps up answering the call from Arturo. His face lights up with a serene smile of satisfaction.

Margherita asks, "Is that your lawyer?" Glenn nods affirmatively, "He made a paper for Elena's husband?" Glenn nods yes again, while smiling like a Cheshire cat. "You got business with him? You are paying him money?"

Glenn disconnects saying, "Thanks Arturo." Then with righteous indignation to Margherita, "That will be the day…" And when he sees that she does not understand he adds, "That fucker will never see a centavo from me, nor from Elena. *Divorce papers!* He's no longer married to Elena. Go to Arturo's office tomorrow and sign her name on the divorce papers and then bring back a copy. It will be my wedding *present to Elena!* I sent the military there to *make him sign* legal divorce papers!"

"You sent the military into her village?!?" Her eyes bulge in astonishment. "He will tell the whole village; nobody will ever speak to her again. One day the villagers will catch her alone and *beat her to death!* **I told you**, *we don't want anything to do with the military!"*

Glenn shouts, "Well I had to do *something!* I could not let him get away with threatening my family. He said he was going to kick her in her *pregnant belly!"*

"We say that a lot to each other: 'I am gonna kick you in the stomach;' how do you say, it's an expression. Now you have a big problem, you got to shut him up. Maybe give him a lot of money and say you're sorry for sending the military. But then you have to keep giving him money all the time."

Glenn says, **"Bullshit!** Maybe I'll *just kill him,* instead!"

Margherita says, "You must do something, and *do it pronto!"*

"Okay, I'll *do something!* He must be very upset after the military forced him to sign Elena's divorce papers . . ." Glenn thinks for a moment then tells her to put on his spare space-suit as he puts his on. He leads her to Alcarracho, his Jet-Basket, loads some things onto it and then they fly east, high over the valley, following the train tracks down to Elena's village. Margherita points out Elena's big house that she inherited from her grandfather – her mother's father. Margherita explains that he did not want Elena's father, to end up owning it; that's why he willed it to Elena instead of her mother."

Glenn says, "So, It's a grand house with a great view. We could all retire there to raise our children when we finish the nuclear-waste launchings." Then she points out Elena's husband's house. The front door opens to the street, but there is a back door to a small backyard with an outhouse in the far corner. Nobody in the town notices them as they are flying high above. He shuts off his engines and quietly floats Alcarracho down into the backyard. There are chickens running around loose and squawking loudly. He ties a large net to the railing then throws it just outside the house's rear door. He climbs out of the Jet-Basket and lays the net flat on the ground so that it does not obstruct the doorway. He climbs back into Alcarracho and raises it above the doorway. Then he lays down in the open gate and, using a long handled grappling hook, bangs hard on the door. He quickly stands-up and closes the gate. Elena's ex-husband comes out the door in his underwear, angrily demanding who is banging so violently on his door, interrupting his siesta. Glenn elevates Alcarracho's lift balloon rapidly and the net lifts him up and wraps around their captive, swinging him wildly from side to side, banging him into the roof of the house. He screams in terror. Margherita is astounded, as she demands to know what Glenn is going to do with him.

"I should take him up there," he says pointing his fingers up to the sky, "and watch him freeze to death; and then drop him into the jungle for the *animals to eat!*" Margherita is pointing down into the village at the people coming out in response to his screaming. They can all see him flaying wildly inside the net hanging below Alcarracho. His feces and urine are dripping from the netting.

"The whole village knows that it's you, you'll *end up in jail!*" Glenn spies a sturdy solitary tree growing out of the cliff side about 50 feet below the top. From there it is several hundred feet straight down to a rocky basin. A fall would be certain death. Glenn lowers Alcarracho to the tree, ties 2 ropes around two separate sturdy branches and then threads the ropes around the top of the net; then ties it again to the same two branches. The net is swaying from side to side and banging Elena's X into the side of the rocky cliff. He is continuously crying to don't let him fall and begging for his life. Now the net is secured to the tree, so Glenn cuts away the ropes that secures it to Alcarracho's railing. Elena's husband screams in terror as the net drops a few feet and then slams into the cliff side. Glenn flies the Jet-Basket a hundred feet away, floating over the valley, leaving Elena's husband hanging 20 feet below the tree swaying in the breeze and banging against the cliff. Glenn removes 2 automatic rifles from a compartment and hands one to Margherita. They then take aim at the cliff side near the captive and shoot repeated burst into it. The bullets chip away the rock sending debris everywhere around Elena's X. They pause to listen to his screams, and laughing, resume shooting again when he pauses. Then they fly away.

The whole town is now coming out, responding to the gunfire and his frightened cries. They are slowly leaning over the railing and looking down at him hanging in a net from that solitary tree, like a captured jungle monkey. His hanging weight had drawn the top of the net tightly closed so he could not climb out; and if he could, he would still have to climb up

20 feet of rope to get up to the tree and then somehow climb another 50 foot up the sheer rock face of the cliff. It was impossible.

As they take off their space-suit helmets, Margherita looks at Glenn with questioning eyes. Glenn says, "That should teach him a lesson that he will **never forget!"**

"Are you just going to leave him there?" Margherita asks incredulously.

Glenn speculates, "Maybe I'll get our friendly Condor family to go and hang out with him. He will keep them well fed for a couple of weeks." Her eyes bulge. "Okay, maybe I'll come back tomorrow and get him; but – NO! -, I don't want to have anything *to do with him!"* Then he adds, "I can get the military to come up and rescue him?" Margherita shakes her head 'no' with even greater alarm in her eyes. Glenn spies his rope ladder rolled up in a corner of the Jet-Basket. He flies back over the village plaza not far from where all the residents have gathered. They are shouting down to Elena's X, trying to calm him down, assuring him that they would somehow rescue him. Glenn hovers 20 feet above the plaza, picks up his automatic rifle, then opens the gate and rolls out the rope ladder with his foot while firing a spurt from his AR-15, aiming it out over the valley. Everybody ducks down in fright; then slowly stand up as they see the rope ladder unroll on the plaza ground. Glenn holds the rifle on his shoulder as he raises Alcarracho, and everybody watches as it fades out of view. Margherita laughs with relief as she hears Elena's husband tearful crying fade away into the distance.

There is a big mess of confusion as the villagers try to figure out how to use the rope ladder to rescue Elena's X. And still bigger confusion deciding who's going to do it. Needless to say, they are afraid of falling, but they are also afraid of not helping him. Pedro, surprisingly after his frightful experience with heights, volunteers, knowing that his prestige will be enhanced among the village gang. When they return, Margherita wearing the space-suit, runs to Elena who is still cleaning-up in the kitchen. She assures Elena that she is now legally divorced as her husband signed the divorce papers. He will no longer bother her or threaten her as the Boss-Man literally scared the shit out of him. They walk into Glenn's office laughing unreservedly as Margherita tells her what her fiancée romantically performed for her. Elena kisses Glenn saying, "I will have to go home and find out what happened to my X."

Glenn asks Margherita, "Give Elena your phone so she can report back to me."

Margherita looks injured; but Glenn quickly adds, "You should buy a new cell phone, anyone that you like. Call me tonight after you get settled into your hotel. Here is $2,000. That should be plenty." Both she and Elena are wide-eyed with astonishment as she gladly surrenders her phone to Elena.

Then they drag Glenn back into his cabin where they all get undressed and shower together. Elena leads Glenn by his pecker to the bed and she and Margherita kiss and lick him all over his body. Elena mounts him but keeps a hand on his pecker to prevent him from penetrating too deeply, she does not want to risk hurting their baby. Margherita is between his legs licking his testicles; Elena gets up, turns around and then feeds Glenn's penis into Margherita's mouth. She loudly and gladly reciprocates sucking and moaning with a passionate **"HHUUUMMM!"** Then Elena reinserts the head of his penis into her pussy and grabbing Margherita's hair with her other hand, slowly pulls her forward. Margherita is licking up the length of his pecker, onto Elena's grasping hand, and then on to Elena's clitoris. Glenn is thrusting his hips forward, but Elena is restricting his penetration with her hand. He finds it frustrating. Elena quickly climaxes, swirling her hips alternately around while twerking her buttocks rapidly. She lays back on Glenn and rolls to his side; Margherita catches his penis with her mouth and sucks it in deeply tilting her head from side to side and tickling his balls while moaning with anticipation. Glenn groans in delightful relief. Then Margherita climbs on top of him and inserts him to the hilt and she grinds ferociously on his pecker; her tits swirling in sync with her gyrating hips. She quickly orgasms, and Glenn sits up and tares into her titties, sucking hard and then dragging his rough, unshaven face across her nipples, she orgasms again. After a moment she resumes her gyrations and tickles Glenn's balls. Elena watches in disbelief as they each orgasm simultaneously. Margherita falls forward on top of Glenn and wraps her left arm around Elena pulling her closer to them. Elena whispers softly into both their ears in English, "Hey, that's *my fiancée* you're fucking!" They all laugh, totally relaxed. They lay together like that and fall into a light sleep.

They wake up to find Elena licking each of their genitals in turn, as if to sample or taste the presence of one upon the other. All three apprehensively look deeply into each other's eyes. Then Margherita says, "Isn't that a nice way to wake up."

XVII

❖

CONCLUSIVELY,
THERE IS A CME

Glenn is escorting his two loving mujers to the train which is whistling departure time. He kisses Elena passionately then as he is hugging her, Margherita hugs her from behind and warmly French-kisses Glenn. As they board the train, the Professor approaches Glenn, "I have just got a notification through my Astrophysics Association that a CME was recorded leaving the Sun within the past hour; it looks as though it will pass well away from the Earth, millions of miles below our South Pole. Anyhow - thank goodness for that."

Glenn asks, "Do you think we need to lower Skyhook just as a precaution?"

"No, I don't think so. But we'll keep an eye on it." But then the Professor elaborates, "They travel at about 1,000,000 miles an hour so it should take more than three days for it to get anywhere near us, so we have time. But just to be on the safe side, I would arrange to get Jane down from Skyhook within two days."

"Shit!" Glenn says, "What the fuck am I going to do with her now?" Glenn pauses, and then asks, "Could that be the CME the Electric Czar was talking about when I flew with Margherita to Acapulco?"

The Professor says, "I don't think CMEs are that predictable, certainly not that far in advance." He climbs into the train as it pulls away and Glenn shouts after him, "Do you think that it might interfere with our launched barrels."

The Professor shouts back, "If anything, it will burn them up before they reach the Sun's corona; I don't think that it matters if they are annihilated a day or so sooner. I would imagine their atoms would still fall into the Sun. That is an interesting thought though. Glad to see that *you're thinking!*" The Professor shouts with a smirk as he leans out of the accelerating train.

Then Glenn puts on his space-suit, carries his spare space-suit with him and rides up with Bernie who is going to work on Skyhook. He asks Bernie, "Do you think we can trust Jane to order Elena's wedding stuff on the computer - without trying to contact her relatives or the CIA?" Bernie assures Glenn that he has nothing to worry about with Jane. Glenn quietly thinks while gazing across the wide Pacific horizon and the setting Sun, "I'm so stupid, to be risking *everything* for Elena's wedding party!" As they are arriving at Skyhook, he tells him, "Okay, Jane is your responsibility, and you have to keep watch over her. Bring her down with you in my spare space-suit at the end of your shift and have her help Elena with her wedding plans." He enters Jane's prison-cabin saying that he must use the telescope. He notices Jane has a bruise above her elbow that looks like a sucker-bite, a hickey. "What a strange place to fulfill your passion." He thinks as he involuntarily scrutinizes the shape of Bernie's mouth, imagining it sucking on her arm. Bernie follows him, curious to see what has provoked Glenn's *strangely penetrating gaze* at him.

Glenn is not alarmed with Jane in front of him and Bernie behind him as he had been before. He invites them to join him, and they climb the stairs up to the telescope cabin. Glenn manipulates the computer controlling the telescope and focuses on his nuclear-waste barrels that are closest to the Sun. With the Sun filter on, the corona glows green. Then he sees a stream of green sticking out from the Sun's corona: it is a relatively wide blast of plasma. It looks as though it will pass his stream of barrels as he continues to watch it for another half hour; but then it suddenly funnels, or gets sucked into, or veers off its previous course into the barrel's stream. They watch with their mouths agape as barrel after barrel explodes in a machine gun like sequence. Glenn is flabbergasted: "The barrels are traveling at about 1,000,000mph as they get closer to the Sun's South Polar Region and the CME's plasma is traveling in the opposite direction at about 1,000,000mph. The hot plasma is exploding every barrel in front of it." Glenn shouts to Bernie, "Go down and stop the launchings immediately."

Bernie's asks, "Why, that's about 90 million miles away?"

Glenn shouts, "Just do it!"

Jane volunteers, "It's just a precaution, you don't want those nuclear-waste barrels exploding and contaminating that empty space. Its debris may never reach the Sun."

Glenn watches it for hours, all the plasma from that mass ejection seems to be sucked into the narrow stream of his barrels. And as far as he can tell, the CME is still spouting plasma from the Sun's corona into it. He does not know if it is a same original mass ejection or if there is now a plasma stream coming from the Sun's corona up his launching channel. Glenn speculates, "The barrels were launched on 3 separate trajectories as a safety precaution to prevent them from forming a magnetic/gravitational-siphoning-channel the way the Big Cannon's launchings apparently did; but of course, they come closer together as they approach their common destination. These barrels were launched magnetically, and no doubt retain some magnetic residual effect. Could the Sun's magnetic plasma be drawn up into my barrels magnetic stream; away from the Sun's immense gravity? Not likely. But, if the plasma is magnetic, wouldn't it have a negative-end attracted to an external positive source and the reverse on *the other end?!?* – **Too confusing!?!** But if this CME was caused by a magnetic explosion, then it should be comprised of a given quantity of plasma – magnetized or not - which means: it should be ending."

Glenn's reverie is interrupted by his helmet communicator; Margherita is calling. He puts his helmet on and answers her call. Her seductively deep throaty voice turns him on in spite of all his problems. She has purchased that new cell phone and is having dinner in her hotel room. She has safely stored that tiny bottle in the hotel room's little refrigerator and wishes she were having dinner with him. Glenn explains he is busy with Jane & Bernie on the telescope. Margherita can only imagine that they must be romantically gazing at the stars, remembering that he doesn't have Elena nor her to sleep with tonight. He senses her concern and states that he is now leaving Bernie and Jane alone together in the telescope-cabin - asking them to phone him if there is any change.

Glenn continues talking to Margherita as he is returning to the Hacienda, when he gets a message on his helmet's heads up display that Elena is calling him. He tells Margherita to hold on, places her on hold, answers Elena, tells her to hold on, then re-connects Margherita into this 3-way call. The women are terribly confused, thinking how is it possible for the other one to be physically right next to Glenn; never having imagined that this 3-way phone conversation was possible. They keep asking where the other one is located; then accuse Glenn of lying about his present location.

Glenn has a hard time getting them beyond their amazement; he is exhausted, but he wants to know what Elena has to say about the fate of her X husband. By the time he arrives at the Hacienda he finally gets the definitive answer on Elena's X. "Pedro climbed down the rope ladder, with a safety-rope tied around his waist. He pushed the end of another safety-rope thru the net and tied it around Elena's X's waist then Pedro cut the netting allowing her X to climb out thru the hole and onto the ladder, ahead of Pedro. Then together they ascended back up the rope ladder. Pedro didn't seem to mind her X's shitty underwear in his face." The girls are laughing uncontrollably as Glenn is getting out of his space-suit and going directly to bed. They are engaging him in their conversation, but despite his valiant effort to participate; they hear him snoring, already in a deep sleep. They shout at him through their phones. He finally wakes up enough to disconnect his phone and immediately passes out. The girls are also disconnected, but Margherita calls Elena back and they talk and laugh for hours. Content that Glenn is safely alone, away from Jane; they say they have never been so happy. They are cousins, grew up together, best friends forever. They tearfully share their feelings of deepest love for each other – they could have never done that in person: face to face . . .

After Glenn had left them alone in Skyhook's telescope-cabin, Bernie tells Jane that he convinced Boss-Man Glenn to allow her to return down to the Hacienda; but, she must help Elena with her wedding plans. He emphasizes that she is his responsibility; and he is confident that he can convince Glenn to contact her parents if she cooperates.

Jane is thrilled to be getting free of her prison, even though she is only going to be on probation, the Hacienda will be her half-way house. The western horizon rolls eastward, obstructing the telescope's view. They shut down the telescope as the Sun has set long ago and they can no longer see the barrels in the fiery CME as our western hemisphere is now facing deep-space, away from the Sun. He shows Jane how to use the space-suit and instructs her in putting it on. She decides that she will skip attaching the fecal bag, thus keeping her pants on. They ride the Loon-Evator down to the Hacienda and Jane takes up residence again in her old cabin.

When Glenn sees his workers getting off the train the next morning, he is amazed at the number of people, some brought their in-laws and even their cousin's families. Glenn is pissed. The Professor defends apologetically, "It is not a problem, they are used to living in close cramped quarters. Most of their houses are just one room with a bathroom outside and water from a communal well. Many of their dwellings don't even have enough headroom to stand upright. Trust me, this will be like living in luxury for them." Glenn cannot stand the idea of so many of them being jammed into one cabin, so he orders another 15 for the next day's delivery. They spend the next 2 days laying the PVC pipe and doing the electrical connections. Glenn orders another sewage storage tank and changes to a daily water delivery. The Professor's wife uses two of the cabins for her school. She brought all the children that are living in her dormitory. Virginia is happy to spend time with Glenn and Jake, and also glad not to be separated from her schoolmates. She has already become fluent in Spanish and is very helpful as an assistant teacher. She is immersed in her relationships with the children; it's as if she is enjoying her first childhood.

XVIII

❖

CORONA MASS EJECTION

The Professor and the workmen are surprised to see Jane in the kitchen helping to prepare breakfast. They all notice the passion bruise of what looks like a mouth imprint near her elbow. The men are speculating:

"Why does she have that passion mark there?"

"Wonder where else she might also have them?"

"Maybe on her ankles?"

They laugh drawing Jane's attention to the fact that they are talking about her. As Juan is saying, "So, that's how she got the Boss-Man to let *her come back!*" She defensively raises that arm up as she pushes her hair back, inadvertently placing her bruised elbow next to her ample breast . . .

Now the men all bust out laughing, simultaneously coming to the same conclusion saying:

"Her lover must have been drunk as he missed his target by about 3 inches!" They are holding up 2 fingers as if to measure the error her lover's lips made while laughing hysterically.

Jane understands their Spanish and their humiliating laughter as they ogle her. She *is outraged!* She turns to the Professor; he stops laughing and quickly walks away thinking, "That manipulative bitch is not going to force me to choose between her and my employees."

She turns to Sancho saying, "How can you let these pigs talk like that about me?"

Sancho, still laughing, says, "What are you talking about?" feigning ignorance.

She yells, "You are *their boss* . . . tell them to *show* **some respect!**"

He stops laughing, his face turns red as he retorts angrily, "You wouldn't mind your friends enjoying a laugh like this - that is your *white* **Gringo friends . . .** It's just because we are Latinos that you feel *superior to us!* What about when you grabbed my ass in front of everybody: did you show me *any* **respect!!**" Jane stomps off to her cabin with tears in her eyes. "Cry all you want, that *may work* on *Gringo Men*, we don't *give a shit* how much *you cry!*"

Later that day the Professor approaches Glenn saying, "I got an email update last night from my Astrophysics Association: it confirms that CME will pass well below our South Pole." He sees Jane making coffee in the kitchen area, "I see you brought Jane down. Be careful, your hot-blooded fiancée has returned. Somebody could *end up dead!*" Glenn looks at him askance. "You sent your fiancée and your girlfriend away last night and now this morning you have her with you. What's a matter; you can't sleep without a warm female 'comforter'?"

"What!?!" Glenn queries, "What the fuck are you talking about? You said I should bring her down as a precaution, so I *brought her down!*"

"Oh, just a convenient coincidence that your lovers *were away?!?*" Glenn is befuddled and shakes his head saying, *"Let's change the subject . . ."*

He thinks a moment and then asks, "Could that be the CME the Electric Czar was talking about when I flew with Margherita to Acapulco?"

The Professor is irritated, *"**No!** I already told you; I don't think that CMEs are predictable *that far in advance . . ."*

Glenn is thinking, "Maybe it was the Alien who warned me about the CME; or was that just a dream? But maybe the Alien has the technology to predict when a CME will erupt." As the Professor is walking away, Glenn shouts, "And you don't think that it could interfere with our launched barrels?"

"No, I already answered *that question, too!* Do I have to repeat the same *conversation over and **over** again?!?* The worst-case scenario is it may make them explode before they reach the Sun's Corona; but what difference would that make. I presume that the molecules of nuclear-waste debris would eventually fall into the Sun; everything should gravitationally be pulled into the Sun . . ."

Glenn retorts, "Well your **worst-case** scenario is happening *as we speak!* It is exploding our barrels at about 85,000,000 miles away. Bernie, Jane and I spent hours yesterday evening on the telescope watching them blow up in rapid succession – *one after another!!*" The Professor stops dead in his tracks and turns to face Glenn. "I stopped all launchings until the CME passes us, just as a precaution. Is there a way we can track this ionized nuclear-waste debris to see if it is falling into the Sun?" The Professor just shrugs, turns and sheepishly walks away.

Glenn's tells Bernie, "Did I just win an argument - or is the Professor *cracking up!* But, just in case he is right, we need a backup plan. Got to anticipate that this new 'Big Syphon2' will somehow or other miss our valley of balloons, or that all of the Skyhook's balloons will not choke it out of existence."

Bernie enthusiastically suggests, "Let's re-position the 40-mile-wide by 50-mile-long Skyhook H-cube-balloon array so that it lies along the equator, lengthwise east to west instead of north to south. That will give the Whirlwind2 a 10 mile longer impact area."

"All of the 10ft Hydro-cubes are tied to each other," Glenn replies, reversing his prior mind-set, "the Syphon/Whirlwind should pull them all into it. It can't possibly miss our mountain top as it only travels a maximum of 35 miles from north to south on any given day." Bernie gives a quick exasperated shake of his head and walks away. Glenn mutters, *What?!?* Another prima-donna having a temper-tantrum . . ." He questions his anger, "I feel guilty about shooting down Bernie's suggestion, but I wanted to further explain that the balloons cover my Valley where I have the no-fly zone - repositioning of Skyhook would extend them beyond that no-fly zone. But I'm not going to chase after Bernie to explain that to him!"

XIX

THE WEDDING

When Elena sees that Jane has returned, she commandeers her to quickly plan the wedding; to be held at the Hacienda using the Loon-Evator platform for the ceremony. She likes the idea of raising it up a few feet and having the spectators looking up at her. She feels that all her life her relatives have been looking down on her; "Especially since my father started raping me⁓

As if I was responsible ⁓

as if I seduced him . . ."

Jane has no problem with the concept of 'spending whatever you want' and immediately gets on the computer and starts looking at the wedding dresses; she's picking out dresses for herself and Virginia as bridesmaid and for Margherita as maid of honor. Also picking out elegant dresses for Elena's mother, Sancho's wife and tuxedos for Best Man Bernie, and ushers Sancho and Jake. She proposes Elena consider the Professor's daughters as flower girls and his son as the ring bearer. CIA Jane is anxious to show Glenn how cooperative she can be, and that she is working on the Internet without trying to make any personal contacts. She advises Glenn to order a small diamond wedding ring and suggests several modest possibilities . . .

then she asks Elena which one she likes . . .

Margherita returns the next day to find that the wedding has all been arranged for the following day. She is disappointed that there was no invitation for her mother, sister and children. However, she is grateful that she does not have to explain why her lover is marrying their cousin. Also, she is very excited about the Doctor's hopeful procedure; something about being inseminated with her own fertilized eggs. But she must seduce Glenn tonight, the day before his wedding, because she needs another dose of his sperm for the Doctor to give it to her in what he called an 'intrauterine insemination procedure.' He said something about 'cervical mucous' being too thick, and they can get past it, into her womb, with this procedure. Maybe Glenn will understand all of this better than she does – just as long as she gets pregnant with his baby – she doesn't care. So, she will take the train after the wedding on Sunday. She *shivers* with anticipation, "Monday I'll be *invaded* by the Doctor's *big spatula* again and then *my pussy* will be *blasted* with Glenn's *refrigerated* bottle of *juice*. Then, by the next month I should be pregnant." She tries explaining all this to Glenn as she is seducing him while holding onto the little refrigeration bottle.

He asks her critically, "Are you *ovulating*?!?"

She is hurt and denies with indignation, "I have **never** done anything *like that!*"

He is flabbergasted saying, "You've got something wrong: it is either 'IUI' or 'IVF'? – One or the other; not both ~ which one am I paying for?"

She retorts, "*OH **SILENCIO**!!* Keep your mind on my tits, your dick is *not even getting hard!*" she says fondling him. "I donna do nothing wrong . . ." She gets down on her knees and starts sucking on it.

Glenn says, "Elena is going to be mad at you, draining me the day before our wedding."

Margherita explains, "Yo comprendo that Elena's in a hurry to get married before her belly starts showing and you are worried about baby being made before marrying. But that donna stop *me getting pregnant!*" Margherita's eyes narrow as she says, **"Fuck her!"**

Glenn retorts, "Yes . . . Exactly; that's what I'm supposed to do tomorrow night while you're on your way back to Pequito - *after my wedding!*"

"But she's already pregnant, why should *she care!*" Then he is surprised to see she is vigorously flicking her tongue while deftly placing his balls in her mouth and humming a chanting intonation. Then she starts working his pecker with her hand. Glenn *gasps* in *shocking* appreciation for her moist vibrations *reverberating* through his loins . . . and *he climaxes immediately.*

She stops her tonguing with a surprising yelping sound while suddenly squeezing on his dick, ***pinching*** off his ejaculating spasm . . . He slowly groans in anguish, *"M O T H E R r rr – F U C K E R R r rrr !"* as painful pressure throbs in his dick. She places the lid of the bottle between her teeth then twists it open with one hand then points his dick into the open bottle - then finally – slowly eases her clenching grip on it. She catches his fluid in the bottle and lets the lid fall from her mouth.

"Why you shoot so fast?!?" She baby-talks poutingly, "I so sorry, I no want to hurt you; but, I no can lose your juices . . . We need *every little drop."*

He leans back with his face distorted into a scrunched-up frown muttering, *"You - fucking - demonic - bitch!"* as his last spasm drips into the bottle. She smiles up at him from between his knees and returns the lid to the bottle. Then she gently lifts his already shriveling penis and delicately licks the tip and then finishes with a soft kiss to it.

Continuing her lilting baby talk, she says, "I make it up to you *next time,* I sorry that I *hurt you."* Glenn looks at her with a harsh vindictive expression. Then she says in her normal voice, "or I will have Elena treat you extra gentle tomorrow night: *extra special."*

Glenn cannot imagine anything more or new that would be extra special; but his curiosity is piqued. "What is she going to do, bring a sheep to bed with us?" then he suspiciously thinks, "Or sacrifice *a chicken?!?* Or worse - maybe a ceremonial *sexy snake dance!?!"*

Margherita changes the subject as she gets up and puts the bottle into the refrigerator, "Sancho says, that Pedro told him, that Elena's ex-husband is mad because he will lose the house if Elena gets married, or if she has any children. He will no longer have any claim to it. He says even though he signed divorce papers they can be undone as long as she does not re-marry or have any children. - Sancho thinks he may try something to stop your wedding. Her X still doesn't believe that she is pregnant -because *he couldn't* get her pregnant."

"Well, I doubt that he will do anything after the last scare we gave him. But, *let him try!"* Glenn says defiantly.

Margherita says, "Elena would see him dead before she would let him have **her house!** The wedding is tomorrow, you have a Priest coming up on the morning train, it will all be legal; what could he do about it? I don't think that he would try to kidnap a Priest . . ." Then as an afterthought she adds, "I've got to go try on my new dress for the wedding. I heard that your CIA Jane had the clothing store, the wedding store, send up 2 tailors to fit us with our new wedding clothes – costa mucho dinero per tu. Elena talked for hours on the phone with me last night, she's worried you'll be angry about mucho, mucho cost . . . I'm sleeping with Elena tonight." Then, with a leering sparkle in her eyes, she adds, baby talking again, "I hope *your balls* feel better in time for *your honeymoon* tomorrow night!"

Laughing, she runs out the door without waiting for Glenn's response.

He shouts, "You *fucking* **vicious <u>cunt!</u>**"

The next morning's train whistle, announcing its arrival, awakens Glenn. After showering all alone, the Professor barges into his room complaining about all the people getting off the train, "How are we supposed to maintain social distancing, these people don't care anything about the COVID-19 virus. There must be *50 people!* They should all be *wearing masks!!*"

Glenn replies, "Stop exaggerating . . . Calm down, it's a day of celebration and we'll get through it as best we can. Besides there have not been any cases of COVID-19 reported in these mountains yet."

The Professor yells, "They are coming from Pequito – *the city, **not the mountains!***" Glenn shrugs with a vacant look of indifference.

Even though it is a day of celebration, Sunday, there is still work to be done. The nuclear-waste cars have to be un-coupled from the train, fresh water has to be pumped into the storage tank from the train's tank-car, and the sewage-tank has to be pumped out into the train's sewage-tank for dumping when it gets back to Pequito. Breakfast and lunch had been brought up on the train, as opposed to having the bridal party make it. Bernie, Jake and Sancho arrive at his cabin with breakfast as the Professor is leaving. Jake is already wearing his tuxedo. Glenn asks, "The wedding is not for another 8 hours, are you going to be comfortable like that all day?"

Jake says, "The first time in my life I have the occasion to wear a tuxedo so I'm making the most of it."

Bernie says, "Are you ready to take the 'big plunge'? We can still smuggle you out of here." They all laugh. They sit around Glenn's cabin enjoying breakfast together. They discuss what to do now that they've held up on the launching of the nuclear-waste because of the CME. Bernie informs Glenn, "Jane and I went back up to Skyhook's telescope-cabin and saw that the launched barrels are still exploding in the CME. But Jane confirmed that it is much closer now than before, when it was 90 million miles away - now it is exploding them about 50 million miles away."

Jake says enthusiastically, "I want to see it too."

Sancho spits-out, "I do NOT want to see anything if I have to go up higher – ***NOT EVEN ONE*** *step higher!"*

They all laugh as Jake pats him on his back.

"So, our last barrel launched," Glenn speculates, "should be colliding with the Corona Mass Ejection within a few days. The Professor should calculate that."

Bernie says, "Good idea, he might *grant* your *wish,* - after all, it is *your* ***wedding day!?!"*** Jake and Bernie laugh as Glenn smiles wryly. Sancho stares inquisitively as he doesn't understand what can be funny about the Boss-Man asking an employee to do some work.

They decide to walk around the Hacienda while Jake continues the conversation, "Additionally, we have to maintain our irrigating Gusher-Spray, and we have to worry about 'The Big Syphon2'; it is still circling the Earth every 24 hours sucking up air & water. Nobody is concerned about it lowering the sea-level as it will improve the places that were already flooding." They search their cellphones for news on where 'The Big Syphon2' is located and what damage its Whirlwind is causing:

'There are instances of loss of life but it's not exactly clear that the Whirlwind2 is directly responsible and not exactly clear that those governments were notifying people about evacuating; nor providing the mechanisms for evacuation. Those governments are refusing to take any responsibility saying it started in the USA and they plan to pursue prosecution in the World Court for international terrorism. Candidate Prump is blaming his own government for this problem saying that only he can fix it.'

Glenn says, "That *lying **prick!***" as he feels outrage mixed with a pang of guilt. They pass near CIA-Jane who is getting lunch in the kitchen. He is terribly concerned about the loss of life and injury and is asking Bernie, "Can you and Jane see if we can help those people - somehow pay for their medical expenses, funeral expenses, rewarding death benefits to the family - something or other like that?"

Jane volunteers, "We can set up a 'Go Fund Me' web-page, asking for donations . . ."

Glenn curtly silences her, "We don't need to *beg* for **money!!** *Use 'Mother Nature's Blog'* to fund *everything!*" Jane demurely returns to her cooking.

Next thing they know its lunchtime; Bernie and Jake go get lunch and bring it back to the cabin. They continue they're festive gathering. Then it's time to get dressed for the wedding. Jake stays with Glenn and assists him in getting his tuxedo on. Sancho and Bernie go to their cabins to get dressed. Then they come back to escort Glenn out from his cabin, through the kitchen area that is now filled with elegant tables and chairs surrounding a portable (roll-up) dance floor; to the Loon-Evator site, which is surrounded by rows of folding chairs. All this, Glenn surmises, was apparently brought up on the morning train. He reluctantly acknowledges that CIA Jane has done a wonderful job. He is just about to greet the Priest who is admonishing, "I'm sorry that I missed you at this morning's mass - that I gave *for you* . . ."

Then suddenly there is music playing . . . Looking up on the Loon-Evator's loading platform, he sees there's *an* orchestra?

"An *orchestra?!?*" he exclaims,

"A *fucking* **ORCHESTRA!?!**

*That **cunt*** hired an orchestra - how much *does **that cost!?!***"

Fortunately, Elena nor any other woman are near; so that nobody other than the Priest hears him.

Glenn glares at Bernie and just nods his head. Still gawking, he turns to the orchestra, mouthing *"A fucking orchestra!"* They are playing Latin somber music. The Priest, Sancho and Bernie usher Glenn to the platform, it sounds like a funeral march to Glenn. Then Sancho hurries back up the aisle to insist the bride and her mother stop talking and start the ceremony. Now sweating profusely, he signals the orchestra to begin the wedding ceremony music. First there are the flower girls: the Professor's two daughters, modestly but elegantly dressed; marching between the row of spectators and dropping flowers from their flower-basket at the edge of the aisle. Then the ring bearer: the Professor's young son in a short-pants-tuxedo, is carrying a pillow with an *enormous* **DIAMOND** *ring* on it. Then comes Elena's mother in a tastefully mature, elegant evening gown; escorted by Juan, Glenn's train conductor. Then comes 14-year-old Virginia, her elegant gown designed to conceal her ripe voluptuousness. Then comes CIA Jane – the extravagant wedding planner and dress designer - in her fabulously sexy gown. Then comes Margherita, the Maid-Of-Honor, in her matronly beautiful gown. Glenn cannot help but notice her luscious breasts jiggling with each step she takes. He has a flash-back to the first time he saw her, riding the mule; her flesh jiggling with each of the mule's steps.

Then the orchestra breaks out into 'Here Comes The Bride' and everyone stands up. Elena has a beautiful white sequined wedding gown; Glenn is hoping they are not real diamonds. She is escorted by Sancho; they march down the aisle together. They arrive in front of the Priest and Bernie pushes Glenn forward. He goes to Elena, removes her veil, bends down and kisses her. - She starts to cry. - They turn to face the Priest who signals the congregation to be seated.

They obey with a brow-beaten acquiescence as Sancho coyly leaves the altar and climbs the stairs to the control platform. He raises the Loon-Evator up 5-feet, and stops it as the loading ramp folds closed. Then returns to his seat. The orchestra finishes playing, and the Priest begins the Spanish 'Dearly Beloved' ceremony.

Glenn feels goosebumps, suddenly the hair on the back of his neck stands up and his stomach quivers with a panicked anticipation . . . He is doubting, "Could I be this emotional over the wedding?" Then he hears a splattering and sees their wooden deck between his and Elena's feet splinter, followed immediately by a loud crack. He's seen that splintering before . . ."

He screams,

"Somebody is shooting at us!"

He grabs Elena and pulls her to the ground and they role away from the Priest while he is yelling to everybody, *"Get down! Get down!! Somebody is shooting at us!"* More shots ring out with splintering impacts appearing. There are some loud booms interspersed by a different sounding crack and then impact. Apparently, it is more than one type of weapon firing. Glenn craws to the stairs, then hurries up the stairs to the control panel and throws the lever to the down position. This lowers the Loon-Evator down 5-feet to ground level and opens the loading ramp. Margherita had hovered over the children and herded them over behind it and now manages to pull them away so that it can open without hurting them. Then she and everybody else scurry down the loading ramp. The Priest is among the first to fight his way down the loading ramp, roughly passing by Margherita and the children. Glenn climbs down from the second level and grabs Elena and hurries her off with more bullets landing around them. It is now obvious that she is the target. Sancho and Bernie go down the ramp and follow Glenn towards the Jet-Basket. Jake stays with Virginia. CIA Jane instructs everybody to overturn tables and chairs in the kitchen area and to hide behind them. Glenn, Bernie and Sancho take off in the Jet-Basket and start heading North where they expect these invaders must have come from; although there is the military guard inside the tunnel. He cannot imagine how the shooters could have gotten in; he cannot see any sign of them.

But Sancho is not looking North; he is looking South. He sees a train on the tracks leading towards the southern tunnel. Then he sees smoke from the next gunshots coming off the top of the last car. He yells to look there and when Glenn sees them, he reverses direction. Then he searches in the cupboard under the bench and pulls out the two automatic rifles that he in Margherita were using to punish Elena's X. He's handing one of them towards Bernie, but Sancho forcefully grabs it away from Bernie and quickly goes to the southern edge of the Jet-Basket and pulls the trigger. Glenn is following him; he carefully spies the train thru the scope and then pulls the trigger. Neither of the AR15s fire as their clips are empty. Glenn returns to the cupboard and fishes around through empty clips that he had forgotten to refill. He finds two full clips, Sancho takes one from him and mimics Glenn attaching his clip. And then he hurriedly scurries past Glenn and begins shooting southward in a wild meandering spray of bullets. Glenn is taking careful aim again thru the telescopic lens, as he is trying to compensate for the basket's swinging motion, and fires small bursts which he can see hit the train. This causes great commotion on top of the train, and it begins accelerating South as several men stand-up and run and jump from one car to another towards the front of the train - away from Glenn's bullets. Glenn continues shooting at them until his clip is emptied; but apparently has no success in shooting them. The train disappears into the tunnel and Glenn flies the Jet-Basket after it, going over the mountain ridge and sees it coming out the far side. He can clearly identify Pedro and Elena's ex-husband. There are a few other men there too. He can see that they have two rifles. One is a shotgun, but they were never within range. It was Elena's X who was firing the other one, a high-powered hunting rifle with the telescopic lens – he is *aiming it up at them now!* Sancho is urging him to turn around, saying there is no point in pursuing them since we don't have any bullets and they have guns to shoot at us. Glenn's got pistols in the cupboard but he thinks better of trying to pursue them with only pistols against their high-powered rifle. He turns around as bullets splatter through the floor of the wicker basket. Bernie and Sancho grab the railing and squat down, flinching from the wicker basket's flying splinters as Glenn accelerates northward, back over the protective mountain ridge and into the valley.

As soon as they arrive back at the Hacienda, Jake and Virginia are pleading with Glenn about not ruining the whole day and to quickly resume the wedding. He finds that there were no injuries from the shooting except for a cello, french-horn, baritone-horn, a trombone, a base-fiddle and some drums. Apparently, the orchestra wisely used them as shields as they followed the fleeing wedding party down the ramp and into the kitchen. Jake asks, "You reacted even before the shots were fired at you? How did you know?"

Glenn shrugs saying, "I felt something – a premonition – I have learned to respond to these feelings as I have had them before."

"I don't believe in that stuff, I tried meditating for years in the hope of developing some sort of ESP (Extra Sensory Perception), maybe even psychokinesis . . . a waste of my time."

"Me too, I tried all kinds of Buddhist chanting and Yoga meditation. I don't know if it helped with my premonitions or not. But I was fascinated to hear about something called 'Quantum Entanglement': separating atoms from a molecule and then changing the spin of only one of these atoms, also causes the other atoms to change; even when they are separated ~ to anywhere in the *world* – and presumably, anywhere in the *universe* – *instantaneously* ~ automatically changing *by itself* . . ."

Jake says with a bewildered sneer, "That's some *amazing shit!* The Professor will have to show me that one. Think I can talk him *into it?!?*"

Glenn's eyes sparkle, "Not today, please . . . we've had *enough murderous drama* already!" They laugh together.

Jake adds, "Yeah, this is some *heavy shit* . . . we'll resume this conversation after your brains *recuperate* ~ from your *honeymoon.*"

Elena and her mother are gazing over the large assembly of spectators. She is marveling at this elaborate, luxurious wedding *for her daughter*: "More than I could have ever done for her . . ." They see Glenn laughing, "You have made your husband very happy . . ." she tearfully gives her daughter a kiss on the cheek, adding, *"and me too."*

Elena says, "We never have to be separated again. And how happy are you going to be living here, helping me to raise your *3 grandchildren* – **maybe more!"** They embrace and then dab the dears from each other's eyes.

Sancho takes command and instructs everybody to take their former positions and to resume the ceremony. They *can't find the diamond ring*: the ring bearer dropped it in the confusion. The Professor comments with *incriminating intensity* that they **also** *can't find the Priest:* ~ He finally crawls out from under a cabin. Margherita happily offers Elena an alternative ring from off her finger whispering, "It is proper – *no?* You said I am the father of your baby . . ." They both laugh as Elena hugs her with tears in her eyes. The Priest performs the ceremony in Spanish, but it sounds familiar to Glenn, and he imagines that he understands everything that is being said, but must be prodded to respond, to which he says firmly in English "I do." Then the Priest produces the lost wedding ring; it seems he wasn't too frightened to pick it up during the shooting. Glenn is *flummoxed* by the *size of the diamond* as he puts the ring on her finger; thinking, "CIA Jane *fucked me up* again! I'll have to pay for another one at least as gaudy at this one if Margherita gets pregnant. *SHIT!!"* The Priest pronounces them husband and wife. Glenn is recovering, he slowly turns and hugs Elena, then lifts her and kisses her passionately. Everybody applauds and cheers. The orchestra had been playing a noticeably sour 'Ave Maria' on their shot-up instruments during a quiet lull in the ceremony; but now play a jubilant 'Ode To Joy' – also a little sour –. Then they all follow the bride and groom to the kitchen area where the tables and chairs have been set up once again; everybody sits and begins a feast catered by an army of waiters and cooks and others that CIA Jane had ordered. Glenn eyes CIA Jane caustically for this **ostentatious** wedding feast . . . He would not dream of saying anything to upset Elena's happiness. Her mother is beside herself with joy.

She has other relatives too . . . Elena's estranged father shows up with expectations of moving back-in on the family; but her mother puts a stop to that quickly. He obviously was trying to capitalize on her new wealth. He cheerfully approaches Elena with his arms open as if to dance; she dismisses him saying, "All my dances are reserved for Glenn: the ***ONLY MAN*** I want in my life."

Margherita dances with several men, once with Glenn; but, many times finds herself dancing a three-some with the bride and groom. She's glad to show everyone that she is NOT the scorned woman; that she is happy for Elena's wonderfully blessed future.

There is a champagne toast by Bernie in both English and Spanish – produced and directed by CIA Jane, who also plays Mistress of Ceremonies – introducing each dinner entre option – showing off her bi-lingual skills. There is dancing and drinking and joy for all, including little Ricardo who's having a good time dancing with the flower girls. Glenn notices the Professor's young son; he is also dancing with his sisters – reluctantly – as he too is trying to dance with Ricardo. He had given Ricardo a gift of his orange water pistol, who keeps it in the cummerbund of his tuxedo. He playfully whips it out and squirts the little boy in the face whenever he gets too close. The Professor and his wife see this with a grimly apprehensive concern. She is wondering, "At what age does sexual imprinting occur in children? Some psychologists claim it is irreversible . . . probably the homosexual ones."

The Professor is wandering, "Did we leave him in the company of his sisters too much? Has his mother been *babying him too much?!?* If only we could have had the boy before having the girls . . ."

There is a bit of a spectacle as Elena's mother refuses the obvious overtures of her slightly inebriated former husband, trying to get her to dance. He is trying to be romantic, and then he is shot down by her curt refusals. Everyone watches as he slinks away muttering, "I was just asking what's going to happen with our family's house . . ." returning to the bar. Juan continues to eyeball them, suspiciously.

Sancho seizes on the opportunity, talks to the orchestra leader, then takes the bride to the dance floor. As the music starts Glenn joins them, dragging his new mother-in-law off her chair and dancing his parody of the 'Mexican Hat Dance'. It gets a lot of laughs until a small paring knife flies out from her sash/belt and slides across the portable dance floor. She tries to ignore it and continues dancing, encouraging Glenn to strut-his-stuff. He is thinking, "Is my new mother-in-law *stealing* my silverware?!?" Everybody sees it, it grabs everyone's attention. Juan sense of foreboding is elevated. But the Professora Natzinger saves the joyous occasion by quickly sending her students onto the floor to show-off the proper way to do their 'Latino Heritage Dance', which she insisted they all learn to do as good as any professional.

The party ends with the cutting of the cake and ice cream and coffee. Juan festively blows out a tune on the train whistle as the wedding celebration ends. Margherita is feeling elated as she hurries to Glenn's refrigerator, retrieves his bottle of sperm, puts it in a cooler bag with ice, and then runs to the train pausing only to kiss the newlywed's goodbye. She is going back to her luxury hotel in Pequito for the night and then to the Doctor's office bright and early the next morning. Glenn suddenly notices his wedding night's irony - he is feeling pangs of suspicious jealousy, "Margherita seems *too happy* to be returning to that big city hotel - *alone?*"

Then Margherita walks past her friend's passenger car and climbs onto the orchestra's passenger car. She accepts a seat between two lively musicians who are happily making room for her to sit. The festivities continue for them on the train as they are both hitting on her. She knows she looks *desirable to these strangers* and is enjoying their attention. She laughs with abandonment at their suggestive humor. Margherita's eyebrows arch and her eyes shine as she is struck with this once in a life-time opportunity; particularly with the handsome younger man in her *fancy hotel room* (?or? . . . maybe even - *both of them!*). She will *never* see either of them again . . . But, - considering her *pussy's appointment* with the Doctor's *big spatula* in 10 hours, and *Glenn's sperm* being chilled in her purse – she decides to simply enjoy the flirtation . . . she smiles wryly as the passion evaporates from her eyes.

All the caterers pile onto the train after their exhaustingly long workday, leaving behind a big mess. The folding tables and chairs will be shipped out the next evening. All the food that is leftover is taken by the employees to their cabins. Elena's mother escorts Elena's uninvited father to the train. He is apologizing for his past transgressions, "I know I wasn't the perfect father or husband . . . But I *can't believe* they *deprived me* **the honor** of giving away the bride; after all – *She is **MY DAUGHTER!**"*

She says, "No one invited you to the wedding . . ." then loudly announces as they approach the train, "You *ruined all of our lives*, we never want *to see you again!* Because of you I had to choose between allowing her to marry that piece of shit or letting you ruin her by getting her pregnant. Then I had to leave her alone to do house cleaning for rich people in the city just so that I could earn money to keep her house . . . While you went off *chasing other young girls!* I am staying *alone* in Elena's cabin, and . . . don't you **ever come back** to this mountain again – **NEVER!!**" She is publicly humiliating him. He wants to punch her face in, as he had done many times before, but instead he hurries to the train with her screaming right behind him. Then, as he is climbing up the steps into the train's nearest passenger car, she pulls that small paring knife out of her sash and **<u>stabs him in the ass.</u>** He screams and falls forward crying and cursing her. Then, she defiantly walks away . . . *smiling.*

Some passengers come to his aid and see the small knife protruding from his bleeding right ass cheek. They all move away as they don't want to be involved with the military-police. Juan, the conductor, says nonchalantly, "He is lucky that it wasn't his throat. We will drop him off at a town where there is a nearby infirmary; everyone should simply say he had the knife in him when he crawled onto the train, and we don't know how it happened."

XX

PELENA'S CATHARTIC
SYMPATHETIC REVENGA?

The train makes a few stops at the small mountain villages as everybody but the caters and the orchestra gets off. Margherita is still engaged with the two musicians when the train makes an unscheduled stop. A slight glimmer returns to her eyes as the passion again stirs in her loins, she is thinking, "Maybe I can get the younger one to follow me to an empty car or bathroom where I can give him a quick blow-job. I'll at least have a memory to savor during my fantasies." Then the conductor enters their car and, as everybody else is sleeping, he asks her two companions to help carry a crying drunk off the train to a nearby infirmary. Margherita tags along – not wanting their party to end. She is surprised to see that the crying drunk *is Elena's father*, and then they are all shocked to see the *knife sticking out of his bloody ass cheek*. She has a Deja-vu instant of clarity, seeing that small knife falling from Elena's mother's gown and sliding across the dance floor to the refrains of the 'Mexican Hat Dance' . . . "AAAHHiieee!!!" she screams in astonished delight!

Then the two musicians are *flabbergasted* when Margherita starts **laughing hysterically**, leaning against the wall for support. She is laughing so hard she can't stand up. She collapses onto a bench then slides to the floor with rollicking laughter. They are carrying the crying drunk out as she rolls onto her belly *howling* with *side splitting laughter* and starts kicking and *pounding* her fists on the floor with *bizarre maniacal hilarity.* The two musicians *eerily share* wide eyed expressions as they are more psyched by her *insane laughter* than by *the knifing* . . . The conductor, Juan, is totally aloof - which further adds to the *ghoulish* scene . . .

XXI

THE HONEYMOON

The newlyweds leisurely stroll back to Glenn's cabin. The sudden quiet and loneliness is anti-climactic after the evening's festivities; and they both find themselves missing Margherita already. Elena curses her X for telling her father about their wedding. She apologizes to Glenn, saying, "I not know he would come here; I not seen him since I was a young teenager at my wedding. Maybe my X make him to come thinking he could stop our wedding; or make me give him my house, so they could sell it – or maybe share it. How *stupid he is!*"

Glenn says, "You didn't do anything wrong. He'll lose all claims to your house when you have my baby. I don't know how your X knew about the South train tunnel into my valley – I mean: OUR valley!" He looks at her romantically as they go into his cabin. They make a good show of lovemaking while undressing each other. Elena gives him a humming blowjob while she orgasms by grinding her pussy against his shinbone. Glenn is thinking while orgasming, "Lucky my *balls* **RECOVERED** from Margherita's *merciless – PYTHONIC – **GRIP** – WHILE –* SHE - was - milking – myyy - peckkerrrr dry y y . . ." as they both drift off to sleep - exhausted.

XXII

❖

P!?JUSTIFIABLE RAPE?!?

The next morning Glenn instructs Arturo to tell Grizelda (Ricardo's mother ~ who rescued him from the shark and - unwillingly – from his PTSD trauma) to evacuate from the port city to his Valley to be safe from the COVID-19 Pandemic - and also that she'll be with her son. Arturo follows up with the fact that she refuses to ever go back to 'that shitty mountain and those disgusting mountain goat people.' Also, he can go see her on the boat if he wants to visit with her. She said she will just take small groups of no more than four people, keep her mask on, and social distance. And if she's got no customers, she will ride out into the ocean and weigh anchor and fish on her own. She also says as soon as the Whirlwind passes North of her, she will run the boat North so that she will be far away from it - North of it - when it passes to the South at noon on the next day. Then she will sail back to her port and resume business as usual.

Glenn questions, "Do you think she'll be safe if she does that?"

Arturo quips, "Safer than you will be up on that mountain top. You better make arrangements to get everybody North to Colombia or South to Peru the day before September 21st. North would be safer, because God knows if transportation will be possible back through the devastated area, and you don't want to have to keep going further and further South every day to get away from it."

Glenn says, "Yeah, let me think on it. That was a curious expression: 'those fucking mountain-goat people.' Do all your people think of the mountain residents like that."

"No, we don't think of them *like that!*" Arturo replies indignantly, "I think she meant to say they want to fuck like mountain goats, and she is never going back there because of how they treated her - or what they did to her."

Glenn's brow furrows with the thought of the bruise on her ass where he violently kicked her, "Was it 'what **they** did to her.' Or was it *'what I did to her?'* - But she did say I could go visit her on the boat. And forget her ever coming back here again . . . I wonder what she's talking about?" The next day he asks Juan if he knows anything about why Graziela would not want to return to our Valley. "She was happy when she left me? Did something happen to her on the train ride to Pequito?"

Juan replies self-consciously, "I will ask the other conductor about it; but maybe your wife, Elena, might know something about it. They were sitting together, *talking.*" he says with a revealing smirk.

Glenn asks Elena that night at dinner, "Do you know why Graziela would not come back to our valley to be safe from the COVID-19 virus? Graziela says that 'We people are like fucking mountain-goats up here'. She says she never wants to return here again and that her son and I can go visit her at the boat."

Elena says, "Bueno! - Good! You can go there and fuck her whenever you want . . . We don't want that fat, big titted bitch around here. She thinks that she's **the Petrona!!** Do you remember how she was shaking her ass at everybody and jiggling those big tits in our faces and laughing at us because she knew she was making all the men hard."

Glenn looks at her cock-eyed, then says, "That explains why you don't want her here; but why is it that she does *not want to* come back here?"

Elena now carries the aura of the Petrona; she has *No Fear* of blatantly *telling Glenn the truth.* "Graziela knows that if she shows up here again that she will get more of the same . . . When we knew she was leaving and not coming back, we all grabbed her and fucked her on the train ride home. You remember, when Margherita came to your cabin that night after the train left with that fat whore on it. Did you think we were gonna let her get away with shaking her ass and tits in everybody's face . . . shaming me and Margherita?!? We were just waiting til you were done with her to *prende revenga.*"

Glenn is surprised but somehow or other not shocked. He feels that he should fire them for what they did to Graziela; but he also feels that they had some justification for what they did. And, ~ is it just his curiosity that is piquing? "What exactly did they do?" he wonders. Then he demands, "Tell me exactly who did what to her - step by step - blow by blow." Elena's eyes light up with anticipation as she relays the incidents on the train ride to her village:

'When Graziela got on the train that evening I asked her why she was leaving, and she told us all how glad she was to leave this place and this disgusting mountain and that she was never coming back again. That's when Margherita jumped off the train to be with you; she was not going to stay with you while you had that fat whore sleeping with you. So, I went to the front car of the train and told Juan to stop the train after we traveled past the tunnel and then to join us because we were going to have a good-bye party, as Graziela was leaving and says she's never coming back here again - that we are disgusting people. So, when he stopped the train and came back to us, Sancho and Juan grabbed Graziela's arms and pulled her to her knees. Then I grabbed her by the hair and punched her fat face. We took her clothes off her and I sat on the bench and pulled her by the hair into my pussy and made her lick it. Sancho started fucking her in the ass. It was funny, seeing Sancho's hard-on sticking out past his fat belly. He knelt behind her and laid his belly on top of her fat ass, then as he pushed his cock into her asshole she squealed into my pussy. It made *me cum!* Then he smacked her on her ass to make her keep twerking it; it made his belly jiggle just like her ass. I was so confused; I didn't know whether I was cuming or laughing. And then Juan took my place and had her suck his cock and lick him everywhere. Then the Professor came over and made her suck his cock too. He was singing some strange song in both Spanish and English: "You know what boys like, You know what guys like, You got what boys want, *SUCKER!*" Then he would smack her really hard while pulling her hair. Then he repeated this over and over until he shot in her mouth and screamed at her to swallow, to *swallow it all!* Then we made her twerk her naked ass and shake her naked titties some more and then Juan fucked her and then went back to drive the train again. And then the Professor fucked her in the ass while singing that song again – it was like he was crazy, a little scary. He smacked her, hitting her on the big bruise she had on her ass, every time she stopped twerking her ass. He is the only one who deliberately smacked her where it would really hurt. Then I made her eat my pussy again all the way back to my village. Then Juan brought Felix, his relief train conductor, to Graziela telling him how she shakes her tits and twerks her ass; even while fucking her. Then she was giving him a – how do you say – is it blowjob? - as we all got off the train. I later heard that he stopped the train once again and fucked her before arriving in Pequito. It was just the two of them - she didn't say no . . .'

Elena summarizes, "She was a good fuck; we all forgave her, because she delivered on the promises her body made. If she comes back here again to fuck you, she's gonna get more of the same from all of us, and *she knows it!*"

Glenn shakes his head in amazement; he couldn't imagine the Professor involved in this. Then remembers that he was singing that old song that sexually taunted all males, calling them 'SUCKERS'. A female had recorded it with that young, sexy, lilting, mocking voice. But he is more amazed by the throbbing erection that Elena's narrative has given him. Glenn feels shameful about kicking Graziela and leaving her with that painful bruise on her ass. But then, he accepts that testosterone has given his pecker a mind of its own. He now finds himself eyeing Elena with a vindictive passion. His throbbing pecker *knows no shame!* He grabs Elena, lifts and throws her on to the bed as she screams with fearful delight. He quickly removes his pants. She is eyeing his engorged penis. He rips her clothes off then quickly forces his pecker into her tiny pussy as she cries out with an orgasm. Then he pounds her pussy mercilessly and cums deep inside of her. She orgasms again as he finishes with an earth-shaking bellow of relief . . .

She slides her hand down to soothe her throbbing pussy as his shrinking penis slides out of her, saying "I hope you did not hurt my baby."

Glenn feels a pang of guilt as he lingers between wanton ecstasy and oblivion. He ponders, "Does it mean Elena is as masculine as me . . . or that we are both just *loathsome animals*; being *so aroused* by the retelling of the *violent rape* of little Ricardo's mother . . ."

XXIII

MRS. NATZI

The next morning at the employee's breakfast the Professor's wife mentions, "A news report spoke of polluted water in Newark N J, Flint Michigan and elsewhere and that candidate Tom Stever was commenting on it. With all these people you got here now we're going to need more fresh water."

Glenn assures her, "I ordered more frequent deliveries. - I hear from Jake that Candidate Prump is cruelly demeaning his opposition, even their wives?!?" trying to keep the conversation going.

Then she says, "Some religious fanatics are calling the Covid19 pandemic deaths – 'the Lord's culling - due to over population'; others are calling it 'the apocalypse'." Glenn says that there will always be a few fringe fanatics. She says it's more prevalent than that, and then reads a quote from a news report from her laptop:

> 'In 2004, General William G Boykin, the United States deputy undersecretary of defense for intelligence, made headlines from his loaded remarks about his rant including use of apocalyptic language when describing a military victory against a warlord in Somalia: "I knew that my God was bigger than his. I knew that my God was a real God and his was an idol." He later insisted the 'Idol' referred to greed and violence rather than Allah and he received nothing more than a letter of concern and mild rebuke

for his actions. In 2004 another report expressed concern about Christian Evangelical's proselytizing within the Air Force including a chaplain warning the cadets: "those not saved by Jesus would 'burn in hell's fire'". The report warns, "There's no religious voice, but the conservative and fragile evangelical Christian voice, and only it has the right to lay claim to the environment... And it is able to do that by working within the Air Force Academy power structure." Complaints of the military religious freedom foundation, a watchdog group preserving religious liberty in the military, have doubled since November 2016 with members protesting the increasing evangelism in the military. Secretary of State Pompeo's defenders rightly point out that he like any person of faith is entitled to practice his faith while in office; but the chaplain's vision of the relationship between America and the Islamic world as fundamentally "a relationship between good and evil" is at odds with the very nature of the Secretary's office. His dualism is "explicitly opposed to pluralism and tolerance", favoring instead a neat dichotomy of people into godly versus diabolical heathens. Pluralism and tolerance are precisely what makes diplomacy work.'

As she finishes reading the article, she looks up anticipating a response.

Glenn comments, "That's very interesting, but still not too alarming. *It's an old article!* But it's nice to have an intelligent conversation with someone that won't bite your head off." Noticing that the Professor's wife seems to be upset, he adds, "You seem to be worried about something, is there anything I can do?"

Her voice betrays a grave concern as she states, "I guess there is no way to ease into this: my husband's young brother, Rabbi Jerry Natzinger, is a Hasidic Jew living in Spring Valley, New York. His religious group has bought up and taken over that area, turning it into a strictly religious Orthodox Jewish community. They actively discourage any Gentiles by following them around and deliberately making them uncomfortable, even threatened. We hid out with them at their house when the reporters were harassing us. The Gay-Pride organization had orchestrated a campaign against us saying homo- phobes, the Professor and I, must be unfit parents; claiming we cannot be stopped from teaching our children to hate. They were threatening to have our children taken *away from us!* For some reason, the Rabbi got my husband to plot the course of the Whirlwind down to specific dates and locations. Then we moved here."

After assessing Glenn's grave expression, she continues. "It gets worse. As a result of his brother explaining the science of your 'Big Syphon' on TV, Rabbi Jerry became an evangelist. He believes your Whirlwind is the 'second coming of Jesus' and the beginning of the Rapture: where God takes up all the faithful into heaven; leaving all others on Earth to suffer the Apocalypse. He spoke with the Professor on the phone last night saying that this Covid19 pandemic is a further sign of God's judgment. He is begging us to take our children and join him. Of course, we denigrated his convictions and refused to join him in his religious Pilgrimage. We presumed that it would never materialize into anything serious. He has about 2000 followers, and they are on the train known as 'the beast'. They are traveling to southern Mexico where they hope to meet 'God's Whirlwind', as he calls it, at its 'high-noon' location. He thinks this is the Rapture and that God's Whirlwind is going to pick up all the faithful and take them to heaven. Some of these poor Pilgrims have died falling off the train; it happens daily on The Beast to the illegal immigrants who take this train north to the United States - these desperate people squeeze into it and pile up on top of it. Faux News has a reporter embedded with the Pilgrims doing live TV broadcasts. Of course, the Professor is very upset and wants to do something about it to stop his brother: but what can he do. They have 2 small children . . . They arrived in Southern Mexico during the night."

Glenn follows her to her new cabin where their 3 children are meandering around. The Professor is glued to the television. There are reporters everywhere broadcasting all the Pilgrims' comments. They are constantly throwing questions at the Rabbi who is kneeling and praying and rocking back and fourths. His wife and two children are next to him. The Professor sees his mother behind them and shouts, "Look, there's your grandmother. Oh *my God!* He's going to get **her killed too!!**" Now their children are paying close attention. "What am I *going to do?!?*"

His wife says, "It's too late to do anything. Let's hope that it wobbles away from the predicted path and misses them entirely."

The Professor notices Glenn as he calmly states, "There has not been a lot of history of it causing death; I think they will be all right."

The Professor argues, "All those other people avoided it; these fools *want it to hit them!*" Then to his daughters he whines, "Look, that's your uncle and your aunt, those are your too little cousins, that's *your grandmother,* my mother!" They stay there and watch the TV as time slowly drags by. Then a tornadic cloud appears on the eastern horizon.

At one minute before noon the Rabbi screams. "There it is, **God is coming!**"

All the other Pilgrims start screaming. "Jesus *save me!* **Jesus!** God *take me!* **Please God!**" All the reporters jump into their vehicles and hunker down with their cameras running. The Whirlwind is upon them in a cloud of dust as sand is blowing everywhere. There is the sound of growing anguish and then screams with continuing prayers . . . as the dust settles.

An elderly woman is asking, "Are we there? Is this heaven??"

Everybody is right where they were. Some people lost pets but managed to hold onto all their children. One woman, Maria de la Luz Aquilar, is crying, "Thank God that my husband beat me, pulling our two older children *away from me.* He saved them from this madness." She saved her infant baby by laying on top of him. Now she's crying, "I want *to go home!*"

Reporters on the vehicles with their cameras going are taunting the Pilgrims. One is asking the Rabbi who was dusting his clothes off and looking for his hat – "Did you see God? Do you like it better in heaven than you did here on Earth? Was God good to you? Or did he just *smack you around a little bit!*" They break into ribald laughter.

The Professor's mother is saying, "I can't see; I need water, I can't see, the sand *is in my eyes!*"

Her daughter-in-law shouts, "Children, don't rub your eyes; we have no water. God was supposed to provide for us."

The Rabbi bursts into tears saying, "I can't believe that God has forsaken us. I swear He spoke to me. I did *what He wanted!*" Many people are coughing and spitting out the sand. Children were told not to rub their eyes, but they can't resist and grind the sand into them. Within a half-an-hour reporters have broadcasted this mayhem all around the world. They pack up their equipment and drive away, leaving the 2000 crying Pilgrims there in the desert.

"Oh my God, now what are they going to do?" The Professor pleads, "I've got to go there, I got to help him. He helped us when we were fleeing from the 'Gay-Pride Terrorists'. We've got to *help him now!*"

His wife cries, "What can we do, we can send him money, but *where do we send it to?!?*"

The Professor insists, "We'll go back to our village, and we'll get all our cash and banking information. I will go into Pequito somehow and catch a flight to Mexico. I know approximately where they are located from the news reports. I should get there by tomorrow morning at the latest. Meanwhile you can order tents, and food; and water, and heaters, - and have it shipped over there - so that they don't freeze - in the desert - at night - and oh my God - what are we going to do - I got to go - there are hundreds of babies, they are lost in the desert – I have to go now - immediately. Come on **let's go!!**" he sobs tearfully to his wife as he tries gathering himself together for departure.

Glenn interrupts, "Wait, maybe I can help. There's got to be a better solution than that. There's no way you can get it done on time without the help from the military. These pilgrims will be thirsty - and freezing cold overnight. Wait . . ." Glenn says gently touching the Professor's shoulder, "Let me make a phone call; I have an idea that might work."

The Professor cries, "**No**, *I've got to go.*" as he frantically rummages around the cabin.

"Please, don't go!" She cries and clings to his arm; their children are now alarmed and grab onto them. She pleads, "*Calm down* and *listen* to him; see what he's got to say, he said he can get the military involved."

The Professor retorts, "They are in Mexico, not here *in Pecuador!* He doesn't know anybody in *the Mexican Military!!*"

"I can ask the Pecuadorian Military to contact them. General Garcia is my contact." Glenn is thinking, "I really don't want to talk to him after his last 'go fuck yourself Gringo'. - I will call our lawyer and have him try to arrange it." He gets Arturo on the phone and explains, "I want to help Rabbi Natzinger's Pilgrims in Mexico, but at the same time I want to remain anonymous; and not let anybody know of my location."

Arturo says give me 20 minutes. 20 minutes later he calls back saying, "Okay, I have spoken to General Garcia, who spoke to a Mexican General who has troops in that area. As we speak, he is taking a convoy of trucks and buses there; they will pick-up everybody and transport them to a city where they can get lodgings."

Glenn says, "Okay, thank you, *great job!*"

Arturo then abruptly adds, "But payment must be made in advance. He will not pick up anybody until they receive the full fee."

Glenn winces as he asks – "And how much is that?"

Arturo answers, "$1 million deposited into this Mexican General's personal account."

Glenn's face betrays the alarm that he's feeling: The Professor looks at him, then his wife, then each of their 3 children. Glenn walks out of their cabin speaking harshly into the cell phone, "Did you try to negotiate the price?"

He says, "Yes I did, and that's the best I could do."

Glenn is angry, "Well I hope you negotiated a better deal for yourself than you *did for me!*" as he walks towards his office.

Arturo replies blandly, "10%, it's the standard fee on these types of deals. These Latino Generals have conferences where they party together; they gladly take care of each other. And don't forget, he is going to have to kick money down the line to his officers. And also, up to General Garcia and the Presidents of Mexico and Pecuador."

Glenn grudgingly says, "Alright, have him transport everybody north towards the United States border. Give me the info for the wire transfer." As he enters his office he calls his Swiss banker, effects the million-dollar transfer, and then tells him that he has some precious metals to deposit and asks how to do it. The banker says he will have an Assayer go there, and value it together with him, and then we will immediately deposit that amount of cash into your account. It will be insured at that moment. He will personally take the precious metal for processing. Needless to say, this must all remain very confidential. Glenn makes arrangements for the Assayer to be on the next morning's train.

Then the Professor's wife barges into his office saying, "The Rabbi is telling my husband that the Mexican Military can't leave until they get orders from their General. That everybody is loaded into the vehicles, but they're just sitting there. The Military didn't even bring them any water. Everybody is crying from the sand in their eyes."

Glenn says, "I believe they'll be moving shortly."

They walk back together to her cabin where the Professor is on the phone. He had been somewhat relieved speaking to his brother, but once again his blood pressure is going up as evident by his flushed face. As they enter the door, they hear a sudden loud commotion over the phone and engines roaring and a loud squawking over a short-wave radio, followed by "Si Générale". The convoy is moving, and the Professor's wife is looking at Glenn with a mystical appreciation for his clairvoyance.

XXIV

❖

GRINGO SUCKER

The Mexican Military takes the Pilgrims to Paredon, a beach resort town that is directly west. They drop them off in the middle of town and pull away from them. Senora Luz Aquilar's husband grabs their baby away from her as she exits the bus. He then viciously slaps her in the face with his free hand and continues slapping her in the back, steering her towards their car.

A woman approaches the Rabbi saying that she is from the local Chamber of Commerce and can offer them rooms for up to three days at the local hotels. Their HERO, the Mexican General who rescued the Pilgrims, had instructed her to meet with the Rabbi. The town had been evacuated because of its proximity to the Whirlwind; so, it was glad for this sudden business. Glenn thinks, "I instructed Arturo to transport them North towards the US border and further away from the Whirlwind - not South. As luck would have it, they went WEST instead; probably because the military commander was able to arrange extra profits for himself. Now that thief is being praised on international new as a charitable hero for rescuing the Pilgrims. - *Stealing my charity!*"

The Professor's phone rings again, and he is informed by his brother that they have been abandoned. His wife wrestles the phone from the Professor who is livid with rage, she pushes it into Glenn's reluctant hands. Soon he is in conversation with the woman saying that she'll need $1 million deposit into her personal account to provide food and lodgings for all these people for three days, in the meantime hopefully they will be able to make arrangements of their own. Glenn tries to negotiate quietly with her on the Professor's phone – this is much more than the advertised rates; but she demands $1 million paid in advance. He is sure that Arturo had spread the word: 'they have a Gringo sucker on the line, and he can be bled at $1 million per stab.' Glenn finally acquiesces. He goes back to his office and has his bank wire the money to her.

After his phone call with his brother, the Professor is relaxed and is comforted by his wife and children. Meanwhile Rabbi Jerry is praying and fasting seeking God's guidance. He knows that God has chosen his Pilgrims. He is certain that God could not have abandoned them.

The next day the Professor announces that the Pilgrims are all staying with his brother, and he insists upon paying for his brother's folly. Glenn insists, "Do not worry about it; anyway, you were right. I didn't know what to do with that centrifuged gold, so I just ended up throwing it on the pile. It's worthwhile to spend it on these religious fanatical Pilgrims. After all, there are children amongst them that need to be cared for."

Meanwhile the Rabbi is praying and fasting, seeking God's guidance. He knows that he and his Hassidic/Christian flock are 'God's Chosen People'. His faith is beyond any challenge: God could not have forsaken them.

~   {Anything that can go wrong will go wrong.}   ~

Things are getting back to normal when the Professor approaches Glenn saying, "My brother the Rabbi called me again. It appears that the best they can do is get transportation to the United States border where they will have to go through a lengthy immigration process, to verify that they are in fact citizens and that they have every right to cross the border. Needless to say, the immigrants that are waiting will not be happy with the pilgrims going to the head of the line. And, in an act of religious devotion, they had burned their passports when they left the United States, believing they were soon entering God's Kingdom." He still feels compelled to rescue his brother.

The Professor's wife comes running after him saying, "There is that Covid19 cruise ship that was stuck on the West Coast. It was loaded with passengers who were not allowed to disembark until just yesterday. Now that ship is stuck in the ocean with a skeleton crew, as most of the crew also disembarked. We could possibly have it pick up the Pilgrims and take them back to the States. They should have no problem getting through customs; it is well known who they are as they are all over the news." The Professor looks at her and shrugs his shoulders shaking his head negatively. She insists, "At least it's a solution. You can still bring your brother here from the States whenever you want."

Glenn instructs her, "Try getting that ship on the ship to shore radio. Don't let anybody else get involved other than the Captain. I want to speak to him privately."

She goes to Glenn's office and works on the communication through the computer; within an hour she has it set up. Glenn tries promoting the Pilgrims as a service to the Captain. "These people will be able to handle all of the custodial cleansing – the disinfecting of your ship - do all the laundry – do all the cooking. These Pilgrims will be rescuing your ship, they'll make it commercially operational very quickly. All you have to do is pick them up from Paredon Mexico and drop them anywhere in the United States."

"That sounds okay, I can be there by tomorrow afternoon. They can board after I receive $1 million paid into my personal account."

Glenn is trying to contain his outrage, "How is it possible that this new provider is also asking for $1 million? Are all these people in touch with each other through some kind of *'sucker's network'* that they subscribe to?" Glenn argues heatedly, but the Captain is firm. He points out that he has to buy food, and more fuel. Glenn insists, "There should be a 10% discount for the standard finder's fee that all you Latinos charge for referrals."

The Captain says, "I am Greek, not Latino: and the price is *still $1 million!"* Glenn makes the wire transfer. The ship arrives off the coast of Paredon, Mexico and announces that it's available to be boarded. There are no docks there for a large cruise ship. The Chamber of Commerce lady is back in the middle of things, she is on the phone with the Professor again. His wife wrestles the phone away and runs it to Glenn, explaining that now they must pay someone to ferry the Pilgrims out to the ship. He refuses to talk to her saying to get the Rabbi back on the phone again. The

Rabbi says she was going to hire local party fishing boats to ferry them to the ship, which is only a short distance offshore.

Glenn tells him, "Go to the local bank and pick up $25,000 which I am wiring there, and take it in cash –personally - to the docks with all his people and hand out the money yourself. Do not pay more than $10 per person. They should be glad to get the money; but you will have to negotiate."

"Oh, believe me, I know how to negotiate!" The Rabbi replies. By 6 o'clock that evening the Pilgrims are completely loaded on the ship and Glenn is surprised to find that the Rabbi got them there for $7.50 per person on average, no charge for the children, so that he has about $10,000 left over. Glenn is irritated that the Rabbi is a better negotiator than he is. The Rabbi talks to the Captain and arranges for his Pilgrims to start cooking and cleaning and doing what needs to be done on board the ship with the direction of the Captain's skeleton crew.

Then he discusses the course they are taking. "Straight North, to the US Pacific coast into any port that will allow me to disembark you all."

The Rabbi asks, "Would you do a service to God and give my religious Pilgrims a final opportunity to worship; please, allow them one more view of God's Whirlwind." He pauses waiting expectantly . . . "The Whirlwind certainly can't do any harm to a large ship like this, all my Pilgrims survived its impact, and we were in its direct path, in the open desert."

"Will God be paying extra for this service?" After a little more pleading and hopeless haggling, the Rabbi waves that $10,000 in cash under the Captain's nose. The ship turns 180° and heads south. The Rabbi is up praying all night. He knows God has chosen him to lead these Pilgrims, God would not abandon them.

The next morning Bernie joins Glenn walking to the kitchen for breakfast. "What? No, extended honeymoon?" Glenn smiles in response. "By the way, my Mother Nature's email received an Astronomy News Flash saying that the CME has just destroyed the SOHO - Sun Observatory Satellite."

"What an unlucky break. Its orbit around the Earth took it through the Sun's CME blast? I thought the SOHO died years ago; it wasn't supposed to last this long . . ."

"That's true" Bernie replies, "but they were able to upload new software that revived it, including *pseudo gyroscope* replacements. They have been having financial problems since its budget expired years ago."

"Too bad, we could have donated to it; it's dead now . . ."

"Yeah, too bad. It was monitoring the Sun 24/7 for a quarter century; we learned a lot from it."

Glenn is puzzled and turns towards the east's glowing sunrise beyond his crater's rim; he sees an **unusually bright vertical streak** piercing through the clouds. "What? SOHO monitored the Sun even while it was orbiting on the dark side of the Earth?"

"No, ah . . ." Bernie gently corrects Glenn's assumption, "Ah . . . It doesn't orbit the Earth; SOHO orbits the Sun at the L1- Lagrange Point, about a million miles above the Earth – stuck gravitationally between the Earth and the Sun, on the plane of the equatorial/ecliptic."

"Really? We saw that the CME got deflected onto the path of our launched barrels, we saw it exploding our barrels . . . which is far to the south, away from the equatorial plane; millions of miles below the plane of the ecliptic. I stopped the launching of the nuclear waste to end that pathway, and keep the CME away from the Earth." Glenn's stomach churns with this revelation.

Bernie replies cheerfully, "No, it exploded the last of the barrels two days ago. I have it recorded on the DVR so we can watch it. I connected the telescope's monitor into our TV's channel 12. Jane and I also programmed it so that you can operate the telescope from your computer in your office."

Glenn speculates, "Bernie must have gotten it wrong; it's *NOT the CME:* he means Virginia's Big Syphon2 must have destroyed the SOHO Satellite; it swirls from the Earth to the Sun on the equatorial/ecliptic plane; directly through that L1-Lagrange point. The CME is far south of that, millions of miles below SOHO's orbit. It was Virginia's blasting the toxic waste barrels from the Arizona Big Cannon that started up the second 'Big Syphon' on the plain of the ecliptic/equatorial: the L1 Point is a million miles into that path – that's where the Soho Satellite was destroyed . . ." Glenn ponders, "Therefore, that means the CME was millions of miles south of the SOHO Satellite . . . ? Obviously, it can't be both the CME and the 'Big Syphon2'; it must be the Big Syphon2's Whirlwind that destroyed the SOHO Satellite." He doesn't know why, but the hair on the back of his neck is aroused by goosebumps. He's enduring a nerve-wracking apprehension, "Is it because I'll have to ask the Professor about this. Or is it just this strange condition of being married ~ and becoming a father? Or is it the thought of CIA Jane having access to my computers?" After breakfast he has Bernie show him that video of his last launched barrels being destroyed. He resolves to use the telescope tonight and test its remote operation from his computer. He'll spy on the CME and verify its location as it passes millions of miles below the Earth. He gives a dismissive glance towards the east's glowing sunrise, beyond his crater's rim; at that ***unusually bright vertical streak*** piercing through the clouds.

XXV

A TIME OF RECKONING
AND JUDGEMENT

That same morning on the upper deck of that Covid19 Ship, a lonely figure is stepping to the beat of his chanting, while clutching his prayer shawl around his shoulders, and caressing his prayer beads. His whole being is consumed with the fervent chanting of his prayers. He hadn't slept in days. He is looking east and, beyond the horizon, sees *a thin brilliant line* bursting through the clouds, rising-up above the sunrise. He remembers:

> 'The *FINGER OF GOD* etched the Ten Commandments
> in the presence of Moses.'
> Then his eyes narrow into an intensely piercing, but
> celestial gaze:
> 'As far as the inhabitants of Earth are concerned, the
> second coming of Christ will not be a joyous event
> ~ but one of *terrible judgment!'*

Then he remembers:

> My brother predicted: 'The Whirlwind will cross the
> Panama Canal onto Summit Golf Course which borders it'.

Then, his celestial gaze expands to one of *profound enlightenment*. At one third of the way up, ***that bright line*** is changing *into a finger*, turning up, it is *turning towards him*, then it stops in a heavenly iridescent glow:

"It is the finger of God – **and** *˷*

He is pointing at me! ˷

GOD has chosen ME!! ˷

We Are GOD'S CHOSEN People!!!"

An elation spreads across his weary face as he knows that his fasting and prayers have definitely been answered . . .

The ship is nearing the Panama Canal, still heading south. The Captain has been enjoying his pending wealthy retirement: he has been drinking heavily. The Rabbi asks him to take us through the Panama Canal. The Captain is not enamored with the Rabbi's glowing radiance saying, "It's going *to cost you!* The last time I went thru the canal they charged $483,000

˷   better get your **rich friend** on the Phone!"
The Rabbi serenely replies,
"Fear not, God will provide your just rewards . . ."

The drunken Captain is thinking of charging another million dollars and has his first mate steer the ship east, into the canal, ignoring the red stop lights. He is not concerned that there are no ships ahead of him, nor the fact that there are no personnel patrolling the canal's entrance; no one to hook-up to the trains that pull the ships through the canal. They had been evacuated in anticipation of the Whirlwind. The Rabbi assembles all his Pilgrims on the top deck, preparing them to disembark. They start singing 'The Battle Hymn of the Republic': 'Mine eyes have seen ♫♪ the glory of the coming of the Lord.' Rabbi Jerry had studied the map and the weather predictions of the Whirlwind. He concluded that it should cross the canal between Summit Park and Summit Golf Course on the south side of the canal; east of the Centennial Bridge. The ship stops moving upon approaching the closed lock. The Rabbi seizes the opportunity and has his Pilgrims deploy the gangway, then leads them to shore while singing "His truth is marching on, Glory, Glory Hallelujah." They follow the Rabbi southwest, away from the ship's crew, who are screaming at them. In response, they change their song, singing sweetly:

♩♩ "Yes Jesus loves me . . ." ♩♩ then adding emphatically,
"NOT YOU! – We are Born ♫ Again Christians – ♩♩

♫ Yes, Jesus loves me . . . ***NOT YOU!!*** - we
are ***GOD'S CHOSEN PEOPLE!!!***

Yes, Jesus loves me . . . ***NOT YOU!!*** ♫ The Bible tells me ♩♩ so . . ."
♫
The last of the Pilgrims brush by the ship's crew in a parade, now singing, ♫ 'Onward Christian Soldiers.' The Rabbi leads them west onto the main road. They march onto Avenue Omar Torrijos Herrera Street and then directly south for an hour onto the Summit Golf Course.

Faux News Reporter Paura Pingim is with her crew in Panama City. She refuses to evacuate as she wants to catch the wrath of the Whirlwind on live TV. They are listening to the report of the SOHO Satellite's destruction by the CME, when they get word of the Covid19 ship illegally entering the canal. Then they find out that it has the Pilgrims on board. They climb into their satellite trucks and speed towards the canal, hoping to video them on live TV. Maybe this time there will be less dust and they'll see the Pilgrims being hurled around in the air. They catch up with them as they are marching south towards the golf-course. She is commenting on live TV and videoing them as they slowly drive along beside them. They are shouting questions loudly over the chorus of Pilgrims who are now prayerfully singing the ♩♩ 'Ave Maria'.

Rabbi Jerry Natzinger announces, "I have fulfilled God's mission - We have arrived at God's Gateway - We will see His Pearly Gates in 11 minutes." They all kneel and begin to pray.

It is 10 minutes before noon, the latest predictions have it crossing the Panama Canal immediately before Summit Park.

Back at the Hacienda, the Professor is surprised to see his brother is on TV again, "He's in *Panama?!?* He's marching across a golf-course, with his 2000 Pilgrims following him . . . They were supposed to be *on the* **Covid19 ship** in route to **the U S A!**" He calls his wife and children to watch the TV with him.

The Professor's youngest daughter, watching her grandmother on live TV, says, "Why is Grandma singing that *Christian song* - doesn't she know that *she's a Jew?*"

The reporters in Panama follow them onto the golf-course while asking harassing questions. Faux News' Paura Pingram asks, "Aren't you a Jew? Why are you singing that song praising Jesus?"

In response, the Pilgrims resume their song, singing sweetly:

"Yes, Jesus loves me . . ." then adding emphatically ***"NOT YOU!!*** –

We are Born Again Christians –

Yes, Jesus loves me . . . ***NOT YOU!!*** –

we are ***GOD'S CHOSEN PEOPLE!!!***

Yes, Jesus loves me . . . ***NOT YOU!!*** –

The Bible tells me so . . ."

And then Paura Pingram yells over their boisterous singing, "Didn't you zealots learn from your prior experience in the Mexican Desert . . . God *did not want you* before; what makes you think that God *wants you now?!?*"

XXVI

❖

?THE FINGER OF GOD?

Further East, off Panama's Caribbean coastline on the distant horizon can be seen a hot disturbance in the clouds: they are glowing radiantly gold, almost too bright to bare. Looking out at the ocean one can see that its surface is *terribly disturbed*; then there is a *tremendous heat wave.* The nearby jungle suddenly becomes a shrieking cacophony of squealing monkeys. Within seconds we can see the surface of the ocean is *actually boiling* and swirling up into a glowing hot mist. Then there is a loud bubbling noise mixed with *steamy screeching.* The Whirlwind comes ashore, the beach's sand melts into glass, everything ahead of it is igniting. Further ahead of the Whirlwind in the San Lorenzo Protected Jungle, the trees abruptly lean westward away from the blast of the heatwave. Then their branches reach up, as if in shocking trauma. Then row after row, going westward, they suddenly *explode into flames.* This firestorm crosses the land, over Gatun Lake, boiling its surface. God's Whirlwind follows behind its burning heatwave, its fiery, hot swirling winds blowing outward in every direction. It blasts onto the land then across the canal igniting Summit Municipal Park.

The Faux News Paula Pingram shouts to her satellite truck crew, "I *cannot believe* our live broadcast of the *plight of these Pilgrims,* is being **pre-empted** by some *fucking weather announcer's* breaking news. How could this bitch possibly have a *better story?!? Wait!* She is warning us to get away from here ***immediately!***" She puts her on speaker:

'Somehow the CME has been funneled into the Whirlwind's Big Syphon and *its million-degree plasma* is **incinerating everything within 5-miles of its path!** It's moving around the Earth at a *thousand miles-per-hour! Get out of its way! – quick!!*'

They look up to the east and see a towering *streak of brilliance* going up out of sight: it is coming **right at them.**

She is shouting, "Keep the *fucking cameras rolling* - continue the live broadcasting . . . *you pussies!*" as they all frantically jump into their vehicles. They start driving Northwest towards the Canal Bridge, they know it's their only escape route. In the east, they can see the Whirlwind is a giant swirl of *glowing hot steam*. Then Paura Pingram tells her Faux News satellite truck crew, "This is our famous *'Oh the Humanity'* **opportunity!** Make a *fucking U-turn – NOW!!*" As their driver reluctantly obeys, she commands, "Get my face on a close-up." Then dramatically announces to her TV audience, "Our satellite truck crew has bravely decided to return to our continuous live reporting of these Pilgrims. The Bible states, 'The Lord Giveth, and The Lord Taketh . . .'" As her crew apprehensively gasp in terror.

The Professor is in his cabin, glued to the TV; watching the troublesome exploits of his brother, when he hears the weather announcer's news report:

'Somehow the CME has been funneled into the Whirlwind's Big Syphon and *its million-degree plasma* is **incinerating everything within 5-miles of its path!** It's moving around the Earth at a *thousand miles-per-hour! Get out of its way! – quick!!*'

Astounded, the Professor ponders, *"Why should that happen?!?* The CME blew out from the Sun's South Polar region, now it's up to the plane of the ecliptic . . . around our **Equatorial region!?!** What made it change its direction? That's a long way from its *original projected path?* I know there's a magnetic quality to the CME's plasma, it's polarity might interact locally, but not to this degree. It blew up the last mag-lev launched barrel days ago: 50million miles away and millions of miles below the Earth's south-pole. It should not be attracted to the weak magnetism of Glenn's Whirlwind - *if any?!?* I guess even its water vapor and our atmosphere's molecules moving thru the solar wind would create a magnetic-field, like electrons moving thru a wire; but nothing strong enough to divert a *high-speed blast of a CME?!?"* His searching scientific mind relinquishes control to his emotions. "They're telling the reporters to get away – *quick . . .*

What about <u>MY MOTHER</u> AND MY BROTHER'S FAMILY!?!"

At the same time Glenn is in his cabin lamenting his extorted donation of $3,025,000 to Rabbi Natzinger's Pilgrims while intently watching the live TV from Panama. He hears:

> 'Somehow the CME has been funneled into the Whirlwind's Big Syphon and *its million-degree plasma* is **incinerating everything within 5-miles of its path!** It's moving around the Earth at a *thousand miles-per-hour! Get out of its way! – **quick!!***'

"What **the *FUCK!?!*"** Glenn says in disbelief, "The CME came from the Sun's Southern Corona, and deflected northerly to my launched barrels, now it has deflected again and has come all this way north – millions of miles to our equatorial region - to *join the Whirlwind's Big Syphon?!?* Those are two - distinctly separate – phenomena: separated by millions of miles . . . This ***FUCKING CME*** has a **mind of its own!?!** "
Then paraphrasing the Faux News reporter, **"And The Sun Taketh!"**

Everybody at the Hacienda is watching as Elena had spread the news of the Professor's loco Rabbi brother and his Pilgrims aboard the Covid19 Luxury Cruise Liner. Little Ricardo (the Hacienda's 'Town Crier') runs to each cabin laughing and yelling, "The ship went in the *wrong direction!* It was supposed to go North to the USA, instead it went south and entered the Panama Canal! But; the *stupid gringos* - the *Canal **is closed!*** Turn to channel 2 and watch it on live TV." They all share his ribald humor and start watching the frantic chase on live TV as the Faux News satellite trucks speedily return to these Born-Again Pilgrims and their Live Broadcast.

The CME has penetrated down to the Earth, and it is spreading its main ingredient – *hot plasma* – propelling it in every direction. Instantly *boiling away* the water in the locks, it continues across the canal. The Covid19 ship is beyond its flaming pathway. Even so, the *heat radiates ahead* of the Whirlwind. The ship is at first *enveloped in the hot steam* of the canal's evaporation, and then it's *metal skin blisters*, and then it *bursts into flames* as it *flounders and falls* against the wall of the canal with *incredible metallic screeching*. On the bridge with the first mate, the Captain is mercifully too drunk to realize that the water buoying their ship *is boiling away*. They are holding on for dear life, watching through the *steamy mist* as the deck and gunnels before them *are blistering*, then *warping*, and then *bursting into flames*. The windows shatter and *pulverized glass rips into them*. The heat ignites their bodies in an instant. *Screaming in painful* shock, while running a few frantic steps,

they collapse –
  dead;–
    their *brains baking* –
      their *eyes boiling* away –
        their clothing and *flesh burning* into a mix of spitting flames.

As the Whirlwind approaches Summit National Park, the Pilgrims look up and see in the distance:
    a towering tornado, –
      a radiant golden glare piercing through a thick mist, –
        swirling all the way up to the Sun. –
And what is below that? –
    Is it just flames and smoke? –
      Or is it the caustic, pungent fire and brimstone of Satan ––
        advancing rapidly onto the golf-course.

They're all kneeling and praying following the lead of their Rabbi; the hot wind is getting more intense . . .
    - But the Rabbi is smiling . . .
      - He is breathing deeply while turning to gaze upon his flock –
        - His evangelical passion has his face aglow with *radiance . . .*

- His joyful smile becomes **insanely *maniacal* . . .**

- and now, the Rabbi is . . .

>> *!!LAUGHING!!* <<

~ His wife and children beside him and his mother behind him . . .

~ . . . they are *all* ***laughing hysterically!!***

~

It's an unpredictable burst of sudden, ***jubilant laughter***; everybody behind them is also ***LAUGHING!*** Looking at each other and then looking up to the finger of God glaring brilliantly in front of them. It does not even hurt their eyes.

They all turn, looking upon each other with the facial expression of tremendous open *laughter!* It is a ***RAPTUROUS JOY*** they *all share!!* Their hands, extending up to God, ignite into flames as their laughter continues. Their ecstatic wet eyes are reflecting those dancing fingers of flame as their exuberant faces ignite. Row after row of 2000 devout Pilgrims ignite in that same ***rapturous joy*** . . . And then the Rabbi and his family, followed by row after row of Pilgrims, collapse into a burning heap and become part of that pungent smoke . . .

The Professor watches while trying to call all the numbers he had to get in touch with his brother.

His wife and children are watching as the Pilgrims start laughing hysterically; she sees them sharing that *Rapturous laugh.* She succumbs to that involuntary urge, joining the Pilgrims on TV, prayerfully raising their hands up to God. But then she jerks her hands down as she watches the laughing Pilgrim's hands - extended up to God – ignite . . . and then their faces . . . and then their bodies – the field of religious devotees turning into a flaming heap of steaming mist . . .

{'OH - THE HORROR!!!'}

The Professor runs from his cabin screaming . . . his wife chases after him – the children after her - screaming and crying as they flee into the desert . . .

running far away from everybody . . .

from everything . . .

The Faux News crew in their satellite trucks are broadcasting live video with their telescopic lenses and directional microphones, they can see the distant conflagrations as they are commenting. Then the heat hits them, too. At first, they also begin laughing uncontrollably, but then their laughter changes to screaming in horror as they are ignited, and then their crying faces erupt in flames, and then they cease to exist.

Their live TV transmission ends as the satellite trucks explode into flames. The Whirlwind continues setting everything on fire. It's crossing over the International Airport - flames bursting out of Jet Planes - and then it rips through Panama City igniting everything. All those people who refused to evacuate are also enjoying a good laugh; and then scream as their eyes boil away.

The Whirlwind's Fiery Syphon proceeds into the Pacific Ocean, boiling a 5-mile radius of its surface with its million- degree temperature, as it continues westward at 1000 mph.

Glenn can NOT understand it.

News commentators around the world can NOT understand it.

Were these mostly Christians, truly *'Born Again'* into **God's Rapture?!?**

Did they truly see the face of God?

Did they experience such *joyous Rapture* that they **erupted into laughter?**

He saw it, live on TV - they could NOT contain their heavenly joy . . .

Now, after the world has witnessed it, there are more Pilgrims deciding that *THIS* is the

TIME of the RAPTURE

NOW is the time to go to God!!!

Religious zealots are recruiting on TV: 'We are not going to evacuate - we are not going to hide from *God's Whirlwind*; we are going to take whatever transportation possible *to intercept it!* And then, we will join hands and

joyfully enter into - *God's – Rapturous – Fiery - Whirlwind!!'*

Glenn collapses into a chair, muttering, "This shit is really *getting out of hand . . .*"

XXVII

❖

A VINDICTIVE GOD?

Elena shakes Glenn from his catatonic reverie; she is pointing out the window at the Professor running far out into the desert with his wife dragging behind pulling his arm, and all 3 children holding hands and running far behind them. Glenn says, "Si, he could be having a stroke or a *heart-attack!*" Elena shakes her head angrily. Glenn responds, "He just saw his mother and his brother's whole family being burned alive; his wife has got *to calm him down* somehow!"

Elena yells, *"No,* it is not safe for them to run around out there; there are **poison serpentas!"**

"I think they got bigger problems than snakes . . ."

"No, Gringos don't know how to walk out there. We follow behind each other in a straight line so snakes can move away from us. The snakes don't know which way to go to escape the Gringo's running feet, so they get scared and bite them. Go get the truck and bring them back – *PRONTO!!"*

"But the snakes don't come out in the daytime, il sol es mucho *mucho caliente!*" he tries to reason with her using his feeble Spanish. "You **don't understand** . . . That's *live news* on the TV, it's the **Professor's family**; it's *not a movie!"*

Elena *slaps him* on the back then **pushes him** towards the door shouting, *"Go! - Go!!* - The serpentas get scared hearing feet above them and want to escape . . . Take *the truck! Via RAPIDO!!"*

Glenn complains, "Alright, okay . . . Don't push me – you stupid, *fucking – hysterical . . .* **midget** *bitch!"* Then he mutters through clenched teeth as he stomps to the truck, "I ought to *smack the shit out* of you; you scrawny *little fucking **spic***, you think you're gonna **push me** *around!?!* I'm *twice* **your** *size!!*

The 3 children had been holding hands running far behind their parents, unable to keep up. Then the 12-year- old left the other's hands go and running faster left them behind, her feet pounding the hard ground following in the footsteps of her distraught parents. The 9-year-old sister tried to keep up, letting go of the young boy. But the 7-year- old boy couldn't keep up, even though he tried, with tears streaming down his face. He was running with mostly closed wet eyes and wobbling one side to the other.

The 15-inch mountain 🐍 eyelash viper is dark skinned with flecks of a lighter grey, and a diamond shaped head.

They spend their solitary days under the sand and prefer to come out only at night to hunt insects, and small animals – lizards, mice, whatever. The thundering feet above collapses the sand around its shallow snake hole, and it flees in panic. It dodges its way between the heavier vibrations, inadvertently moving towards the receding weaker vibrations. But then the weakest vibration suddenly moves towards it. The serpenta recoils . . . then *strikes,* **sinking its fangs** into the warm flesh under a cotton sock, just above a tennis shoe. - The little boy *screams in shocking pain*, turns and limps away as the snake withdraws its fangs. It follows after the boy, but then senses a different resonating vibration and fearfully scurries back to its snake hole.

Glenn had seen them separate from each other and saw them spread apart as he was driving the truck towards the Professor while thinking, "I just got married and the *bitch is pushing me around* already!" He breathes deeply then switches to practicing his argument to calm down the Professor and get him back to the Hacienda, "It's not safe out here and your children won't return without you." Then he sees the boy trailing far behind everyone. The boy abruptly turns with an unexpected frantic motion of his arms, then he is suddenly running askew while dragging his right leg.

Glenn leans on the horn and steers towards the boy. He has gotten everyone's attention and then they see their little boy. They see he is running further away from all of them and that he is painfully limping.

Then he falls to the ground. Glenn screeches to a sudden stop beside him and jumps out of the truck. He sees the crying boy's bloody sock and kneels down next to him asking, "What happened big guy, did you hurt yourself?" Glenn pulls the bloody sock down and sees the pair of telltale oozing fang holes.

{'OH-THE HORROR!!!'}

Glenn's *excruciating emotions* are resisting a *scream* as he turns his face to the sky *pulling on his hair* with both hands . . . "AND TAKETH AGAIN!" Then he regains control of himself and gives a quick look around. He lifts the boy, peering over his small body, *fearfully looking* for any sign that *the snake* might still be *attacking*. He puts him into the passenger seat, rummages through the glove compartment and removes the snake bite kit. There is a vial and a syringe, but he doesn't know how much to use. He fills it halfway and injects it into the crying boy's ankle between the 2 fang punctures. He runs to the driver's side and climbs in, beeping the horn frantically. Then he speeds back towards the Hacienda as he glances at the rear-view mirror, watching the boy's family. The parents each pick-up a daughter and are running back towards the Hacienda.

All the workers are coming for lunch, but then run away in fright yelling, *"Loco Gringo!"* as Glenn speeds into the kitchen area and slides to a screeching stop.

Elena is first to get the door open as Glenn shouts to Sancho, *"Serpenta,* **snake bite**, *the little boy* . . . How much anti-venom – medicina - do I give him; I gave him half . . . is it too much?"

Sancho asks, "How big was the snake?"

"How *the fuck* do I know!!"

"Ask the boy!"

Glenn lifts him out and lays him on the table asking gently, "How big was the snake that bit you?" The boy betrays *severe fright* as if he didn't know he had been bitten. Elena hugs the boy reassuring him in Spanish that he's okay.

Sancho asks, "Should I suck the poison blood out of his foot?"

Glenn wails "I already *injected* his foot with *the medicine!* . . . **Fuck this!!**" He calls General Garcia on his cell phone, as Elena instructs Juan to take the truck and pick-up the Professor's family pointing to them running in the desert. Glenn hears a firm - Senior Glenn . . . - but quickly interrupts shouting "*Snake Bite*, small boy's ankle, about 6 years old. **Fly Doctor here!** Tell him to call me, I injected him with half a syringe of anti-venom; I don't know what **else to do?!?**"

"Right away." He replies gently then adds, "Put a tourniquet below his knee." Elena is already instructing Sancho to do that. Glenn collapses into a chair; the color is draining from his face as tears well up into his eyes.

> Within a minute, the phone in Glenn's hand buzzes. The Doctor says, "A nurse from the airport is flying there now, make sure the runway is clear and turn the lights on, even though it is daytime. I will follow as soon as I can get to the airport." Glenn explains what they did so far, the Doctor says, "Good, give him the rest of the syringe on the out-side of the fang holes. Keep him calm and let his leg hang down till the nurse gets there."

Glenn sends Sancho to turn the runway lights on. Then he runs towards the approaching truck waving it down. He explains, "A nurse and Doctor are flying in, I have already given your boy the anti-venom, applied a tourniquet and I am now going to inject the rest of the anti-venom at 2 other locations as the Doctor instructed. But the Doctor said to keep him calm; so, don't *get him excited!* No **screaming or crying!!**" Now they begin to realize that their boy had been bitten by a poisonous snake. They all scream and start crying all over again. Glenn restricts them from running to him, saying, "Dry your eyes and stay calm - and keep *him calm* so his heart doesn't *pump the poison* to his vital organs.

Glenn runs the half-filled syringe back to the crying boy who is being comforted by Elena's embrace. He injects the boy's ankle as his parents and sisters hesitantly approach him, feigning calm. The younger sister tells him, "You're okay now, we are here with you – so, you can stop crying now . . ."

He screams at her, "*It HURTS!!*" This comes as a shock to everybody; this need for a statement of the obvious. ~ Flabbergasted; they all try to conceal their astonishingly flagrant laughter. Now the boy bursts into dramatic, emotional wailing as his mother takes him and hugs him close to her.

The air force jet arrives with the nurse, all the workmen are excited to see a jet landing nearby. They are surprised to see such a quick response. They all know of someone who died from a snake bite. They doubt that a Pecuadorian child would have been given the same attention. The Professor carries his son into their cabin with the nurse and pilot following, carrying medical bags and commenting that the swollen ankle is already starting to turn blackish. They get the boy on an I V Drip and induce a sedative. The boy falls unconscious, then the nurse cuts his ankle across the snake bite, allowing it to bleed freely. Guilt engulfs the Professor; he cannot control himself. He turns from his son, to his daughters, then to his wife, runs out of the cabin, cursing and crying; then composes himself, goes back inside, and then repeats the whole traumatic episode. The pilot leaves with a blood sample and returns in an hour with the Doctor who tells Glenn he's been in contact with the nurse, and they fear the boy's foot may have to be amputated. The boy should go to the hospital; but, with the Covid-19 infections there, maybe it's better to keep him here. Glenn runs to his office sobbing, "Please God, don't make me have to tell that to *the Professor's family.*" Elena follows him, then hugs him; trying to comfort him while not comprehending about the possible amputation. After a minute he composes himself and instructs her to take food to the Professor's cabin.

Half an hour later the Doctor burst into Glenn's office saying, "I don't know *what to do* with your Professor Natzi?!? He has been prancing around crying and blaming his wife and daughters for leaving the boy. He keeps shouting that **he killed** his mother and brother's family . . . I didn't even mention the *amputation yet!* He has got to be sedated, he threw all the food out the cabin door, saying how could anybody eat with their son like that. I can see his blood pressure is soaring, though he won't let me take it. He could have a stroke or a heart attack; anything can happen. I want to start draining his son's ankle, but he won't let me. The pilot tried to make him sit down; I thought they were going to fight." Glenn looks at him perplexed. "I sent the pilot back to get blood for transfusion . . . Well, he's your employee; *maybe he'll listen to you.*"

Glenn says, "That'll **be the day!**" Then he adds, "We will just *upset him more* if we try to insist."

The Doctor stresses, "He couldn't be *any worse*, something has got to be done - **NOW!**"

Just then Mrs. Nazi comes running and shouting, followed by her daughters, then Sancho. "You got to help me; he is going crazy. He pulled the girls from the cabin by their hair and then he kicked me in my legs, pushing me out so he could be alone with our son. He's muttering a Jewish **Death** Prayer. I'm afraid he's going to *kill himself **and my son**!* He wants to join his *mother and brother!!* **What are we going to do?!?"**

They all start walking quickly back to her cabin. Glenn is asking the Doctor if he can stick him with a tranquilizer.

He replies, "I'll need 1 minute to prepare it." as he runs ahead.

"Can all you girls hug him and sit on top of him, put all your weight on him, make him lay down?" Glenn is formulating the plan as he speaks. "I'll lay across all of you and grab hold of his arm. Sancho: then you grab his wrist and pull his arm down flat so the Doctor can stick a needle in it."

"The Head Rabbis in New York City were teaching the elder members to slaughter animals the humane way," Mrs. Natzi crying explains, "just in case they may have to repeat the Masada procedure, where they mercifully stabbed their families rather than allowing them to be taken by the Romans. Rabbi Jerry refused to do it because it was too gloomy, and they should get beyond the holocaust horrors and embrace a positive future including a heavenly Resurrection." She pauses to catch her breath, sobbing, "My husband continued the instruction, stabbing a sheep, insisting that one day we may need an honorable exit from this world; that between Global-Warming, Gay-Pride and their fanatical liberalism – there may be no sanctuary."

The Doctor is outside the cabin kneeling next to his medical bag and other debris that the Professor had thrown out of the cabin. He is filling a syringe while looking up towards the Professor with fearful alarm. Then Sancho cries out, "Professor!" as they see him pushing the struggling nurse out of his cabin door with a big knife in his hand. She falls backwards to the ground.

"RUN! *NOW!!*" Glenn shouts, *"before he locks the door!"* Mrs. Nazi gasps in terror, then sprints ahead, followed by her daughters and Elena.

Glenn and Sancho, in a frightful panic, struggle to keep up. They all bust into the cabin before he can lock the door. His wife and Elena jump up on him as he is turning around, he drops the butcher knife growling with shocking anger; then his 2 daughters jump onto him as he falls backwards onto the floor. Then Glenn dives with all his weight, landing sideways across all of them and wraps his arm around the Professor's left bicep. He can't budge with all that weight across his torso. Sancho grabs his left wrist and leans all his weight back, stretching his arm out. The Doctor avoids the screaming Professor's kicking feet and kneels down and stabs the needle into his left forearm. The livid Professor gives one more violent kick, and then his eyes glaze over, and shut.

The Doctor says as they are getting up off the Professor, "You'll have to get another bed in here so that we can tie him down and keep him there - sedated for a long period of time. I'll probably have to amputate their son's foot, otherwise he may die." The mother hears that her son may lose his foot; she *is crushed*, reduced to a *whimpering mass* of devastation, as she craws over to his bed. She falls on her son pressing her lips to his pale cheek and *clinging* to him, soaking his face with her *sorrowful tears*. Thankfully, he is still sedated and is unaware of her emotions. Her two daughters are *desperately clinging* to her, their tears co-mingling with hers, *painfully demanding* to know what is going to happen to their brother. The Doctor introduces a fluid that is forcibly pumped through his veins and arteries below the tourniquet. Sancho gets busy getting another bed and arranging ropes to tie down the Professor.

The pilot returns with the blood supply and the Doctor immediately begins the transfusion directly into the boy's leg. In this short time, you could see some color return, the blackness is fading. The Doctor tickles the boys left foot and he wiggles it in response. Then he does the same to the affected foot and he wiggles it much less. The Doctor says, "That is a hopeful sign; but, his toes *didn't move!* Confident that he has gotten the bad venomous blood out of the boy's leg, he removes the tourniquet allowing the blood to flow naturally. The Doctor says he will stay with him through the night and see if the damage to his foot moves up his leg: if so, he'll have to amputate. Glenn runs to his own cabin in tears.

The workmen are amazed at all the attention this one child is getting. If Panama City was occupied by whites instead of Latinos; all this attention and medicos would be going there. Three separate flights: a nurse on one, Doctor on another, blood supplies on the third flight with a dedicated plane and pilot. And now the Doctor is going to spend the night with him along *with the nurse?!?* They know this would never happen for a Pecuadorian child. Their children get bit by snakes and if they're not near a hospital - *they die*; or have their *limbs cut off* - and **then they die!** When Sancho relays the Professor's condition, ("I had to tie him to the bed!") they smirk saying that only the rich can afford to be so emotional that they must be sedated; the poor people endure. Then Sancho relays the story that he heard Senora Natzi tell by way of explaining why her husband threw them out so violently; and why he had the knife. She told of the Masada Mountain fortress that the Jews held in ancient times that was surrounded by Roman soldiers and was about to be totally invaded. 'So rather than be taken as slaves and being viciously brutalized, raped and murdered, they chose to have their men kill everybody instead; using a knife in the same way that they mercifully kill their farm animals.' She feels that the Professor had chosen to do that rather than see his son wither away painfully, and then kill himself, so that he could then join his mother and brother. 'Although Jews do not believe in a heaven, as such, his brother sect did believe in the second coming of the prophet Jesus Christ, and then dwelling with him in the house of the Lord forever.'

Sancho then wryly comments, "That sounds like heaven to me. . ."

Elena takes control by directing CIA Jane and Virginia to do the cooking in the kitchen while she assists the nurse in the care of the child - and the Professor - and also his family . . .

XXVIII

❖

THE FIERY SYPHON

Millions of monkeys are dead; burnt to a crisp. Panama City & its airport are gone, smoldering debris is all that is left. Thousands of people have simply ceased to exist – but above all else, COMMERCE MUST CONTINUE. The U S Navy's Demolition Division tows the collapsed burnt-out hull of the Covid cruise liner out of the canal's lock and then sink it into the deep Pacific. There is no thought of rummaging through it. Bridges over the Canal are mere stick figurines - macabre imitations of modern art. Firefighters, military and volunteers rush into the Fiery Syphon's burning trail of devastation trying to minimize the damage. Too soon, the remaining heat was unbearable, they had to wait for night fall. Also, road and train track maintenance workers follow them to quickly repair the infrastructure that was burned and melted in the horrendous heat of the Fiery Syphon. They try to treat the few survivors who were far enough away who only got skin burns from the heat. All the injured animals are immediately shot dead as there is no provision for their recovery. The Gusher-Spray will help with the next high-tide on the Pacific coast, but it's not enough to squelch the fires entirely.

Rapture Pilgrims show up in small villages in Africa, letting villagers know about God's Fiery Whirlwind; inviting them to join the Rapture. Then there is a mad effort to flee. They are pissed that their government had not informed them to evacuate. Some people don't go the full 25 miles away from its predicted center and instead of instantly catching on fire and burning to death – ***they bake.***

Now that the Fiery Syphon is terrorizing the world, all nuclear shipments to Pecuador are cancelled, as well as other shipping. Only the religious fanatics aren't afraid of the Whirlwind's Fiery Syphon. They want to experience the Joyous Rapture and go to God just as the Jewish Rabbi did with his Born-Again Christian flock. It is burning a path through some Malaysian Islands and across Africa; a five-mile-wide trail of total destruction of all civilized and forested areas. Deserts are turned to glass. Beyond the 5 miles, fires are raging. Glenn is torn between blaming Virginia for restarting his Big Cannon in the Southwest of the states, blaming fate for restarting his Big Syphon, then blaming himself for its creation in the first place, AND blaming a nonexistent God for taunting him with humanity's destruction. "And the threat of the boy's amputation: just an additional kick in my stomach, a tiny extra measure, rubbing salt in my wounds . . ."

Glenn instructs Arturo, "Have all of the nuclear-waste on the docks shipped into my Valley around the clock because the Fiery Syphon strikes Pecuador on September 21st." Responding to his objections, "If the heat from the Whirlwind's Fiery Syphon were to explode the barrels on the docks, it would cause irredeemable pollution. At least in my Valley we can contain the pollution within this controlled, remote area. We've got to anticipate that this 'Fiery Syphon' will somehow miss our valley of balloons, or that all of the Skyhook's balloons may fail to choke it out of existence."

The next day everyone is quite distressed with the situation of the Professor's family; and no work is going on which adds to Glenn's depression. Now, at least a few of his workers will be kept busy unloading the nuclear waste.

Though Elena is quite busy, she and Margherita realize that Glenn has a problem since he doesn't even want to have sex anymore. Bernie, Jake and Sancho try to hang out with him during the day. Glenn finds their patronizing presence disconcerting. It comes up in conversation that his air conditioning had not been running much except when his cabin was crowded. Also, that the region has been much cooler; very unusual. Sancho comments that the grass has not been growing as well. Jake says, "How could it, with 50 square miles of balloons overhead blocking out the Sun."

Glenn says, "We will have plenty of heat soon . . . After the September 21ˢᵗ Fiery Syphon's destruction blows through here, we will replace the balloons with clear plastic ones, hopefully allowing much of the Sun's rays to penetrate down to our mountain region again." Then he says, "Last night I dreamed of picking up the Professor's son and examining the snake bite in his ankle; and then I see the snakes die in our Frozen Ice Storm raining down from our Gusher-Tower . . . I vow to one day end the **snake's reign of terror!**" he says dramatically. "We will *freeze them to death!* We will spray the Gusher-Tower into our valley . . . But, in order to do that we have to spray it below the level of our Skyhook's balloons. But I can't figure out how to do that without dismantling it, and I do not want to interfere with the other irrigation sprays we have scheduled."

Sancho objects to the idea of killing the snakes, "They are God's creation; they were here even before people came and they have every right to live here. People dying from snake bites is just a fact of life that we must live with."

Bernie tries to tell him that there are vast areas where there are no poisonous snakes killing people. That the people had removed them. Sancho insists, "It's God's work that removed them because of the weather - or whatever - and people who try to control God's creation **are doomed!**"

Jake comments, "Sancho, you are beginning to sound like those *religious fanatics!*" Then he says, "Candidate Prump's campaign is blaming the Democratic Administration failure for the Fiery Syphon and that only he – as 'God's Chosen One' – can fix it. *Can you believe it!* That Tax Dodging, Charity Stealing, pussy-grabbing promiscuous predator, Seducer of Adolescent girls and over all disgusting, self-centered individual: ***God's Chosen One?!?!***"

Sancho prayerfully mutters, "El via de Dios, es mysterioso . . ." Bernie & Jake bust out in outrageous laughter – Sancho's mortification radiates.

Glenn asks, "What did he say?"

"El via de Dios, es mysterioso . . ." Jake translates, "God works in mysterious ways . . ."

Then Bernie adds with cynical laughter, "'Mysterious' . . . *NOT FUCKING **PREPOSTEROUS!***"

Glenn fixates on Sancho's raging glare. He resolves to get everybody out of his cabin by finding work for them. "Have the cavern made accessible to the train so that we can stack the nuclear-waste in there. When the Fiery Syphon comes it will probably blow up everything in the ports including our nuclear-waste and contaminate the whole area . . .

Even the atmosphere!! Bernie, you should post a warning on your Mother Nature's Blog for all toxic waste storage sites to be moved underground, 25 miles away from the Fiery Syphon's path. The weather stations around the world should further disseminate this announcement. You should explain that all local toxic waste is being moved to some isolated, underground spot (like our cavern) where - if it does blow up - it will not be an environmental catastrophe. We can continue filling up our Valley. But first we'll fill up the cavern, which is quite large; we didn't even explore the other rooms there. Now that the Gusher-Tower is funneling all the seawater up and away from the cavern, it should be safe to utilize it. Let's go there and check it out now." He drives the truck there with Bernie, Jake and Sancho. They see that the Military Engineer had made a ramp down into the cavern using the fallen lava rock and concludes that the new railroad track can be laid on it.

Bernie designs a lay-out of the tracks allowing access to every corner of the deep cavern with switching to a separate return track for the empty railroad cars to exit. He also includes a thick, movable, cement barricade; which will be able to completely seal the cavern from the blast of heat and wind of the Fiery Syphon. This barricade has an electric powered motor and rides the railroad track, then switches to a side-rail, out of the way when the cavern is open. Using that same Military Engineer again, it will be completed within a week while constantly working around the clock and running trains. The cavern will hold all the nuclear waste, stacking the skids as high as the forklifts will allow. The port is being cleared of all nuclear waste, so the port city is safe as no more shipments are coming in. And, Glenn's payment is contingent upon each pallet arriving in his Valley; so, at least that much money is flowing once again. The Pecuadorian Government got their commission and import tariff tax with the unloading of the ships into the port; but Glenn doesn't get his payment till it arrives in his Valley; the president gets his 10% 'handling fee' kick-back at that time also.

XXIX

❖

THE NEW PROFESSOR
NATZI

It develops that the boy's leg is recuperating but, he has lost mobility of his right foot, and he walks with a limp.

The Professor is slowly being taken off tranquilizers and is getting used to the idea of seeing his son limp around the cabin. He is still tied to his bed and is told that he had a stroke, which is almost a lie; and they also tell him that he had a seizure - which is a lie - and they tell him that he has to take blood pressure medication regularly and remain calm.

However, the boy's limp is not the only tragedy from the eyelash viper incident. As the Professor comes out from his narcotic stupor an obvious change in his personality is apparent. He is supple, pliable, malleable, manageable - he is talking without any fervor, or intention to dominate.

The Professor's wife comments at the employee's breakfast that she had to get out of their cabin for a while. She misses the man he used to be. She whispers to Glenn in a suggestive tone, "For the first time in our lives, he has no desire for me." She feels guilty of thinking of such things as her eyes get wet with tears; "But life goes on and nature takes its course. I am thankful my son is not any worse off than he is. Thankful that he did not have to have an amputation. But everybody seems to be making the best of it - except for the demise of my husband, as I knew him. He has been left with no personality whatever. He has been maudlin and although responsive, not motivated, nor determined, nor preachy, nor concerned about the welfare of mankind; not even his constant anger at you: 'EL Cheapo Glenn'. Your past failures - to do the proper testing, nor your money grubbing - gold prospecting, nor your unsafe centrifuging while floating 20 miles up above the equator – nothing bothers him. It's like his personality has died."

Glenn's eyebrows raise when he realizes that the Professor had been constantly complaining to his wife about him. "He called *me 'El Cheapo'?!?*" But then thinks he preferred him the old way, compared to this insipid, malleable shell of a man she is describing. Glenn is anxious to get him back to work; but is concerned that maybe his mind has deteriorated because of all this. Glenn needs to ask him about killing all the snakes using seawater from the Gusher-Tower. "Could he calculate how much it would take and could we possibly freeze them out? I don't want to make my valley uninhabitable." Glenn places his hand on her shoulder saying, "I've been avoiding your husband, let me visit with him for a while." They walk to her cabin. Upon entering Glenn knows why he has been avoiding him. The cabin reeks of the Professor's feces: it must be time to change his diaper. Glenn overcomes his nausea - Mrs. Natzi does not seem to notice it. He pulls up a chair by the Professor's bed, saying, "How are you feeling, any better?" He nods his head, affirmatively while watching the TV news. Glenn tries to engage him with talk of the ongoing work. Getting little response, he ventures a comment about the boy's leg who is meandering around the cabin, his limp betraying the fact that he has no muscle control below his right ankle. "I see your son is getting around on his own now." The Professor's gaze turns forlorn as he winces in agonizing, guilt ridden, pain. Glenn mercifully surrenders and turns his conversation to the boy and his mother.

While they are making small talk, the subject of the Rapture is reviewed on TV. She says, "Isn't it amazing, the joy they displayed" then whispering, "while *being burnt alive!?!*"

Glenn says, "I can't understand it. It's getting hard for these governments to make the religious fanatics evacuate. There has got to be some other explanation for their joyous laughter - The reporters in the satellite trucks started laughing too, but then quickly started screaming in pain."

Then a familiar, but distant voice whispers, "It was the nitrous-oxide, laughing gas, the intense heat combined the atmospheric Nitrogen and Oxygen into nitrous-oxide."

Tears well up in her eyes as she whispers, "That's the first sentence I've heard my husband speak since we tranquilized him."

Glenn turns to him, trying to be casual, "Laughing gas – same as the dentist use as an anesthesia? That's a surprise. So, you think everybody is going *to die laughing* as it continues to *cook our atmosphere?!?*"

"No," the Professor explains, "It will continue to transform into other chemical compounds as its temperature increases. If the Whirlwind's Fiery Syphon's plasma is in fact maintaining its million-degree temperature it will then atomize everything. I'll have to think on what the consequences of that would mean."

"*Wow!* A million degrees burning a path across the surface of the Earth!! Yes. Please concentrate on that and let me know what you can surmise. Also, I was wondering how much Gusher-Tower seawater we would need to spray into our valley to kill all the snakes . . ." Glenn backs out of the cabin saying his goodbyes. He goes to his office where Bernie is busy scheduling the upcoming Gusher-Tower's irrigations to spray in front of and also behind the Fiery Syphon to try and minimize the fire damage. But, of course, they can only spray during the time of Pacific Coastal high-tides. "The Professor said the heat from the Fiery Syphon turned the atmosphere into nitrous-oxide - laughing gas - just like the dentist use. That's why the pilgrims were laughing before they burned up."

Bernie is surprised, "Professor Natzi *can talk?!?*"

"Yes, for the first time - full sentences."

"And he's talking science?" Bernie sighs in relief. "I was afraid he would never speak again, or if he did, it would be some religious nonsense."

Glenn says, "I'm relieved too, but he's still very fragile. Mrs. Natzi still has him tied up. It hurts to see him like that. Maybe it's time to untie him? Look into this Nitrous-Oxide possibility - that this laughing gas is what caused the Rapturous laughter. Get it into Mother Nature's Blog as the explanation of this phenomena - in the hope that it will stop these fanatics from trying to kill themselves."

"The atmosphere is 80% nitrogen and 20% oxygen, it's plausible that with the varying temperatures it would combine into all of those nitrate compounds." Bernie restating the obvious while he is already keying it into the computer, "It says that nitrous-oxide is a greenhouse-gas 300 times worse than carbon-dioxide. It is a pollutant released from combustion engines at 250C; about 480 degrees Fahrenheit. I guess the Whirlwind blew this gas out ahead of it allowing it to cool, then the people breathed it in before the deadly heat arrived a few seconds later. It makes *sense to me!*"

"Alright . . . Any explanation is more plausible than **the Rapture!**" Glenn replies somewhat relieved. Then suggests, "Why don't we add that the 'Whirlwind's Fiery Syphon' will be extinguished on September 21st's vernal equinox as it's crossing the equator. That should give people *some hope!* . . . But then; that's probably a false hope - that we shouldn't encourage."

Bernie's enthusiasm surges for his blog to have this new, exciting, lifesaving prediction – and then disappointed. "No, - it's not a false hope . . . We're going to - *to suffocate it!* - It can't get past our 2,000 square miles of balloons that we have floating above us – they are just *waiting to choke it!*"

Glenn is shaking his head negatively, "No we better not, we're not sure how this may workout and we don't want to have to make an apology afterwards. It may deter people from evacuating ahead of it in Asia, and around the rest of the world."

He takes a pair of scissors and returns to the Professor's cabin, asking, "Have you figured how much Gusher-Tower seawater we need to kill the snakes, and could we possibly freeze them?"

The Professor says, "Yes, 51 minutes." Glenn quietly snips his bindings with the scissors and gently massages the abrasions from the bindings as the Professor reviews his calculations aloud. "If I remember the square footage of our valley correctly." He begins mentally calculating aloud how long it would take to lay down 20 inches of gusher water, presuming they would eventually drown in that. "Or, if it turns to snow and ice, it will require much less than 20 inches." Then he calculates how many minutes of water it would take to rain down the 20 inches into the Valley. Concluding, "And, if it did all stay in the form of snow, it would leave 35 inches on the ground. Somewhat less, depending on the amount of ice remaining in the spray."

Glenn thanks him while helping him sit up in bed, then says to his tearful wife, "We *must kill* all those snakes one way or the other. We figure that after the Fiery Syphon destroys one or more sections of Skyhook's H-cube balloons, we can direct the Gusher-Spray through that puncture hole, down into our valley. That would be immediately after September

21st when the Fiery Syphon will be crossing the equator and must inevitably pass over our valley." They both help the Professor into the bathroom. Glenn gladly leaves the stench of their cabin. He is anxious to find the girls and announce the Professor's recovery and his solution to the 'Rapturous laughter - laughing gas' mystery.

The next day Glenn is flabbergasted to hear that Mother Nature's Blog predicts the Whirlwind's Fiery Syphon will not survive passage over the Andes mountains in South America on September 21st, the equinox. He angrily approaches Bernie, "I thought we said **NOT** to make *this prediction!* It will lull people into a false sense of security - they may not be able to evacuate in time. Remember, it is just a question of hours before it arrives across the Pacific to Malaysia and then Africa! Those people need days to evacuate - **NOT HOURS!!** SEND OUT *THE APOLOGY NOW!!!*" Bernie reluctantly does as he's instructed.

XXX

SPACE SHUTTLE

Astrophysics News Headline May 24, 2016:

India's Mini Space Shuttle successfully completes test run as country joins race to make reusable rockets

Arturo informs Glenn that the Space Shuttle is arriving on a flatbed of the morning train. It causes a furor of excitement through-out the Valley Hacienda. Suddenly the Professor leaves his cabin and becomes animated again. He can't believe his eyes; can't imagine Glenn had purchased it. Finds it hard to believe El Cheapo Glenn spent all that money on a whim. He takes complete charge for the first time since the snake bite incident. He supervises every aspect of setting it up and investigating its usage, then giving it electrical power and charging its batteries. He is thrilled like a little kid; still with this insipid personality, but now showing excitement and interest. He enjoys getting into a spare space-suit, climbing into the cockpit as if to fly it. He's practicing what he would do with the controls to accomplish avoiding a threatening meteor, re-entry into the atmosphere, flying to the Moon and how he could possibly land there. Glenn is gratified to see that his - 'DONATION' - of $50,000,000 that he spent on the Shuttle is invigorating the Professor, and he enjoys being with him - as opposed to hanging with Bernie and Jake and Sancho. For days they practice what it would be like to go outside space-walking in their space-suits while orbiting the Earth: attaching their safety-ropes while instructing each other thru their helmet communicators. Now Glenn reminds him that he did have that experience when the Big Syphon had thrown him out into deep-space, and he thought he was going to die. The Professor is somewhat disinterested in his actual history compared to the fantasy they are able to imagine. It's as if he doesn't want reality to clutter their fantasy. They exit the Shuttle, and the Professor carefully closes the hatch. Glenn speculates that they could never launch it as they don't have the booster rockets to accomplish that. But the Professor comments casually saying we launch every day from Skyhook without rockets; we could do the same with this. Of course, we would have to wrap it in nanotube cable to create its magnetic-field for propulsion. That makes Glenn's mind explode with a myriad of bizarre possibilities. He quickly removes his helmet. He shakes his head to recover his earthly clarity as the Professor removes his helmet saying that the nanotubes would prevent them from opening the Shuttle's cargo-bay doors. Then the Professor questions, "How are we going to protect our beautiful Shuttle from the Fiery Syphon? When it gets close, it will certainly destroy it." As they climb down to the ground, "I think the best way to protect it would be to launch it, remotely. It is small enough to fit on the Loon-Evator; we can slowly tow it into position on to the launch-pad using the forklift."

Then it hits Glenn, "Yes, it is small enough; I thought NASA Space Shuttles were bigger than this – I didn't know they made them this small?"

The Professor shows his first signs of humor since the snake bite, *"NASA?!?"* He guffaws, "I don't think you can afford to buy one of their Shuttles! This one comes *from INDIA!!!"* he shouts, laughing heartily.

Glenn freezes in position as his face turns white with shock, his eyes bulge as he thinks, "It's not from **NASA?!?** I paid $50,000,000 for a *fucken miniature* Space Shuttle from *INDIA!!"*

Everyone is gathering for dinner and watching as the two *spacemen* return from *playing* on the Boss-Man's new toy. They see the Professor's dramatic outcry. It sounds like laughter, but they think he is most likely crying in anguish, given his recent trauma. They all gather around him and are relieved to hear him laughing. He relays the story of Glenn's confused purchase in both Spanish and English and everyone is joining in his merriment. *"OH SHIT!!!"* Glenn grimaces with humiliation, "Now everyone is going to know what a *fool I have been!!*" He stomps to his cabin avoiding the jubilant crowd. He calls Arturo on the phone:

"You ***MOTHERFUCKER!!!***"

Arturo responds laughingly, "It took you this long to realize it – wait – *WAIT!* Before you have a stroke. I saved you about $40,000,000 . . . Nasa's Space Shuttle is 80' wide, 60' high, 125' long, and weighs 165,000 lbs. How can you transport it? You would have had to clear everything away from the railroad tracks 90' feet across and widen your tunnel into your valley. It just wasn't feasible. I'm sure this Mini-Shuttle is adequate to fulfil your fantasies." He pauses as he can sense Glenn's seething anger on the other end of the phone. "Do you have any idea how much time I waisted researching *your $50,000,000 toy?!?*" Glenn slams the phone down, hanging up on him. Then he gets out of his space-suit and logs onto his Pequito bank account. He sees the purchase Arturo authorized is for $12,679,000. This eases his anger somewhat.

Then Elena & Margherita saunter into the cabin laughing cheerfully . . . *"SHUT THE FUCK UP!!!"* he screams at them. They silence immediately, looking at each other with concern. They avoid looking directly at him while they set up the dinner on the table. Now he suddenly feels his pulsating erection pressing tauntingly against his confining underwear. As they are timidly walking by, he grabs each of them by the hair and pulls them towards the bed. They grab his hand to minimize the hair-pulling pain as he sits down and drags them to their knees. They spy his angry erection outlined against his pants as he pulls them to his crouch then releases their hair. They silently undo his pants, sliding them down as his raging penis springs free. They remove his pants and underwear while apprehensively licking his threatening member, their fingertips defensively caressing his abdomen, his inner thigh, cautiously moving towards his scrotum, as if to tame his savagery. He lies back, spreading his legs wide open, and wraps them around both women at their waist. Then with a vanquishing, "AAAGGGHHH!", he vindictively squeezes the woman together. He snarls wantonly as he mercilessly clutches Margherita's tits through her sweater. He begins to remove it and Elena deftly unsnaps Margherita's bra. Glenn viciously rips her sweater over her head as his eyes lock onto her tits bursting free of her bra. He *climaxes* with a shocking *screech* of anguishing release as the alarmed women each struggle to quickly capture his orgasm in their mouths while they continue their tonguing of its angry, gushing eye . . .

As he drifts off to sleep, they continue their soothing tonguing of Glenn's shriveling penis and then all around and below. Their tongues frequently meet and then explore each other. The glint of apprehensive fear fades from their eyes revealing a flashing spark of passion. They have absorbed his angry intensity. They climb up onto the foot of the bed undressing each other silently. Margherita gets behind Elena, laying her big boobs on Elena's shoulders. Elena presses them against her head with delight. Margherita slides her arms under Elena's and gently caresses her nipples. Then she pulls her back to the middle of the bed and lays her down. She bends her head down to Elena's tits and licks them. Now Elena has Margherita's tits hanging down in her face and she sucks and bites the nipples. They echo a contagious sigh as their fingers slowly explore their way to each other's vaginas. Then Margherita licks and nibbles her way down to assist her stimulating fingers. Elena does the same while lying on her back as Margherita slowly slides down her body. Then Margherita plunges her face into Elena's crotch while grinding her loins into Elena's face. They both orgasm . . . then pause . . . then begin again ...

Glenn awakens to being entangled in a confusion of sweaty backs, long hair, numerous arms and legs, and juxtaposing butt-cheeks. His women are moaning and rolling around all over him in the water-bed. He escapes from their writhing imbroglio and scrambles from the bed thinking, "What a strange configuration of '*The Beast* with two backs' . . .

So, this is married-life . . .

Do they even know I'm here?. . .

I'm hungry . . ."

The next morning Glenn is enjoying the employees' breakfast as the Professor's wife is gratefully saying, "I can't imagine what it must have cost you to buy that amazing Space Shuttle?!?" (Glenn wonders if she is being a smart-ass.) She continues with a contented – sensual smile, "But it has improved the quality of my married life, almost back to normal."

Her eyebrows raise as she coyly rolls her eyes. Then she says, "It seems that the Professor can endure our son's limp much better; now that the Space Shuttle's presence has somehow eased the guilt eating at his emotions. He spent last evening explaining its operation to our son, which has renewed their communicating. He says Daddy is teaching him so he can be a space cadet when he grows up. Now all the other children are asking my son to give them a one-on-one tour. It's making him popular, and happy too; it kind of makes up for his limp . . ."

A fleeting thought flashes thru Glenn's sub-conscious mind, {"Will he prefer the little girls or little boys for his one-on-one tours?"} Glenn manages a pleasant smile, then it changes to a sly smirk as he replies, "Where is the Professor this morning; or is he still in bed – *recuperating* from your – aaahh – **reunion**?"

Juan, the train conductor responds, "He took your space-suit and went up on the Loon-Evator first thing this morning with Sancho. We were very surprised to see him do that." His wife and Glenn are also surprised as he was adamant about staying on the ground, telling Glenn to hire professional Astronauts for that kind of work.

Glenn gazes toward the Loon-Evator's landing area and notices Jane studying their beautiful Space Shuttle. Jane is shocked looking up at the Shuttle on the flatbed railroad car. She says to Glenn at breakfast, "I don't understand; I thought you were a humanitarian . . ." she pauses waiting for Glenn to justify this extravagance . . . His silence is maddening, "How could you have spent millions on that Mini-Shuttle - *a toy* - when there are refugees suffering in camps around the world?!?"

Glenn says matter-of-factly, "Send the refugees back to their home country - *problem solved.*"

She replies indignantly, "You know it's not safe for them to return home; that's why they left in the first place."

He continues matter-of-factly, "Well then, solve the problem in their home country instead of making problems for other countries."

She retorts, "And what - more wars and violence, and living in refugee camps for generations. You must like to see the gun manufacturers **getting rich** *off their misery!?!* . . . And it's your *Fiery Syphon* that is setting **the world on fire!** . . . You really *piss me off!*" Glenn has had enough of this congenial employee breakfast; he carries his food to his office to eat alone.

Back for the employee lunch in the kitchen area, Glenn loudly instructs Bernie, "Have Mother Nature's Blog organize and pay $1,000 for each sterilization for any adult of child-bearing age. Somehow collect their *'tubes'* from their tubal ligation and vasectomies along with their medical records to verify surgery was actually done."

Jane shouts, ***"That's terrible!*** You'll have *alcoholics* and *drug addicts* lining up for **the money!"**

"Exactly!" Glenn retorts, "These are the people who *should not* be having children!" Then he says to Bernie, "Have the Family Planning Clinic personnel suggest proper investment usage of the $1,000. The clinics will be glad for the business, it shouldn't be too expensive as it's an outpatient procedure. Maybe $300."

Jane says smugly, "So you'll have the poor people in the poor countries give up their right to Parenthood."

"Nobody wants to bring children into the world and make them miserable; it's the accident of birth that is causing all these problems. These people should be RELIEVED to NOT be birthing children that they can't afford to care for." Then again to Bernie, "Make it so the clinic opens an exclusive bank account, locally for each of the patients, and we pay the $1,000 into their bank account, AND restrict their bank account so that they can only withdraw $100 per month. This will start them on a good plan of money management and using banks so as not to be tempted to spend it immediately, to be frugal, and make it difficult for someone to steal their money. This way, they can't use the money to leave the country." Then haughtily to Jane, "The problem is overpopulation. Within a generation or two the refugees will be called back to their home countries when the population falls. Also, our irrigating deserts should help solve the refugee problem."

Bernie had been feverishly taking notes to keep up with Glenn's tirade of instructions. He laments, "This will cost hundreds of millions of dollars."

Glenn is thinking, "I just saved $40,000,000 on that Space Shuttle." But says out-loud, "Now you know where all that Gusher-Tower gold you've been centrifuging is going."

XXXI

THE 14-YEAR-OLD COUSIN

The next morning's train brings shocking news. Elena's young cousin Miguel (who was teasingly called Sally) was kidnapped buy a bunch of men and thrown over the cliffside to his death, right where Glenn and Margherita had terrorized Elena's X. Nobody would identify the men who did it. Elena's X had not been seen since that episode. They had all been confident that he would not have the nerve to return again as he'd been so humiliated; his power within the town was destroyed. Elena was crushed. Her X knew of her fondness for the young boy. She was convinced that he had something to do with this. He was exacting his **revenge** upon her. Margherita recalled how this sort of thing had happened before with suspected homosexual men. She and Elena had discussed years ago the possibility of the boy growing into a homosexual. Elena had not been alarmed by the prospect at all as she had her own homosexual inclinations, probably brought on by her father molesting her. Margherita relives her first time. As a young girl Elena's father had dragged Elena, screaming in protest, into her bedroom. She'd been humiliated to be raped in the presence of her cousin and best friend. Margherita had tried to intervene, but her uncle, Elena's father, had grabbed her and pulled her to the bed - releasing Elena — who'd rolled to the floor, crying hysterically. He'd stripped Margherita's blouse off, sucking and admiring her perky, young tits. Then he quickly took her cherry. The terrified Margherita had been forced to submit. The pain was unbearable, but she endured and *perversely enjoyed* his subsequent attacks. She hated her uncle, just as she hated her own father. They were pigs - with no concern for their family's welfare.

Elena's mother had finally extracted vengeance for her daughter by stabbing his fat ass.

XXXII

❖

THE EQUINOX ARRIVES

Bernie had been tracking the Fiery Syphon and had been following the fires that ensued from it. He had the Gusher-Spray attack the fires first and then he would have it inundate the projected path of the Fiery Syphon. Of course, he could only affect that during the time of high-tide. Everything was ablaze. It kept the fire-fighters busy around the world. On the coast of Colombia in the city of Barranquilla there is a prison where recent rioting had resulted in the deaths of inmates and guards. It was severely overcrowded and there was fear of the Covid19 infections. Also, there were drug cartel prison gangs killing each other. Now the prisoners were again rioting in fear of the Fiery Syphon. But they were assured by the government that they would be transported out in the morning hours before it arrived. It had been planned to evacuate everybody from the path of the Fiery Syphon. They were all locked in their cells that night as usual; but their cell doors did not open in the morning and before long they realized that all the guards had disappeared . . . and they were locked in their cells . . . and *nobody was coming* to evacuate them. It was a horrendous scandal; they were all burned to death as well as everybody else in the fiery path who was not evacuated. The government justified it saying that they couldn't risk these violent murderers being transported. The prison guards refused to move them as 6 of them had been recently murdered by these prison gangs.

Glenn had planned for only Sancho to remain with him inside the Gusher Cavern during the fiery equinox, so that they could immediately begin repairing the damage to their valley's railroad tracks. This would enable the rest of his employees to return. But he didn't like the idea of evacuating CIA Jane. God knows what she might have done once free of her captivity outside the valley. Margherita wanted to stay with Glenn, Bernie wanted to stay, CIA Jane said she wanted to be with Bernie. But Elena wanted to leave. She betrayed an irrational, primitive fear. Her face flushed and her eyes were sparked with anxiety. She was only concerned for the welfare of her baby and wanted to get as far away as possible. CIA Jane explained to her in Spanish that the Fiery Syphon was 12,000 miles away in the Indian Ocean and that they had 12 hours to get to safety. Elena replied caustically, "I don't know what *you are talking about!*" When Glenn and Margherita tried to calm her down, explaining she would be safe 25 miles to the north, she screamed frantically, **"Just get me out of here!!"**

So, Glenn reconsiders and tells Sancho to evacuate with his family on the train tonight and to try keeping Elena, his pregnant wife calm. Of course, the Professor and his family would all evacuate. Jake & Virginia wrangle all the school children on the train to escape the Fiery Syphon. Margherita and CIA Jane will stay with Glenn and Bernie in the Gusher Cavern which now contains all their nuclear waste. They had been rushing to stockpile all their remaining nuclear-waste in the Gusher Cavern before the Fiery Syphon hit. It was a 24/7 effort. The workmen refused to be in the cavern during high-tides due to the gusher surging up the tower making a tremendous roar. It scared them; thinking that the whole thing was going to collapse. Therefore Jane & Bernie worked one high-tide shift while Glenn & Margherita worked the other high-tide shift. So, they were now used to the roar and will have no problem staying in the cavern for more than 12 hours while waiting for the Fiery Syphon to wreak havoc as it passes by, and then goes out to sea.

The night before the equinox the train is loaded with all the inhabitants of Glenn's valley except for Bernie, CIA Jane, Margherita and Glenn, they plan to drive to the cavern and seal themselves in it behind the massive cement gate.

They are confident that it will protect them from the million-degree heat. As the train pulls out, the Professor sneaks off from the last car and hides himself, lying flat on the ground. He watches as Glenn and the other three wave goodbye to the train. Glenn is furtively grabbing Margherita's ass, while he instructs Bernie to drive, as they are walking to the truck. Walking in front of them, Jane is maintaining a respectable distance from Bernie. Then Glenn jogs to his office and returns carrying a pouch full of loaded clips and two AR15s and two pistol belts. Margherita asks why they need guns. CIA Jane is quick to answer, "People can go crazy at times of stress. I can handle an AR15 . . ." betraying her secret CIA training.

Glenn & Margherita climb into the rear of the truck. He says with a bitter twang, "Margherita is already familiar with them." while eyeing her with a suspicious leer.

Bernie and Jane are getting into the cab of the truck. Bernie eases the tension saying, "Yeah, you saw how crazy Elena got . . ."

Margherita states defensively, "Elena *is not loco*; she is only afraid for her baby!"

CIA Jane patronizingly replies, "That's all we're saying, it is a very stressful time because of Glenn's 'Fiery Syphon's assault." Then she whispers to Bernie, "Glenn just left his wife on the train a few minutes ago, and he is already going to *screw Margherita in the back of the truck!* Jesus – She acts like **she's the Petrona!**" as they begin to drive south. Bernie resists the urge to tell her that those 3 regularly have sex together.

The Professor stands up as the truck's tail-lights fade in the distance. He goes to the Loon-Evator and loads the Mini-Shuttle from the flatbed railroad car onto the Loon-Evator's cargo platform. Using a forklift, he is able to tow it into position. He is so engrossed in his task, he doesn't notice that there are suddenly a lot of snakes on the move all around him, heading South. Then he puts on a space-suit and begins to float the Loon-Evator up the 20 miles to the Skyhook.

Looking out over the railing, the Professor can see the train with his family going down the mountain, North towards the border with Columbia. He is confident that they will be safe there. The Fiery Syphon had passed there at noon earlier and the government of Columbia and Pecuador are working together to repair all the roads and railroad tracks, ensuring the citizenry would be able to evacuate safely. Then he turns to the South. He is surprised to see the truck disappearing, "They must have already arrived at the southern end of the valley. They are taking refuge inside the cavern - which is packed with all the nuclear waste . . ." He watches as the truck lights disappear under a strangely dark oscillating cloud – "Can they be there already? They must be driving into the cavern, with that huge cement door closing behind them, hopefully protecting them from the million-degree heat." He is consoled knowing that they will be safer than he will be. It's a beautiful full moon-lit night and he enjoys the serenity of it reflecting off the mountains and the ocean beyond. He barely notices that the desert to the south has a peculiar rippling quality to it. He finds it strange, experiencing this serene calm with the pending devastation arriving in less than 12 hours. "Maybe it's the serene calm before *my own pending doom* . . . I guess I will be **joining my mother** soon . . ."

Margherita immediately assembles a tarp and some blankets into a bed in the back of the truck. They crawl under the blanket, their faces glowing with anticipation. They have only been driving south a few minutes and Glenn is ferociously grinding his face into her naked titties, she is undoing his pants and sliding her hand down to his groin. Then she catches a glimpse of 3 huge birds crossing in front of the Moon. She becomes transfixed on them as they turn in formation towards them. They are flying down as she yells, "MIRA!! (LOOK!!)" and they land on the truck's tailgate. Glenn sits-up and recognizes the mother Condor and her 2 babies from their previous encounters. His scientific curiosity is peaked by these birds suddenly joining them; but, he is confident they are not going to attack. However, his *penis* had *been more than peaked* by her fondling of his testicles. He assures her that everything is alright and pulls her back down resuming his onslaught of her breasts while guiding her hands back to his groin.

Momma Condor gawks intently:
>   {An intercourse not well designed
>   for beings of a golden kind . . .}

As Glenn is sliding Margherita's pants down, he hears Bernie yelling, "The *desert is alive* ahead of us . . ."

Glenn rolls off Margherita and pushes her head towards his swollen pecker. He yells back to Bernie, "It must be snakes . . . You should know they come out at night. Maybe they are having an orgy. Keep driving, I won't tell Sancho if you run over some of them." He guffaws a slight laugh at his own humor, as her tongue laps the tip of his pecker, pinching off his breathing. His unseeing glare is locked on the trio of Condors, who are gazing back at him with a curious fascination:

~   {Without a cry, without a prayer,

With no betrayal of despair . . .}   ~

Then CIA Jane shouts with alarm, "There must be *a million* of them!" as Glenn and Margherita sit-up suddenly there is impact under the wheels and debris flying up beside the truck from the front wheels, and then behind the truck from the back wheels. Suddenly the condors are actively catching this flying debris with their beaks and whipping it from side to side, ripping it in half and swallowing it. Then catching more and flinging them away from the truck.

Glenn screams, "Vipers – ***poison snakes!!***" They get to their hands and knees and crawl towards the front of the truck, pound on the rear window and yell at Jane to open her door. Bernie slows the truck as Jane opens her door. Margherita climbs over the edge of the truck holding on to the open door and slides into the truck's cab. Glenn is quick behind her. They squeeze in together and close the door, giving no thought to their nakedness. Bernie begins to accelerate again. The condors take over the back of the truck continuing their battle against the snakes. Glenn tells Bernie to drive faster, as the little poisonous snakes are being thrown into the air everywhere behind them.

After a bit, CIA Jane notices the sky ahead of them is dark with a fluttering - undulating cloud of blackness. "What is that?" she questions pointing up. The next thing they know they are in a huge flock of bats, many of whom have joined the snakes on the ground in a struggle for survival. Jane exclaims, "We can't even see where we *are going!*"

Despite this bizarre encounter, Bernie tries to calmly assure her, "All we need to do is follow the main railroad track, and I have driven it many times before. We must have driven into a mass migration. Or is it mating season? Maybe they ARE having an orgy?"

Now the truck is throwing up bats and snakes in combination which poses no challenge to the condors in the slightest. Then beyond their lights they see larger bats and Margherita's brown eyes bulge in recognition, as she clutches her bare breasts, screaming, "MURCIELAGO VAMPIRO! - MURCIELAGO VAMPIRO!!" repeatedly. As a child, tales of these frightening beasts gave her nightmares.

Jane mimics her scream, "MURCIELAGO VAMPIRO??" repeating the words in Spanish and then translating with a dawning awareness as her blue eyes swell larger than Margherita's,

"VAMPIRE BATS?!? . . .
VAMPIRE BATS!?!

VAMPIRE BATS!!!"

Glenn cries out, "**Jesus H. Christ**, *THERE ARE THOUSANDS OF THEM!*" as Margherita and Jane repeat their fearsome bellowing with saucer-like eyes.

Bernie is flabbergasted, then finally realizes that it's true, his voice cracks as he shouts, "***Holy Shit*** – they are supposed to be extinct in our hemisphere . . . What *is this* . . .

A FUCKING HORROR MOVIE!!!!

XXXIII

MAG-LEV THE
SPACE SHUTTLE

The Loon-Evator floats up 20 miles to the Skyhook and the Professor uses the forklift up there to tow the Mini-Shuttle onto the magnetic levitation tracks. Then he loads the two spools of nanotube wiring that he had brought up and wraps it around the center of the Space Shuttle, in the hope that it will create a magnetic coil that will assist in the mag-lev's launching of the Space Shuttle. He takes care not to block the hatches that house the landing wheels when they are retracted. He decides that he will launch at 11AM while the Fiery Syphon is still 1000 miles to the east. Then he programs instructions into his laptop computer, set to control the Railgun. "I will launch in a southerly arc at 18,000 mph which will send me away from the million-degree heat, into a low Earth orbit, and it *should* bring me back to approximately the same spot (it's last point of acceleration) within an hour and a half; in 90 minutes - just like the satellites do. By that time, 12:30PM, the Fiery Syphon will be 500 miles west, boiling the Pacific Ocean. I don't expect to be alive at that point . . . The Shuttle will continue on that orbit until it degrades, possibly crashing into the Skyhook . . . or whatever is left of Skyhook after the Fiery Syphon demolishes it. Or the Shuttle will crash elsewhere . . .

But my children will know that their father was up there in space, flying it . . .

    that their father tried to save it, so that his limping son might one day fly it . . .

        their mother will take some solace in telling them that their father finally became an Astronaut . . .

            Not exactly a hero; but . . ."

The Professor climbs aboard the Shuttle. While waiting in the air-lock, his space-suit is deflating, and he programs his laptop computer to do a virtual fly-over of his projected flight. He climbs into the pilot's seat while watching the Shuttle's virtual flight and noting the time it takes to fly from one landmark to another . . . he doses off strapped into the pilot's seat in his space-suit.

XXXIV

VAMPIRE BATS

In the truck, everyone is screaming as the windshield shatters from a huge vampire bat crashing into it. "Keep driving! - Good man! - Keep driving: - FASTER!!" Glenn says breathlessly, ***"MUST – GO - FASTER!!"*** Then dead silence . . .

Finally, Bernie speaks hesitantly, "I think we are getting close . . ."

Then Jane says, "LOOK!" pointing up, "Most of the Vampire Bats are climbing up higher."

Between the melee of flying animal debris bouncing up off the front of the truck, Glenn can see his new southern train tunnel, and the Gusher-Cavern entrance 140 feet beyond it. "It looks like most of the vampire bats are flying over the cliff to get out of the valley; but, the smaller bats and the snakes are all heading into his new southern tunnel to flee the valley." A glimmer of hope displaces the fear in his eyes, "You have to let me out before you drive into the cavern so that I can drive the cement-gate down the railroad track to seal the cavern entrance." The others exchange glances of devastating terror . . . "There aren't as many of the vampire bats now, I'll grab the AR15 from the back." he turns and looks through the rear window and is surprised the Condor family has disappeared. The vampire bats must have won the battle...

Bernie relieves the tension by explaining, "I'll stop next to the exterior-side of it. My rail mounted cement-gate perfectly seals the cavern entrance, so you can open and close the Gusher-Cavern by driving it into position on the tracks - from duplicate control-decks on both sides of it; either the inside control-deck or the outside control-deck. It has an electric motor; it gets the electricity from the railroad tracks it is riding on." He adds anxiously, "I designed it." He takes a wide turn and stops the truck in front of the cement-gate, 90 feet away from the Gusher Cavern's entrance. Glenn cautiously opens his door, then stands on the running board and hugs the truck as he reaches around into the back, feeling around for the AR15 machine guns. He is fearfully watching all the fluttering bats around him as he sticks his hand under the tarp. Then a sharp pain tells his sub-conscious that he's been bitten, he sees fluttering under the tarp as he whips his hand back. He plunges his bleeding hand into the ammunition pouch and grasps a fully loaded clip as he glimpses the AR15s rifles and then grabs one.

Glenn jumps off the truck and runs waiving the weapon defensively above his head while firing indiscriminately. He runs up the few steps to the control-deck on the exterior side of the cavern's cement-gate. As he stops moving there is a collaboration of the bats sweeping down towards him. He fires the AR15 as he is simultaneously starting the electric motor and driving the cement-gate down the tracks towards the tunnel entrance. He sees the truck is already driving into the cavern. There is fluttering all around him and he's firing constantly. A huge bat falls at his feet, it is gnashing its teeth at him. He yells in fearful disgust as he empties his clip into it. The bullets are ricocheting with a pinging noise off the metal. He violently kicks the quivering bat away. Glenn ejects the clip then loads the other one and continues firing. He sees that he's 5 feet from sealing the entrance and shuts off the gate's electric motor. He climbs down the stairs firing at everything that moves around him, running around to the inside of the gate. As he rounds it, he sees that Margherita is already out of the truck and firing with the other AR15 at anything and everything that's moving. He shouts at her, she pauses, then resumes firing around the remaining cavern opening as vampire bats are following after Glenn. He climbs up the inside stairs of the cement-gate and turns the motor on again as she is firing all around the exterior edges of the gate. Bullets are ricocheting everywhere. As she runs out of bullets, the cement-gate totally seals the cavern entrance, squashing a vampire bat; it's gruesome head and one wing remains stuck on the cement-gate. CIA Jane sees that they are enclosed within the familiar cavern and there is nothing flying or crawling on the ground around them, she gets out of the truck and promptly sits down on the ground and starts to cry in a cathartic relief of terror. Bernie joins her on the ground, comforting her.

Then Margherita also starts crying and runs to Glenn. They are safe now as the cement-gate has sealed the cavern entrance. They barely notice that they are shouting to overcome the roar from the Gusher-Tower. Then Margherita notices Glenn's bloody hand. She screams out in Spanish, "The vampire bat has bitten you; they carry *deadly disease!* It will make **you** *go crazy!!*" Glenn looks at his bloody hand nonchalantly, not realizing he has been bleeding in the terrifying melee. He unconsciously begins to move it towards his mouth to lick the wound. She grabs him forcefully saying, "No - deadly poison - deadly disease - we have to clean it." Bernie stops comforting Jane and gets the first aid kit from the glove compartment of the truck and rushes over to Glenn. He pours hydrogen peroxide onto the wound and wraps a tourniquet around Glenn's forearm. Then he squeezes the wound forcing more blood out. Glenn reacts in pain and reflexively pulls back the weapon in his other hand as if to club Bernie. They all freeze for a second . . . Bernie is the first to laugh and the others join in. He pours more hydrogen peroxide into the wound. Then he pours iodine into it. Glenn winces with pain and again brandishes the weapon menacingly. He doesn't join them in their laughter, he kneels down in pain. Margherita says, "We've got to get you to the hospital or fly the doctor here; just like you did with the Professor's son."

Glenn says, "That's not possible. The Fiery Syphon is coming within the next 10 hours. Everybody is busy evacuating."

Then CIA Jane screams, pointing to a massive fluttering motion from under the tarp in the back of the truck. Margherita moans in apprehension, grabs her AR15 and pulls the trigger pointing it at the back of the truck. Bernie cautions, "Watch out for the gas tank!" The gun is not loaded. She throws it to the ground and grabs Glenn's AR15, and again tries shooting indiscriminately into the back of the truck; but it's also empty.

Glenn stands up saying, "All the ammo is in the pouch in the back of the truck. We've all got to approach it, whomever is closest to it must grab the ammunition pouch and the rest of us will distract the vampire bat. Jane starts crying again as she walks towards the truck. Margherita is visibly quivering with fear. Bernie turns up the lights inside the cavern and joins them in very cautiously surrounding the back of the truck and hesitantly creeping towards it . . .

Then a fluffy white neck appears from under the tarp. Margherita gives a sighing gasp of relief. Glenn recognizes it's one of the condor babies. There's more fluttering and suddenly all three birds pop out from under the covers. Glenn collapses to his knees with relief knowing that his wound is not from the vampire bats. He had been pecked mercilessly by the same mother Condor. He survived with is flesh hanging down from his scalp. So, this little bite on the back of his hand should not be a problem. One of the baby condors had managed to get Margherita's pull-over sweater over his head and Margherita suddenly becomes self-conscious about her boobs hanging out in front of Bernie. She angrily climbs into the back of the truck cursing in Spanish at the birds and pulling on her blouse. The mother and other bird begin pecking towards her, but she kicks at them angrily until she manages to free her sweater which rips as she pulls it away from the baby bird's beak. She exits the truck and immediately puts it on over her head and pulls it down. Her torn sweater is completely revealing her left boob. Glenn starts to laugh when he sees that and then Bernie and Jane join in. Dead silence from Margherita, she is angry, but then starts laughing too as she realizes her boob is exposed. They are all laughing hysterically in grateful relief from there terrifying ordeal.

They pull the blankets and tarp away from the condors who protest loudly. Margherita makes one large bed for them, and they lay down: the two women in the middle and the two men on the outside. Bernie follows Glenn's lead and snuggles close to Jane. Their intimacy is like an antidote, recovering from their traumatizing ride to the safety of the cavern. They settle down for a long sleep . . . they're exhausted. They welcome the relative quiet as the Gusher-Tower's roar turns to a gurgle and then ceases; the high-tide surge has ended.

Their sleep is like a gift   ∼   from the Grace of God . . .

{Oh courage, could you not as well,

Select a second place to dwell;

Not only in that surging sea,

But also in the heart of me.}

They are too soon awakened by the familiar but hideous loud vibrating roar of the deep ocean water surging up the lava-tube, then up into the Gusher-Tower, gushing with tremendous pressure and spraying out the top of the tower, 22 miles up into space. They're used to its roar but find it hard to get back to sleep. Their emotional exhaustion should enable them to return to sleep in spite of the roar. The Fiery Syphon will be arriving in just about 2 hours. Bernie explains that he programmed it to spray along its projected path; but not in this valley because it is covered with their H-cube balloons. When it passes, he will have it spray in the valley to extinguish whatever is burning. Glenn says, "There is not much that can burn in the valley other than the animals & insects. It might melt the sand. Of course, it will destroy all of our network of H-cube balloons: Skyhook and Loon-Evators 1 and 2. And most likely everything in our Hacienda. Maybe even this Gusher-Tower!" He sees the look of consternation they are exchanging. He explains, "We should be safe behind this cavern's granite walls. They've been here for thousands of years. They are thick. After all, they were forged with volcanic lava. Besides, it is forecasted to pass over the northern end of our valley." Glenn is distressed, "I hope the million-degree heat doesn't melt our Gusher-Tower or collapse it? We could drown before opening the cement gate." as he checks his watch - 10:40AM.

Bernie says, "Most of those vampire bats were flying above the cliffs. The snakes on the ground - that were not fighting each other and whatever bats that were closer to the ground, all were heading into the railroad's southern tunnel; they were all avoiding the entrance to this cavern."

Jane nods affirmatively, "It's as if these animals know, the cavern is not on their migration route. For whatever reason, this mass animal migration is programmed to go further South than this cavern."

Bernie speculates, "What could be causing this sudden massive migration? Bypassing our cavern and going straight into the newly constructed railroad tunnel; how did those snakes even know it was there?"

Glenn says "This is some weird shit . . ." as Margherita is placing food on the blankets for them to enjoy.

Jane shows she is regaining her composure, "I've heard that animals have premonitions about natural disasters and react to them in advance. Rats desert the ship before it sinks, animals get nervous and flee in advance of an earthquake. Of course, domestic animals don't have that option, but they do get frantic in advance of an earthquake. I don't know about volcanoes, but I think birds do fly away before an eruption occurs. All three of those big condors hitched a ride with us. Their premonition must have been that they are safer with humans . . . that has got to be an evolutionary mystery . . ."

"It's the mother and her two babies; a boy bird and a girl bird." Margherita enlightens Jane, saying, "The mother's love for her babies is beautiful to see."

Jane asks, "How do you know that? I mean which is the boy and which is the girl?"

"Just by looking. What? Can't you see the difference between them? Can't you see some different coloration, you must open your eyes and look closely. The lighter color is the girl, she is a little smaller too."

Jane disparages by raising an eyebrow and snidely speaking to the two men, "The more primitive among us are most likely to be in tune with nature."

Glenn tries to ignore her caustic tone, "I wonder if anybody observed the birds fleeing before that La Palma volcanic eruption in Spain's Canary Island. So, you think they are anticipating the Fiery Syphon's arrival and are fleeing from it? There have been no reports on any activity like this in the news with the first Big Syphon, nor with this Fiery Syphon."

Jane retorts smugly, "I guess the news has more important things to worry about than animals running away with all this devastation that *you have caused!*" Glenn glances at Bernie's shocked expression and feels vindicated for keeping her prisoner. He's glad he didn't entrust her with any weapons.

He leaves his half-eaten food and goes to the truck, picking up the weapons and ammo. As he is returning to the picnic, the mother condor seizes the opportunity and swoops down snatching Glenn's sandwiches, then flies indifferently near Glenn's head, returning with the food to her babies. They are all stunned with this sudden appearance of the giant bird. Glenn, realizing that she has stolen his food, raises his AR15 . . . pauses . . . and then says to the birds, *"HMMPH??. . . You're welcome . . ."* The other 3 bust out laughing as they quickly finish their own food. Glenn turns his head repeatedly between the picnickers and the condors in the truck, *"Talk about frenzied - erratic behavior . . ."* He looks at his watch, it's 11AM.

XXXV

ON THE TRAIN

Before noon on the Equinox morning the train is climbing a mountain just over the border of Colombia. 24 hours ago, Bernie had the Gusher-Tower's Spray saturate the area where their train was escaping. They had expected to be much further north than they were, but there are problems along the track. The train goes very slowly as there is debris and the wooden supports under the tracks are smoldering and the rails are sagging. Juan, the conductor, jams on the brakes as he sees ahead that the old wooden railroad bridge had burned down. Juan has to back up and then switch to another track which takes them to a metal bridge. It shows signs of having burned and blistered from the prior day's heat, but Juan thinks it's sturdy enough. He gets everyone off the train. Then he slowly drives across the blistered bridge. Then the passengers all walk across seeing that the train is safely on the other side. Elena is emotional as Sancho and his wife hold onto her walking across the railroad ties. She is traumatically telling of the premonition she envisions of them *all being blistered* like the bridge they are on! She is reluctant to climb aboard the train again. They fearfully observe there are more mountains ahead. As their train is going deeper into this mountainous region, they can see *smoke billowing* into the sky; they had been informed that the Colombian military had put out all the fires and *it was safe* to travel. The train is laboring up the tracks. As they round a bend, they can see there are still *flames burning* down the side of the next hill, but there is none on their mountain, and this track will take them high above and beyond those flames. They are all looking down watching the conflagration reach the gorge in between the mountains. They feel safe as there is a sizable stream running through it. They feel that it will prevent the fire from crossing on to their mountain. But the flames easily leap across it and *rapidly start climbing* up the mountain. Before they know it, it is *underneath them* and rapidly *blazing up* at them. And it has already gotten ahead of them. As they round the bend at the top, they can see the tracks ahead are *engulfed in fire.*

Juan stops the train and begins to back it up. Now the flames that he had already passed below the track, *are coming up beside them* - as they are backing down the mountain. He accelerates going backwards: he *cannot* see what is behind him but knows that if he stands still, they will be *immolated.* Elena sees trees *bursting into raging flames.* Her eyes fearfully reflect their *shimmering blaze.* She has a flashback of the pilgrims *burning alive.* She screams, *"MY BABY!!"* while *clutching* her abdomen. Now the heat grows more intense, the jungle *is blazing* on both sides of the track. Juan goes *full speed in reverse* down the hill, more afraid of *burning to death* than of derailing the train. *Pandemonium breaks out* with the intense heat; they try to close the windows against the *caustic smoke.*

As the train *accelerates backwards* down the track, the *wheels screeching* around the unending *sharp bends,* everybody grabs onto their seats, *screaming in anguish* as they are being *tossed around* with each *perilous turn.* Mrs. Natzinger lays her weight across her 3 children *to hold them* in place. "We took this train to flee the wrath of the Fiery Syphon . . ." Religious zealotry invades her mind, "It *immolated* my husband's family – *Where is he?!?* Now it's taking *our babies* for another *sacrificial immolation* . . ." Everybody is *screaming* forming an inhuman resonance with the *callous screeching* of the train's wheels.

They finally get back down the mountain, *roaring through flames* and smoke. They reach a point where the jungle has already burned; it is just smoldering. Juan slows the train to a crawl. There is fallen tree debris smoldering on the tracks. The train slowly pushes it out of the way as they keep moving. They must stop for the heavier debris. Breathing the caustic smoky air is bad, especially for the men who are working outside clearing the tracks. Juan is challenged with either going south into today's Fiery Syphon, or north into the flames of yesterday's assault. Finally, they see the Colombian military working on repairing the tracks. Somehow or other his train had gotten ahead of the military. Juan is livid with rage, reliving the terror they had just endured. Tears well up in his eyes, "This military came here to protect us; but the cowards stayed far away from the danger . . . - They should have stopped us from going into that *mountain inferno!!*"

Juan backs the train over that blistered metal bridge, then stops. He figures it's as safe as anywhere as this jungle area has already been burned to a crisp. Elena is crying like a baby, Sancho and his wife hold her, safely sandwiched between them. The Professora gets off of her children reassuring them that they are alright. She sees there are many injured passengers, so she organizes Jake, Virginia and some others to render aid.

XXXVI

❖

BACK ON SKYHOOK

The Professor's computer wakes him up as it is executing the instructions timed for 11:00 AM. It begins charging up the magnetic levitation operation. He sees out the Shuttle's front window that sunlight is penetrating through the overhead balloons that support the tracks of the Railgun. The Shuttle will be accelerated through its circular track until it achieves 18,000 miles-per-hour and ejects him south into his polar orbit. He puts on his helmet and lowers the sun-visor. "I expected that I would have been levitated immediately above the Railgun and should have already been accelerating up the track . . . This Shuttle is not a toxic waste barrel - It *weighs 12 tons!*" He quickly bangs instructions into his computer to maximize the electric flow into the levitation magnets surrounding the Railgun's starting position. As soon as he activates it, the Shuttle begins to slowly rise and then is abruptly jerked directly up. He is thankful that he practiced using the seatbelt every time he sat there, otherwise he would have been thrown against the ceiling. He quickly retracts the Shuttle's wheels. Now sensors tell him that the magnetic-field around the Shuttle is building, and he is beginning to move up the track . . . *it is working!* However, he does not seem to be moving quickly enough; he does not feel the acceleration. But all he can see is the tracks, then suddenly bright sunlight ahead, and instantly he is out above the blue atmosphere, climbing higher into the blackening sky.

Looking down he sees the Earth far below him, the jungles of Brazil growing smaller. Then suddenly he's over the South Atlantic Ocean.

Concerned he wonders, "I should be flying directly South as I programmed the mag-lev launching. *No time to think?!?* I can't understand why it is going off course to the east?" He pauses, "It must be the magnetic-field I created around the Shuttle; it's deflecting it, causing deviation off my course as I am coming closer to the *very weak* South Magnetic Pole. **That is unacceptable!**" He transfers his computer control to the Shuttle's joystick; adjusting the switching within the nanotube coil's wiring that he has wrapped around the outside of the Shuttle. (The nanotube wiring had been especially designed with unique switching capability every 100 feet, which could direct the current in any combination of 6 different direction: 1 forward, 2 left, 3 right, 4 up, 5 down, and 6 backwards. Each of these individual switches is directly addressable thru the computer, and can also be shut off to block current flow. The computer, combined with this joystick, can instantly manipulate all of these switches to accomplish variations in its magnetic-field, allowing the Shuttle to be guided in response to any external magnetic-field.) He is able to adjust his magnetic-field to minimize deviation, but then he decides to simply reverse the magnetic-field - which pulls him back onto his original course. Saint Elmo's Fire suddenly engulfs the Shuttle as the current's directional flow is changing, but then that glowing electrical potential is reabsorbed into the coils as the flow reverses. It had momentarily obstructed his view. He can see now that he is already rounding Patagonia's Strait of Magellan? "I can see Antarctica. **Wow!** *That was quick!*" He looks at his watch, "One-sixth of the way around the world already in *only 9 minutes?!?* I can't be traveling that fast. He checks the Shuttle's GPS speed, it is going as programmed, just over 18,350 miles an hour. As he rounds the South Pole, his orbit has reached its highest point on the ark, the apex, at 207 miles in altitude.

He too soon flies over Antarctica, crossing the southern Pacific Ocean, then over Australia and north up the Pacific. He cannot believe how quickly it is going as he is crossing the Equator. He sees that the Shuttle is again being magnetically deflected off course to the East. *"Oh Shit!"* He tries adjusting, *"Fuck it!"* but then reverses the Shuttles magnetic-field. Once again St. Elmo's Fire briefly envelopes the Shuttle. He passes the Hawaiian Islands on the East; it is back on course. Now he can see Kamchatka Peninsula out the left window. Then he sees North America on his right and Asia on his left, seeming to come together ahead of him. Now he is over the Aleutian Island and begins rounding the Artic. He is only 95 miles in altitude as he crosses the North Pole. He rounds the Artic ice cap and crosses over North America. He sees his altitude is dropping drastically. "AM I GOING *TO CRASH* IN THE STATES!?!" It's down to 35 miles as he sees the Florida Peninsula streak by his left window. His altitude is down to 28 miles as he crosses over Central America. The Shuttle's speed is down to 17,725 miles-per-hour, and he is only 24 miles in altitude when he flies over Columbia. Then he encounters an external magnetic-field that latches onto the Shuttle, causing it to accelerate while turning it 180 degrees. He is *streaking down* toward the mountains of Pecuador!! **"GOD HELP ME!"** he pleads, as he quickly reverses the Shuttle's magnetic-field. St Elmo's Fire returns, blocking his view for a second. Then, "OH *GOD, I'm crashing at 18,000 miles-per-hour. NO!!"* just as the Shuttle is about to plow into a massive construction. "But I'm still 20 miles up - high above *the mountains?!?* . . . What is this? It looks like it's made of *floating square balloons?!?* I am crashing *into* **SKYHOOK!"** The next thing he knows the Shuttle is enveloped in constantly violent electrical arcing. *"I am looking into the abyss of death . . ."* **He is terrified!!** Panic stricken; he shuts off all power. And then the electrical arcing slowly fizzles out . . .

He can see that the Shuttle has stopped . . . it is floating back at Skyhook's mag-lev starting position. With the final arcing of the collapsing magnetic-field, he feels the Shuttle gently landing on the Railgun tracks. Totally befuddled; he frantically sprints to the Shuttle's exit. He tries forcing the outer door open, but he must wait for the air-lock to equalize. He is unaware that his space-suit is inflating. The door finally opens, and he climbs down the ladder. Then runs into the familiar safety of Skyhook's cabin. Again, he must wait for the cabin's air-lock to equalize, now he becomes aware of his space-suit deflating and alarms are sounding. At last, the door opens, and he runs in and throws himself into the big lounge chair. He looks at his helmet's internal display; his heart rate and blood pressure are high. The current time reads 11:52AM . . . 8 minutes before the Fiery Syphon arrives, no time to do anything. He thinks to call his wife; to say goodbye to his children. But then, what's the sense in upsetting them now. "Just be content in knowing I will be following after my mother and brother." A pregnant pause . . . then he speculates, "How was the Shuttle flying at 18,000 miles-per-hour and then it came to a dead stop - floating above the Railgun's mag-lev point of origination. I can't believe it. After launching me, I did not shut off the mag-lev operation, it remained magnetized waiting for the next launching. Instead of which, its magnetic-field *pulled the Shuttle* back to its point of origin!?! I can't believe *I'm still alive?!?"* He is struggling to remove his space-suit's helmet. His whole-body shudders: then once again with the frightful awareness that he is now in the direct path of the Fiery Syphon's million-degree heat, and he hasn't time to do anything about it . . . "And my Mini-Shuttle will still be destroyed - after all that I've been through . . ."

XXXVII

❖

BACK IN THE CAVERN

Glenn looks at his watch as they are all laying down again, feigning sleep. It's 11:35AM; 25 minutes before noon - it will soon be here. They don't notice, but begin sweating profusely. Within a few seconds they feel the ground under them getting very warm and then quite suddenly - fiery hot. They all jump up at once and get to their feet. Bernie shouts, "What *the **FUCK?!?!***"

Glenn replies, "The heat in advance of *the Fiery Syphon!* It must be heating the desert floor outside; it's transferring its higher temperature along the ground into here . . . *Run down the ramp* into the center of the cavern! *Get away* from the outside heat!"

Margherita gathers the blankets & tarp from the ground; then, she yells, ***"AAAiiiEEEE!"*** as she heaves them into the back of the truck. Her hands are *burning hot,* she sees the blankets are smoking. Her feet *are baking,* and she starts running down the ramp. Bernie sees the tires on the truck are starting to smoke and he jumps in and drives it down the ramp.

Jane moves aside to allow the truck to pass and leans against the exterior wall. *"AHH AH! It's **fucking hot!!"*** she shrieks with the shocking pain. They run down the ramp feeling intense heat radiating from the walls and the ground beneath them. The railroad tracks make *crackling sounds* as they expand and buckle from the heat. They lean up against the fork-lift that was left in the cavern after stacking the nuclear waste. The center of the cavern is cooler, but the heat is reaching there, too. Jane points up to a darker corner of the exterior wall, they can see what appears to be a *molten reddish* color. "Is that rock *melting?*"

Glenn, dumbfounded, asks, "Can it be?" Then they all climb up onto the fork-lift as he recalls, "Lava is *only about 1500 degrees* Fahrenheit! The temperature might go **up to a million degrees** outside that wall!!" Now they can see steam or smoke emanating overhead from the rocky roof. There is a *cracking of the rock* as it is heating, and steam is coming out the cracks. Apparently, the rocks had been holding moisture. "But we're inside a mountain; a whole *fucking mountain?!?*" Some rocks begin *falling* from the ceiling where the cracking has occurred. "Is the roof of the cavern *going to collapse!?!*" Glenn does not know what to do - everybody is looking to him for answers. The fork-lift's tires are smoking.

Bernie turns to Glenn with breathless hesitation saying, "It's not even 12:00 o'clock, - and we are going to burn-up like the pilgrims - like the Professor's family - in Panama - before the Fiery Syphon hit them - *even before High Noon!*"

Jane cries, "It's like we are in *an oven*, Glenn brought us here **to bake** *in this oven!*"

All four of the fork-lift's tires simultaneously burst into flames . . . they frantically jump off and move away towards the Gusher-Tower.

Suddenly the condors are flying around the cavern *squawking loudly.* The truck's tires start to smoke again. "Oh my *God!*" CIA Jane harshly cries out as Margherita blesses herself and, with a *pleading fervor*, begins reciting the 'Hail Mary' in Spanish. Everyone is lifting their feet, one foot then the other as their *feet are burning* through their shoes, again. Then they see *puffs of steam* coming towards them from every direction across the sandy floor; behind that, they can see the sand melting into a *viscous glassy* surface, ~ **coming towards them** . . . They back away, then up against the Gusher-Tower. . . *There's no escape.* Margherita's exposed breast *is bouncing* as she lifts her feet while blessing herself; *praying fervently*: **"*Padre nuestro*!! Que estas en los cielos!! . . ."**

Now Jane, remembering those pilgrims, begins singing faintly: "Yes, Jesus loves me - *Yes . . .*"

Glenn screams at them, "***STOP – I CAN'T THINK!!***" He's recalling an old quote: 'There are no atheists in fox holes.'

He sees a flickering glow coming from the elevated adjacent cavern. He reflects, "It's stacked to the top with skids of nuclear waste." He glances around the interior walls of this cavern, also covered with skids of nuclear waste, almost up to the ceiling. Then he spies a bottom wooden skid holding the stacked barrels of nuclear-waste - *smoking* – then **spontaneously igniting** . . .

They hear *crashing sounds* and see nuclear-waste barrels *rolling down* from the adjacent cavern . . .

Bernie *can't believe* his eyes as he sees the ends of Jane's hair *starting to glow*, like a hot *electric wire*; then smoking, then *his eyes pop* as her hair spontaneously *bursts into flames*. **"I got it, don't worry . . ."** Bernie says, trying to stay calm, as he is smothering her flaming hair with his hands. "It must be your *hairspray* . . ."

She is oblivious to his actions . . .

Glenn is struggling to breathe deeply,
- his eyes are meandering aimlessly,
  - he is mentally exhausted.
    - "I am so confused . . ."
      - his body yields to submissive fatalism . . .

He hears the deep voice of Jim Morrison in the back of his brain singing, 'This is the *END, MY FRIEND* . . .'
- His knees give out as he collapses back against the Gusher-Tower.
  - The others gasp in fearful denial - transfixed they glare down at Glenn . . .

Is that a sigh, or is he exhaling his last breath . . .?
- They will not live to see this equinox's high noon.
  - The Fiery Syphon is going to burn them alive - before it *even gets here!*
    - Shock trauma begins numbing each of their brains . . .

Glenn feels a *cooler wetness* spreading on his sweaty back;

    ~   "What a relief, a tremendous burden simply dissolving away . . .

        ~   the acceptance of my doom . . .

            ~   I am *'going gently* into that goodnight'?" . . .

                ~   A smile begins to develop on his face:

"It goes: 'DO – *NOT* - GO GENTLY INTO THE NIGHT'!

    ~   *STUPID!!*

        ~   Is that my final sarcasm?"

They are shaken as they see Glenn's urine permeating through his pants, sputtering out on to the hot sand; then suddenly they are each involuntarily pissing out their own hot urine.

        ~   Then Glenn's eyes spark with a flash of realization:

            ~   "It's *CONDENSATION* I feel, from the outside of the tower . . .

                ~   It's running down my back . . ."

                    ~   He remembers, "The deep Pacific Ocean water:

                        ~   it's *freezing cold!"*

                            ~   He jumps up and *sprints away . . .*

    ~   The others *are aghast* looking at him!

        ~   Is he *deserting them* to this fiery fate?!?

            ~   He reaches an electrical- box mounted on a far wall.

        ~   *He throws the switch.*

                ~

Then, the next thing they know their bodies are being *flushed away* by a freezing high-pressure surge of deep ocean water. Glenn dives into the flow and grabs onto Margherita. Bernie holds onto Jane. They are all relieved that their feet are not burning but are shocked at the sudden impact of the freezing water. Glenn had opened the maintenance door at the base of the Gusher-Tower. The fork-lift fire is extinguished. They half craw, half swim, half walk through the cold water and then hold onto the truck which is beginning to float in the rising water.

Bernie cautions, "The gusher filled up this cavern before: we are going to *drown in here!* We have to open the cement-gate."

Glenn replies, *"NO!* It's not even noon yet, we have to wait for the Fiery Syphon to pass and the heat to dissipate." They are all staring at him with doubt in their eyes. He had told them they would be safe in this cavern.

Jane cries, "So *we drown* in here or **burn to death** out there! That's *our choices!?!*"

Glenn shouts, "LISTEN! Can you hear it? The Gusher-Tower is still roaring. Not as loudly, but, can you hear it? I think that roaring sound means that the gusher is still surging 22 miles up the tower and spraying into the stratosphere. Most of the water is spraying out the top, so it should *not fill up* the cavern. We've got to get into the back of the truck, try and keep it level." As they are climbing into it, "Get all the way into the back. There's too much weight from the engine - it will tip forward and sink."

The three condors dive into the cooling water. Then, with a few flaps of their wings, join them, settling onto the tailgate. The hot bed of the truck cools from their cold, dripping wet bodies, while they warm-up from its heat. They sit in the back of the truck as it floats around the cavern. The water continues to rise. They can no longer hear it surging out from the maintenance door of the Gusher-Tower. They sit there for minutes in pensive silence. Bernie is thinking, "This high-tide gusher started at 10:15AM, it will go on until 3:55PM, four more hours, and the cavern already has 12 feet of water in it . . . I think it is *going to fill up!*"

There is a single narrow stream of sunlight coming through the ceiling where it cracked before and rock came falling out. Margherita points it out and says happily, "Sunlight" she chuckles saying, "Why am I happy to see sunlight?"

The truck is now floating gently in the circular current created by the water gushing out of the Gusher-Tower's maintenance door. Occasionally it bumps into an exterior wall, and they can feel the heat emanating from it. The edge of the rising water sizzles as it meets the baking walls. As the truck bumps into an exterior wall, heat immediately transfers into its red painted frame. The paint blisters as the heat spreads. They splash water onto it and see the heat sizzle, leaving a crusty salty deposit.

Glenn is positioning everybody around the back of the truck to maintain a level balance, trying to keep it from tipping over and sinking. Each movement makes it rock precariously. The four tires are buoying it up, but apparently the right front tire is not as buoyant. The mother condor observes Glenn's directions and seems to comprehend what he is trying to accomplish. She flies from the rear tailgate and lands on the roof's left side and then gently steps to the corner where the windshield and the door meet, doing her part to adjust the weight. Then the mother gestures towards her baby-boy and it gently steps sideways to his left arriving at the other corner of the tailgate. Everyone exchanges incredulous glances; they are too rational to imagine the birds are communicating, that they are trying to help with this delicate balancing act. There's nothing left to say, as noon arrives. They are all just gaping at that one beam of sunlight coming down into the water. It is strange, how beautiful and rewarding that one stream of sunlight can be, reflecting through the water, shimmering back into their eyes - they're all transfixed on it. As the truck is gently turning and bobbing, Momma bird squawks at that laser-like ray of light. Her babies squawk in reply.

Glenn speculates looking at his watch, "It's now 17 seconds past noon, the Fiery Syphon must have passed already?"

The truck is floating around again, and that golden ray of sunlight is on the path to strike the girl condor perched on the right-hand corner of the tailgate. Suddenly Momma bird squawks aggressively, and her baby-girl gracelessly steps sideways towards the left. The ray of sunlight passes over the tailgate's corner, then the girl bird returns to her right-hand perch. Margherita's gaze glows with empathy for the Momma bird, for some reason Momma fears that tiny ray of sunlight and is trying to protect her baby-girl from it. As the floating truck almost completes a 360-degree rotation, the ray of sunlight is now approaching the left corner of the tailgate where her baby-boy is. She squawks at him, but he does not respond as his sister did. She springs up and flies over, grabbing her baby-boy with her beak around its neck and lifting him with one swaying motion, deftly throws him directly into Glenn's lap. Then she lands in that spot her baby-boy had occupied, on the left-hand corner of the tailgate. Suddenly that single beam of sunlight changes from golden to a greenish-orange. It intensifies to a degree that it *hurts the eyes* - the water is *spitting steam* where it enters. It immediately *cuts across* the tailgate's left corner and is *slicing into* Momma condor's tail-feathers. A little smoke comes up as she *squawks in pain*. She *bolts up* with a *skreiching scream* then dives into the cold water; her tail-feathers sputtering. The tailgate is smoking with a glowing, red-hot slice where Momma condor had been, everybody starts splashing water on it. That laser-like hot beam sizzles 25 feet across the water and then changes back into that gentler golden beam as the water stops sputtering. Then blobs of molten lava drip from that crack in the ceiling. They splash into the water *violently blasting boiling steam* as they sink. An acrid stench like metallic chlorine abruptly permeates the air. Everybody involuntarily closes their burning eyes and covers their searing nostrils with their hands. Glenn crouches over the baby bird protectively. When they have to breathe again, they inhale through the fabric of their shirts. A molten blob hits the metal roof of the truck and burns a hole through it - setting it and the passenger seat aflame. The stench quickly dissipates after the last blob of molten rock sinks into the water. Bernie anxiously douses the truck's flames.

Now they notice Momma condor is drinking the salty water. Then she flies back to the tailgate. Before landing, she spits a mouthful of water directly onto that sliced opening; then hovers as it sizzles. Everybody is splashing water onto it as she sits down there again. Glenn is astonished as he is holding her baby-boy condor. Mamma condor squawks to her baby-girl on the right corner of the tailgate. She responds, jumping off the tailgate and awkwardly walking between the people, she settles onto Glenn's lap next to her brother. Momma condor reaches her head high and spreads her big wings all the way across the back of the truck, as if providing shelter. Everybody is looking at her, including her babies. Momma condor's eyes glaze over, and she falls backwards into the water: Dead...

It was over in an instant . . . Glenn is thinking, "Apparently that was a small slice of the Fiery Syphon's burning ray cutting through the crack in the ceiling. It cut into her like a surgical laser, killing her from the pain, or the shock, or vital organs being destroyed. She must have been in *terrible pain*. But she was able to fly after being burned . . . Mercifully, shock smothers pain. Even terrifying pain – **mercifully . . .** I had experienced painful terror - existing beside that shark for days, but apparently shock overwhelmed my terrorizing pain and enabled me to function. The mother Condor had done her duty while she was in pain by transferring the welfare of her babies to me. She felt my compassion and empathy for them."

As if she could read Glenn's silent thoughts, Margherita says, "God is telling you to protect these babies. You had said that we should protect them because they are becoming extinct." Her face is aglow with spiritual zealotry. They all see the babies' mother laying on top of the water, her scrawny feet sticking upside down out of the water with her neck and head sunk underneath. The babies, mournfully squawking, each bury their head into Glenn's armpits, snuggling as close as possible. Then everyone is silent . . . Quiet respect; while trying to fathom this surreal, bizarre experience.

Finally, CIA Jane says accusingly, "That hot beam of light was *your 'Fiery Syphon'* passing over us . . . I thought we would have heard more of the melee outside, the wind sucking up the sand, maybe rocks sliding, maybe animals screeching and screaming - *something!?!*"

"What could we hear from inside this cavern. We saw all the animals migrating away; there are no people, and the desert sand - we saw it melt into glass here, without making a sound. What would be making noise, other than the wind, and we were so engrossed watching the Momma Condor die, we probably just didn't hear it." Glenn doesn't understand his own defensiveness. "It would've sounded like a vacuum sucking up air - what does that sound like absent the electric motor. I guess we might have felt it sucking the air from the cavern through that tiny hole in the ceiling if we were paying close attention."

Margherita says, "I felt my hair moving a little by a quick breeze."

"See . . ." Jane chimes in, this time without sneering, "It proves what I said before, the most primitive among us are more inclined to be in tune with nature, have premonitions and experiences from the natural world."

Bernie replies, "This Fiery Syphon is anything but natural. I can't imagine this planet has ever experienced anything like this before, life would not have survived."

Glenn says meaningfully, "Life can be very determined to survive all kinds of horrors; maybe sometimes wishing that it had not survived it..." He endures flashing images of his abuse of Graziela, he feels shame every time he looks at her son Ricardo. And now, he feels humiliation at the stirring in his pants as he reflects on that violence he made her endure. He winces as he thinks, "Why is it now illuminating my brain with lustful passion. This is disgusting..." He is shocked that his pecker could be responding to that abusive memory at a time like this. "It *truly does* have *a mind of its own!* But then, she seemed to get 'turned-on' by my abusiveness. - *AND,* why do *I NOW* have the urge to reach out and *pull Margherita* by the hair?!?"

They remain sitting quietly with no more traumatic events occurring. They are in a stupor, half asleep, lost in their own narcoleptic trance, each trying to lean their head on the metal truck in such a way as to enable sleep.

After a while they float by the cement-gate and Glenn manage is to tie a blanket around the gate's control-deck railing and ties the other end to the truck's tailgate chain. The truck won't float around the cavern now. They didn't realize it, but the interior lights had shut off due to the rising waters shorting-out the electrical boxes. But there is one fluorescent light above the cement-gate's control area that automatically turns on when the gate is closed as it is now.

Then, after several hours, everybody jerks with fright with the impact of the wheels settling into the sandy floor. Bernie says, "At least we don't have to worry about drowning anymore, the water is receding back down the Gusher's lava tube. If you listen, you can hear a difference in the sound. It's more of a gurgle than a roar." He checks his watch: "It's after 4:00 PM. It should end soon as the Pacific tide is receding. We must have electricity here as this fluorescent light is still lit. It's coming from Loon-Evator2's center cable thru the outside railroad tracks. That's a good sign, that track must still be intact; even though they have buckled here inside the cavern. When the water completely recedes, we can close the Gusher-Tower's maintenance door. Then I suggest that we open the cavern's cement-gate and survey the damage."

Glenn responds, "Yes, but since I am the oldest, I will go out by myself at first and see what it's like. We don't know - there might be radioactive rays emanating from these rocks that got baked by the Fiery Syphon. For all we know, it might be unfiltered radio-active sunlight that's been funneled directly through our atmosphere - like through a wormhole."

Bernie gives him a radiation detection alarm to wear from the truck's glove compartment, noting, "It's already registering a little above normal radiation. It must be from being sealed in here with the nuclear-waste barrels." Glenn opens the cement-gate, but it won't move beyond a few feet; maybe just enough to drive the truck out. Then they recoil as the heat hits them like a sledge-hammer. The temperature soars to 127 degrees Fahrenheit. He discards the radiation detector as it becomes burning hot as he walks outside the gate. The baby condors are following behind him; he at first gestures and then runs at them as if to make them return inside the cavern, but they ignore him and continue to follow outside. Glenn sees that the tops of the railroad tracks have melted. They'll have to be replaced. Loon-Evator2 is nothing but a little smoldering debris, but the center cables are intact, the outside insulation is still smoldering as far up as he can see. There must be enough of Skyhook still floating up there to gather some electricity and support the weight of the wires. The valley's desert sand has baked into a glassy surface. The top of the cliffs going north show signs of molten lava cooling off. Glenn comes back inside the cavern, and he finds that Jane is running the truck; she's turned on the air conditioning. Glenn cautions, "Make sure you're not wasting all the gas, we still have to drive back to the Hacienda and if it's destroyed, we may have to drive out of the tunnel in the north."

Bernie whines, "I told her, but she won't listen." Glenn opens the passenger side door and grabs Jane by the hair, pulling her out of the truck, and throwing her down to the ground. He shuts off the ignition. Everybody is sweating profusely.

Glenn growls, "As Bernie said before, we have to wait, we have to shut the Gusher-Tower's maintenance door after the water recedes."

Bernie implores, "We got to get out of here; I'll dive down and close it."

CIA Jane's humiliation is conquered by concern, *"Are you crazy!"* as she gets up from the ground, "Do you want to be *sucked down* into its lava tube *with the water!!"*

Bernie retorts, "We'll tie a rope around me; you all will hold on to me."

Glenn commands, "There's no sense taking foolish chances. We'll just wait out this heat until the Sun sets." Everybody wants to get back to the Hacienda, or some sort of civilization; but they must yield to the Patronne's ruling. There are some drinks left in the little refrigerator and they quickly finish them off. Then Margherita takes a rope and ties it to the rear of the truck and holding onto it walks down the ramp into the receding water, just to cool off. The others quickly grab onto the rope and follow behind her. The baby condors awkwardly walk, following behind Glenn.

The cold water provides wonderful relief; they all follow the baby condors lead, ducking their heads under to cool their brains off. But it's too cold and they begin shivering. They come out and sit for a few moments and rapidly heat up again, then return to the water. This process keeps them busy for a while and they're somewhat amused watching the baby condors flounder in the water. They are not strong enough to prevent themselves from floating away in the current: then with a squawk they fly back to Glenn. Finally, the sunlight's glare is fading around the cement-gate. Bernie jogs up the ramp and looks outside the gate. He notes the temperature, "It is now down to 105 degrees Fahrenheit. I think that temperature is tolerable" he says to Glenn; "The Sun is behind the cliffs. At least we will be in the shade, if we leave now."

Glenn is thinking, "The temperature has been known to drop 50 degrees overnight in the desert; it would be good to get back to the Hacienda and see what we're dealing with in daylight, there probably won't be any electricity." He nods and tells Bernie, "You'll have to come back when this cavern drains to close the Gusher-Tower's maintenance door." They all pile in the truck with joyous relief to be escaping the nuclear-waste's tomb of torture. Bernie drives into the entrance-way but finds that he cannot maneuver around the cement-gate. Then Glenn drives the truck slowly up against the left-hand side of the cement entrance gate; he puts it in four-wheel drive and slowly revs-up the engine; it doesn't budge. Then everybody else gets out and pushes their weight up against the gate. The condors gawk at them from the back of the truck. It finally moves a few feet then slides off its track with a thud . . . It's not moving any further. Glenn tries to maneuver the truck, but the cement-gate is against the rear right fender. The other three get behind and feverishly begin bouncing the truck with their body weight, they force it up and down. Then Bernie groans, "NOW!" as it is springing up, they force their feet into the ground and lift it to the left. After 3 more heaves they get it to move four inches. The Condors flap their wings and slam into each other with each heave, squawking bitterly. Margherita is yelling a malicious stream of Spanish cursing at them as she feels they are lustfully looking at her bouncing naked boob. The fender is now away from the cement-gate and Glenn is able to drive out into the desert. They jam into the cab of the truck and their sweaty bodies instantly begin to shiver from the air conditioning.

XXXVIII

THE SINGED VALLEY

They take in the devastated panorama as they are driving north. Jane gives a running commentary in English, and Spanish for Margherita. "Look at the mountain cliffs on the left. It looks like the Fiery Syphon came down more South than West, melting that wide path along the cliffside for miles, from the base over here, up to the top of the cliffs back at the cavern." They drive several miles, "Look at the ground here. It is baked, but also the ground is raised as if it was being sucked up and baking at the same time, kind of like rows of ice cream cones."

Margherita questions, "What's an ice cream cone?" They all laugh in surprise. "I don't know what it is, I never seen one, I never even heard that said before."

Bernie says, "I am going to order a railroad car full of them from Pequito for everybody at the Hacienda when they get back."

Glenn is trying to get some information on the truck's radio; nothing but static. They try their cell phones, but they were ruined in the water. Bernie pulls his laptop computer out from under the seat and plugs it in. He gets a weather report:

> 'The Fiery Syphon went up the mountain just southwest of Pequito as predicted; but then it wobbled to the South as evidenced by the fact that it materialized on the southwestern coastline 18 miles further south of where it was projected to go; burning everything to a crisp.'

Bernie reacts, "Oh my God, that was supposed to wobble only 5 or 10 miles off of its projected path. Evacuating 25 miles north or South of it should have been safe. But if it wobbled 18 miles off its path crossing over the mountain, the additional 8 miles may not have been enough to protect everybody. They say the murderous heat extends 5 miles on all sides of it. - Well, at least it didn't go north, as far as we know, where our train was heading."

Margherita doesn't quite understand but is making the connection between the train and the Fiery Syphon, she cries, **"Elena!?!"**

Jane assures her, "It went South, but Elena was going directly north, away from it. All the heat came South towards us; she is at least 60 miles north of us by now." They drive over that quarter mile wide section of blistered glassy desert sand with an occasional semi-melted boulder, clearly outlining the path that the Fiery Syphon had taken. And then beyond that, back to a flat glassy like surface for about 6 miles.

Then the familiar landscape returns . . .

Bernie ventures, "Could it be; our Hacienda was spared?" They see ahead of them burnt remains of Skyhook's balloons on the ground. Then, Margherita gasps in disbelief. On the eastern side of the valley, hanging down from the sky, they see a wall of Skyhook's balloons, going up out of sight, disappearing into heaven. They had been exploded, obviously, but did not burn-up as they were not in the direct path of the Fiery Syphon. Glenn wonders about repairing all those balloons, like he had done before, after the Big Syphon hit on a prior equinox. He's not looking forward to climbing on them and re-attaching them to Skyhook again, as he had to do when he first started building it - and then again after the first Big Syphon destroyed it. He has help now . . . people working up there with him; but he feels that it's too dangerous to ask of them, to be climbing around on the edges the balloons, 22 miles straight up in the air.

They can see some arcing in the shadows, flashing inside the debris. He is comforted knowing that there's still electricity flowing and hopefully they still have electricity at the Hacienda: the air conditioning might be working. They pass by this debris field, and looking up at the sky, can see that all of Skyhook's H-cube-balloons to the southwest were pulled towards the east: as the easterly balloons collapsed, their falling weight pulled in the balloons from the west - as they continued to collapse from the heat - and formed that wall of collapsed H-cube-balloons.

Everything at the Hacienda appears to be as they had left it. The girls run to the kitchen for water and food, they're starving. Now Glenn notices something is different. The Loon-Evator is gone. The flatbed railroad car that had his Mini-Shuttle on it, is empty. The ramp is down. The forklift is nearby. Obviously, it was not taken or destroyed by the Fiery Syphon as there's no sign of debris. Glenn looks up into the sky: "*FUCK! – Could it have been my friendly Alien? . . . What the fuck!?! That was only a dream?!?* I am sure he wouldn't need my Mini-Shuttle to escape the Fiery Syphon. But - *I was dreaming?!?*" Jane brings him a sandwich and iced tea which he quickly swallows. "More." he tells her. He checks on his Jet-Basket everything is intact. He strips down to his socks and t-shirt. She brings back more food as he's getting into his space-suit pants. His mind is spinning as he is stuck in a vicious cycle, searching for answers. He needs to sit down; but instead grabs onto Jane's shoulder for support. She is shocked at his leaning on her while nonchalantly displaying his full-frontal nakedness.

Bernie had eaten and then had gone to the bathroom. He returns just in time to see Jane's alarm. "Glenn, you're turning into the caricature of an 'Absent Minded Scientist'." he says feigning humor. Glenn's eyes are a glaze of confusion.

Margherita comes running as she suddenly realizes, "Donde es la Loon-Evator?"

Glenn points up with a bewildered expression muttering, "Aliens . . ."

Jane seems to be the only one who comprehends him as she guffaws incredulously. Bernie is following Glenn's example by getting into his space-suit, but he modestly keeps his pants on. He looks to the loading area and sees that the center electric supply and control cables are in tack – no damage from the Fiery Syphon, "Who took the Loon-Evator?" as he is getting into his space-suit, "Everybody else is supposed to be on the train *in Columbia?!?*"

Then Jane shouts, "*Where is that **fucking MINI-Space Shuttle?!?***" pointing at its empty railroad flatbed car.

Glenn's stupor begins to defog as the others are approaching his state of bewilderment. He's thinking, "They seem to be as upset as I am, but the Shuttle **cost me** *$13 million.*"

"Wait, let me get my space-suit on; I'll go with you." Jane says. Glenn is inclined to tell her to stay behind, but then, worried that she may run away with the truck, he agrees.

Margherita exclaims, *"Me too!* You are not gonna leave me all alone down here." as she is putting on a space-suit. All four of them climb into the Jet-Basket. Recalling when she was dangling out over the edge, high in the sky, Margherita squats down on the floor and holds onto the toilet in the corner. This being CIA Jane's first time on the Jet-Basket, follows her lead and clings to the other side of the toilet. Bernie reminds everybody to lower their helmet's sun shield. They float above 15000 feet. Nobody notices the two condors have joined them until the girl-bird flops over unconscious, her brother is squawking nervously. Glenn lifts her up and throws her over the edge, her brother flies down after her; everybody is shocked that Glenn can be so callous.

But then they see far below the two birds flying in circles. "It must have been the cold or the lack of oxygen at this altitude, but she's alright now." They float up the 22 miles to the Skyhook. They see that the Loon-Evator is docked there, with its loading ramp open. "One mystery solved . . ." Glenn is thinking, "Now I will have witnesses to confirm my *friendly Alien's* existence." Glenn recklessly guides the Jet- Basket up in between Skyhook's loading-bay and the Loon-Evator's ramp. It's a tight fit and its lift balloon bounces off the Skyhook on one side, then the Loon-Evator on the other side, making the Jet-Basket sway precariously from side to side. Glenn is not alarmed as he has experienced much worse than this; but the others betray fearful glances.

XXXIX

❖

NOT MY FRIENDLY ALIEN?

They tie on to Skyhook, climb over its railing and walk through its loading-bay. Bernie and Jane are supporting Margherita's arms as she had never experienced this 'near-space' environment. Glenn is, at first, relieved to see his beautiful Mini-Shuttle is in the mag-lev launch-pad area. Then he is alarmed, "It's lying flat on the rails, it's wheels must be retracted - or *broken off!* It is facing inward – the wrong *direction for launching?!?* What is that covering its exterior? Is it some kind of *fungus? NO . . .* It's nanotube cable wrapped around it . . ." Then CIA Jane sees the Professor through the window, inside of Skyhook's cabin. She bangs on the glass and runs to the door; the others follow her and anxiously await the air-lock to adjust. The four of them go inside, taking their helmets off, joyfully greeting the Professor. He's sitting in the chair as if in a daze. Glenn demands, "You're supposed to be on the train with your family: *what happened?"* No answer . . . "You tried to launch the Shuttle? *Obviously!* You had it facing *the wrong way - You were going to launch it backwards? – dumb-ass!"* Glenn can't help being disappointed; he fully expected to see his friendly Alien.

The Professor ignores the expressions of concerns from the others saying blandly, "I did launch it, I flew it one orbit, and it brought me back here automatically - I don't quite understand it myself. I've been preoccupied with waiting for the Fiery Syphon to kill me."

Glenn doesn't believe him. He challenges, "How could you have done that?" Jane goes and gets more refreshments and food for everybody from the refrigerator, and they all sit around and listen to the Professor's explanation of what happened. Lastly, he asks what time it is, and then raises the question as to why his clock was 35 minutes behind all the others when he returned.

Jane says, "You know time slows down with speed. Maybe you were going faster than normal speed."

"I would have had to been going much, much faster; no, I was wide awake all the time, it could *not* have been a *full 90 minute flight* - like it was supposed to have been. I completed one full polar orbit and my watch verified that it took less than 55 minutes. My watch is 35 minutes behind yours."

Glenn speculates, "The Professor has become a delusional lunatic. Maybe he has not recovered from the trauma of his son's snakebite – The Fiery Syphon arrived about 20 miles to the south, but up here in near-space, was it somehow able to cook his brain? Or maybe it really was the Alien that rescued him?" He walks around the cabin, searching for evidence as he challenges, "So you fired up the Space Shuttle's jet engines and guided it back onto the Railgun's tracks? Wasn't the Railgun set for launching instead of landing; how could it have returned against the magnetic-field?"

"I reversed the Shuttle's magnetic-field as I could see I was accelerating on a crash collision course. I had previously reversed it as I was being magnetically deflected off the polar orbit by the Earth's magnetic south pole, then I reversed it back again as I was being deflected off course by the north magnetic pole. Then I saw I was going to crash; I saw my speed was accelerating. I reversed it again as I thought I was crashing into Skyhook, and the next thing I knew I was enveloped in electrical arcing and couldn't see anything. Then as it subsided, I found that I was stopped, hovering at our mag-lev's launch-pad. So, I shut off the power to all the magnetic-fields and it landed as you see it now on the Railgun's tracks." He adds apologetically, "I forgot to lower the landing wheels . . ."

Glenn looks at him incredulously, "The Earth's magnetic-field is only about 1/10,000 the strength of a *simple bar magnet!?!* How can it effect the Mini-Shuttle speeding at 18,000 miles-per-hour?"

"I don't understand it either. Could it be the computer's artificial intelligence sensed my high-speed return and reversed the launch procedure? – I'm perplexed . . . Even the Sun's magnetic-field is only

1/1000 the strength of a bar magnet. But they block all the universe's perilous electro-magnetic waves. There must be some other factor that combines the Earth's magnetism with its gravitational mass; that the Minnie-Shuttle tapped into. How else can we explain why the Earth's magnetic-field extends into space 75000miles; the Sun's extends out billions of miles. I am mystified . . ."

Glenn shakes his head in puzzlement, "So you lost 35 minutes on a 90-minute flight - it had to have been a 90-minute flight – *as a minimum!* - *AND* you didn't suffer anything from the inertia of the takeoff. *You should be dead . . .*"

The Professor replies, guiltily, "Well, I expected to be dead; I guess I was waiting for Gabriel's horn to summon me . . . I wasn't sure I was alive until you showed up here. Although, I didn't even think about the inertia killing me. I didn't experience *anything* – **NOTHING!!** I bounced a bit when the magnetic-field built up and the Shuttle began to levitate. It scared me; I don't know why – I should have expected that. Fortunately, I had fastened my seatbelt. My computer showed the magnetic-field continued to build; and then I was launched . . . I was single stepping the launching instructions, and I hit launch, and the next thing I knew I could briefly see a blur of the tracks, and then I was *out in the sky!* My body did not feel any inertial pressure – **NOTHING** – It was like *I wasn't moving at all?!?"*

Glenn contests, "You must not have set your watch correctly..."

The Professor protests mildly, "No, I had the alarm set, it woke me up as the system was becoming activated and I checked my watch: it was at 11:00AM." Seeing Glenn's disbelief, he becomes angry, "My watch was correct, and it has been working ever since . . . I programmed the mag-lev to start power up *at 11:00 o'clock!*"

Jane is protectively chastising Glenn, "Why won't you believe him, if he says his watch was correct - it *was correct!"*

The Professor is at first offended by her bold intrusion into their scientific, intellectual debate; but then gratified by her desire to protect him. Then she asks, "When you saw all that arcing, or electrical sparking, as you were coming back in, was it along the lines of flux – you know - like you see with the iron filings outlining the magnetic-field."

The Professor replies matter-of-factly, "No, those metal filings that you see describe something that does not exist within our 4-dimensional space/time."

Bernie queries, "I guess that means those lines of flux exists in another dimension."

Jane is puzzled, "What do you mean they *don't exist* - you could see it with the metal filings."

"You can't touch it, wait – God-damn-it . . ." Exasperated that he has to explain the basics to her, "If it does not occupy space, nor have mass, doesn't weigh anything - therefore – it does not exist in our dimension." Jane is dumbstruck.

The Professor is becoming more irritated, "We can discuss 'Time' in 'Einstein's Theory of Relativity': In space-time - ah - and losing 'Time' the faster you go – 'Time' slows down - the faster you go your mass increases, you need more energy to move that additional mass, until it will require an infinite amount of energy to propel that continuously increasing mass . . . But, you think I might have been going faster - more than one orbit but - ah no - I had landmarks plotted – along the way - that I was able to see - there is no question - I only did one orbit . . ."

Bernie interjects his youthful logic, "You agree that the Earth's magnetic-field is only about 1/10,000 the strength of a simple bar magnet and even the Sun's magnetic-field is only 1/1000 the strength of a bar magnet!?! You question how can it effect the Mini-Shuttle speeding at 18,000 miles-per-hour? Isn't it obvious, the Mini-Space Shuttle's magnetics has broken through to *another dimension!* A '*magnatraction'* dimension – or a '*magneton'* dimension! Maybe the Shuttle's extreme level of magnetism broke through to another dimension where the Earth and Sun's extreme magnetism exists. It's apparent that only a small portion of the Sun's extreme magnetism filters through to our dimension. Look at the *strength* of those magnetic storms on the Sun. *Jesus! They blast the CMEs into deep-space!!* We would expect these heavenly bodies to have *extreme magnetism* ~ not just a *small fraction* of a simple bar magnet. Professor, is there such a thing as a '*magnetic dimension'?*"

The Professor is thinking, "Next he'll be suggesting a *magnet-man super-hero.*" He responds with extended open hands combined with a muddled quiver of a head-shake.

Glenn ignores Bernie's juvenile speculation, He demands, "And, how did you endure being weightless?"

"I was strapped in the pilot's seat the whole time - I don't know, I didn't even think about it."

Glenn glances around the room, avoiding eye contact, muttering skeptically, "Well, why don't we just check the mag-lev's computer record of the Railgun's launch activity and see what we got. It will have recorded how much electricity was used, and what time it was used, and the strength of the magnetic-field, and – ah - the projection of the Railgun."

They key into that info: it started at 11AM and verifies everything the Professor said, including the mag-lev computer's elapsed time of 92 minutes. "Yes; I expected to be killed by the Fiery Syphon when I got back before high-noon. I was sitting here waiting for it at noon; I was pissed because I did all this to save the Shuttle and it was still going to be destroyed. But then, when nothing happened, I thought I must be dead already. I was waiting for oblivion to consume the rest of my consciousness. I was *getting bored* waiting for it to happen . . . My laptop computer, which I had with me inside the Shuttle, shows that it was only a 55-minute flight; 35 minutes short of what it should have been. And furthermore, it shows that the Mini-Shuttle's magnetic-field stayed on for a little more than 55 minutes. The video I recorded shows it is true, that I did one polar orbit." ~ He pauses to observe everyone's attentive expression, "At the start of my launching – here on Skyhook - the Railgun's computer showed the jump in electrical consumption at the levitation phase and then consumed a lot more electricity with the launching. Its magnetic-field remained constant for 93 minutes - and then it shows a *big influx* of electricity - *flowing backwards* - into the mag-lev's electrical supply. That was *when I landed!*" He further explains, "I reversed the magnetic-field on the Shuttle, and it was going against the magnetic flow and that induced electric current in the surrounding magnetic-field in the opposite direction - which flowed back into its magnetic-field generator. It looks like the Railgun regained virtually all *the electric energy* I used to launch!"

Glenn concedes, as there is no argument against the data. "*Son of a bitch...* you actually did *orbit the Earth!* It shows that you were flying a little more than 90 minutes. I can't believe you didn't suffer from *the inertia.* Are you *suicidal?!?*"

The Professor replies calmly, "I don't know - maybe my sub-conscious didn't want me to consider it . . ."

"It shows that you took-off *going 18,000 miles an hour* in less than *2 minutes . . .*" Glenn voices his intense frustration. "You came in for a landing at *over 18,000 miles an hour* and then you came to a *halt in less than one minute.* How could *you survive* that? Your organs should have been *squished . . .* Your brains should have **smashed** against the inside of **your skull!!**"

The Professor is in a quandary, "I didn't even feel it; nothing - no impact whatever until I shut off the magnetic-fields - when it had landed – hard on the tracks. Then I felt that impact; It scared the *shit out of me!*"

They review the videotapes that he had recorded out the windows of the Shuttle, and they could hear his comments to himself. Bernie says, "You are officially an 'ASTRONAUT' now, as you completed one Earth orbit." The Professor's face lights-up with awareness. Then Bernie pontificates, "We have to think of Spacetime as a 4-dimensional fabric that exists everywhere. (During that eclipse of the Sun, Einstein showed that Spacetime is warped by gravity.) The dimensions are: 1 = up, 2 = down, 3 = depth and 4 = time, as in occupying that same spacetime geographical position yesterday or today or tomorrow. It has to be a factor of passing through that Spacetime-Fabric in such a way that you accelerated the Space-Fabric, causing the slowing down of the Time-Fabric. *It must be an inverse ratio!!!*"

There is a long, pregnant pause as everyone was listening intently while observing his youthful glow of intellectual discovery.

"Take a shit . . ."

Glenn says in a pensively thought-provoking tone.

Then he slowly turns to face the Professor, ". . . and look for blood."

"Good idea." The Professor acknowledges as he goes into the bathroom. They can hear him urinating. he calls out, "No blood there . . ." Then, "Wait . . . EERRR, ah, wait . . . ERRRRR, aahhh, wait . . . *EEEERRRRRRRR*, aaahhhh . . . *NOoo*, everything is normal; *no blood there either!*" Another pregnant pause, then, "You want to come and *see for yourself?!?*"

⁓

They surreptitiously look askance from one to
the other; then divert their gaze . . .

⁓

CIA Jane finally breaks the silence, "That's a good idea, we'll swap the toilet's sewage tank and we can have it tested for blood. We'll send it to a lab in Pequito for testing." She solicits help from Margherita as she translates their task into Spanish; obviously, not very concisely . . .

Margherita busts-out into dubious laughter, "You can *TEST the Professor's* **SHIT** *all you want,* **but I ain't helping you!**"

Jane's eyes pop as she wonders if the words *'test his shit'* could have been better translated . . .

Bernie joins Margherita's laughter, then volunteers, "I'll swap-out the sewage tank."

Now everybody is laughing – Margherita thinks, "They are laughing *too much* . . . are they *laughing at me?*"

Glenn continues theorizing with the Professor, "There must have been something different than just your 'acceleration'. You had 35 minutes less of elapsed time, simply by going faster. Jesus, the atomic clock lost less than one second when they took it to the Moon and back – going much faster than 18000mph. But in one orbit you saved 35 minutes off your lifespan – that's 35- minutes you did NOT age - that you **DID NOT** *live thru.*" (Glenn's subconscious percolates: Experiment: accelerate faster & faster with one of two identical twin lab-rats. But; they already did that with Astronaut Scott Kelly versus his identical twin. He came back from space after a year in orbit, a little younger than his brother. Were they able to measure it biologically in his DNA? In his telomeres?) Pondering 'space/time fabric', Glenn says, "Remember the article you wrote . . .

Einstein said it's a fabric - and traveling through it faster, slows down time: that 'inverse ratio' crap! Or if you're making a hole through it, that would be like a wormhole, that means you're not going thru spacetime and there is no elapsed time, you would arrive at the other side of your trip instantaneously. A wormhole penetrating through the fabric I think is the theory behind time travel – into the past, or into the future." Then he thinks, "But my 'Friendly Alien' said the past is dead and gone, you can't ever go back in time. (Or was that a dream?)" Glenn's thought process fades into emptiness . . . Then it returns invigorated, speaking directly to the Professor, excluding everybody else. "But again, it makes sense that if you're traveling through spacetime fabric faster – therefore traveling through more time - you should be aging - not saving time. So, rather than passing through more spacetime fabric the faster you go, maybe your speed is just pushing that fabric aside. Like you explained in your article: As you're not traveling through it, but pushing it aside; explains why you gain mass. That's a better explanation than that 'acquired mass bullshit' simply materializing from nowhere. That mass you're gaining is the resistance of the spacetime fabric, as you are pushing it aside. - The faster you go, the more fabric you push aside - the greater the apparent mass that you've gained - because you are gaining the mass of that fabric which you're pushing aside. The faster you go, the more fabric you have to push to the side, the more resistance you encounter - the more mass you appear to gain." Glenn finalizes, "And the more spacetime fabric you are pushing aside, the less time-fabric you are passing through: therefore, less aging – less time endured, less time-fabric passed thru . . . Yeah, that makes sense, so how fast do you have to be going to have saved that 35 minutes out of your life?"

The Professor ignores that question and counters with another. "But obviously, something has to be different. I had no indication that I had gained any mass while accelerating."

Glenn is looking out the window at his Mini-Shuttle. He responds pensively, "Yes, obviously – though - the only thing different is that ugly – fungus looking - wire you wrapped haphazardly around it - you created the magnetic-field with the nanotube wiring . . ."

The Professor's eyes bulge, *"Eureka!! I CREATED AN EXTREME MAGNETIC-FIELD!!!"* Everybody's gawking between Glenn and the Professor.

Glenn says, *"Yes!* - Instead of speed pushing aside the fabric of space/time, your magnetic-field must have created a hole in space/time. Or maybe spacetime is *not a fabric*, but a magnetic-force-field that the Shuttle's magnetic-field deflected, or changed the environment, so that you were no longer traveling through that spacetime magnetic-field; kind of like entering another dimension. But you could see everything; even if you were in another dimension, you had visual perception into this dimension."

The Professor's excitement is making his face flush red, "Nothing makes sense; but the 'Super String Theory' claims that there are at least 10 different dimensions; some claim maybe thousands of different dimensions. Magnetic-fields and gravity function, as Einstein said, from that 'spooky distance without making any physical contact'. Maybe they make the contact through another magnetic dimension; that makes more sense than anything else we could think of. Scientists have found a huge magnetic-field existing between galaxies where there is absolutely nothing but empty space? It must come from another dimension. Maybe not necessarily entering another dimension – possibly just getting outside of this dimension? Maybe being within the small, enclosed Mini-Shuttle's magnetic-field; it squeezed me out of Earth's spacetime dimension - not necessarily into another one - just out of this one?!?"

Bernie says, *"Wow! That's what I just said:* **a MAGNETON DIMENSION!!"** They are all glaring at him with blank stares. **"Complex shit!!"** "Wormholes, Dark-matter, Dark-energy! Maybe this magnetic-field should be considered dark-energy?" The Professor tries to tune out this distraction as he is overwhelmed in technical considerations.

Glenn can't deter his entrepreneurial yearning, "The solution to economic space travel . . . Apparently, the Professor was able to guide our Mini-Shuttle by exploiting its magnetic-field against the Earth's magnetic-field. My rogue nuclear-waste barrel is oriented to the Earth's north magnetic pole when its orbit is north of the equator, but it shifts orientation in the southern hemisphere as it is apparently attracted to the Sun's magnetic polar field. The planets are held on the plane of the ecliptic by the Sun's concentration of equatorial gravity and maybe also its magnetic polar fields? Do the planets that have less - or no magnetic-field - orbit off the ecliptic?" Then he raises a question with the Professor, "How did the Mini-Shuttle maintain its magnetic-field without the constant flow of electricity once it was outside of the mag-lev environment?"

The Professor responds, "I don't know, maybe induced from the presence of the Earth's magnetic-field just like it is induced from the mag-lev's magnetic-field. Or maybe the solar wind blowing around *my* nanotube coils was enough to induce the required electrical flow to maintain its magnetic-field. I'll design some experimental tests to clarify how it works and I'll take it out again for another orbit. I want to take my son with me . . . he'll be thrilled to become an Astronaut, too."

Cia Jane explodes, ***"ARE YOU INSANE!?! YOUR WIFE WILL KILL YOU!!"***

Bernie calmly says, "You can't bring him up here without a space-suit made for his size. But I'll go with you; I would like to add 'Astronaut' to my resume."

Glenn says, "The Fiery Syphon has passed now. We've got to start launching the nuclear-waste to the Sun again. It's a lucky break that our mag-lev wasn't destroyed by it. Also, I don't know how much electricity we're getting after it hit, but there's about 30 square miles of balloons to be re-floated. I'll be working off the Jet-Basket in the stratosphere to rebuild Skyhook and re-establish the electricity supply. Our train should be back from Colombia with all our employees by midnight tonight so we can start launching tomorrow afternoon. Hopefully, we can get the military to start working on fixing our railroad tracks: maybe even tonight. And Juan can replace the damaged main railroad tracks with the undamaged rails in the east of the valley. Meanwhile Bernie, you can fly in the Jet-Basket to the Gusher-cavern, open the cement-gate with a forklift, and close the Gusher-Tower's maintenance door. Then you can load the Jet-Basket up with as many skids of nuclear-waste as possible and fly it up to Skyhook." Glenn's mind is racing to the renewal of their enterprise. "Jake and Sandro can start launching the nuclear-waste barrels again tomorrow afternoon, working 12-hour shifts. Also, Margherita can drive truck-loads of skids to the Loon-Evator for launchings. It will be slower; but at least we can keep it going until the military repairs the melted train tracks. We saw through the telescope that our last launchings have all burnt up in the

Sun's corona or were destroyed by the Fiery Syphon's CME." He pauses, then adds as an afterthought, "Maybe it's not a good idea to be launching while the Fiery Syphon is still active. But maybe our exploding Skyhook balloons destroyed it, like we had hoped it would. Although the radio reported it surviving long enough to come out on the western side of the Andes mountains and then go out to sea. We'll have to get more news on it. - Anyway, I'm flying the Mini-Shuttle tomorrow morning for one orbit. Professor, start thinking about those experiments and measurements we need to figure this shit out." Then he adds as an afterthought, "I will fly it tomorrow morning on my own. The Professor and I both cannot be gone at the same time, otherwise our whole operation may come to a halt . . . AND - I want to be an Astronaut *too!*"

The Professor has to get back into his space-suit. The others put their helmets on and go out to the launch-pad as Glenn tells Bernie, "Single step the mag-lev to float up the Mini-Shuttle so that I can lower its landing wheels. Then, if it's not damaged, you can tow it out with the fork-lift and reposition it to launch again."

As Glenn is climbing aboard, Bernie counters, "When we float the Mini-Shuttle, we should be able to turn it around by using our weight, just like I move the railroad cars around on their tracks, only here there is no friction resistance to overcome."

Simultaneously Jane is commenting, "I was concerned about the Professor's well-being but, if anything, he's more agile and alert - and happy . . . Have we heard anything from the train?"

Glenn nods a positive reply to Bernie then a negative to Jane while thinking, "We really stumbled onto something great here: the Professor did not suffer any inertia-pressure trauma. Was it because inside the magnetic-field he was in another dimension, and there was no speed? No traveling within that dimension that he was enclosed within, even though outside of that magnetic-field he was traveling at 18,000 miles an hour. He had accelerated to that within two minutes; it should have killed him 20 times over again." Glenn climbs up into the Mini-Shuttle and powers it up. Then he signals Bernie to start the mag-lev. Withing a minute it levitates off the ground, and he lowers the landing wheels. Glenn is thinking, "Now, I am within the Mini-Shuttle's magnetic-field: my time should be different."

Bernie goes to the Shuttle's nose, and he directs the two women to each push on a wing. As the 3 of them begin leaning their weight into it; the Shuttle easily starts to turn, from center to the right . . .

{But will the strong magnetic-field cooperate?}

The Professor is picking-up his space-suit's helmet and happens to observe thru the window what they are doing. He frantically pounds on the glass screaming, **"STOP THAT!** – *STUPID!!* – **STOP!!!"** They are engrossed in their novel task: trying to manually rotate a levitating, 12-ton, space Shuttle. They are 22 miles up in the stratosphere where there is no air to carry the sound waves, they cannot sense the Professor's frantic pounding on the window . . .

As the Shuttle responds with a gently delicate rotation from center of the Railgun towards the cabin on the right - everything is suddenly enveloped in **violent electrical** *arcing and sparks!* Each space-suit is being attacked by *lightning bolts*, illuminating them from head to toe. Inside their space-suits they can hear *the sizzle* of the high voltage, psychedelic, **bluish-silvery arcing!!** They fall to the floor and roll away; but the *electrically confounding* lightning bolts remain attached, reflecting its *terrifying flashing*, off of every square inch of their space-suits!

From the pilot's seat inside the Mini-Shuttle, Glenn cries out, "HOLY MOTHER OF GOD!?!" as he is *astounded* by this electrical storm's *blinding arcing* . . .

The Professor runs into the air-lock and puts his helmet on while yelling at them, "*Move away*, continue *rolling away* from it . . ." Glenn gets a glimpse of Bernie's space-suit rolling away, still engulfed in that electrical travesty, a lightning bolt *tenaciously stretching* out to him. Then, without anybody touching it, the Shuttle rotates back - left to center - and the arcing clears for a second. Then the arcing storm *engulfs everything again* as the Shuttle continues to rotate left towards the mag-lev controls. Then clears once more as it returns – right to center - again.

Glenn can now see the other 2 space-suits rolling away. *"Margherita!!"* he screams. Glenn runs to the Shuttle's air-lock. The arcing rhythmically illuminates the interior of the Shuttle as it sways side to side decreasing its degree of rotation. The lightning bolts finally relinquish their ownership of the space-suits, and the arcing fizzles out as the Shuttle returns to its original position and finally stops. The Professor exits the cabin in his space-suit and gingerly steps around the still electrified space-suits on the ground; he sees little arcs from them going into the floor. The Professor powers down the mag-lev computer and the Mini-Shuttle settles gently down on its landing wheels. Glenn comes out of the Shuttle's air-lock and climbs down the ladder. An electrical discharge leaps from his foot as it gets close to the floor. He and the Professor lift CIA Jane by her arms and legs, there is a little more arcing into the ground from the ass of her space-suit. They carry her into Skyhook's cabin's air-lock, then carry Margherita in and lay her beside Jane. Then they get Bernie, but he is able to walk with their support. He lays down across the other 2 as Glenn activates the pressurization of the air-lock.

Bernie says, as they are waiting for the air-lock to open, "I don't know what happened, but I think I am alright."

The Professor replies, "Your space-suit should have acted like a 'Faraday Cage', funneling the electricity around the outside of your space-suit then into the ground. It should not have penetrated inside the space-suits."

Glenn says looking down at them, "Hopefully it's just the shock-trauma and not the actual electrical-shock. I had a similar experience when I was constructing the Skyhook."

Then Jane responds saying, "I think I am alright . . . I don't know?" They look down at her as she leans on Margherita's space-suit to sit upright.

Then they notice they can *see inside* Margherita's helmet; her eyes are *wide open* in a *dead stare.*

The air-lock pressure equalizes, and they open the inner door as Glenn quickly removes her helmet. His hands cup her face in alarm as he looks into her lifeless eyes.

"YOU ROTTEN MOTHER-FUCKERS!!"

she suddenly screams; followed by a tirade of Spanish cursing. As she is scrambling to her feet, everyone runs into the cabin in dreadful *fear* of her; Bernie locks the inner door trapping her inside the air-lock. She is *screaming* and *pounding* on the door; her dead eyes are now *glittering* with *insanity.* Bernie tells her in Spanish to calm down and he'll open the door.

She screams, "You're the *stupid cocksucker* that told me what to do! *I'll tear your Fucken heart out!!*"

Bernie retorts, "It was Glenn that said we should do it . . ."

Glenn says, "Thanks a *fucken lot!*"

She continues with livid rage, calling him every name she can think of. When she calls him a *'fagot'* he responds vehemently, "How can you call me that in front of Jane; you know how I feel *about her!*"

Jane has fully recovered and says, "I have had enough of this nonsense . . ." and runs up to the telescope cabin. She is anxious to see if the CME is still connected to the Sun.

This does not deter Margherita as she screams, **"Open this door!"** then - *"I got to PISS!!"*

Bernie negotiates with her, "You can piss - only after you calm down." When her voice is less intimidating, Bernie has the Professor open the door as he cowers behind the couch. Margherita runs past the Professor and Bernie quickly shifts further away from her. Shaking her outstretched fist, she rushes past his frightened gaze – into the bathroom.

She comes out, breathing heavily, glaring at Bernie, then at Glenn. "How do I get *my ass out* of this **fucking space-suit?!?**" she demands. Glenn helps her.

The Professor says, "That was pretty stupid: you knew that the Shuttle's magnetic-field was going to align with the mag-lev's magnetic-field. Changing that magnetic alignment caused the field to breakdown with all that violent arcing."

Glenn replies, "I guess I should have, but my mind was elsewhere... This has been *some fucking day!* Let's get out of here." He summons Jane, "We are leaving now, come here immediately, unless you want to be locked in here again." She hurries back.

The Professor, and the two women walk down the ramp onto the Loon-Evator; but Margherita will not let Bernie on, screaming, **"You are a piece of shit!!** That's why you *got shitted-out* of the Skyhook! Go with Glenn in the Jet-Basket . . . I'll throw your *ass over the side* if you try to get on here with me!"

Now his manly-hood is challenged, and he replies, *"I'd like to see you try it . . ."*

Then Jane intervenes telling Bernie, "Ride with Glenn and give **her primitive temper** a chance to calm down."

The Professor says chuckling to Glenn, which they can all hear through their space-suit radios, "I don't know if you should trust her anymore: *she's a terror!*"

Glenn says, "I guess that's the price you have to pay for having *a hot Mama!* Come with me Bernie, I'm waiting for you."

The Loon-Evator and the Jet-Basket float down, side by side, towards the Hacienda. At 35,000 feet Bernie notices an unusual cloud below. As he is drawing Glenn's attention to it, he sees that it is coming from the South of the valley and suddenly they are engulfed in it. It is freezing cold, kicking their space-suit's heating unit into high gear. As they pass through it, ice is forming on all services and suddenly everything is getting heavier. The balloon motors kick in to heat up their gas to expand and maintain their buoyancy, and release more of their compressed gas from their tanks to maintain elevation. They do not want to descend so fast and lose control. Then they come out of the cloud and find that they are in a snowstorm. It is a peculiar snowstorm: the flakes are gritty with sand. They hear Margherita's voice on the radio marveling; she had never seen snow before. She is trying to remove her helmet; but Jane explains "You'll have to wait as we are still too high, and this altitude can kill you like it almost killed me."

Glenn is examining the icy flakes and determines how these flukie-flakes materialized, "Bernie, we did this."

Bernie realizes immediately, "Something's wrong at the Gusher-Tower and its nozzles have reverted to its default position of squirting straight up. The Gusher-Spray must have gone hundreds of miles into space directly above us and it's just now falling back to earth in the form of snow and ice, with its sediment-sand included in its snowfall. The control platform must have burnt away from the Fiery Syphon. But the nozzles were constantly being cooled by the Gusher- spray so hopefully they were not damaged. That spray was supposed to be directed to the path of the Fiery Syphon to mitigate its damage. Well, you wanted to freeze all the snakes to death . . ." Although Glenn had wanted to spray the valley and cover it up with snow to kill all the poison snakes; he did not want it wasted at this time on that, while the Fiery Syphon's fires were burning everywhere.

Margherita cannot wait and again tries to remove her helmet at 18000 feet altitude, but Jane explains again, "The space-suit's safety lock won't let you remove it at this altitude. If it did you would die, like I almost died." Finally at 2000 feet they remove their helmets, and they are catching snowflakes in their mouths. They taste salty and have a grittiness to them. Jane is complaining, "These are not normal snowflakes; they taste funny."

Margherita is laughing with delight at this exciting phenomenon and refuses to allow her crazy comments to distract from it. Then her eyes widen with surprise as she says, "Jane, your nose is red, your *cheeks too!* Why do you **look like a clown?"**

Jane laughs saying, "Yours too." Margherita gets a mirror and looks at her face and can't believe it. She has never had a red nose and red cheeks like this before, and it is freezing. She laughs with joy and goes back to capturing the snowflakes in her mouth.

They land at the Hacienda. There is already 5 inches of snow covering everything. Jane shows Margherita how to make snowballs and then they throw them at the Professor; then at Bernie and Glenn as they are getting off the Jet- Basket. Margherita is taking a particular delight in whaling them as hard as possible at Bernie. She is laughing hysterically, **"Como fantastico!"** She has seen ice on the mountain tops from a distance. She knows that somewhere it will snow, but she has never experienced it before.

Bernie anxiously updates his 'Mother Nature's Blog:

'Warning: evacuating only 25 miles may not be enough, the Fiery Syphon climbed west-southwest up the Andes Mountain; but then inexplicably wobbled and traveled further southwest across the mountain peaks. But then it returned to its predicted path, so we expect it will continue on that path. Maybe it was the high mountains that threw it off course?'

Margarita commands Jane to help her in the kitchen to make sure everything is secure from the snow; never having experienced it before. Jane protests saying that she must review the video that she took of the Near-Earth Asteroids, because something interesting is happening with some Aten - Earth Crossing – Trojan Asteroids. Margarita dissects her statement then arrogantly translates it: "You gotta look at video of *'ass-hemorrhoids'* & *'Trojan-rubbers',* so you can *test* the Professor's *shit!?!*

Do you think I'm **STUPID!** If you don't help me with this, you don't get *anything to eat!*"

Jane is protesting, "There's nothing to do except wipe the snow off, then cover everything with plastic. The canopy over the kitchen area should have kept most of the snow off . . ."

Margarita doesn't wanna hear it. "Come with me you *lazy bitch!*"

Jane complies pouting, "So you think that you are the new Petrona just because *Elena is not here!* You just wait until she gets back . . ." Margarita eyes her suspiciously, not quite understanding what she meant as she was speaking English, not Spanish.

Glenn decides to go with Bernie as re-establishing the Gusher-Tower's targeting spray along the Fiery Syphon's path is the most important mission to accomplish. They refuel the truck and the Jet-Basket then return to the cavern again, towing the fork-lift behind them. They close the Gusher-Tower's maintenance door, as the next high-tide will be coming soon, and they don't want it to flood the cavern. The seawater in the cavern had all flowed back down the Gusher's lava-tube. Everything is pretty much the same, the seawater had extinguished all the burning skids. Only one stack of skids had collapsed when the bottom skid had burned-up, toppling over those stacked on top of it. Only one busted through its metal bands and its six barrels rolled down the slope to the lower cavern. But these barrels did not break open; their nuclear-waste was still safely contained.

Then Bernie and Glenn put their space-suits on and float the Jet-Basket up to the top of the Gusher-Tower to assess the damage from the Fiery Syphon's equinox attack - it is total. The Loon-Evator2 is gone, however its cables are still hanging. There are exploded balloons everywhere. They are hanging down - attached to the balloons on Skyhook's east that are still floating 22 miles up in the stratosphere - still providing electricity. The Gusher-tower's control platform is totally gone. The electric supply wires are burnt-off the Gusher-tower's motorized nozzles. Using tools on the Jet-Basket they unbolt the motor and take it with them to be repaired in the Hacienda. Now they are torn between the possibility of damaging flooding from their spray or the consequences of doing nothing to minimize the scorching fires. Bernie suggests spraying it out harmlessly over the Pacific. Glenn's thinking of the terrible heat they had endured, "I am figuring a flooding rainfall is better than a raging fire. So, let's lock it into the East

Coastal position, hopefully it will spread out as it falls into the thicker atmosphere. Remember how it flooded the Peruvian coastal mountains. You must come back here before each high-tide and manually re-direct it to the Fiery Syphon's latest predicted path."

They return to the cavern and using the forklift, are able to lift the cement-gate up onto the track and then tow it where it is usually parked. Now the entranceway is totally clear, and they can drive the forklift in and out - and the train tracks going into it can be repaired. They use the forklift to pick up skids of nuclear-waste loading them into the Jet- Basket. Glenn cautiously floats the Jet-Basket; "It is not strong enough to carry all that weight. I am concerned that it may rip through the Jet-Basket's woven wicker. I'll only take 2 skids." They stack six skids on the back of the truck. As Glenn is trying to gain elevation, he sees the Jet-Basket cannot maintain the altitude carrying the weight of 2 skids. He concludes that their efforts would be better spent repairing the train tracks so they can move skids in volume. So, he flies back to the Hacienda at ground level following the truck and they unload the skids of nuclear-waste onto the Loon-Evator.

They finally get some late evening news. They were surprised to find that there were fires still raging all along the Colombian border to the north of them where their train was going. They are thankful Margherita doesn't hear this news. She would be further enraged if she knew Elena might be in danger from these fires.

Glenn and Bernie sit at the dinner table as the Professor is just finishing. He assures Glenn that he's got the experiments planned for his Mini-Shuttle orbit tomorrow morning. He goes back to his office to continue working. Margherita gently places Glenn's food in front of him as CIA Jane slams Bernie's food down in front of him. Jane confronts Glenn, "You better talk to your girlfriend... I don't like the way she's bossing Bernie around. I can take her shit, but Bernie doesn't have to. Now that Elena, *your wife*, is not here, she thinks that she is the *God-damn Petrona - the QUEEN . . .*"

Margherita yells, "You *loco* **Gringa Bitch**, why you got to bother him?!? Don't you see he's *tired!?!*"

Jane leers at her, "She fucks with me I'll *tear out her jugular!*"

Glenn says, "Humph - 'tear out her jugular' – But yet you still deny that you are *a fucking CIA Agent.* Since when did you become so high and mighty? You are a prisoner here - you've got nothing to say."

Bernie picks up his food and heads to his cabin, too exhausted to endure petty squabbling. Jane ignores the CIA comment, "I may be your prisoner, but I am *nobody's slave!*"

He counters, "I could have you thrown in jail for life for *attempted murder!*"

She exclaims, *"What?!?* I shot your helium storage tank, *not you.* If I wanted to shoot somebody - *I would have hit them."*

"You blew it up while I was *diving* behind it - but you were *shooting at me . . . **That's attempted murder!**"*

She says, "I was out of my head, I didn't know what was going on."

He retorts sarcastically, "I don't think this country accepts *temporary insanity pleas . . .* You'll do well in a local prison for the next *40 years.* I'm sure these local jailers would love to have an *arrogant young Gringa* to entertain them . . . Stop causing me fucking aggravation; or I'll use my considerable influence to have your *sophisticated ass* locked up! - Just try to get along."

Margarita is tired of Jane's whining, thinking, "You stupid, bleach blonde, *Gringa Virgin;* you think you can compete *with me!?!*" She approaches Glenn from behind, wraps her arms around him and flagrantly reaches down to his groin and erotically tickles him. He involuntarily fondles her boobs against his face. She lifts her sweater up exposing her naked boobs and then pulls her sweater down over his head, squeezing his head between her boobs. Jane is looking on with a peculiar gaze of fascination. As he removes her sweater, Margarita slides down and nimbly opens Glenn's pants and delicately lifts his pecker and testicles. She starts licking them and humming with a gratifying 'Hhuuummmm'. Margarita eyes sparkle as she watches Jane's gaze become frozen. Glenn is torn between gaping at Jane and then down at Margarita. He stretches his legs out, lifting his buttocks, enabling Margarita to pull his pants down low and free one leg. She continues sucking and licking him all over his penis, then fondles his testicles while placing them in her mouth, then goes down below sensuously tickling everywhere with her quick tongue. Now Glenn is astounded at his voyeurism as he can't take his eyes off of Janes shocked face. Margherita pauses to inspect and then proudly displays her elongated, engorged accomplishment to Jane. And now her talent: She slowly slurps taking the whole length of it all the way into her mouth. Then she demonstrates how she is able to simultaneously lick his balls, turning her head while tonguing back and forth, circling left then right, then in and out. Jane is transfixed; {is it voyeurism . . .}. Glenn orgasms with a ferocious cry of relief . . .

Jane stomps off to her cabin. Margherita helps Glenn get his pants back on. They finish eating and go to his cabin and fall asleep. Too soon Glenn feels Margherita mounting him and inserting the head of his already erect penis. She's grasping his sunrise piss-hard-on, breathing heavily saying, "I got to get all I can - while I can." While completing the insertion, her vagina twitching on his penis. Glenn questions her with his weary gaze. "I have to go back to our fertility doctor again . . ." pausing and gasping with gratification. "He might tell me no more sex." She groans with a wiggle of her hips. Her tits jiggle, Glenn's hips reflexively thrust forward. Her face is glowing, "I think his big spatula did the job on my pussy . . ." Squealing orgasmicly, *"My period **is a WEEK <u>LATE</u>!**"* Glenn is surprised to find himself also orgasming with this announcement. Deep in her pussy, Glenn feels a wildly new sensation: a gentle rhythmic nibbling on the head of his pecker while tightly clamping onto its shaft, as if her uterus is seizing and milking him. He marvels as his mind ecstatically explodes with *joyful feelings* of *blissful contentment*. His consciousness is being drowned in *loving endorphins . . ."*

{Must be *Mother-Nature's* reward for fulfilling her plan . . .}

Then *serenity* . . . Then his urine escapes as he drifts off to sleep . . . She yelps as her pussy unclamps his pecker and she re-directs his urine flow into their empty coffee cups. She laughs recalling their mornings when she was taunting him and made this happen in the tent. ⁓

Late that night the train returns from Colombia. They are too tired to marvel at the new experience of snow. Sancho complains, "Glenn said he was going to freeze all the snakes to death; it's not what *God intended!*" Juan mercifully does not blow the whistle, and everybody quietly ambles off the train, trudging through the snow into their own cabins, grateful for the luxurious comfort of their own beds.

Elena creeps into Glenn's cabin and debates for an instant if she should force herself between Glenn and Margarita's nakedness or snuggling on Margarita's side of the bed. She settles for sandwiching Glenn between herself and her cousin. Then she quickly falls asleep. They wake-up in the morning and Glenn immediately notices the smell of charcoal. Margarita asks, "Why do you stink like smoke?" Elena is very groggy but relives her harrowing experience on the train – screeching backwards down the mountain through smoke and flames, and her fear for her baby. She is now sporting a noticeable bump beneath her belly button. She feels some remorse about letting her new husband leave for work without her sexually satisfying him. But she allows sleep to envelop her, feeling certain that Margherita had already *fucked his brains out.*

CIA Jane is preparing breakfast in the kitchen area. Bernie informs Glenn, "The Professor went up in the Loon-Evator before sunrise to install his experiments for the Mini-Shuttle's orbit. I am supposed to take you up in the Jet-Basket, and then I have to fly to the Gusher-Tower and adjust its spray. Sancho has the truck. He is building a new control platform that we will float to the top of the Gusher-Tower. I will use one of the Professor's old computers to control the Gusher-Tower's nozzle array motors and install it during the next low-tide.

Jane serves Glenn his breakfast saying, "I have some interesting information to show you when I am not too busy slaving for your royal household."

"What? Did the *CIA* stop *paying* your wages to your *family?!?*"

She ignores his snide comment, "I have telescope video of your favorite asteroid: '3753Cruithne'. It was impacted by another Aten Asteroid: '2010TK7', 1000-ft diameter".

"Really?" Glenn is genuinely astonished. "That's the 'HORSESHOE ASTEROID', it makes a horseshoe shaped orbit that comes close to the Earth every 700 years; but Earth's gravity pulls it beyond our orbit, alternating it between an inner, narrower, faster orbit; then an outer wider slower orbit. It's due to be coming near soon. I think it will be making that hard right-angle turn; changing its orbit to the other side of the horseshoe."

"I showed the video to the Professor this morning; he thinks its horseshoe days *are over!*"

Glenn is anxious to see this video, but doesn't want to give CIA Jane the satisfaction, "Okay, I'll take a look at it after I finish my breakfast." Bernie positions his computer so that they can all watch the video, then plays it. They can see 2 points of light; one is very small. The smaller one is accelerating towards the bigger one. It disappears behind it and then everything streaks out of the field of view. "That's disappointing - it doesn't look like much of anything."

Jane retorts, "What were you expecting, exploding fireworks from *14million miles away?!?*" After a long pregnant deafening silence, "It's a good thing you taught me to use the telescope's sun-shield. These asteroids are on the Sun's side of our orbit; we would have never been able to see this without using the sun-shield."

Glenn finally reacts, "Get your space-suit on and ride up with us; see if you can find it again with the telescope. Then you and the Professor can plot its course."

Bernie stops the video's constant replay and then the morning breaking news plays:

'There was so much coverage on the pilgrims being burned to death in Panama that other news didn't get out until just now. Northern Venezuela was also hit by the Fiery Syphon and the people for the most part were not able to successfully evacuate. They are blaming their Kleptocratic (*'Communist'*) Dictator for that failure. He was confronted with the problem, and he assured that everyone would be taken to safety. However, there was nowhere but Columbia to go to, and of course, he didn't want any more of his citizenry fleeing with his government into Columbia, as the supporters of his opponent had done. That morning he had constant announcements for Venezuelans to evacuate at least fifteen miles north or south as the Fiery Syphon was projected to burn everything along their northern coastline. There was no suggestion as to public transportation or available boats. The roads going south were all jammed with traffic. It burned across northern Trinidad, the Peninsula DeParia, Carupano, Cumana, Caracas, Valencia & Maracaibo. Then it crossed into Colombia cooking the prisoners at Barranquilla; most of their citizenry was all safely evacuated the day before.'

They are all listening intently as CIA Jane condemns Glenn, "See what *your fucking invention* has done - you're **killing *millions of people!*"** Glenn's face pales with this horror. *"Quiet!* I need to hear this." The radio commentary continues:

'Northern Venezuela has burned, the dictator waited too long to tell poor people to evacuate; his rich government cronies had already taken all the available transportation south. A few dozen ships sailed north. The poor were notified in the morning to travel south 15 miles, or north into the Caribbean Sea 15 miles. But none had the resources, nor the time to do that. Those few who tried to get away in small boats, into the Caribbean Sea, burned or boiled, or mercifully drowned. Most of those that escaped south, got burned in the next day's Fiery Syphon. Their dictator is refusing to give any accounting of the disaster. He is however blaming his political opponents who were exiled to Colombia, for working with the United States to weaponize the weather against Venezuela. Like they had done before to Cuba. And which they will certainly continue to do to Venezuela and also Brazil, as the U S doesn't like the government there either.'

Bernie spits out, *"The lying bastards!"*
The news continues:

'The impending threat of an even greater disaster when this 'Fiery Syphon' is projected to hit Rio DE Jannero and Sao Paulo. Millions of people live in dilapidated housing on steep cliffs. It is densely populated. The shallow swamps will certainly boil, and the foliage will burn. The Brazilian Jungle will blaze, there is no hope of controlling a fire in those dense jungles. How sad as these people have already been suffering a higher death rate from the lack of Covid19 medical care; and the lack of vaccinations.'

Jane looks at Glenn with scathing contempt. In response, Glenn turns to Bernie saying, "I need you to hire every cruise ship available on the East Coast and run them as ferries between Rio de Janeiro & Sao Paulo area to whatever northern ports will take them. Or further South is better; far below the Tropic of Capricorn where they will be safe from the 'Fiery Syphon' through December 21st; when it will start to move north again. We need to use all of our resources via Mother Nature's Blog to make sure that they have tents to sleep in and food and sanitation facilities at whatever refugee camps that must be set up for them. We better get moving now, get your space suits on. I've got to study Jane's video of the asteroids colliding."

CIA Jane naggingly condemns Glenn, "You still want to *fool around* with your *Mini-Shuttle* and the *Chruithne asteroid* collision?!? Don't you have **better things to worry about!?!**"

Glenn shouts, at the top of his lungs, *"YES - I* still want to *play around* on *my expensive toy*, **and yes** I still need you and the Professor to plot the course of those two asteroids! *So get your ass moving!"*

Bernie tries to calm the tensions, "Well, I got enough to keep me busy for the foreseeable future. At least it's the warmer season in the Southern Hemisphere, we don't have to worry about them freezing. Maybe we can even arrange for them to be vaccinated aboard ship." Glenn nods his approval.

They ride the Jet-Basket in silence up to Skyhook. Glenn questions why the Professor brought up a dozen more spools of nanotube cable. "Yah," the Professor explains, "I thought that I may have to replace some of the Mini-Shuttle's magnetic coils, that some of the wiring may have melted when it re-entered the atmosphere at 18000 miles-per-hour. But apparently, the magnetic-field somehow or other got around the re-entry heating; ordinarily it causes the heat-shield to glow red-hot upon re-entry – you know - due to the friction with the atmosphere."

Glenn questions, "I thought that it's the slowing down that converts kinetic energy to heat?"

The Professor ignores the inquiry, continuing, "Even if some of the coils melted below where I can see, the computer shows that all their switches are functioning properly. Electricity is still flowing every which way thru the switches, same as before. I am able to guide the Shuttle in every direction within this magnetic-field using just the joystick; the computer automatically controls all the switches to accomplish the guidance needed. That's computerized artificial intelligence for you. It is manipulating the switching so that I can point the Shuttle in any direction: up, down, left, right, spin it around – with lots of electrical arcing . . . It's *amazing!* I installed the magnetometers around the exterior of the nanotube coils and also on the inside of the Shuttle. I measured the variance in the magnetic-field on each device as I worked the guidance joystick in every conceivable direction. Now, we can compare the magnetometer readings against the new readings that will be recorded as you fly around on your orbit. I was torn between flying to the left, or to the right of the Earth's magnetic poles as we only have one orbit, so I'm sending you on the other side of my orbit; we may learn something new."

Glenn asks, "Any reason why we can't do more than one orbit?"

The Professor replies calmly, "I think this is ambitious enough, there's always tomorrow."

Jane retorts, "Not if you believe this morning's newscast; the 'Fiery Syphon' hit Venezuela's northern coast. And it is on course in December to destroy the Rio de Janeiro - Sao Paulo area, killing millions. And then, it'll turn around and be right back again, after the December 21st Solstice, when it starts coming North again. You didn't hear this morning's breaking news? They are saying that it is too dangerous to even live *within the Earth's tropic zones!* Glenn's invention is decimating the Earth more than *all the plagues* and **all the world-wars combined!"**

"Holy shit!" the Professor exclaims.

Glenn looks towards Jane, muttering to himself, "That fucking cunt better *stay away from me!"* But everybody can hear him over their radios.

Jane responds by running to the telescope cabin saying, "I have to track what happened with the asteroid collision."

The Professor is glad to shift the conversation, "Yes, Jane showed me the video this morning. Although that TK7 asteroid is only 1000-feet in diameter it must have knocked Chruithne off its course. I'm not sure, but at least one of those asteroids crosses the path of Venus. It approaches Mercury on one side and Mars on the other side of its elliptical orbit. I don't see how it could have escaped their gravitational pull, deflecting its orbit, making it virtually impossible to predict their paths with any degree of certainty. But it looks to me from what little I saw on the video that Chruithne was butted closer to the Earth's orbit. It never got within 12 million miles of the Earth before. But I think it's gonna get much closer now. We may even be able to see it with the *naked eye!*"

Glenn mutters, "You talk like that's a good thing."

Bernie chimes in, "I don't like the idea of asteroids coming closer to the Earth. Remember one exploded over that Russian city injuring some 1500 people. That didn't even impact the ground. And from what Jane tells me this one has a 3-mile-wide diameter, much wider than that one over Russia. And it is made of iron, or some kind of a *metal* asteroid. Which is much denser that the Russian one; something like ***130 billion tons!***"

The Professor says, "I don't know about iron, but I have heard there could be iridium; which is *even denser.* Selenium, lithium and iridium are rare elements used in modern batteries. Chondrite Meteors contain carbon and maybe some DIAMONDS. Maybe a lot more with the impact pressure if they go crashing into the Moon?"

Glenn's entrepreneurial mind lights up, "Isn't that desperately needed for computer circuitry and electric vehicles. It must be worth a fortune, if only that asteroid could be mined."

Bernie says, "I've got to get to the Gusher-Tower." Glenn reminds him to stay safe and take extra O2 canisters as he leaves on the Jet-Basket.

The Professor reviews everything on the Mini-Shuttle with Glenn and shows him exactly what he did by way of guiding the Mini- Shuttle and reversing its magnetic-field simply by using his computer from the pilot's seat. The combined magnetic-fields should pull him into a safe landing, just like the tractor beams did in Star Trek. Glenn says, "OK, let's get this *show on the road!"* The Professor reminds him to fasten his seat belt, then exits the Shuttle and operates the mag-lev computer. They watch as the magnetic-field builds all around it, then floats it above the Railgun's rails. Glenn raises the landing wheels, sits back in the pilot's seat, takes a deep breath and presses the launch keys.

Glenn sees in an instant: Railgun-tracks, then the early morning blue sky, then the blackness of space. Looking out his right-hand window he can see the Pacific Ocean. Out his left- hand window he can see the Andes mountains streaking by beneath him. Then suddenly he is approaching Antarctica and he can see the deflection of the South Magnetic Pole. He works the joystick steering away from the deflection, and then towards the polar deflection, as instructed by the Professor to test the magnetometers. Then as he passes the South Pole, he can see it slowing his speed, magnetically pulling him back. He reverses the Shuttle's magnetic-field and experiences the blinding shroud of electrical arcing followed by Saint Elmo's fire, illuminating the nose and the wings. The Professor was interested to see if the Shuttle's magnetic-field reaction would be different flying on the daylight side of the Earth versus the night-time side of the Earth. He said the Earth's magnetic-field is blown heavily to the dark side of the Earth by the Sun's solar wind. Glenn notices a buildup of the Shuttle's magnetic-field which he gathers can only be accounted for by that dark side difference in the Earth's magnetic-field. In no time at all he is crossing the equator, and then over the North Pole. As he flies back into daylight, he can see that the magnetic-field does not build up as quickly, after his reversal, like it did in the dark side of the Earth. He is questioning: if the solar wind helps to build the magnetic-field around the Earth, it should also create the magnetic-field around him in the Mini-Shuttle – even if he is flying high beyond the Earth's magnetic-field. It is obvious now that Earth's magnetic-field is not only responsible for deflecting the Shuttle's magnetism, but also it transfers the Earth's magnetism to his Mini-Shuttle's magnetic-field, keeping it strong.

For the first time he hears the Professor whose been yelling at him. "It is time to reverse your magnetic-field once again. You will be accelerated towards the Skyhook and as you turn into it - you need to reverse your magnetic-field immediately upon seeing the Skyhook".

Glenn responds matter-of-factly, "That was too quick; I'm going to do another orbit." The Professor protests, but Glenn challenges him whimsically, "I am whizzing by The Baja Peninsula . . . *You better shut off the mag-lev's magnetic-field! You don't want this thing to be magnetically dragged-in from the Pacific side of Skyhook ~ AAAhhhhh? . . . I don't think* *your extreme magnetic-field understands – nor cares – that there **is no access to the Railgun tracks from the west!!**"*

He dismissively throws up his hands and then follows Glenn's orders. Glenn flies another orbit, enjoying the view while experiencing weightlessness.

The Professor warns, "You would intentionally risk *crashing our Shuttle!?!* Just to get your *own way?!?* If we lose radio contact, I won't know when to turn on the mag-lev tractor beam to pull you in. It seems you are getting giddy with the power of space flight. That could *get dangerous!*"

"Let's just try to remember *who is paying who* in our *employee/employer* relationship! I think there is no problem radioing when we are in the same hemisphere. We need to gain some experience if we are ever going to fly this thing. I feel fine, I am eating a sandwich and drinking a hot cup of coffee from a sippy cup while floating around. I see you loaded-up on food supplies. Were you planning on taking an extended flight?"

The Professor ignores his question, saying, "You got to change course, or you will scare the shit out of the Astronauts on the International Space Station." Glenn follows his new course directive. "You got to be careful, they had to fly around some space debris from a satellite that had been destroyed. Look out your right-hand window, you might see the sunlight reflecting off of it. It's a failed Russian Satellite of some sort which I guess they wanted to keep secret, so they fired a missile and blew it up. Its debris is flying every which way at thousands of miles per hour. Czar Putzin didn't even warn anybody, and they have Russians living on the Space Station."

Glenn replies, *"Oh Shit!* I can see it, *it's really close.* I can fly alongside of the debris field. It's like picking your way through traffic." The Professor is protesting, but Glenn steers next to it, "**Wow,** there must be a *thousand pieces!*" Then the Mini-Shuttle's magnetic-field pulls the debris towards him . . . *"Oh Jesus! **No!!**"* Glenn's mind screams as his urine escapes into his space-suit's fecal bag . . .

But then, the debris magnetically attaches gently to the Mini-Shuttle's coils . . .
      ***"I can't believe my eyes,** I just recovered some of the debris!*
         I bet that I can do a spacewalk and bring it inside.
               We can sell it *for a million!*"

"You must be DRUNK!" the Professor shouts, *"Don't even think about it!!* How much *fucking money* do you need . . ."

Glenn steers within 25 feet of each piece of this debris, continuing to collect it all, saying, "A lot more than we have if we are going to successfully evacuate Rio."

The Professor replies, "That's impossible, there has to be another solution . . . " then as an after-thought, "If you wanted to make some real money you could retrieve the SOHO satellite that is in that fixed 'L1' orbiting location between the Earth and the Sun, about a million miles away. It could be repaired and re-launched – saving hundreds of millions to rebuild it."

"If it is stuck there constantly between the Earth and the Sun, shouldn't it be blocking the Fiery Syphon?"

"It's too small to completely block it. I would think it must have been burnt to a crisp by the Fiery Syphon's CME by now. Also, it is not in a fixed position; it is stuck in that 'L1' position, but it is orbiting around it in a 200,000-mile spiraling loop, perpendicular to the plane of the ecliptic."

"Why can't they just keep it in that one 'L1' orbiting spot?"

Shades of the old Professor's irritation escape, "Go get a *fucking Doctoral degree* in Astrophysics and *then **maybe*** you'll understand!"

Glenn's eyebrows peak as he re-thinks, "Maybe I like the *meek Professor better!?!"* Then he changes the subject, "While I am up here, let me fly by our rogue nuclear-waste barrel and see if I can latch onto it too. Tell Jane to get the coordinates so that you can guide me there."

"I think *you're crazy;* but alright!" While he is talking to Jane, Glenn puts on his space-suit helmet, replaces an O2 canister silencing the alarm, and then floats into the air-lock. He ties on to the safety-ropes as he and the Professor practiced and opens the exterior door and peeks out into the darkness of deep-space. He catches his heart in his mouth as he *gasps for breath,* he has seen this before when he was lost in space, but it is still overwhelming. His blood pressure alarm flashes in his helmet. "Are you alright?" The Professor queries, "Your breathing sounds erratic?"

Glenn takes several calming deep breaths, then fabricates an explanation, "I tried to take a step and surprisingly stumbled; you have to get used to weightlessly floating around." He hesitantly craws out onto the wing, there *is arcing* between his space-suit and the nanotube wiring coiling around the wing. He is *alarmed,* but doesn't feel anything, just hears the electrical *sizzling sound* coming thru the aluminum fabric of his space-suit: it is also slightly magnetized and has a little adhesive quality that enables him to craw instead of floating. Glancing to his right, he can see the city lights of Asia below him. Making sure that the safety-rope is securing him, he inches his way to the satellite debris. It is magnetically stuck to the wing, but he is able to lift it with a little tug. He places the debris into several large canvas cargo-bags. He makes several trips, dragging it all into the Shuttle's air-lock. When he gathers it all, he closes the outer-door, then opens the door from the air-lock into the cargo bay, then he tosses these cargo-bags into the cargo bay.

Then Glenn receives the coordinates to his rogue barrel. The Professor is saying, "It's over 100-thousand miles above the Earth; maybe beyond the Earth's protective magnetic-field - why risk it. It's not going anywhere."

"Jane will *never forgive me* for not cleaning up my pollution! To her it's like not cleaning up your dog's shit . . ."

"*Very funny!* And I will never forgive you if you *lose our Mini-Shuttle!!*"

"The *Shuttle?!?* What about *my life?*"

"Who gives *a fuck* about *your life?!?* It's just a question of time before you *kill yourself* with all your irresponsible activity. I bet your still contemplating going on a spacewalk *all by yourself* to retrieve that satellite's debris off the wing!"

Glenn replies dourly, "<u>You Think So,</u> *huh!?!* Why not think about what would happen to it when I come in for a landing. When we reverse the magnetic-field, that debris might fly everywhere at 18000 miles per hour and destroy our Skyhook."

The Professor eagerly suggests, "That's a good experiment. Reverse the magnetic-field now, see what happens."

Glenn admits, "TOO LATE! I already did the spacewalk; I hauled all the debris into the Shuttle's cargo area." Then he sees the new coordinates on his computer screen. "That's more than 100 thousand miles away – how fast do you think this baby can fly?"

The Professor can't conceal the excitement in his voice, "Judging by our experience with the Railgun, the only limitation on speed is the length of the magnetic rails. But you're not moving on magnetic rails up there; you're propelled by the various magnetic-fields of the Earth - the Sun - and

God only knows what else – which *are somehow* all combining together, *substituting* for the *magnetic rails*. I guess this experiment will take you outside of the Earth's magnetic-field and that will tell us something. But I don't see anything to slow you down so maybe your speed is virtually unlimited. You will be flying high above the South American continent; we will track and video you through the telescope. You are changing your current orbit's trajectory. This would require a lot of fuel in other space-shuttles which are propulsion guided, not magnetically guided. I am anxious to see how it effects our Mini-Shuttle's magnetic-field."

Glenn points the Mini-Shuttle towards the new coordinates and begins accelerating. Before he knows it, he is flying 65,000 mph. He slows down and the computer reversing polarity causes more electrical sparking as he comes gliding next to the rogue barrel. Glenn can't believe how they were able to pinpoint its location with such accuracy. Within two seconds it gravitates onto the wing, attaching magnetically. Glenn replaces his helmet, enters the air-lock, attaches his safety rope, opens the outer door and tries to casually jump down onto the wing. His effort sends him flying up above the shuttle 100 feet before the safety ropes snaps taunt. He is shocked as he expected to land on the wing, instead he propelled himself strait up. He now finds himself spinning faster and faster in a circle as his momentum tries to carry him beyond his tether. Hand-over-hand on his tether, he pulls his spinning body down to the roof of the shuttle where his legs painfully slam into it causing him to stop spinning. His inflated space-suit bounces off and his lungs seize in fright. It's not the spinning ordeal, nor the pain in his legs that is crushing his heart. He is awestruck as he gazes over the top of the Shuttle and sees South America below him where his Fiery Syphon is just entering the Pacific Ocean off the coast, south of Pequito; and its blazing radiance towering up past him, all the way into the Sun. It has left a flaming trail from the Atlantic to the Pacific across the continent.

Glenn watches, mesmerized as the Fiery Syphon speeds off into the west, becoming a thinner and thinner string of fiery plasma stretching between the Sun and the Earth . . .

Glenn manages to pull himself back down to the Shuttle's door-way and then he crawls out onto the wing. His mind is numbed by this chaotic second spacewalk. He slowly drags the rogue barrel into the cargo compartment and lashes it down so that it can't move. While he's at it, he methodically lashes down the cargo-bags of satellite debris. His mind is relinquishing its numbness and he starts feeling proud of himself: he has survived that ordeal. He's hungry. He warms a container of coffee and slowly eats a sandwich. He gazes at the Earth out the window, he watches the moon set in the west. He drifts off to sleep. Glenn feels his head scraping against something. As he wakes-up he abruptly turns his head and jams his nose against a wall. He is upside-down and has floated against the bathroom door. He pulls himself upright and shakes-off his stupor. As he sits in the pilot's seat he grumbles, "Professor, you *might have mentioned* that I would be flying *into the high-noon **Fiery Syphon** when* you sent me here!"

He sneers, "*I told you not to do it!* You are more than 100 miles south of the Fiery Syphon's path . . . How *the fuck do I know* **what time you're in** up there . . ."

Glenn is baffled by his response and begins to fly back to the Earth. Now it appears to him that he is closer to the Moon than he is to the Earth. "Some sort of *optical illusion?!?* But I can clearly distinguish its mountains from their shadows." He is tempted to fly a quick orbit around the Moon, but then decides that is too rambunctious. Surprisingly, he finds that he has more consistent radio contact with the Professor than when he was closer to Earth. "The horizon seems to be the factor, the further away I am, the wider the horizon is. I gather I'll have communication as long as I am on the same side of the Earth as South America."

Glenn is suddenly worried about radiation poisoning this far outside of the Earth's protective magnetic-field. He checks the radiation detectors on the inside and outside of the Mini-Shuttle. There is no reading whatever; apparently, his magnetic-field is deflecting the radiation around the Shuttle. He excitedly shares this revelation, . . .

~   but the Professor is not responding as expected.   ~

"Jane and I were just reviewing the new orbiting path of Cruithne and TK7, which has gravitationally captured it. They are both headed to what will inevitably be **a *collision course* with the Earth**. It's just a *question of days* before they *are captured* by the *Earth's gravity,* and they will orbit a few times **before crashing into us.** I can't tell exactly where, but - it is going to *be* **cataclysmic.** It's *half the size* of the one from 65 million years ago *that destroyed* most of the *life on Earth.* I expect it will have a *comparable effect.* Whatever the impact and heat wave doesn't destroy, the *nuclear winter* that it causes will **kill everything** else off, except maybe rodents, who can live underground, and insects . . ."

Glenn is lost in a long, quiet reverie as his mind assimilates this new information. Then he says, "Just what we needed; another **mass extinction** ~ to add to the:

'Fiery Syphon' ~
          'Covid19' ...
                    ~ AND ~
                              ~ Presidential Candidate Prump's Coup d'etat!"~

XL

PRAY TO LA LUNA: INTERCEDE?

G lenn mutters to nobody, "Well; at least Jane will not hold me responsible for this extinction."

Then he hears Jane's voice over the radio, *"No!* I don't blame you for this. But you're in a position *to do something* about it!" Her voice becomes rasping, "In a few more hours cities in Brazil like Macapa, Belem, Castanhal and others *will be annihilated!* You are up there *in space!* You can fly in front of it and *block it* or *deflect it,* or **something** . . ." She bursts into tears with this last plea.

Glenn replies sarcastically, **"No thanks!** I don't want to be cooked in space any more than I wanted to be cooked on the ground."

She pleads again straining with torment, "But then, in a few days an asteroid is going to kill everybody . . . Let *me go home!* I want to be **with my parents!!"** bawling like a baby.

"The Professor could be mistaken, or maybe the Moon will intercede and boomerang our asteroid into deep-space or capture it. It wouldn't be much of a tragedy if it slammed into the Moon. Maybe that would fix the problem of the ocean tides causing it to accelerate in its orbit." Glenn is rambling on. "You know we are losing our Moon; it moves further away a couple inches per year. As it gets further away from the Earth, we will lose its stabilizing effect. Then the Earth will wobble erratically causing horrendous storms and tides - and we don't know what else. It may cause our magnetic poles to reverse. The Earth could lay on its side rotating so that the poles become the equator, the Ice Caps would melt making the oceans rise 200 feet."

The Professor interrupts, "You're babbling . . . No sense looking for a silver lining. All this idle speculation is not going to help. Jane, I'll need you here with me to continue tracking these asteroids while we try to minimize the impact somehow. I know the U S Government has nuclear fall-out shelters in Area 51; and maybe Yucca Mountain now that they are shipping all of their nuclear-waste to us. We can shelter some younger couples inside of the Gusher-Cavern with enough supplies for 10 years or so. Maybe you and Bernie can help re-populate the world. Become the new Adam and Eve of the 21ˢᵗ century. But wait, maybe Jane has got something there . . . If you can navigate the Mini-Shuttle magnetically, why not an asteroid? You are flying around in space without using any fuel. Maybe we can wrap an asteroid with nanotube wiring, like I did with the Mini-Shuttle. The solar wind will provide the electricity to magnetize the asteroids coils, and then we can magnetically fly it to that SOHO Satellite's L1 position and block the Fiery Syphon."

Jane sobs fervently, **"I'll research it!** What asteroid shall we pick? Which one do you think we can magnetize? Can we do it before December 21ˢᵗ when Rio de Janeiro's gonna be wiped out?"

"Well Cruithne seems to be the ideal candidate; if we don't get this asteroid moving within a few days it will be *too late* to worry about Rio de Janeiro ~ and *the rest of the world!"* The Professor gives a deep sigh, then continues, "Suddenly, I have a staggering amount of work to do. Glenn, I'm sending you info on this asteroid's data; it is about 30 million miles away, approaching point 'A' on the diagram. We have a couple hundred miles of our nanotube wiring down here. I will use the Railgun to launch these spools of cable into orbit trailing after Cruithne. You can fly there and attach the cable to the asteroid somehow wrapping it around." Glenn is surprised that he still has access to the internet's satellites from this distance. He looks it up on the internet:

> '3753 Cruithne is a Q-type, Aten asteroid in orbit around the Sun in 1:1 orbital resonance with Earth, making it a co-orbital object. It is an asteroid that, relative to Earth, orbits the Sun in a bean-shaped orbit that effectively

describes a horseshoe, and that can change into a quasi-satellite orbit. Cruithne does not orbit Earth and at times it is on the other side of the Sun, placing Cruithne well outside of Earth's Hill sphere. Its orbit takes it near the orbit of Mercury and outside the orbit of Mars. Cruithne orbits the Sun in about one year, but it takes 770 years for the series to complete a horseshoe-shaped movement around Earth. It orbits the Sun in 365 days. It's an Aten class asteroid discovered October 1986.':

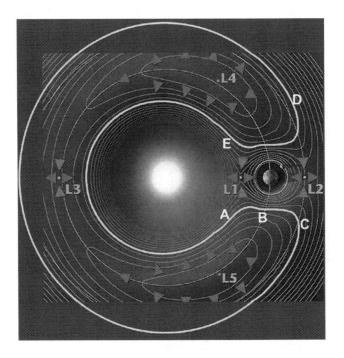

Glenn studies Asteroid Cruithne's orbit diagram and deduces that everything in the diagram, - the Earth, the Cruithne asteroid, the L1 thru L5 Lagrange points, *even the horseshoe pattern diagram itself*, - are **all orbiting counter-clockwise** *around the Sun*. Asteroid Cruithne's horseshoe orbital path is in lightest color blue; its path represents the horseshoe. The gravitational Lagrange points (L1 thru L5) remain fixed (equidistant) relative to the Earth's motion as it orbits around the Sun. The Earth remains in that open end of the horseshoe, rotating the whole horseshoe as it orbits. Therefore, Earth orbits along its path – always in-between the blue-line points A, B, C, & D, E, - passing by Lagrange points L4, L3, L5 and then thru point B, at an average speed of 67,000mph.

Cruithne moves faster, than the orbiting Earth on the inner orbit from point E to point A. Then, as it catches up - Earth's gravity pulls it from point A, past point B – (at the closest distance of 12-million-miles from Earth) - then to point C, where the **Earth** *speeds away* from it. Because Cruithne moves slower on this outer (wider/longer) orbit from point C, finally (trailing slower behind the Earth) Cruithne arrives at point D in 770 years; when it once again is pulled by the Earth's gravity to point E, where upon – **Cruithne** **speeds away** from the Earth, because it is now on the inner – shorter/narrower orbit. This varying orbital speed is what creates the horseshoe pattern. Earth is always orbiting in between this rotating horseshoe's gap, in-between Lagrange points L1 & L2.

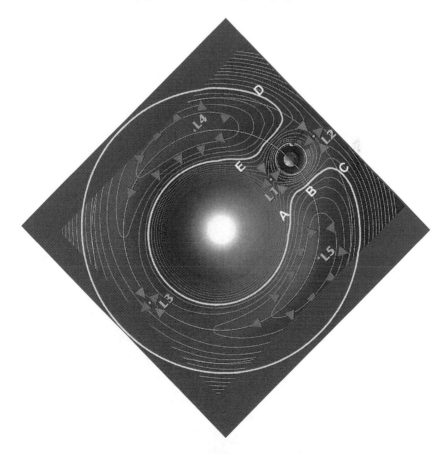

Glenn thinks, "That 'L1' point is the Soho Satellite's orbital center. This whole horseshoe pattern is rotating counter-clockwise with the Earth's orbit. Asteroid Cruithne is now approaching point 'A' on this diagram and will crash into the Earth because Asteroid TK7's impact into Cruithne has increased its forward speed. That's the Moon at the 1 o'clock position on its orbit around the Earth. The Professor seems to think it will hit the Earth instead of the Moon: Why?"

XLI

❖

PLASSOING CRUITHNE?

"**S**o, you want *me to lasso* this 3-mile wide asteroid *and hogtie it* with hundreds-of-miles of nanotube cable . . . Well, I guess that's *a little better* than me sitting in direct line with the *'Fiery Syphon'*; better than <u>*being cooked*</u> by it. I presume you will <u>***allow me***</u> to be hiding behind the asteroid while using it as a shield to block the *blasting Sun's <u>million-degree</u>* CME!?!

<u>SERIOUSLY?!?</u>"

The Professor softly laments,

"Unless you have a better idea? "

After a pregnant pause, the Professor apologetically continues, "I would do it myself, but no one can accomplish what I need to do from down here on the Skyhook . . ." Another pregnant pause, "I am sending you the coordinates for our last sighting of Cruithne; you can start flying there now. Jane will go to the telescope and track it, then we will give you its updated coordinates. Meanwhile, I will start connecting 5 spools of cable, the end of one to the beginning of the next one, consecutively; and launch as a group. This will then be a 5 mile long, continuous, single nanotube-coil, contained on these 5 wooden-spools. Maybe I can assemble some sort of explosive harpoon that you can shoot deep into the surface of

Cruithne firmly attaching the cable into it. You have got to be careful to wrap it tightly around the asteroid so that it doesn't unwind and fall off."

"And – EXACTLY - how would I do that?" Glenn inquires bewildered as he pushes the joystick forward and the Mini-Shuttle flies in a direction towards an asteroid about 30 million miles away from the Earth.

The Professor answers, "You would have to anchor it around a suitable rocky perturbance or a huge bolder. Then fly the coil around the asteroid, unwinding the cable while wrapping it tightly around and securing it onto the asteroid."

Glenn is shocked, "You actually want me to do *a spacewalk* - to go climbing **onto an asteroid?!?"**

Before he can answer, Jane reveals her CIA training. "Glenn has two AK47 machine gun/grenade-launchers at the Hacienda. Maybe I can modify them to launch your harpoon instead of a grenade? I'll have to separate the nitro-cellulose propellent from the grenades. Glenn also has a crossbow with metal arrows; maybe the arrows can replace your harpoon?"

As he's flying rapidly away from the Earth, he notices that the South America continent is now in darkness. He asks, "What time is it down there Professor?"

He says, "It's after 10PM at night; what time do you have up there?"

"My computer shows that it is only 12:35 in the afternoon, I'm wide awake. So, for you, 15 hours have elapsed since I was launched this morning. But for me, it's only been about 5 hours . . ."

Bernie's voice intrudes, "*'FAR OUT!'* to quote John Denver – in other words *'AMAZING - MIND BENDING'!"*

The Professor grunts, "I wish I had the time to philosophically reflect on it . . ."

Bernie is undeterred, "Think about this: If Glenn is traveling 3 million miles: If it takes those coils two or three days in OUR time, but for him in the Mini-Shuttle's magnetic-field only 10 hours of HIS time - how fast is Glenn actually traveling versus how fast are your coils traveling? - I guess *it's all . . .* **relative?"**

The Professor baulks, "These coils of nanotube wiring must also form a magnetic-field around them and leave Earth's space/time dimension just as the Mini-Shuttle apparently did . . . Well, the computer is recording everything, we can analyze it later and come up with an answer. This is some interesting shit we are encountering. This is the type of research I always wanted to do."

Though he feels that foreboding dark shadow creeping up his spine, Glenn lightly quips, "Well, I certainly don't mind doing a little space exploration. I'm going to fully accelerate this thing as far forward as this little computer-joystick will go; let's see how fast it is. Do you think it will slow down automatically, just in case I fall asleep? Can't we kind of put it on automatic pilot so that it will slow down automatically."

The Professor says, "Yes, it is on automatic pilot already. When you enter the coordinates and push the joy-stick forward, you fly there automatically."

Jakes voice intrudes, "*No shit?!?* Glenn thought **he was flying** the thing!"

CIA Jane displays the knowledge she gained from working with the Professor, "Glenn was flying it, accept when he entered guidance coordinates. Then it goes into automatic pilot, steering the Mini-Shuttle to that location."

Jake adds, "So, he can relax and doesn't have to constantly man the piloting computer . . . Cool!"

Bernie sounds off, "Instead of tracking the Asteroid, it would have been cooler if we could have been watching the Shuttle on the telescope to see if it leaves this dimension. That is: does the Mini-Shuttle visually disappear, or does it simply fly away. We still don't understand what is happening, are you presently within our dimension now when you are flying; or only when you are stationary? One fact seems to be that our radio communications are not affected by our inter-dimensional differences."

This conversation is diminishing the dread of his onerous deep-space mission. Glenn queries, "Oh yeah . . . Since your dimensional time goes by twice as fast as mine, is my speech coming thru the radio slower?"

Bernie hesitantly corrects, "I would think it should be faster, eerrr, not slower. But no, it's real-time. Just like normally talking to you."

"Same here on the Mini-Shuttle. Apparently, the radio waves are inter-dimensional. We can try switching to another channel on the radio and see if we still have contact."

The Professor shouts, ***"NO!! Stop fucking around!*** *Are you crazy!* You want to risk losing contact at a time like this? All you *spectators,* go find something else to do . . . Jane and I have got to concentrate on what we are doing."

"Okay, okay, calm down." Glenn clarifies, "We were just thinking out-loud. We can try that when I am on the Railgun's launch pad, in the magnetic-field, immediately before launching. Oh, another thought just in case those 5-mile nanotube coils actually arrive; am I going to be safe up here with them flying up at me."

"Good thought, I am going to make a circuit-board for each of them, duplicating the Shuttle's magnetically controlled guidance system. Jane is back with the asteroid's new coordinates. I am sending them to you now. The asteroid is just over 27 million miles away from you. I will be launching the nanotube coils to follow within 15 miles of it." The Professor addresses Jane, "I need you to take the Loon-Evator down to the Hacienda, bring back those AK47s fully loaded. I'll test one here, and if it works, we'll send the other one up to Glenn. Also, have Jake load up all the spools of nanotube cable from the warehouse that he can fit on the Loon-Evator. And, get Bernie to carry all my computer stuff from my office and re-install it up here in the Skyhook's cabin. I can't think clearly enough stuck inside this space-suit."

Jane challenges, "You're going to copy the Shuttle's guidance system onto your own circuit boards? Isn't that proprietary information? Won't you be violating the patent laws?"

Glenn guffaws, *"**Harrumphs!** You can* arrest him *after we **save the world!**"* Then he reveals the combination to his weapons cabinet in his office to CIA Jane; then adds as an afterthought, "The crossbow with a quiver of arrows is in there; send them all up to me too."

As Glenn is activating the new guidance coordinates, Jane gets Bernie and Jake and goes down to the Hacienda, and the Professor is testing the mag-lev with the first coil (5wooden-spools of the cable). "I could only fit 5 spools on the Railgun's launch pad. I rolled them on then activated the maglev. When I floated them up, they slowly turned 90 degrees - all by themself, then attached side by side to each other, lining up into a single magnetic-field. Obviously, they had the current from the magnetic-field flowing thru the nanotube wiring, and the switches at every 100-foot of the wire became activated, *communicating with my computer!* It all happened automatically; I didn't touch my computer. This Artificial Intelligence *is unbelievable!* Then I connected each spool's nanotube wire to the spool next to it. I will be launching using the Railgun to put them in the same orbit as Cruithne; but I will also be giving that same coordinate to the coil's new guidance circuit-board. Maybe they will enter into your dimension and travel faster than their launching speed? My computer shows that you are already traveling at *over **150,000mph!*** Is that what your computer shows?" Glenn responds positively. "You should try to get some sleep; you are going to need to be rested for your spacewalk."

Glenn is distracted as he still can't believe this haphazard scheme is going to come to fruition, "I am looking out my left window and I have a new angle looking at the Moon; I can see part of the back-side of the Moon. I can clearly see a horizontal line across the surface; kind of like something burned across it. Kind of like the trail the Fiery Syphon blazed across our valley and up the western cliffs. But, this is kind of reflecting light."

"**Of course!**" the Professor exclaims, "It's obvious, when the Moon eclipses the Sun at noon, *it blocks the Fiery Syphon!*" He gets the Moon's schedule on his computer. "There is a partial eclipse coming over South America tomorrow; hopefully it will block the CME's million-degree heat."

"Did we luck out? Is the Fiery Syphon gonna be blocked?"

The Professor replies joyfully, "I think so, at least we will have a partial block for some time. Although, I don't know that a narrower stream of CME is gonna be any less devastating than the wider stream that we've been getting. Let's just hope we *get a total block!*" Then the Professor exclaims, *"Holy shit! You're going **over 200,000mph!**"* Glenn checks his computer, confirming the same speed. The Professor checks on the launched spools and determines they are almost approaching 200,000mph, and also still accelerating. You'll get there pretty quick. That's good, it's rapidly approaching point 'A' on that diagram. You will have time to steer the asteroid towards the L1 point and keep it away from the Earth's gravity. If you let it make that right turn towards point B, the Earth's gravity will capture the asteroid; AND, considering its speed and its mass, I doubt that any amount of magnetizing will be able to divert it."

*"**What?!?**"* Glenn repeats apprehensively, "- *'If - **I let** - the asteroid make that - **right turn** – the - Earth's gravity'* . . .?!? - I better take that nap . . ." Glenn mutters incredulously, then he eats again and goes to sleep.

When he wakes up, he sees several messages from the Professor:

'I launched the first coil with the guidance system. I want to wait for it to arrive at the asteroid to make any adjustments, but we don't have time to wait for anything.' –

'I launched 15 more groups of coils and they have all accelerated, just like the Mini-Shuttle has accelerated. That's 80 spools, or a total of 80 miles of nanotube cable. I thought we had more. I could order more but by the time it gets delivered, considering the Fiery Syphons devastation, it will be too late.' -

'I could try to recover nanotube cable from the fallen bursted Skyhook balloons; but, I don't think that we have time for that either.'

Glenn calls and questions if they have enough cable to magnetize the asteroid. The Professor replies, "Hopefully, 80 miles of nanotube wiring coiled around the three-mile-wide asteroid will be enough to effectively magnetize it so that you can fly it to the L1 spot. The third group of spools, that 3rd coil, has the AK47 grenade-launcher fitted with an arrow that I tested firing. It already has the cable attached to the arrow. All you have to do is unwind some of the cable and then shoot it into the asteroid. Then fly the coils around while unwinding its cable. Let's hope that the arrow is strong enough to penetrate the asteroid and secure the cable to it. If not, you'll have to *physically attach it to Cruithne.*"

Glenn's stomach clenches with this alternative. Then he is surprised to hear Jake cheerfully congratulating him on becoming an Astronaut. He tells Glenn, "You were talking in your sleep about an Alien with a 'magnetic pyramid'; you had us worried for a minute. I believe those Alien abductions are true. Jane and Bernie are here laughing at me."

Glenn explains the whole Alien dream experience he had on Skyhook and that sometimes he's not so sure it was a dream. They all share a keen interest in this. Now Glenn is speaking loudly to overcome the embarrassing noise of his urine splashing into his space-suit's fecal bag. "How fast am I going Professor?"

He answers gravely, "I don't know . . . The speed display maxed out at six digits. It just shows a '+' after 999,999mph. You should be slowing down soon, as you are within one million miles of the asteroids. You will be joining their orbit at about 67,000mph going back towards that right turn; which will bring it too close to the Earth. Yes, I can see that your speed is now registering again. Don't you feel anything?" Then a deep breath, "Your speed is slowing down radically." Another breath, "This can't be right, your almost there and you are still over 500,000mph?" Two rapidly deep breaths, *"JESUS!* YOU ARE ALREADY DOWN TO *100,000MPH!?!"* A bated attempt at breathing, *"YOU ARE THERE!!* I can't believe you *don't feel anything?!?"* Then more calmly, "Let me check: the coils are arriving too. You should be able to see them. Look around. You are down to orbital speed now; only 67,000mph. I can't believe you didn't *feel anything*?!? You began a wide 180 degree turn at over 1,000,000 mph and came in behind the asteroids." A long pause, then he repeats, "I can't believe you didn't *feel anything?!?* Are you alright?"

Bernie chimes in, *"TAKE A SHIT!" Everybody ignores his attempt at humor.*

"I didn't feel anything at all, just like *standing still!"* Glenn says with the same incredulous disbelief. "And, I am floating around up here inside the Shuttle, I am *not even strapped* into my seat?!?"

The Professor is shaking his head in doubt saying, "**Not strapped down** – *that's the stupidest fucking thing I ever heard!* - I can't *understand this!"* After a moment he adds, "Bernie joined us up here on Skyhook. Jane has gone to take a nap; she has been working with me all night. It is now almost noon on the East Coast of Brazil. We are watching the news; can you hear it. Listen, its CNN cable news:

'We have a remotely controlled TV camera in the far eastern side of a Northern Brazilian Island, called 'Ilha Do Machadinho', showing live, the ocean off the coastline. Thankfully, another one of 'Mother Nature's Freaky Rainstorms' drenched this whole area earlier this morning. We can now see a radiant cloud of steam in the distance and the water beginning to boil ahead of it. Wait, the iridescent quality has disappeared from that cloud of steam. Wait a minute, wait; the ocean stopped boiling. The heatwave has arrived onto the land, it is blowing the palm trees to the west, and they are *bursting into flames!* But there is no hot beam from the Sun's CME. Here comes the hot swirling wind. Is that the 'Fiery Syphon' ~ but without the fire? The scientists now think the Moon is blocking it. We can pan the camera around; it should have been melted by now; or at least severely damaged. We can see that it is just the tops of the palm trees that are burning. There seems to be very little devastation here.

Now we are switching to our remotely controlled TV cameras on the mainland in Belem. There is wind, but no *fire*, and <u>no heat!</u>

AAHHHH . . .
<u>IS IT TRUE?!?</u>

The Moon has *blocked the* **Fiery Syphon's CME – <u>*Entirely!!*</u>**

The Professor's jubilant voice interrupts the newscast, "What a *<u>lucky break!</u>* Let's hope it continues to block it across all of South America. Otherwise, *it will cook* Southern *Pecuador!* Bernie is helping me here now. He says he had the Gusher- spray irrigate all the way across the continent. He wants to explain the eclipse blocking the 'Fiery Syphon' on his Mother Nature's Blog. Is that alright with you?"

Glenn says, "Okay, yes, I suppose that it won't interfere with people evacuating. I don't think you should suggest that the eclipse will block it for any significant length of time."

"OK, Bernie's going to work on that now. South America is about three thousand miles wide at our latitude, that's means the earth's rotation will take about 3 hours to cross West to Pecuador. That is a long time for an eclipse to last. The longest one I know of was more than three hours. That length of time means that the Moon is furthest away from the Earth, orbiting slower on its elliptical orbit. So, maybe it will last the full three hours. Let's hope!"

Glenn worries, "Murphy doesn't have laws that solve problems. It said 'Wind but no fire, and no heat'? It doesn't make sense that the CME has separated from the Whirlwind because of the eclipse." Then he says, "My steering, according to my computer display, is being maneuvered? It must be trying to avoid other magnetic-fields. I am looking out the window, and yes, I can see something glittering in the distance – and it's *coming towards me fast*. Wait, it is slowing down, it apparently has stopped behind me. I am turning a little so that I can see it: it's the coil of nanotube cable. My computer shows that there is more coming behind it. *Jesus* - there is more than 5, wait more than 10, wait there's all 15 of them! *Wow!* That's curious . . . Why are they all arriving at the same time? So, you say I am piloting this thing now, I am no longer on automatic pilot?" The Professor confirms that, so Glenn begins to gently pilot the Mini-Shuttle and flies to the third coil of cable. You can clearly see there are five spools neatly lined one against the other and as he goes closer, he sees there is a large duffle-bag attached to it. He guides his Mini-Shuttle alongside it and goes into the air-lock, breathing deeply waiting for it to open. His space-suit is inflating as the air is being sucked out of the air-lock.

Finally, the door opens, and he exhales a long sigh as he is overwhelmed by the empty blackness before him. He turns to his right and sees two points of reflected sunlight off the coils ahead of him. Turning to his left he sees a long row of these reflections. Then he involuntarily tremors, as he watches that third coil of nanotube-cable approaching the Shuttle from the rear and then it ominously turns, aligning itself magnetically with the Mini-Shuttles magnetic-field. Glenn is quivering with fear. Is it just the newness of this experience; or is it being so far out in space, millions of miles from Earth? The quiet turning of this ghostly third coil has an eerie, ethereal effect on Glenn. He feels goose-bumps on his neck; urine escapes and splatters loudly into his fecal bag as he clutches the doorframe. Glenn mutters to himself with a quivering voice, "It looks like magnetism is in charge."

He is astonished when he hears the Professor's weary voice. "Are you surprised? All that magnetism certainly has more force than the slight gravitational attraction between you and the spools." Glenn watches with lonely angst as the coil completes a 180 degree turn and then moves quickly onto his wing and attaches magnetically, with a silent but *jarring impact.* Glenn is *tossed aside* by it and manage is to grab onto the doorframe as his lower body is *flung out into space.* He grabs the handhold near the door, realizing that he forgot to *attach his safety-rope!* As his *legs snap out* into the black space, his right-hand is ripped away from the doorframe, but his left-hand tightens on the handle outside the door. His left shoulder is *wrenched painfully.* But he *holds on; "My God,* I was almost *thrown out into deep-space!* My shoulder *hurts.* I forgot to attach my safety-rope. *Fucking stupid asshole* that I am . . ." he anguishes.

Alarmed, the Professor hears the trembling in his voice and asks, "Can you get back inside?!? *Close the air-lock door!* Are you inside yet?"

Glenn is able to painfully pull himself closer with his left arm, then reaches around with his right and grabs the inside of the door frame, then pulls himself back inside. He sees the safety-rope and wraps it around himself, then clips it onto his space suit. The Professor is pleading with him to get inside, to have a cup of coffee, to relax. But Glenn quiveringly says, "No, I'm alright - I got my safety-rope attached now. The coil has magnetically attached to the wing. I wasn't expecting that great of an impact. I am good now; I can do the space walk. I can at least check out your AK47 harpoon launcher."

The Professor cannot hide his concern for Glenn; being all alone up there, struggling to save our planet. But he doesn't want to impede his progress; time is of the essence. With each passing second, Cruithne is moving 20 miles closer to a cataclysmic impact with Earth. So, the Professor tries a new tact, "I am tracking everything using the GPS system that NASA has set up. They have 24 satellites that comprise the GPS system which plots any position on the Earth from their known – near Earth - positions in space. Now we are using them to plot your position in deep-space. I combined their GPS with our computer's artificial intelligence. The magnetometers I installed on the Shuttle detects the magnetic-fields around you and incorporates that into the guidance system. It's really quite remarkable."

The Professor's weary but now calming voice has somewhat distracted Glenn. He appears more tranquil now; his voice is not trembling. "I am crawling on the wing to the coil." he narrates his activity, "I am looking into the bag at the AK47's grenade-launcher. It looks like the gloves of my space suits are so thick that my fingers will not be able to fit inside the trigger guard to pull the trigger."

"I was able to squeeze my trigger-finger in when I tested it," the Professor replies, "just remember to keep the safety on . . . Wait a minute, why didn't I think of this before . . . If I have instantaneous voice communication with you, why not video communication instantaneously with the video cameras which are constantly recording from inside the Shuttle's windows. Let me check that. Yes, I can see something. Wait, let me remotely turn on your outside lighting." The Shuttle's lighting comes on and immediately Glenn is shocked at the harsh glowing outlines of the brightly lit but familiar coil of 5 wooden-spools. "Now, isn't that less spooky?"

Glenn replies with a hesitant but grateful, "Yes, it is. It's blinding, but I guess my eyes will get used to it." He looks around, "I guess my eyes have adjusted, now I cannot see the two coils ahead of me nor the row of coils behind me. Let me try unwinding some of this nanotube cable." Glenn finds that he cannot remove more than 4 foot of the cable as the wooden-spool will not turn. Furthermore, the cable wants to magnetically adhere to the spool. The Professor can see this on the video display.

"You are fighting the spool's magnetism, which is a problem. I must shut off all that nanotube-cable's switches which will block the current flowing through the spool – killing its magnetism. But I should also send you these controls to your computer in case we break communications, for whatever reason, then you'll be able to control that on your own. I will set it up so that you have voice control, then you can dictate commands to it. Let us call it the Nano-Computer and you can address each coil by its number as in you are now working on 'coil number 3'. I sent it all to your computer now. Try shutting off coil #3's current through your headset."

Glenn has been checking the connection between his harpoon-like-arrow stuck into the AK47's launcher and the nanotube cable secured to it. It all looks pretty flimsy. "Professor, are you sure this is going to hold; it doesn't look like a very strong connection." Glenn doubts as he is holding it in the air waving it to the video camera.

"Those plastic ties have held our Skyhook together; I think they should be able to secure that wire to the arrow. Since weight is not a problem up there, your launch should have no problem dragging the cable behind the arrow all the way to its target; as long as you have the wire hanging loose - off the spool. Now, you try the demagnetizing command from up there."

Glenn says, "OK: 'Nano-Computer coil #3: Demagnetize' . . ."

Glenn sees electrical arcing flashing all around him as the magnetic-field collapses around coil #3. The Professor's computer displays a simultaneous gain in the Mini-Shuttle's magnetic-field. Glenn tries to roll the first wooden-spool away from the other four, but they're still firmly attached. "Maybe I should reverse magnetize this spool so it will be repelled from the others?"

The Professor says, "No, we don't want to create a confusion of magnetic-fields. You're going to have to use your weight to pry them apart. You must overcome their cohesiveness and their slight gravitational attraction. But your weight should be enough to separate one spool at a time. I would think you can lift it a few feet above the wing, it should float there, then you will have no problem spinning it. Just make sure that you are firmly attached to the Shuttle, or as you try to spin it, you will spin yourself in the opposite direction. Make sure that you are constantly anchored by your safety-rope." Glenn passes his safety-rope through an eyehook on the outside of the wooden spool so that it doesn't drift too far away from him. Then he places his left foot against the inside wooden-spool and forces with all his might against the outer wooden-spool. The Professor hears him grunting with a ferocious effort and decides it's time for a pep-talk. "Atta-boy, give it all you got! – Its inert mass is *no match* for your *manly determination!*" Finally, he thrusts it up and away from the other spools. Glenn marvels at his accomplishment as he pulls back on it, so it doesn't float away. But then it comes back down landing on the wing's coils.

Glenn says breathlessly, "It looks like it's still being magnetically attracted to the Mini-Shuttle's coils. Or I guess it could just be the gravitational attraction, in the absence of everything else."

"It's probably the residual magnetism. Well, at least you got it separated from the other 4 spools. You should also separate each of them, allowing them to float freely so they can consecutively spin-out their cable, after the prior spool is completely spun-out."

Glenn whimpers, "Can't I at least finish dealing **with the *first one*** before fooling with the others?!?"

"Okay, but remember, the cables are attached together as one 5-mile-long wire." Glenn's only response is heavy breathing. "Alright, we'll deal with that after you wrap the first five miles around Cruithne. Let's try lifting that first one above the Mini-Shuttle ~ Wait, get another safety-rope and tether the wooden-spool to it so that it doesn't float away. Then you could try lifting it."

Glenn boldly declares, "I already attached it to my safety-rope."

The Professor yells, *"Jesus H Christ!!"* But then forces himself to sound patiently understanding. "Please, just get another safety-rope and don't do anything without conferring with me first." Glenn clips another safety-rope to that same eyehook on the outside edge of the wooden-spool. Then removes his own safety-rope from it. The Professor gently inquires, "You are no longer tethered to the wooden-spool? You don't want to be attached to it when it starts to spin . . ."

Glenn spits out, *"I know, I know!"* Then laying down on the Mini-Shuttle's coils, he wedges himself underneath the spool and then pushes it, with both his feet and arms, directly up and away from him. It floats up until its tether-rope tightens and it snaps back, wobbling back and forth, floating 4 foot above the wing. Glenn gets up. The Professor shows some alarm as his screen displays a little arcing between the magnetic-field of the Shuttle's wing and Glenn space-suit. He can hear the electrical sizzle thru the radio. Glenn doesn't even notice it anymore.

Now feeling like super-man, Glenn squats down and then jumps up and grabs onto the free-floating spool. His whole space-suit seems to radiate a macho glow as he puts his feet against the spool, clenches the AK47 in one hand and the attached end of the cable in his other hand. He crouches down again and then flinging his body weight out with an arching of his back, he pulls out the cable, spinning its spool, turning out hundreds of feet of cable. Glenn's safety-rope snaps tight. "OK Professor, how far am I away from Cruithne?" he asks as he uses his safety-rope to pull himself back down to the Shuttle's wing. The spool continues spinning, as more and more of the nanotube cable comes spinning out, disappearing into the blackness beyond his view.

"You *can't* see it?" The Professor asks skeptically, "It is 3-miles wide and you're within one mile of it. The Sun should be reflecting off of it."

"No, I can't see anything outside of the range of these lights. I can't see the other coils anymore either. I was able to see the Sun reflecting off of them before. OK, I will give the voice command to shut off the lights: 'Mini-Shuttle, shut off outside-lights'." The lights all go out and now Glenn's eyes have to adjust to the soft glow of his space-suit's lighting. He can still see the wooden-spool he's working on and much of the loose cable floating around. Now he can see the two coils reflecting sunlight ahead of him and the row of coils behind him. He looks ahead again; he still cannot see anything beyond the 2 coils.

"Bernie's voice intrudes, "Can you see any stars; I can't see them on your video display."

Glenn says intently, "Wait a second; I think I saw a flash for an instant. Now wait, I see it again, but it appears to be a little to the right. Now I see it again where it was before on the left. Maybe that is Cruithne wobbling in such a way as to reflect sunlight on one side, then on the other? It must be directly between me and the Sun's glare. Cruithne is blocking the Sun from me, exactly what we want it to do for the Earth with the Fiery Syphon, except that we don't want any flashes coming at us like those few flashes are coming around it." He pauses and listens to Jake, Bernie and the Professor's pensive breathing. Glenn questions, "Whatever happened *with Asteroid TK7?*"

Jake questions, "Did it get destroyed when it collided, or did it simply attach to Cruithne?"

Bernie ponders, "Do we even know what happened to it? Maybe it flew off into deep-space, in another direction?"

Jake theorizes, "Or maybe it was smashed into smithereens and there's nothing left of it?"

The Professor calmly states, "Maybe that flash you see is its debris field orbiting around it?"

"*Oh shit!* Don't tell me I have to worry about being ***bombarded*** *with meteorites? How far away is it, anyhow?"

"You have been moving closer to it all the time, you should be within firing range now." Glenn stares into the blackness; now he sees a flash that is much closer, and he sees that it is much bigger.

Jane was awakened by the Professor's yelling at Glenn. She is in the telescope cabin and listening thru the intercom. Her excitement of Glenn's perilous spacewalk reveres in her voice. "I am now using the telescope's computer display and I see two erratic points of light from the asteroids, one is constant but the little one disappears and then re-appears in what is no apparent pattern? I guess that is TK7, or debris from TK7. But it looks to me like it is about the same size, *very tiny,* but the same size as TK7 when I saw it before. But now their movement has a little erratic pulse: like *a slight tick."*

The Professor asks, "Glenn, can you see anything consistent with that flash of light? Is it reflecting off the same thing? Is it the same size? The same intensity?"

Glenn stares assiduously and sees the flash as he had seen it before – repeating. Then at one point he doesn't see it on the right but then appears on the left again. He relays this to the Professor, "No it doesn't seem to be the same quality of light; as if it's reflecting off of different surfaces – maybe – almost like – a flickering. But its reflection does seem to be about the same size."

"The Professor states, "Well, that suggests that it is just one object orbiting the Cruithne Asteroid. Yes, maybe it is TK7 rapidly orbiting Cruithne, and I don't understand why you cannot see it consistently. Maybe you are blinking and missing the light . . . Maybe it's *spin* N *I N G !* . . ." The Professor's voice escalates into a crescendo, *"TK7 might be bouncing off of Cruithne*!?!"

Then he shouts a command: *"Mini-Shuttle computer:* **reverse polarity –** *back-up – back-up - BACK-UP!"*

Glenn is overwhelmed as *instantaneously* everything is enveloped in *blinding electrical arcing . . .*

Then it stops . . .

"What was *that?* . . . *Was it* **TK7?** *~ DID IT HIT ME?!?"*

~ Glenn doesn't understand what's going on; he needs to be able to see! "Mini-Shuttle: turn on forward flood-lights!"

~ The lights come on and Glenn can see a *huge globe flying up at him!*

~ It is the *1000-foot diameter TK7*, suddenly brightly illuminated, it's *growing larger* in front of his eyes!

~ Glenn is unexpectedly *thrown into space* as the Mini-Shuttle's abruptly backing-up is whip-lashing his safety-rope!

~ He sees the wooden-spool that he has attached to the other safety-rope experiencing the same whip-lashing.

~ Then it is *flying directly towards him!* He gets his feet in position just in time *to push off against the spool!*

~ **Screaming** as it *impacts him*, - he and it - simultaneously **crash** into the side of the Mini-Shuttle!

The wooden-spool recoils away from him. The other four companion spools have been propelled away from the Shuttle. The sudden jolt of the Shuttle's reversing direction and it's changing magnetic-field has them flying away into space. But then, once again their connection to the spool tethered by its safety-rope, in sequence, snaps each one of them back down towards the Shuttle.

~ Glenn grabs on to his safety-rope and hand over hand frantically pulls himself towards the Shuttle's air-lock!

~ He crawls thru the doorway and closes the door behind him!

He is *quivering in shock*, but he is able to gain self-control, feeling the relative safety of being inside his Mini-Shuttle. Looking out the window, he sees one of coil #3's wooden-spools coming towards him. He feels its crashing impact against the outside of the Shuttle. He breathlessly commands, *"Nano-Computer: coil #3 magnetize"* The nanotube's electronic switches activate and the solar wind blowing by these cables induces a current that slowly builds up to a magnetic-field, and once again, these scattered spools align themselves. He apprehensively watches as they gravitate back to re-attach magnetically to the Shuttle's wing, including the rogue wooden-spool he had anchored with the safety-rope. He opens the inner air-lock door. Glenn floats inside the Shuttle and abruptly starts to *cry burning tears* with uninhibited *sobbing*. Then he is *embarrassed* and removes his helmet so that no one will hear him crying. He looks out the window as he tries to regain his composure. Everything is as it was before, except the loose nanotube cable, with the AK47 grenade-launcher attached, is now lying across the Shuttle's wing - magnetically stuck to it. Jane is now fully awakened by the loud frenzy. She demands that Bernie & Jake update her on what she missed while napping.

The Professor commands the Mini-Shuttle to stop moving backwards. They can see on his computer display, the view out the Shuttle's front window. The TK7 asteroid is spinning wildly as it is orbiting Cruithne, coming ominously close to the front of the Shuttle - maybe even closer than before - then it quickly goes back down and around, disappearing behind Cruithne. Then seconds later, it reappears on the other side with a quick flash of sunlight. Now Glenn can make out the edges of Cruithne as TK7 comes flying out towards the Shuttle once again. The Professor responds to Glenn's fear saying, "It did not get within 50 yards of you. You are safe. That's half a football field away; don't be alarmed."

"Easy for you to say . . ." The words stumble from his mouth in spite of his desire to appear courageous. "*I'm in deep-space . . .*" he cries through bated breath.

"Of course, we all know that, we understand the strain you are going thru. But now we really need you to function.

You've got to steer above, ah, that is, above or below Cruithne. Try to get on the eastern side also so you can see it in the sunlight."

Glenn whines, "How can I do that?!? Which way is east, or up, or down, or west? There's *no direction* here!"

The Professor says, "You now know where the Sun is, it should be out your front window, behind Cruithne."

Glenn wails in response, "I'm trying *to **not** look* at it!"

"Yes, I understand, but just try to remember where the Sun is - relative to you. For our purposes, East will always be where the Sun is as you're looking at it. We will call that direction 'East' - North is above you; South is below, and West is directly behind you - when you are looking towards the Sun. We must maintain some sense of direction. Now we need you to fly slowly north - not forward, but straight up; that's north Orient the Shuttle straight up slowly inching forward on the joystick. When the Shuttle gets above Cruithne, you will come into the sunlight."

Now TK7 comes flying *directly towards him* again! He resists the urge *to scream;* his urine splashes loudly into his fecal bag again. Then Glenn's bloodshot *eyes bulge* as they all see TK7 circle away, skimming very close to the surface of Cruithne ~ then impacting it and rolling off with a slight debris field also bouncing away. *"**Holy Mother of God!!** Did you see that?!? I feel like I'm the target in a **fucking shooting gallery!** But instead of bullets,* they are **hurling boulders** the size of *skyscrapers* at me!"

The Professor chooses to ignore his rant. "When we get above it, you'll be safe to launch the nanotube cable. Then we will be tracking TK7 so that you could wrap the cable around Cruithne without coming near TK7. I never expected TK7 would be orbiting – eerrr – certainly never – aahhh - bouncing off it as it is doing. Eventually I'm sure Cruithne will capture it, but we cannot wait for that to happen. We'll just have to deal with this instability by timing your wrapping of the asteroid with the revolutions of TK7."

Bernie exclaims, "But that bouncing makes it *unpredictable!*"

The *deafening silence* vehemently *cuts through* their discussion as the Professor and Jake glare at Bernie for his naïve comment. Glenn forces himself to calm down, automatically taking deep breaths as he had learned in prior situations. Then he grabs another hot cup of coffee and a sweet fruit & cheese Danish while looking at the monstrous TK7 spinning and bouncing off of Cruithne after circling it several times. "Jesus, how fast is TK7 going?"

Jane responds, "I'm working on it, I'll have it figured out soon. The Professor put a formula on my computer. I have the dimensions of the asteroids and now I just have to enter the timing - when it passes that most easterly position. I'm using a stop-watch, I can't believe it is that fast. I am going to try taking the average time over ten revolutions. Maybe even more than ten revolutions because it doesn't seem to be consistent – I guess its rotation and its orbit changes after each impact."

The Professor *growls emotionally* as he doesn't want Glenn dwelling on the difficulty of predicting TK7's orbit. "But meanwhile you can start by going out there and launching the nanotube cable by firing the AK47 into Cruithne's north polar region. You should be far away from TK7's bouncing up there as it should stay close to Cruithne's equatorial region."

Glenn doesn't think Cruithne has any poles nor an equatorial region. It is spinning wildly in every possible direction as a result of its constant impacts with TK7; but he decides to keep his mouth shut. Now he has flown above that *north polar region*, he has the Sun blazing thru the Shuttle's front window. He rolls the Shuttle over so that it is now upside down above Cruithne. Then he looks down and sees that wooden-spool he had just wrestled with, and just beyond that, TK7 is bouncing up towards him! *"Holy shit! Do you see that?!"* Now the wooden-spool is *crashing into TK7*, bouncing off of it – *exploding* - **splintering** into a *million pieces* and **flying out** in every direction!! Then TK7 goes back down and crashes into Cruithne then bounces and disappears behind it. Gasping for breath, *"Thank God that wasn't me . . . It could have been* – me in this Mini-Shuttle . . ."

The Professor says *"Calm down,* we didn't see anything on our computer screen. Tell us what *you think* you saw."

Glenn wipes his tear-filled eyes while emotionally relaying the fate of the wooden-spool and then adds, "There seems to be something unusual on TK7's surface to be smashing it and flinging the debris off in every direction. It must be a very irregular surface where it impacted; like a mountain peak."

Bernie says, "I thought the spool was attached to the safety-rope. How could it have been smashed into splinters while still being attached to the Mini-Shuttle. That would mean you were within 100 feet of the TK7 asteroid's surface because that's how long the safety-rope is."

Glenn is infuriated by their disbelief. He puts on his helmet and goes back into the air-lock. Frustrated, he proclaims, "I'll check it out . . ." The exterior door opens into deep-space. He attaches his safety-rope and then grabs the other safety-rope. He pulls it in and sees that there are splintered slithers of wood attached to the eyehook, which is still attached to the end of the safety-rope. "Obviously, it ripped out of the wooden-spool when it impacted TK7 . . . Therefore, TK7 was within 100 feet of the Mini-Shuttle... That 1000-foot diameter asteroid would have destroyed me; that *was **CLOSE!!*** - A *near miss!"* Glenn's anger at them has usurped his fear. He is breathing heavily but tries to remain calm as he displays the evidence in front of the video camera decrying, "The wooden-spool *ripped free* of this safety-rope, it's wooden debris is *still visible* on its eyehook, which is *still* *attached* to the end of **this safety-rope!**" Glenn pauses breathing deeply, as they remain silent. Now he's exasperated. He tries not to think of himself becoming chunks of space debris. He is resisting the urge to go back inside the Shuttle. He sees the AK47 with its harpoon-arrow and attached cable; it is challengingly summoning him. He reasons aloud, "If I don't do *this now*, I'll be *too scared* to function. It's time for me to stop acting like a little girl; so, I should dry my eyes, pull-up my panties and *get moving!*"

Though he is rattled, he crawls out to the AK47 laying on the Mini-Shuttle's magnetic coils. With a tug he is able to lift it up and then strap it over his left shoulder. With additional tugging he is able to pull up more of the cable that is attached to its arrow. He sees that the mile of cable is loose from the now splintered spool #3A, and has magnetically attached in a haphazard melee across the wing. With a tug he is able to lift it up. He lays it over his right shoulder and pulling it down in front of him, is able to pull up more cable behind him. But as it hangs over his shoulder, the lower portion of the loop is again magnetically re-attaching to the Shuttle's surface cables. The force of it pulls him down to his knees and then lays him flat under the cable. It is as if he is wrestling with a skinny but heavy Anaconda snake. **"What the fuck?!?"** he says as he is pinned to the Shuttle's wing. He crawls out from under it, saying "I can't launch this thing with the magnetic-field still on. Nano-Computer coil #3: demagnetize." There is electrical arcing as the cable becomes demagnetized. Now, with a tug, Glenn is able to lift the nanotube cable and gently toss it up and away from the Shuttle's wing till all of the mile-long wire is floating in space, several feet above the Shuttle.

Glenn takes the AK47 in full view of the video camera and listens to the Professor's instructions, "Make sure that your safety-rope is connected." Glenn confirms. "Now squeeze your finger into the trigger guard." Glenn confirms that it is a tight squeeze, but he's able to do that. "Now aim directly down into Cruithne. You should be pointing directly into its North Pole. Make sure that your safety-rope is connected, maybe you should wrap it around your left arm for additional protection. Glenn confirms that he is doing it, as he notices his left shoulder aches from that wrenching it had before. The Professor explains, "When you fire the AK47 you will feel a backlash, the reverse propulsion of the grenade-launcher propelling the harpoon-arrow. Make sure that you are completely away from the rest of the cable. You do not want to be entangled by it as it goes flying into Cruithne. Now, are you aiming it into the North Pole of the asteroid."

Glenn says, "Yes. *Jesus,* in this sun-light I can see it's spinning *every which-way,* probably from TK7's collisions. It's making me dizzy – even nauseous. It looks as though it's close enough for me to reach out and touch it."

The Professor glaringly shushes Bernie, but replies glibly, "No, it's not, now *stop hallucinating!*" Glenn suppresses his anger as the Professor continues, "I can see that you are a couple hundred yards above it. With your left-hand, take the safety off the AK47. Continue aiming and squeeze the trigger. - *Fire when ready.*" Glenn slowly squeezes, he can hardly feel the trigger against his finger through the thick glove of the space-suit. Unexpectedly there is an impact against his shoulder, and he is propelled backwards as the arrow fires out with a silent detonation of flashing gunpowder. Glenn flies backwards and his safety-rope tightens around his left arm, and he is slammed against the backside of the Shuttle. He can see the nano-cable whipping out as if it is a snake striking. He manages to grab hold of a handle on the Shuttle as he watches the rest of the one mile of cable being snapped down toward Cruithne. Then that cable ends. The last of that cable is connected to the next wooden-spool which is suddenly flipped up into space a few feet above the wing and it is spinning fast; unwinding its cable into Cruithne. And then it ends, flinging its wooden-spool into space, and then the third spool quickly unwinds its mile of cable, and then the 4th spool, and then the fifth spool, each flinging their wooden-spools into space as the last of the cable rips away from it.

"*Holy shit!*" Glenn hears himself saying.
And then he hears the Professor saying, "*What the fuck!*"
Jane is screaming "What's going on?"
And Bernie is saying, "I can't believe my eyes, *what did we do!?!*"

There is a long silence. Then the Professor says "Glenn, do you hear me? You've got to get closer to see what is happening. We have to be able to understand what is happening. We wanted the cable wrapped up tightly around Cruithne, but all we know is that 5 miles of cable suddenly disappeared." Glenn has the control computer in the air-lock near the exit door. He goes to it and gently inches the Mini-Shuttle down towards the North Pole of Cruithne. He can barely breathe as he sees TK7 bouncing off the surface once again less than a mile away from him. He quivers with the thought of it bouncing towards him again. Glenn is getting closer and the flood-lights from the Shuttle are now illuminating the northern surface of the big asteroid. He has a foul taste of metal in his mouth as his stomach heaves bile up his esophagus and he gags! The Professor hears this and says, "Wait, *stop!* Let's think a moment."

Bernie says, "Can't we try magnetizing coil number three? Even though its cable is off its wooden-spools, it should still get electricity from the solar wind blowing by - and hopefully it is grounded into the metal asteroid. Maybe we can get a reading on it?"

The Professor *skeptically* moans, "That *might work . . .* even though it's not long enough to wrap around the asteroid. The guidance circuit-board I made is still attached to the nanotube wire, which should still enable the computer's communication with it, which should still be able to control the nanotube switches."

Glenn is elated to reverse direction, "Mini-Shuttle Computer: Reverse Polarity, Back-up." There is arcing all around. Then slowly backing away from Cruithne and **TK7** *(wherever it may be),* he says, "Nano-Computer coil #3: Magnetize." The sensors on the Mini-Shuttle immediately detect this new magnetism on the rotating asteroid and abruptly accelerates the backing away from it. Glenn is again tossed to the end of his safety-rope.

The Professor is perplexed as the sensors tell them that this magnetized coil#3 is now moving rapidly away from the Mini-Shuttle, and is now approaching from another angle, and then away, and then again from another angle, and then again... "Oh my God!" the Professor says, "The fucking thing is *spinning so erratically!* The cable can't be doing that by itself, it would coil up into a ball if that were true. I can see that its magnetism is laid out flat, but the whole thing is spinning in a wide circle. The fucking Cruithne asteroid is spinning every which-way."

Bernie is exasperated, *"Isn't that what **I just said!?!**"*

The Professor continues to ignore him, "It's not predictable in any way, I don't understand it – the dynamics of it. - I mean - TK7 is banging into

it, but that's not large enough to cause it to spin this way - I don't think . . .
How are we ever going to *make this work?!?"*

Jane suggests with a tender femininity, "What choice do we have now
except to go ahead with what we're doing? Since it is spinning so much, I
guess all we can do is shoot the cable into it. Thank God Glenn doesn't
have to dodge TK7 while trying to encircle Cruithne to wrap this cable
around it. - The spinning, hopefully, will take care of that problem."

The Professor reflects a moment and then says, "OK, launch away.
Watch out for those wooden-spools when they go flying. Don't let them
come close to you. I was shocked to see that happen; I could have never
anticipated that."

Glenn commands, "Nano-Computer coil #1: Magnetize." While
thinking, "How the fuck can I control the direction where those wooden-
spools are flung to." The first coil launched from Skyhook comes close to
the Mini-Shuttle, but not so eerie this time, not so spooky, then attaches
to the wing magnetically. Glenn is lying flat on the wing holding tightly to
the coils to remain stable as it impacts. Then he crawls to it with his AK47
and takes an arrow from the sack and pushes it into the grenade-launcher.
Using a plastic tie, he ties the end of the spool of cable to the arrow. Then
he slings it over his right shoulder. He commands: "Nano-Computer coil
#1: De-Magnetize." Again, he forces the end spool loose and spins the
cable out. He manually keeps it spinning, unwinding about half-mile
of the nanotube cable. He inches his way back to the Shuttle's door; he
tightens the safety-rope wrapping it around his left arm so that he cannot
be thrown more than a few feet. This will keep him close to the air-lock
where he can hide from the violent thrashing of the wooden-spools. He
carefully points it down again into the North Pole of Cruithne. Then he
takes precise aim while releasing the safety switch and squeezes the trigger.
He's squeezing and squeezing and squeezing; but nothing is happening.
"Professor, nothing is happening. The grenade-launcher is not firing."

"Did you reload it?" The Professor asks.

"No, I didn't, and I don't see any reloads in the bag. I never fired a
grenade-launcher before. - Oh shit . . . Jane, you didn't provide extra ammo
for the AK47's grenade-launcher?"

She replies, "No, you didn't say to make more reloads. I thought you were connecting all the coils together so that you would only need to fire it once. I had to separate the propellent from the gren . . ."

Suddenly the Professor's weariness explodes as he yells at her, "You stupid little bitch; how could you be so *fucking dumb!* Some **fucking CIA Agent** you are!"

Glenn suddenly feels sorry for her. The half-mile of nanotube cable is floating above and away from the Shuttle, except for the end that's tied to the arrow. Breaking the tense silence, he says, "Alright, I'll use the crossbow." He removes the arrow from the AK47 and loads it into the crossbow. He raises the question, "Is the arrow speed going to be great enough to even reach the asteroid? Do you think I need to get closer for this? When I was closer before, shining the flood lights down there, I swear I saw a mountain come whizzing by and almost hit the Shuttle."

The Professor says, "That's possible I guess, with it spinning erratically like that, it might have an irregular surface. It must have hills and valleys as you say. The reading of the magnetic-field from the cable laying on its surface shows that it is spinning erratically, and it also shows that it is contoured irregularly. Some sections of the magnetic-field whizz by closer than others suggesting that it's laying on a hilly surface. There is nothing to slow down your arrow, except to drag the nanotube cable behind it. No air resistance. If anything, the colliding and the gravity attraction of the asteroid will increase its speed. As Jane said: 'No choice but to try it.' So, *fire when ready!*" Glenn again secures himself close to the air-lock. He pulls back the crossbow loaded with the arrow with the cable wired to it. He points it down into the North Pole again and fires. He quickly scrambles inside the Shuttle closing the door. On the video display, they can see the nanotube-cable once again snaking after the arrow and then being whipped down as the arrow penetrates into the spinning surface of Cruithne, whipping the cable down and wrapping it tightly onto the asteroid's spinning surface.

They watch as the subsequent 4 wooden-spools unwind in sequence with each of their wooden-spools being pulled free and flung into space. Bernie asks the Professor what's going to happen with all these wooden-spools. "Well, I can speculate that they might be captured by the gravity of Cruithne, like the first one was when it got smashed to smithereens. Or, since they are presently in an orbit that will take them close to the Earth, they will burn-up in the Earth's atmosphere, after maybe orbiting a few times. They might destroy several satellites along the way. Since we have 79 - wooden-spools left, it is a good possibility that some of them will be crashing into the Earth atmosphere and must inevitably hit a few satellites. We will have a lot of orbiting satellite wreckage to clean up when Glenn gets back with the Mini-Shuttle." the Professor says matter-of-factly. Then he relays to Bernie that Glenn had recovered debris from the blown-up Russian Satellite, which was threatening to collide with the International Space Station.

"Bernie says, *"All right Glenn!* Can I put that on Mother Nature's Blog?"

Glenn says still breathing heavily, "Let's let that consideration go for a different time. Nano-computer coil number one: Magnetize." The sensors now show a second magnetic row spinning erratically.

The Professor says, "All right, you got this all figured out now, let's keep it moving. Every minute that goes by you're orbiting 120-miles closer to impacting the Earth. The Mini-Shuttle is recording the new magnetic-field you just created on Cruithne, but you're going to need a lot more than the ten miles that you have planted on the surface so far. It's got to wrap around the asteroid several times to create a strong magnetic-field. Gotta keep this *show moving!"*

Glenn says facetiously, *"Aye, aye -* Mon Capitan!" He changes his O2 canisters in the space-suit and makes sure his safety-rope is attached. He opens the air-lock exit and brazenly crawls back out onto the wing with the crossbow strung across his right shoulder, and the quiver of arrows over his left shoulder, barely noticing the arcing coming from his feet. "Nano-computer coil #2: Magnetize." Coil number 2 comes over and turns with this magnetizing and attaches with a jarring bump onto the wing. Glenn stables himself by holding tightly to the safety-rope and pulling himself back down to the Mini-Shuttle. "Nano-computer coil #2: Demagnetize." Once again, he pries the first wooden-spool, #2A, loose from the others and then connects the spool's nanotube cable wire to the arrow using a plastic tie, inserts the arrow into the crossbow, spins loose a half-mile of its nanotube wire, goes back near the entrance air-lock, and fires the crossbow into Cruithne's North Pole again. He quickly scrambles inside and closes the air-lock door as all 5 wooden-spools consecutively unwind, whipping each of their wooden-spools into space. It attaches to the surface of Cruithne. Glenn commands, "Nano-computer: magnetize coil #2. Are you getting a reading on that one yet Professor?"

"Yes, it looks like it overlapped at one point with the first one that you launched. That's 15 miles of wire you got adhering to the asteroid; you only got another 65 to go - keep at it." Glenn does as instructed, launching an additional 15 miles, which is coils numbers 4, 5 and 6. As he's bringing in coil #7, he looks at his quiver and sees that he does not have enough arrows. He bitches, "I don't have enough arrows - what the fuck is *wrong with that woman?!?"*

She begins to cry saying, "Nobody told me how many to get, I just took the quiver of arrows that was there in front of me."

Bernie gets protective saying, "What's a matter with you people - we're all doing the best we can, *stop being so critical!"*

Glenn anguishes, "Yeah, but only one of us i*s risking* his life in *this fucking vacuous, empty,* **death trap**: I'm in deep-space - anything could happen, and now *I'm running* **out of arrows!!"**

The Professor says softly, "There are another 10 coils. Let's load them all onto the wing as best as is possible, they will magnetically align even if they extend beyond the wing. They all have to be connected one to the other." His voice cracks with uncertainty, "You can extend your space-walk out along the length of them connecting coil 6 to 7, and 7 to 8, and 8 to 9, etcetera; up to coil #15. Then you'll have them all connected to each other, allowing all fifty miles of cable to be launched with one arrow. It is not your arrow that is unwinding the nanotube cable, it is the spinning of Cruithne that is actually doing the unwinding."

Glenn says, "Well I don't see any other choices. Let me fly closer to them and bring them aboard." He maneuvers the joystick to slow down slightly, allowing each remaining coil to get closer. They align negative to positive as they approach. Then attach magnetically to the other ones already on the wing, coil against coil. Glenn adds a second safety-rope, so he has 200 feet available to him to go further on his space-walk. Starting with coil #7, he takes the end wire and connects it to the beginning wire of coil #8, then takes the end wire of coil #8, connecting it to #9, etc. Once attached, the connections are snapped securely, so that there's no way they could come loose short of the cable breaking. The connection is as strong as if the cable was solid. As Glenn's crawling out to coil #10, he realizes that he is at the edge of the wing and must now climb onto the coils to make the connections. He has to tug each wire to get it free of the residual magnetic clinging, in order to attach it to the next coil. This proves to be a more precarious task while trying to stay perched on top of the coils. Finally, Glenn sees coil#16 has a heavy grappling hook attached to the end of its nano tube wire.

As Glenn finishes attaching coil #15, he notices the Sun is blocked by the Cruithne Asteroid, and he is looking out over the edge into total blackness. He lifts his sunshield. Then his eyes come into focus - he is entranced by the sight of a distantly glowing phenomenon: it's the *Milky Way* ~ He quivers at the thought of 'Sagittarius A': its *enigmatic* **black-hole** ~ *the living Solar-Plexus* of our universe. He becomes mesmerized with this stunningly captivating sight. Then an emotional wave surges through every cell in his body; he feels its vast, all encompassing, heartfelt loving gravity reaching to embrace him. He is completely enthralled with an intensely passionate yearning as tears fill his eyes . . .

~

{Without a cry,

Without a prayer;

With no betrayal of despair.}

~

Glenn becomes aware of a distant voice, stealing from his divine <u>non-being</u> state of Nirvana Consciousness . . .

Then he hears the Professor who has been yelling in his ear. "What are you doing - *answer me* - I *can't see you* on the video camera! *What's happening?* **Where are you?!**"

Glenn answers with a frail quiver, "Okay . . . my – ah -consciousness - is being -ah – drawn into – ah - *absorbed – ah* - into the *Milky Way* . . ."

"Jesus Christ! We are all within the Milky Way Galaxy . . ." the Professor yells as he is exhausted and unable to contain his irritation, "This *is no fucking time* to be **star gazing to get your rocks off!**"

With tears in his eyes, Glenn turns-around while clinging to his epiphany, longing to maintain this ephemeral reality; as he is meditatively clutching each wooden-spool, crawling his way back towards the Shuttle's entrance . . .

As he traverses each spool, he is recovering from his profoundly alluring encounter with that all-consuming Galactic Divinity. He had meditated for years trying to achieve it: That contemplative realm of Nirvana – total silence – total awareness – total **just *being***

But somehow – this was on the edge of complete immersion, of surrender . . .

of - ***NON-BEING*** . . .

this was - ***SUICIDAL!***

Then he has a vision of the 'laughing pilgrims' burning-up and wonders if they were feeling the same emotion that he was feeling . . .

Glenn crawls back to the Shuttle's door after spinning free a half-mile of the nanotube wire. He already has the arrow tied to the #7 leading nanotube-cable and he inserts it into the crossbow. He pulls on the bow-string & arrow by arching his back, loading it into the firing position. He aims it down into the asteroid's North Pole, ready to release it. But the Professor says "Wait, don't fire yet. Let's see if we can time this so that the arrow intersects at some point with the thirty-miles of cable that you have already laid."

Glenn says, "I'm ready, you tell me when to pull the trigger."

The Professor is reading the magnetic waves and he sees a group disappearing directly below the asteroid's South Polar region - he shouts: ***"FIRE!"***

Glenn releases the arrow, launching coil#7's nanotube-cable, as he ducks back into the air-lock and closes the door. He feels goose-bumps as the hair on the back of his neck bristles. The Professor was pretty accurate in his prediction of when to shoot as that section of magnetized cable spins around. Glenn's arrow penetrates nearby, causing the cable to wrap around and over top of the existing cable, making a continuous magnetic connection. Coil#7's five-wooden-spools thrash free and soar out into space. Glenn agonizes, "Can the wooden spools *destroy the Shuttle* if they **slam** into it?!?" Coil#8's wooden-spools are whipped more aggressively into space, then coil#9, then #10, right up through coil#16. Glenn is holding onto the window frame as he stares out with dreadful apprehension. They are all *spellbound* watching these *tempestuous dynamics* in deep-space.

Then they see the grappling hook at the end of coil#16's wire; it is whipped into the Mini-Shuttle's wing . . .

- ~ It *hooks onto* a section of the nanotube wire wrapped around the wing!
- ~ Suddenly the Mini-Shuttle is *jerked side-ways* —
- ~ It's being *dragged into the violently spinning Cruithne Asteroid!*
- ~ Everyone's heart stops beating . . .
- ~ Then that section of nanotube wire breaks and *the grappling hook lashes back at Glenn's face* . . .
- ~ *His eyes bulge* **with terror**!!
- ~ It scrapes along his window . . .
- ~ . . .over to the door . . .

> . . . *hooks onto* the Mini-Shuttle's door-handle . . .
> . . . "It will *rip the* **door off** _the Shuttle!?!_"

Glenn's instantaneous - *helpless* - realization:

> "– **AAHHH**!! - Cruithne is *seizing me*, **reclaiming me** for the **MILKY WAY'S BLACK-HOLE**!!"

After an endless few seconds of being dragged, the handle breaks off and is ripped away. The Mini-Shuttle immediately backs-up . . . backing away to its magnetically coordinated safe distance.

~

They can all hear the *anxiety-filled silence*, and then *feel their bated breath* being slowly released through their radio communicators.

~

Glenn inquires timidly, "Ah - Mission . . . . - ah - accomplished?"

The Professor says, "Yes, as far as you're concerned. I don't think there's anything more that you can do. Just let me finish magnetizing all eighty miles of this nanotube wire and see what we got." Glenn feels his space-suit decompressing and he opens the inner door. He floats inside the Shuttle, takes off his helmet and pulls himself down into the pilot's seat, breathing a sigh of relief as he fastens his seat-belt. The Professor's voice continues over the intercom, "I'm assigning the whole eighty miles of nanotube cable as a single magnetic unit called 'Cru-Mag', and now I'm going to try to induce a single magnetic-field by using the Earth's as a template. TK7 banging into it is causing disturbing fluctuations. Can you see anything up there?"

Glenn answers wearily, "I was just closing my eyes, I could use a nap. Yes, I see electrical arcing on Cruithne that I had not noticed before. As I am looking, I see different areas with various degrees of arcing, not like isolated lightning bolts. So, that's TK7 orbiting it while interacting with the new magnetic-field we created? . . . Too bad Cru-Mag can't capture it."

"Well, that explains that. **Man!** This computer is really flying. The Artificial Intelligence has taken over and I'm not sure what is happening. Oh, it has already designated a north and south pole, although it is still spinning erratically. I will try to align the north pole with the Earth's."

In a second Glenn shouts, "*HOLY SHIT!* THE WHOLE ASTEROID IS ARCING *EVERWHERE!*" dead silence from the intercom, "It looks like it's slowing down, wait, under the arcing I can make out *some features:* hills and valleys. Now it has stopped spinning in one direction, on one axis; and it is *wobbling back and forth* towards the side facing the Sun. It's slowing down; *it's stopping.*

WOW! That was fast.

The Mini-Shuttle is suddenly backing away from it."

The Professor finally speaks, "The computer's Artificial-Intelligence is really some amazing shit . . . Cruithne's spinning energy must have been converted to magnetic energy as it stopped spinning on that polar axis. The Mini-Shuttle detected the increased magnetic-field and backed up to maintain it's safe distance. Now, how do I stabilize the other access of spin? I can just designate a section on the Equatorial side, and have it locked onto the east where the Sun is. Let's try it." Within seconds before their astonished eyes there is massive arcing as the asteroid stops spinning altogether.

Glenn states, "The Mini-Shuttle is backing up again as Cru-Mag's field is increasing. *Jesus*, that really is *incredible*. I can't believe my eyes."

The Professor replies, "I think the magnetic-field must have transferred from the surface to the interior of the asteroid. It has grown hundreds of times stronger than the field we created with the eighty miles of nanotube cable. Now, let's see what we could do about TK7."

Glenn is gawking thru heavy eyelids at all this activity on the asteroid as TK7 comes crashing down onto it. But instead of bouncing off, it rolls and throws up a lot of debris and finally slams into a steep cliff that stops it. There is more massive arcing. Then it rolls back and settles into place. Cruithne rocks from the impact but returns to its stable position. Glenn relays all this to the Professor, adding matter-of-factly, "That was too easy . . ." as the Mini-Shuttle backs away more, evidently TK7's kinetic energy has also converted to magnetism for Cru-Mag .

The Professor in an astonished voice says, "Well, onward to the L1 point... we will have Cru-Mag follow you by magnetically attaching it, so you will be towing it behind you."

XLII

❖

MISSION ACCOMPLISHED?

Glenn inquires, "Mission accomplished? I can take a nap?"

"Go ahead, get some rest."

Glenn is wearily mumbling, "But, the mass of this asteroid should drag me to it, rather than trailing after my Mini-Shuttle's magnetic-field?" He receives his new coordinates to L1 and starts the autopilot. As he passes by, Cru-Mag falls in behind him, dutifully following.

The Professor is responding enthusiastically, "Apparently magnetism is different than gravity and stronger in this case as it is taking precedence over gravity. Onward *to the L1 Position!*" as Glenn falls asleep.

Bernie asks, "We use magnets to overcome gravity, but only in a very close proximity? How are you controlling Cru-Mag from down here?"

"I am remotely using the Mini-Shuttle to communicate simple instructions to the Cru-Mag's nanotube-cable electronic switches, which adjusts its magnetic-field."

"Does it make sense that our radio signals are not impacted by all that magnetism?"

"He's receiving our signal from within the Mini-Shuttle's magnetic-field, maybe it's travelling through another dimension and materializes inside of his magnetic-field without passing through its external force field. I do not really know . . . We were in radio communication with him as he was launched from within the mag-lev's magnetic-field. To my knowledge we never lost radio communications."

Bernie leaves to join Jane and Jake behind Skyhook's cabin . . .

XLIII

❖

UNWINDING

The Professor is monitoring the acceleration of Glenn in the Mini-Shuttle. "Make sure your seatbelt is attached." After a bit, he drones on, "I am surprised we have not heard from the Green-gos. That's what Sancho and the others are calling the triumvirate: Bernie, Jake, and Jane. I guess because they are younger therefore the 'green' part and they are 'gringos' so they changed that to 'Green-gos'. I would have thought that they'd be excited about are successful capture and transporting of Cruithne to the L1 position. Although, they were hanging around here too much with nothing to do since I stopped the launchings. I told them to go find something else to do so that I didn't have to listen to their chatter."

He continues babbling, "So, they went over the invoices of nuclear wastes as we were missing one barrel. Then they went to the cavern on the Jet-Basket and found the missing barrel. Apparently, it was turned the wrong way inside the skid so its barcode could not be scanned. Pecuador's dock workers would not take the *extreme effort* of turning the barrel around. Anyhow they brought it back up here to show you when you get back. I guess you should remember to congratulate them on their effort. They also brought back more train track rails. Evidently, they were fascinated by your story about the Alien dream and are repeating your experiment. That might confirm whether you were having a dream or not. Jane observed that the magnetic force field of a bar magnet seems to emanate from the center of the bar magnet, possibly coming through a different dimension – flowing in a pattern like the infinity symbol. You know, like the number eight - *8* – only laying on its side – but picture it in three dimensions. Also, she pointed out that have been no negative medical effects from the extreme magnetism of Magnetic Resonance Imaging. Anyhow they ran some electricity through the twelve rails and magnetized them behind Skyhook's cabin. They built a pyramid as you described with these twelve rails and Jane got the idea to sit inside this magnetic-pyramid to see if her time in there was shorter than our time. She figured that if the magnetic-field was working to shorten your time experience in space maybe it would work up here in near space. I congratulated her; I'm very interested in the results. They're also talking about that high school that Virginia went to. They're very upset about that and feel compelled to do something about it. Maybe we could get Mother Nature's Blog to report on it, in the hope that the government agencies will intervene to correct the situation. I suggested that; but they insisted that it would NOT work and at best it would be only a very short term, temporary solution. The drug lords are making too much money off of these high school students. And these students have no other real opportunities to make money. What do you think?" - Waiting for a reply, all the Professor hears is the deep snoring of Glenn's much needed, recuperative sleep. "You lucky fuck, I wish I could sleep like that."

XLIV

❖

LAGRANGE L1-POINT

The Professor summons Glenn, "You are arriving at the L1-Lagrange point."

Glenn stretches and yawns, "I feel well rested. I am surprised that I could sleep so well, while floating around up here."

The Professor says, **"Again!** . . . <u>With-out</u> your _seat-belt?!?_" Forcing himself to calm down, "Well, you should be well rested, you went to sleep 24 hours ago in our time, although you probably only slept 8 hours in your time. Now, you have to steer Cru-Mag into a 'Halo Orbit'."

"Glenn laughs saying, "Just kidding; I slept with my seat-belt on."

"You think that's funny, like I don't have enough to worry about!"

Glenn asks, "Halo Orbit? What's that? I thought we were going to remain stationary in that fixed position between the Earth and the Sun."

The Professor says, "I thought you might need a little introduction to these dynamics, so I sent you a few diagrams. Look on your computer."

Glenn quickly scans them saying, "I don't have time to study your _fucking 'Halo orbit' shit!_ Just tell me what I need to know."

The Professor digresses, "Well talk about bizarre, CIA Jane was researching these diagrams to send to you; but, she refused to give you anymore than just the web address on many of them because they are proprietary and you need permission to transmit them. She takes her 'upholding the law' oath very seriously . . ."

Glenn writhes with vehemence, "Will somebody **smack the shit** out of that *stupid cunt . . .*"

The Professor responds with a whimsical "Humph!" and then returns to explaining the 'Halo Orbit': "The Moon's orbiting of the Earth is constantly varying it's 'gravity-well' which varies its L1 location. The Earth orbits further away from the Sun by June, then orbits back to its closest position by December. This constant variation in orbital distance changes the location of the L1-Lagrange point. The Halo Orbit stays on this high-point between the Sun and the Earth's gravity-well; orbiting around that L1 zero gravity point. That's why the 'Halo Orbit' is <u>perpendicular</u> to the 'plane of the ecliptic'."

Glenn is looking at the information that Jane sent to him:

Sun & Earth Gravity Wells = L1 is the stable high-point between them. The Moon's orbit also effects the L1 - its gravity also effects the varying distance of the L1 position between the Earth and the Sun:

https://www.google.com/search?q=Sun+%26+Earth+Gravity+Wells& rlz=1C1CHBF_enUS765US765&oq=Sun+%26+Earth+Gravity+Wells&

A Gravity Well:
<u>https://infinitylearn.com/surge/blog/iit/jee/dimensions-of-gravitational-potential/</u>

Lagrange Points:
<u>https://physics.stackexchange.com/questions/286642/why-are-the-lagrangian-points-l-1-l-2-l-3-unstable</u>

Glenn says, "I can't deal with this *science shit.*"

The Professor is exasperated, "Well, I simply wanted to make it *available* – you don't have to *look at it!* L1's stable point is between the Sun and the Earth's gravity wells. These diagrams are in 2 dimensions; try to picture them in 3 dimensions."

- The Lagrange Points and Gravity Wells:

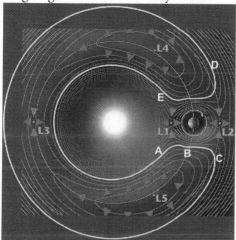

- Halo orbit is 90 degrees off the ecliptic, perpendicular to the ecliptic:

Halo Orbit:

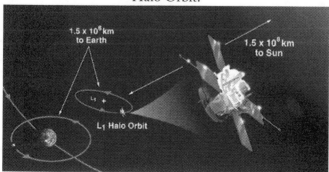

Lagrange points:
HTTPS://WEBB.NASA.GOV/CONTENT/ABOUT/ORBIT.HTML

Plane of the Ecliptic:
https://en.wikipedia.org/wiki/Ecliptic#Plane_of_the_Solar_System

- plane of the Ecliptic: from the Sun's equator out in a flat line, where most of the planets orbit.

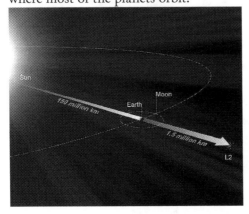

-

The Professor continues, "But it would be much easier to understand if you spent a few moments perusing these diagrams." Glenn groans in anguish as the Professor continues wearily explaining, "L1 is the relatively small spot between the Sun and the Earth where their gravity cancels each other out. Think of it as the high-point between their two gravity wells. Try to imagine it in 3 dimensions. The high-point between the Sun and the Earth's gravity-wells is not fixed in space as Earth's orbit is irregular around the Sun and consequently, the high-point between the two gravity-wells, adjusts its position as the Earth's distance from the Sun varies. So, now try to picture this L1 high-point in the 4th dimension of time: today, next month, 6 months from now. The only way to maintain it is to use this Halo-orbit around that L1 center, but it is a small orbit. The Soho Satellite's 200,000 mile Halo-orbit is perpendicular to the ecliptic, that could NOT block the Fiery Syphon. So, we are going to try orbiting around the L1-Lagrange spot – not perpendicular to it - but on the plane of the ecliptic, wherein we hope to block the Fiery Syphon at least half of the time. I'm not even sure that it's going to work."

Glenn shouts, "It may *not work!* After all **this** *shit I've been through!* ~ All this *Lagrange crap* seems to be irrelevant to the magnetic-force-fields. We have been using magnetic-force-fields to navigate so far. Can't we continue using these to try and hold the asteroid at the exact L1 Spot rather than this Halo-*orbiting crap* around L1. Then we should be able to totally block the Fiery Syphon?"

The Professor is thinking and finally responds, "I don't know . . . Maybe it will work . . . Let's try it . . ."

The Professor sends the coordinates for the exact L1 Spot (making it relative to the Sun, the Earth and the Moon's gravity, while computing its constant variations and also the magnetic fields it will be orbiting thru.) to Glenn's computer on the Mini-Shuttle and then the guidance procedure for backing the space Shuttle into position. Glenn pushes the joy-stick, there is some arcing, and the Mini-Shuttle begins magnetically pushing Cru-Mag asteroid into the L1 position. The Professor gravely explains to the Green-gos: "I have just developed a complex formula that we hope will magnetically adjust the position of Cru-Mag relative to the Earth's orbit, keeping it on the plane of the ecliptic, so that it will constantly remain on that high point between the Sun and the Earth's gravity-wells, without orbiting around the L1 Spot; but rather just keeps it sitting there, exactly on that L1 Point's varying location. That is where the shortest distance between the Earth and the Sun is and that is the path along which the Fiery Syphon's CME is blasting. Watch Glenn on the video monitor as he is now going to maneuver Cru-Mag into that L1 position . . ." Everyone is concentrating on Glenn's intense activity.

The Mini-Shuttle pushes it magnetically into position and Glenn releases Cru-Mag from the Mini-Shuttle's magnetic control. Everybody is holding their breath. He flies above it, and they can see the Fiery Syphon is now burning into the sunny-side of Cruithne Asteroid. The Professor worries, "It must be melting the nanotube wires that are controlling the magnetic-field holding it in place. We don't know what effect it will have on its control. But the computerized artificial intelligence seems to have no problem compensating for what might be going wrong. It is maintaining that fixed position between the Earth and the Sun without halo-orbiting around the L1 point."

Glenn asks, "OK, are we there yet?

Mission accomplished?"

The Professor says, "We have to wait awhile and see, give it a chance."

Glenn says, "*Fuck that*, I wanna come home. You have guidance-controllers on Cru-Mag's nanotube cables, if you can communicate with that directly, then you should be able to make adjustments remotely. Even if we have to pay people to constantly monitor it."

The Professor responds, "How do we know it didn't burn-up, or that it's not going to burn-up - totally. That guidance- controller may be in the direct path of the "Fiery Syphon.""

Glenn says, "Well you have an idea where your guidance-controllers are located within each nanotube coil, simply rotate the asteroid – turning them into the shade – magnetically rotate them into Cruithne's shadey-side."

"That's a *clever idea!*" says the Professor with surprise, "I must be exhausted, I should have thought of that." He checks their location on Cru-Mag and sends the guidance coordinates to rotate the Cruithne Asteroid 98° on the ecliptic and then 36° from north to south.

Now Glenn flies above Cru-Mag; they can see the Fiery Syphon's CME burning into the surface of the asteroid. However, he sees no sign of the Whirlwind. The Professor tells him, "We should not expect to see atomized vapor from it in the vacuum of space."

"Send me the coordinates, I want to *come home.*"

"Turn the Mini-Shuttle 180°, do you see that *blue&white* ball? *That's home.* You should fly there on your own, just for the experience. You need to pile-up flying time for your *space-pilot's license.*"

Glenn laughs, then asks "What are all the others doing?"

"Sancho is working with the other Pecuadorian employees on rebuilding Skyhook's H2-cubes. He had the idea of lowering all of the bursted balloons to the ground and repairing them like we did before - on site - then re-inflating them. He is getting the hydrogen from the upper stratosphere – the mesosphere - the same way we did after the first Big Syphon's destruction. We still had some 30+ helium-tank-carts that we were able to repair back then. He is floating them up into the mesosphere and pumping in hydrogen, then floats them down and inflates the repaired balloons with it. They already accomplished rebuilding Loon-Evator2 and Bernie restored the functioning of your centrifuge operation. The Greengos are busily involved here on Skyhook. They are diligently working on their experiments. I had not seen any of them while you were sleeping. Before you come home, since you're already at the L1 point, what do you think about picking up the Soho Satellite from its Halo-orbit. You are only 100,000 miles or so away from it."

Glenn says, "Alright, send me the coordinates. But I gotta call Margherita."

The Professor warns, "You better call *your wife **first!***"

Glenn says, "Yes you're right." He resets his communicator for private conversation with cell phones and he commands, "Dial Elena." There's no answer. "Dial Margarita." There's no answer there, either. "The stupid girls must have forgotten to charge their phones. As excited as they were to have them, you would think they would have remembered that."

The Mini-Shuttle quickly flies him to the Soho satellite and Glenn comments to the Professor as he is looking out the window, "I see it. I don't know how I'm going to get it into the space Shuttle; do you know how big that thing is?"

"Of course, the solar panel array is about ten meters wide, but you can fold them down. You can take them off entirely if it'll help getting it through the Mini-Shuttle's door." Glenn does another space walk and following the Professor's instructions, recovers the Soho Satellite.

He asks, "Any chance I can simply fix it – re-charge it - and re-insert it back in its proper orbit?"

The Professor answers, "No, but *I could* if I were up there. That's why I should have been the one to go. Anyhow, I'll fix Soho when you get it here. Then *I'll take it back* and reinsert it into th*at L1-Halo-orbit.* The world will just simply be surprised by the fact that Soho suddenly came back online, and is continuing to do its job: hopefully for another 25 years. Do you know that it is responsible for finding more than *four thousand comets*; I bet some of them **are Earth threatening** too."

"Well, I strapped Soho down with everything else inside the cargo area; can I come home now?"

"Bring it on home, Glenn . . . bring it on home..."

Glenn straps himself into the pilot seat and accelerates the Mini-Shuttle back towards that blue&white ball.

Soon he slows the Mini-Shuttle down to 18000mph and begins orbiting the Earth on a polar orbit. The Professor sends him the guidance coordinates as he is flying over the Artic. Glenn can see the Pacific Coastline out his right window. The computer has slowed him down somewhat as he is crossing over Columbia. He sees Skyhook on his right. Then it makes a hard right turn and he comes into Skyhook's Railgun track as the Professor shouts at him to, "Reverse Magnetize." All he sees is total electrical arcing until it comes down to a few sparkles, and he sees that he is back at Skyhook's mag-lev launch-pad. Then, "Don't forget to lower the landing gear; then I'll shut-off the mag-lev." Glenn confirms.

He feels very heavy as he puts his space-suit helmet on and clumsily exits the Mini-Shuttle while cursing at the Earth's gravity. He is expecting to see the Green-gos with the Professor waiting to celebrate their success. It's just the Professor, who tells him, "Let's go check on the Green-gos. They are behind Skyhook's cabin working on their magnetic-pyramid experiment. They'll be happy to see you are back!"

But Glenn is too anxious to see his women and he says, "No, I'll just take the Loon-Evator down. Then I will send it back up to you. What is the latest on the Fiery Syphon?"

The Professor replies, "No news from around the world, I don't see any sign of it, yet. Cru-Mag is holding on to its L1 spot. I am hopeful . . . The Moon totally blocked it over South America yesterday; but it has *been ravaging Africa!* Today the Moon only partially blocked it, so we have some fires burning south of us. Interestingly, the Syphon reversed directions and sucked-down a lot of moon-dust into the Earth's atmosphere. Another *potential problem! But its Fiery CME stayed on the far side of the Moon. Maybe I can check on the effect it had there after I re-install the SOHO into orbit.*"

Glenn floats the Loon-Evator down to the ground and his two mujers are glad to see him, giving him the joyous reception that he expected. They help him out of his smelly space-suit and join him in the shower. Then they take him to bed and screw his brains out. They bring back food to his cabin and enjoy a relaxing meal together. He asks, "Why didn't you answer your cell phones when I called. I telephoned you *from deep-space*: from **a million miles above the Earth!** I was worried about both of you." They react with alarm at the loss of their phones. Margherita doesn't remember where hers is. Then Elena says the same thing. Glenn phones them again and they listen for the ringing but can't hear it anywhere.

Margherita runs to the kitchen telling him to keep calling so that she can listen for it. They can't find either cell phone, and apologizing for losing their expensive phones, they *begin to cry*. Glenn is *gob-smacked-flabbergasted* after his heroic deep-space endeavor as he calms them down, "Don't worry, we'll find them tomorrow; they *are not that important!* Believe me; people are always mis-placing their cell phones . . ." They have a relaxing evening together watching TV and falling asleep entwined, all three of them, wrapped together lovingly.

The next morning Glenn congratulates Sancho on the work that's been accomplished, and then asks, "Where's Bernie?"

Sancho replies, "I have not seen him in days. I thought he was working with you and the Professor up on Skyhook."

Then Glenn notices that the Jet-Basket is gone and thinks, "He must be working on the centrifuge, collecting the precious metal bags." He tries to hail Bernie through his space-suit communicator and also through the computer. No response. "That's surprising... I hope he's alright." he's thinking of taking the truck and driving down to Loon-Evator2 to check on him, but remembers the Professor said they were working behind the Skyhook's cabin on an experiment. He communicates with the Professor to send down the Loon-Evator, and he will ride it back up immediately as he wants to speak with the Green-gos. He adds, "I thought I might see them down here for breakfast, but nobody has seen them for days."

The Professor asks, "Why don't you fly the Jet-Basket up here."

Glenn says, "Bernie must be using it to work on the Gusher-Tower."

"Bernie is over here working on that experiment. I'm sending down the Loon-Evator to you."

The Loon-Evator comes down and Glenn gets his space-suit on and rides it back up to the Skyhook.

XLV

THE EXPERIMENTAL MAGNETIC PYRAMID

Bernie had been listening to Glenn's conversation with the Professor. Then Bernie switches communications to speak directly and privately to Jane and Jake only. He is outside of their magnetic pyramid; she is on the inside of it, intently staring towards the pyramid's point. Of course, they are both wearing their space-suits. The pyramid is now pointed north-northwest and down at an angle towards America's northern hemisphere. He says, "If you're going to do this, we have to do it now before Glenn gets here. I'm sure he'll stop us."

Jane says, "He won't stop me, I dare him to try."

Bernie says, "Don't talk like that, just because I let you have your gun, don't start thinking that you're invincible."

Jane is thinking, "As if you could have stopped me from *getting my gun!*" She is on a cell-phone Face-Timing with Jake, commanding, "Where exactly are you now? Flip the camera; I need to see around."

He whispers as he is pointing out an individual in the lunchroom of the Arizona high school, "I'm in position; can you see the *Drug-Lord-High-Schooler*. I am zooming-in on him now. That's him - I *recognize him* - I had seen him before, and I knew he was *bad news*. He looks just as Virginia described him to me. *There's no mistake*, I am *100percent sure — he is our TARGET*. Maybe I should take his picture and you can verify it with Virginia? I see no sign of your 'Pyramidal-Projection', I don't know what to look for, but everything is normal here - *except for me*. I stick out like a **sore thumb,** an older white guy in the lunchroom, not being a teacher. I'm surprised that nobody has confronted me yet."

Jane says, "It's too late to verify with Jane. I am able to zero-in on you, I'm having a hard time moving the Pyramidal-Projection ray the short distance from you to our target. This projection doesn't want to move a few feet, it moves miles at a time." Then she says to Bernie, "You better go and intercept Glenn before he gets off the Loon-Evator. Stall him, somehow keep him busy. Eventually we will have to explain everything to him, but let's finish off this Drug Lord first; before your Boss-Man has anything to say about it."

Bernie goes to the Loon-Evator and greets Glenn coming up the loading platform. He says, "Come with me Glenn, we have so much to talk about. Congratulations on your accomplishment; it looks like you stopped the Fiery Syphon. The Professor says it's too soon to say for sure, but there have been no reports of damage of any sort since you moved the asteroid into the L1 spot." Glenn follows Bernie back onto the Loon-Evator and into its cabin. Bernie apologizes saying, "I wanted to talk to you alone, away from the Professor. He's very irritable since you've been gone." They take off their helmets and sit down and relax. Glenn explains that we all have to give the Professor some slack as he's been thru a lot. He's hopeful that Cruithne at the L1 spot has solved the problem. He discusses the experiences that he had up there, mule-hauling that three-mile-wide asteroid around. He tells him how he rescued the Soho Satellite and how the Professor plans on fixing it and then returning it back to that L1-Halo-orbit so that the world will certainly be surprised when it comes back online again. He tells Bernie that he can help him unload that satellite plus all the other space debris that he picked up. He even has that rogue barrel nuclear-waste to unload. Then he asks Bernie about the experiments they've been conducting; the Professor had mentioned it to him.

Bernie gives a long sigh, "Yes, Jane wanted to see if being inside the magnetic-field would create the time difference that you experienced inside the Mini-Shuttle's magnetic-field while you were flying around. So far, apparently not, maybe it only works if you're moving fast. We remembered that dream you mentioned: that an Alien dis-assembled your magnetic pyramid three times. We remembered that you inadvertently made the pyramid magnetic, out of the already magnetized metal rails; so, we did the same thing. While she was sitting there inside the pyramid, ah, for some unknown reason, she felt compelled to balance the magnetic force to be functioning so that the point of the pyramid was its north magnetic pole. So, we put individual flow controls on each rail of the pyramid and continued adjusting the electric flow through each one of them, so that it would balance properly. Then to further control it we decided to wrap each of the rails with the nanotube cable just as the Professor had done with the Mini-Shuttle. That seemed to give us better magnetic control . . . Aahhh - Now - pay close attention: do you remember ever feeling **weirdly intrigued** by the perimeter of the **circle** going **inside** and then **outside of each point on the pyramid.** Jane insists we are not allowed to copy it; but let's look it up now at:

https://www.livescience.com/freemasons.html "

Within a few seconds he has it on his computer display. "See the top of the ancient Mason Temple. The circle passing in and out of the pyramid; its like the pyramid is depicting this dimension and the circle is going in and out of this dimension at the points of the pyramid. Now imagine that with a four-sided pyramid like the ancient ones in the Egyptian desert; remembering their intriguing mystery. Now imagine them magnetized as you had done."

Glenn exclaims, "Jane says you *can't copy* this page! What kind of *nonsense* is that? It looks like she's got you **by the balls!!"**

Bernie tries to ignore that comment and stammers on, "**Or the '***All-Seeing Eye'* in the **point** of the *pyramid*; you've seen it in numerous places; sometimes called the 'Eye of Providence'. You should recognize it ~ Look at this picture:"

Bernie gravely continues, "Well, as Jane was looking from the inside of the pyramid towards the point - while still monitoring the time, you know, looking for that differentiation in our time - She was sitting in there for more than a day so we could get a valid measurement. While she was there, ah, she was trying to balance the magnetic force to be functioning so that the point of the pyramid was its north magnetic pole. So, we put individual flow controls on each rail of the pyramid and continued adjusting the electric flow through each one of them, so that it would balance properly. Then to further control it, we decided to wrap each of the rails with the nanotube cable just as the Professor had done with the Mini-Shuttle. That seemed to give us better magnetic control, ah."

Glenn interrupts, "You're repeating yourself; you said that already . . ."

"Sorry . . . I guess I lost track of what I was saying. We've been working long hours, day and night on this. Well, as Jane was looking inside of it, still monitoring the time, you know, looking for that differentiation in time, she noticed that she could see out beyond the rails of the pyramid, from side to side in every direction, but looking towards its point, all she could see was a blackness, what she thought was strange. Then at one point, after several hours of being there, maybe even more than a day, she noticed a change in that blackness. It seemed like there was some fiber to it. Then she noticed a gritty surface area seemed to materialize and then a mountain peak showed up - reflected in golden sunlight - and then a shadow on that mountain - and then, back into darkness again.

All this time inside the pyramid she had been video-taping herself, and she also had that black spot at the point of the pyramid in the video. So, we looked at what she had recorded - this is it." Bernie slowly searches his laptop computer. Glenn is very impressed with their experiment. As he is watching it, Bernie becomes rattled as Glenn impatiently fast-forwards it to the golden reflection off the mountain.

Glenn immediately recognizes it. *"Holy shit!* That's the Moon. It's a better view than I had from the Mini-Shuttle. It's very close, you can almost touch it. Is this through the telescope?"

"No . . ." Bernie insists, "This - this is from *our Pyramidal-Projection!"*

Glenn queries, "I don't understand, how is this possible? Have you discussed this with the Professor?"

Bernie says, "No, he's been too busy and irritable."

Glenn says, "Let's go talk to him now." Bernie protests, "But I have more to tell . . ."

"We'll just have to *repeat* the whole thing *all over again* with the Professor, so let's just go do it with him now." They put their helmets on and walk over to Skyhook's cabin where they find the Professor eating his lunch. Glenn has Bernie review everything again for the Professor and shows him the video from their Pyramidal-Projection. The Professor is totally befuddled.

Then Bernie continues, so we used less electricity and pointed it down to the area of our Hacienda. All we could see was blackness until we adjusted it down to a very minimal amount of electricity and then we saw the surface area around the Hacienda."

"So," the Professor says, "it *is functioning* like a telescope. I gotta see this."

Bernie interrupts, "I've got more to tell you."

They are too excited and say, "You can talk to us while you're showing us on this projector-pyramid, ah Pyramidal-Projection: – whatever."

"No, it's more complicated than that. We wanted to explore, or investigate the lens that we were looking at - or looking through - maybe it was a screen? But we were afraid to touch it. So, we pushed some nanotube cable up against it and were surprised to see that about four feet of it went totally through the point of the pyramid. And then it broke off. But we could see that broken off piece falling to the ground at the Hacienda. We pushed through several more lengths of nanotube cable and the same thing happened. We could see it laying on the ground by the railroad tracks nearby. Then I flew down in the Jet-Basket and looked for these pieces on the ground. I found them and Jane said she could see me through the Pyramidal-Projection. She pushed through more pieces as I looked up. They seemed to materialize out of thin air at about 25-feet above me. I could not see anything else out of the ordinary."

The Professor says, "Unless there's some other explanation, what you're describing is Inter-Dimensional Transporting."

The hair on the back of Glenn's neck is standing up again. "Bernie is speaking too slowly and too calmly for such a resounding discovery, if in fact he believes it himself."

"There's more... I grabbed Ricardo's pet dog, and a few live chickens from the kitchen supply area. I put them inside the Loon-Evator's cabin in open, but airtight boxes. Then when I got up to Skyhook, one at a time, I sealed them in the boxes and Jane threw them through the pyramid's point. We could see them come out onto the ground in the Hacienda area, just as those pieces of nanotube cable had done. We could see that they were alive and well; the dog was running back towards Ricardo's cabin. Obviously, they were all unharmed. I later checked with the radiation detector; *no contamination!* The dog still obeyed Ricardo's commands; you know – sit, beg, roll-over . . . apparently no brain damage."

"But you said that the cable broke off."

"Yes, but that's when we stopped moving it through the opening at the point of the pyramid. Apparently, if it remains in in both dimensions, it'll break off and I presume would kill an animal if he was stuck there, cutting him in half."

"Well, this is some more amazing shit. We're going to be very busy checking this stuff all out and writing dissertations; even books. We are gonna be famous!" the Professor exclaims. "Oh! Speaking of famous, look up the movie 'The Philadelphia Experiment. It is supposed to be a true story that happened in the Navy Philadelphia Ship Yard in the early 1940s. A warship, The USS Eldridge, was put under extreme magnetism to make it disappear from radar, as a cloaking device. But weird shit happened. Sailors where stuck inside the metal of the ship. Their arms, legs, torsos, were enmeshed within the ship's bulkheads and decks. A few disappeared and were never seen again. In the movie they re-appeared in the future. A survivor claimed it was true . . ." Bernie reads the Wikipedia info on it.

Glenn says, "Fascinating. Well, can we *go see* this fabulous *Pyramid-Projection*, or do you have *more* you *have to* tell us."

Bernie can't think of a way to stall any longer, so he says apprehensively, "No - OK, let's go . . ." They put on their helmets, and he connects to Jane whispering, "I can't stall them anymore, here we come, it's now or never."

She growls, "It's gotta be now . . . I think I got him." As they get closer, they see Jane in her space-suit sitting inside the pyramid with Ricardo's orange-colored water pistol aiming down towards the pyramid-point. And there they see the back of a young man's head, getting closer and closer to it, then into his hair, and then a darkness. Jane shines a flashlight on it, and you can see what looks like the inside of a skull, grey matter - brain tissue, pulsating veins and an artery with blood pumping through neuronal tissue. As she moves the control a minuscule amount it appears to be going deeper inside. And then she lifts the water-pistol directly into the beam of light and *squirts* a few ounces of liquid out of the squirt- gun. They see the ominous liquid impacting and then being absorbed into that neuronal tissue and bloodstream.

~   Suddenly there is violent movement!   ~

Jane drops her flash-light while adjusting her computer controls. Now they can see the image of a lunchroom from above as Bernie says fearfully, "Jake is in that high-school lunchroom now. I think he's *in danger!*"

The Drug Lord desperately whips around, screaming, ***"AAAAAEEEEAAAA!!!"*** while searching for something behind him. His eyes are frantic as he squeezes his head with both hands, screeching in pain. He looks around and then spots Jake as an anomaly. He screams, ***"What did you do to me?!?!"***; *then vomits!* Jake has his cell-phone camera on the lunchroom crowd, Jane is looking at that on her cell phone, propped up in front of her.

Glenn interrogates, "Where did she get those pistols from - and that cell phone - isn't that Margherita's. That's Ricardo's water-pistol and she's got another pistol, laying on the blanket next to her. It looks like the plastic Glock pistol I had taken away from her. She must have stolen it out of my locked cabinet when she got the AK47, and the crossbow and arrows for me." Jane drops the squirt-gun and picks-up the Glock.

They can hear the voices through the cell phone shouting get him. The drug Lord collapses as his gang gets up and starts approaching Jake with malevolence. Jake is backing away as he pockets the cell phone. One kid charges – and Jake throws him to the side. Then other ones start coming after him. Jane can no longer see-through Jake's cell-phone as he put it away to fight off the attackers; but she is looking down on the entire lunchroom thru the Pyramidal-Projection. She calmly aims the Glock pistol and starts firing into it. We see in the Pyramidal-Projection that she is shooting the attackers that are going after Jake. They are wincing with pain and falling to the ground, clutching their heads, their shoulders, their necks in agony. Bernie yells, **"Get them Jane!"**

Glenn shouts **"What the fuck is going on!?!** I trusted her and she *stole that pistol?!?"* The Professor is just dumbfounded.

Bernie is screaming, "Jake! *Get away! -* **RUN!** *- get out of there!"*

Jane sees an older boy pull out a gun and is firing it towards Jake. She quickly takes him down with a shot to his neck; then continues firing at the others. "I can't follow you, Jake. You have got to run – *get out of there!* I'll try to keep them from following you." She deftly changes the pistol's bullet-clip and continues firing at everybody who's moving in the direction where she last saw Jake. They are *in agony,* dropping like flies!

Jake shouts as he is breathlessly bounding down the school's stairs. "I'm *running to my car now!"*

Bewildered, the Professor asks, "Where is this? That's not in our valley."

Jane is able to pan back and can see the whole school building and Jake running across its parking lot. He scrambles into his car and drives away. A few students and a female teacher come out and scan the area. Then the teen-ager with the gun bust through the door and *starts shooting* towards Jake's car! The teacher grabs him and *rips the gun* out of his hand!

Bernie shuts off the electric supply to the projection-pyramid. There is arcing as the magnetic-field collapses.

Jane crawls out of the pyramid with the pistol in her hand. Glenn brazenly extends his open hand, demanding she surrender the pistol. She calmly obliges him. Glenn interrogates in revulsion, "You murdered all those *high-school students?!?*"

"*No!*" Bernie interjects, "They were rubber bullets."

Glenn is livid, "They were lethal plastic bullets, I *examined THEM* when I *took them away from you! They were penetrating the Loon-Evator's deck and the helium storage tank.*"

Jane dourly replies, "Some of them were rubber, if you were trained by the CIA, you would know the difference."

"Where did you get those phones?"

Jane smirks, "Stole them from your women."

"How did Jake get to Arizona?"

She laughingly says, "He *stole your* Jet-Basket . . . Don't worry, he'll be back with it in a few days."

They all go into Skyhook's cabin and take their helmets off. Glenn seethes, "So you finally admit *that you ARE A CIA agent!*"

Bernie says, "Glenn - Take it easy on Jane; she has had a difficult time with this project."

"Yes, I am **C I A** . . . AND ... By the way, Bernie is *no longer your flunky!*" She declares curtly as Glenn's face flushes red hot. "But I am a failed agent as I never accomplished anything - *until now.* Investigating your nuclear-waste dump was my first assignment, a*nd I failed* . . . AND I got myself *captured by the enemy!* I was supposed to take *the suicide pill* before allowing that to happen!"

Glenn is exasperated, "What do you mean – '*until now*'? You think that this is some kind of successful undercover operation?"

She replies persuasively, "Yes, ~ but it was just a dry run."

The Professor asks, "What was that liquid you squirted from the water-gun?"

Bernie points to the nuclear-waste barrel; "The one that was missing from the cargo-ship's delivery invoices. It is presumed lost at sea. They can't ever trace it back to here."

Glenn is flummoxed, "Are you saying you *squirted nuclear-waste liquid into his brain?*"

Jane and Bernie respond together, defiantly, **"YES!"**

Bernie adds, "The Russians infect their political opponents with nuclear stuff all the time."

"My God!" Glenn exclaims, "What did you do *to that teen-ager;* that **Drug-lord?"**

Jane coyly replies, "Hopefully *executed him.*"

Bernie adds, "At least we drove him crazy - permanently. I'll be anxiously awaiting his medical examination, or autopsy."

Glenn is shaking his head in disbelief, "But, ah – What do you mean – *'dry run'?"*

"There is an organized cult that is plotting to destroy our American Democracy – to turn it into a Kleptocracy, like China, Russia and those other countries that are being taken over by despots."

Glenn can't grasp what is going on,

~ "But a *'dry-run'*

~ *what are you **TALKING ABOUT!?!?"***

~

Jane replies with overwhelming determination,

~ *"**Presidential Candidate Ponald PRUMP!!!"** ~*

THE END

Printed in the United States
by Baker & Taylor Publisher Services